# THOSE
# WE
# CARRY

## Scott Allen Saxberg

**RE** imagined
**PRESS**

An imprint of
The Thunder Bay Historical Museum Society

Published by
The Thunder Bay Historical Museum Society Inc.
425 Donald Street East
Thunder Bay, Ontario, Canada P7E 5V1


Cover design by
Jerry Todd

Printed in Canada on acid-free paper


Library and Archives Canada Cataloguing in Publication

Title: Those we carry / Scott Allen Saxberg.
Names: Saxberg, Scott Allen, author. | Thunder Bay
Historical Museum Society, issuing body.
Identifiers: Canadiana (print) 20240445627 | Canadiana
(ebook) 20240445635 | ISBN 9781068915406
   (softcover) | ISBN 9781068915413 (EPUB)
Subjects: LCGFT: Novels.
Classification: LCC PS8637.A9928 T46 2024 | DDC
C813/.6—dc23

# THOSE WE CARRY

*For my cousin Mark, lost too young, who inspired
in me the passion to dream big.*

N

Canada

Calgary    Regina

Vancouver              Fort William
              Winnipeg

USA

Chicago    Toronto

Halifax

New York

Europe

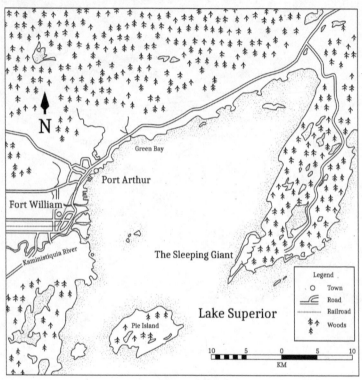

Fort William, Canada

## Prologue

# Witness

Fort William, Ontario, Canada
August 1940

Marv smelled like grass and wet soap. He sat motionless in an over-sized chair beside the judge, feet dangling, just like he was told. He blinked and rubbed his eyes. They were already red and swollen from crying. His mother had carried him back up to the stand once already. He fought the urge to run back to her. It would be embarrassing. He never ran to his mother. His Sunday school clothes were wrinkled, and grass stains covered his knees. The label of his shirt scratched the back of his neck. Marv didn't like the Fort William Court-house, and its cold red brick and white stone windows and columns. Only bad people came here. He wanted to go back and play along the shore again. His mother had let him run around the tall grassy park along the Lake Superior shoreline earlier as they waited to go in. He saw a train of grain cars and watched the ships go by. But his mother made him wash his hands in the washroom, and now the sleeves of his shirt clung wet and tight against his wrists. Marv tried to focus, but bits of grass kept falling down his collar, and the wet cuffs made his wrists itch. He pulled one last time at the cold, itchy sleeve and scratched at his collar. It reminded him of Joey at Christmas, pulling at the sleeves of his new jersey as he crossed the street.

\*\*\*

Marv had just returned home from their Cadieu family Christmas breakfast at the Hoito and was sitting on his front steps waiting for Joey. The Hoito restaurant sat at the bottom of the Finnish Labour Temple and was one of the cheapest diners in Port Arthur. Marv ordered the Finnish pancakes and sausage. It was his favourite. He only ever got it on special occasions, like Christmas and birthdays. In his hand he held a half-eaten piece of toast from the Finnish bakery Kivela, next door to the Hoito. Kivela toast, dried bread covered in sugar and cinnamon, came in a white paper box of a dozen and it sat next to him. Marv licked the sugar from his lips as Joey approached in a new Toronto Maple Leafs jersey. Marv knew Joey had been hoping to get one for Christmas. Joey had a bounce in his step and the bright sun lit up the white home jersey. Marv pretended not to notice.

"You like a piece?" Marv asked, staring down at his toast, not looking up.

"Sure."

Marv lifted the white box up to Joey, and he took out a piece.

"What did you get for Christmas?" Marv asked, biting his lip, holding back laughter from his own joke.

"Come on," Joey said.

Marv thought he was so lucky.

\*\*\*

Marv shook away the image of Joey's surprised face as he looked over the dreary courtroom. It held only a few people scattered across several benches. Marv's uncle sat to the right beside another man Marv didn't recognize. His uncle looked skinnier in his new baggy uniform, and there were no medals on his chest. He was normally quick with a smile or joke, but he only stared down, looking into his hands, holding his cap. Marv's hair was the same brown as his uncle's, and now he had a short buzz cut just like him. Marv thought about trying to get his attention by pointing at his hair but decided not to. He was worried about the two men at the other table. They were dressed in dark suits and sat, whispering. They made him feel like he did something wrong, and it scared him.

The older of the two scary men, in slow motion, stood up. His face showed more wrinkles than the other man. He smoothed out his jacket. Marv could still smell the soap from the court bathroom. It was the same as they had at home, and his mother had used it on him several times whenever he got into trouble saying dirty words. He sat on his hands and bit his lip.

"Marv, do you know the difference between right and wrong?" the wrinkled man said. His voice was like his mother's just before they sent him to bed without supper. Soft and inviting like every adult, and he knew he had to be good. Marv scratched under his leg.

"Yes."

"If I said grass is blue, would I be right or wrong?"

Marv looked at his knees and flicked a piece of grass off.

"Wrong."

"What about this table? If I said they made it with steel?"

He gazed at the top of the table and counted the neat stacks of paper. There were four.

"Wrong."

"What if I said that my jacket was black?"

Marv's eyes met with the wrinkled man's. They were dark.

"Right."

"Okay, let the court register that Marv knows the difference between right and wrong." The man smiled for the first time, showing his yellow-stained teeth.

"You're seven years old?"

"Yes."

"What is your relation to the defendant? The man sitting

there," the wrinkled man said, pointing at his uncle.

"He's my uncle," Marv said as he looked at his feet.

"You know him well?"

"He's going to fight in the war," Marv said with a slight smile, then stopped himself. He put his head back down—no fooling around.

"Do you know what car he drove?"

"Yes, my grandpa's."

"What is the colour of his car?"

"Black."

"Now, I'm going to ask you a very serious question. Do you understand what serious means?" the wrinkled man questioned, resting his hands in his pockets and staring down at him.

Marv leaned on his hands and swung his feet back and forth. He curled his legs behind the chair. "Yes," Marv said and looked back down, noticing a chunk of grass filled with mud still stuck to his shoe, and he poked it with his other foot.

"Did you see your uncle drive by in your grandpa's car?" the wrinkled man said, "Before you saw the accident."

His Uncle Ardagh had surprised them with a visit and his mother had let Marv and Joey stay outside later while they talked. Marv still remembered the smell of beer on his uncle's breath.

***

"Hey, boys," Ardagh said from the kitchen. "How about you guys get some more pop and ice cream? It's been a long time since I've had Brocke's ice cream. What you say, boys?"

"Yeah!" Marv and Joey screamed and jumped up and down all around Uncle Ardagh as he handed them the money.

Joey ran to the neighbour's house and grabbed the wagon while Marv collected the bottles scattered throughout the house. He had more than enough bottles wrapped in his arms to buy an extra pop, and the money from Uncle Ardagh would cover the ice cream. He patted his pocket one last time after placing all the bottles in the wagon and dragging it onto the sidewalk.

Marv lined up on the sidewalk beside Joey and gave one last wave to his mom before he marched down to Sprague Street.

Joey, wearing his Toronto Maple Leafs jersey, stood with one leg on the back step of his white-handled and red-bodied CCM tricycle. Marv had one knee planted inside his red Eatonia wooden wagon and one hand on the folded back red handle. The wagon rattled excitedly like a wind chime with the bottles for the store.

They set both to race down the street, keen to declare the next champion.

"Listen, you two, be back before it gets too dark," Marv's mother said from the porch step, waving her finger.

"Yes, Mom! After we finish our race!" Marv said from the sidewalk.

Marv rolled off the sidewalk and pulled up alongside Joey and his tricycle. The small wagon with a beat-up wood box didn't look like much, with its low beaten-up frame sitting on a black set of rubber wheels that needed to be greased daily. The long handle was bent over the wagon for Marv to hold on to while he pushed and steered at the same time. "Big Red" had won many races in its day, and this next race was part of a constant battle between tricycle and wagon. Some days, they even switched places to add to the excitement and bragging rights.

"I'll take the road," Marv said. "My wagon is slower on the sidewalk, and it'll be a closer race."

"Oh, no, you don't. The sidewalk is too bumpy for my bike. I'm going to do the one-legged push. No pedalling, I promise," Joey explained.

"How about I take the trike, and you push the wagon? That'll even it up. You're much better with one leg on the wagon and one leg pushing from the street, anyway."

"Okay, but let's race all the way to the store this time."

"But stay close to the sidewalk, my mom says."

"Deal."

It was a minor concession to give Joey a chance at redemption from the whupping Marv had given him in the previous race. He might have mentioned it to Joey just a few times on their way back to the start line. They'd already had one warning from his mom, and they only had a short time before they would be called into their respective houses. The sun was low and about to disappear behind the row of houses. Mount McKay had its usual long shadow that signalled the day was about to end.

"No matter," Joey said. "I'll beat you, either way, this time."

Joey tucked in his Maple Leafs jersey on one side and pulled back his sleeves to prevent them getting caught up. He dragged his trike onto the sidewalk beside Marv. They switched positions, and Joey climbed into the wagon on the street.

"So first one to the corner store this time," Marv said as he climbed back up onto the sidewalk. "It's further than our normal races, but I want to buy pop after the big win."

"You'll be buying me the pop," Joey said.

The street was empty and quiet. The wooden sidewalk stretched out along the cold, hard road in front of Marv and Joey.

"On the count of three, we go," Joey said.

"One, two, three!"

Marv, with his head down, had only one thought on his mind. To get to the finish line and beat his pal. Marv pedalled his tricycle as fast as the pedals could move, pressed hard over the handlebars with his tongue out, screaming. His eyes focused ahead on the corner store. The race was on with Joey, his jersey tucked in and determined to win. Joey's advantage was the paved road, his choice with one leg in the red wagon and one leg pumping away, holding on tightly to the front of the wagon. Joey wasn't about to lose. He pushed hard and was bullheaded to win.

Their competitiveness had started well before this race. The boys had been joined at the hip as long as they could remember and never backed down from each other. Pick a day or activity; competition was the glue of their friendship. They fed off each other as seven-year-old boys did, playing multiple games of hide-and-seek, kick the can, baseball, football and road hockey. They were kids, but don't tell them that. Their favourite was playing soldiers and hearing the stories of the war. Wood sticks and rocks were their guns and grenades. The days flew by, filled with pretend battles and their heroes. The Germans invaded from every street corner and behind every porch or bush. How the adults missed them, they never could figure, but they battled every day, sometimes late into the night. The summer days were the best, with longer days and more hiding spots.

The impression left by the war filled their minds with images and drove their imaginations. The details around the uniform were their biggest challenge. Do they wear a hat or helmet, pants or shorts? Who was the sergeant, the enemy, what type of rifle? These were the details that took hours to discuss and work out before the battle. The wounds were sometimes horrific, with lost limbs or guts blown out. All survived, but the carnage and heroism of those days never ended. The girls sometimes caused the boys trouble, but they could usually be convinced to play nurse to the injuries, and all was good. They sometimes didn't mind the attention, although they would never admit it.

Joey had gotten to an early lead but crashed into the sidewalk, and before he could gather himself back up, Marv blew by him with a triumphant shout and built a big lead as he saw the finish line ahead.

He crossed the finish line with a roar of excitement. "Oh,

yeah! Winner of the greatest race of all time!" The lights of the convenience store lit up the street in front of him. He heard glass breaking behind him.

Marv turned and looked back down the dark street, waiting for Joey to pull up beside him, but he was nowhere to be seen. Marv swung the tricycle around to retrace his race, pushing and steering along the sidewalk. He would tell Joey they could have a new race. It was not uncommon for one of them to get their pant leg caught up in the pedals or get stuck after hitting a hole in the road and spilling over the handlebars. It was only fair that they started over. His mom would be fine to let them race one more time. It wasn't too dark yet. He looked out across the road over the houses and could still make out the outline of Mount McKay as the sun still sat on the horizon.

As he looked up to make a push on the tricycle, the headlights of a car moved down the road to pass him, and he instinctively stopped his tricycle and watched the car slow down as it approached. To his surprise, it was his grandpa's car, but his uncle was driving. He gave a smiling wave to his hero, Uncle Ardagh. His uncle didn't wave back, but had a dazed and confused look about him as their eyes met. His grandpa's car turned down the street behind him and sped off in a hastened, sudden acceleration. Uncle Ardagh was with Danny, his best friend. Danny always had a serious look about him, but somehow, he made Marv laugh. This time, he looked scared.

Marv pushed down to the end of the street just as a streetcar pulled up into the intersection. The streetcar lights spilled out onto the road, and several passengers stood up to stare out the window. Their backs were to him. The streetcar stopped at the intersection. After looking both ways down the street, no other cars were coming, he pushed on to see what all the fuss was. He still hadn't seen Joey anywhere.

As he pushed the tricycle around the streetcar, he jumped off, grabbed the handle and kicked the tricycle to a stop, peering around the streetcar. He then saw what the fuss was all about. Joey lay spread-eagled on the road, in his Toronto Maple Leafs jersey. Marv watched in shock as the conductor jumped out and bent down beside his fallen best friend. Marv, stunned and silent, pushed his tricycle up to where Joey lay still.

"Joey," Marv said, "Are you okay?" Expecting Joey to get up and say, "Just kidding!"

"Is this your friend?" the conductor asked in a soft voice, without turning his attention away from Joey.

The trail of blood showed the direction and distance Joey had been dragged along the road. His Toronto Maple Leafs jersey was now torn, red with blood, and was pulled up over his shoulders. Blood covered his face. His body was crumpled and spread out like a rag doll thrown to the ground. He was still breathing as his chest was moving in and out. He was moaning softly with every breath.

"Yes," Marv said, slumping, and hid his face in his elbow. He couldn't make out Joey's face anymore, and it was confusing to him. It was his jersey and wagon. But not his face.

"We were just racing," he blinked, and tears formed in his eyes as he crouched over Joey. The conductor stood up and turned to hold and lift Marv away from Joey, who still hadn't moved.

"Is anyone a doctor? Let's get him to the hospital, now!" the conductor ordered to the surrounding crowd. Another man stepped forward, picked up Joey.

"I'll take this one to his house, and we can find their parents," the conductor said to the crowd as the other man lifted Joey into his arms and rushed away. Joey, folded in his arms, still had not moved, and was quiet as they carried him away.

"Where do you live, son?" the conductor asked.

Marv stared down at the smear of blood where Joey used to be, then down the street and pointed. He looked at the streetcar and the huddled group of adults staring down at him through the glass. Marv turned back to search for the lights of his house, but tears had formed in his eyes, and he had trouble making them out. It was getting dark, and the lights of the other houses blurred his eyes.

The conductor, holding him tightly by the hand, walked steadily toward his house, dragging the tricycle behind them.

They staggered their way back to his house. It was fully dark now, and his mother would be worried. Only the glow of the neighbouring homes lit the way.

"Where is Joey going?" Marv whimpered.

"Don't worry, he's safe. They're taking him to the hospital. Don't worry, he'll be alright."

It felt like time stood still as the conductor picked up his pace down the street until Marv's mother shouted from the porch step, "Marv, is that you?" and ran out onto the road to meet them.

"There's been a hit and run," the conductor explained to Marv's mother as he set Marv on the porch step. "What is your friend's name again?"

"Joey."

"What's happened to Joey?"

"They've taken him to the hospital," the conductor said. "Do you know where he lives?"

"Across the road, over there." Elaine pointed as she moved to hug Marv. "Are you okay? Are you hurt?"

"No, Mom, I'm okay," Marv said, hugging his mother.

"Marv, you go back in the house," Elaine said, taking charge. "It'll be better if I go with you to his mother and father." They rushed to the house across the street. Marv would never forget standing on the porch and hearing the cries of Joey's mother.

\*\*\*

Marv pushed away the memory and looked over at his father and mother, sitting in chairs behind his uncle in the courtroom.

He thought about the look on his uncle's face. The bottles scattered across the dark road. The people staring at him from the brightly lit streetcar. A few brief moments and pictures played over in his head. The blank stare and dead-eyed look from his uncle frightened him. It sent shivers up his back. His stomach ached, and he struggled to think past it.

Marv cried for days after and woke up with bad dreams of Joey. Several days had gone by before the questions started. What did he see that night? He hadn't put it together. It was his uncle, one of his heroes.

The street was quiet throughout the rest of the spring, and he stayed close to home, his mother constantly checking on him when he was outside. It wasn't until the end of school that his grandma and grandpa arrived at the house, in the middle of the day.

This was when he learned what had happened. No one understood how. His grandma and mother cried together, and the family gathered at the house. His uncle, who had stayed away for over a month; how could it be?

Marv shifted his gaze back to his uncle and to the wrinkled man who asked the question. It couldn't have been him. Why was he here? What did it matter? He looked again at his father, who gave him a double nod of his head.

The wrinkled man moved closer and put his hands on the railing that separated them and asked again, "Before you saw the accident, did you see your uncle drive by in your grandpa's car?"

"Yes," Marv said, staring at the wrinkled man's yellow fingers.

"Are you certain? Are you sure?"

Marv looked again at his uncle and then at his parents.

His father mouthed in Finnish, "Se on okei." It's okay. He knew he had no choice but to answer.

"Yes."

"Thank you, son, that is all the questions we have. You may step down."

Marv climbed off the chair and walked by his uncle, who, to his surprise, had tears in his eyes. Marv smiled at him, and his uncle gave a blank stare before attempting to smile back, then lowered his head to the empty table. His mother whispered, "Brave boy," and reached out for a hug as he passed by. Then he was out of the courtroom and into the dark hallway on a cold wooden bench, alone.

# Chapter One

# Bomber

Farnham, England
March 1944

Ardagh Cadieu drained the last of his Guinness and looked at the bottom of his glass. He felt empty inside. The feeling never seemed to fade, no matter how much he drank. He thought he could escape Joey's accident by joining the war. But the images still mixed in his head. Jim's frozen stare. Jean's final look of disappointment. Marv's slumped shoulders. It was an accumulation of events that changed his life forever. He had no choice but to join the fight, and after four years of waiting, it was like living in purgatory. The layers of guilt and shame grew harder to break. The borrowed Royal Air Force officer jacket felt tight over his shoulders and pinched his arms. He pulled at his sleeves.

"Hank, does your brother always look this sad when he drinks?" Boyle asked, grabbing Ardagh's shoulder. "Did he lose a popsie? He has a face like a slapped arse!"

"Yeah, a girlfriend, something like that," Hank said, placing a full pint of Guinness on the table in front of Ardagh. "He is an arse, but he'll be okay."

"Bastards," Ardagh said, pushing away his empty beer.

Ardagh hardly recognized his brother Gerald. They kept

calling him Hank instead of Gerry, not to get him confused about being a German. Hank was a top gunner and flight officer on a Lancaster bomber. Boyle was a flight sergeant and the pilot. It was a risky business. The statistics of air force casualties were not in their favour. They would be lucky to survive the thirty missions.

This was his first-time visiting Hank at his base. He had plenty of leave while training for the big show in Europe but was bored by the same day-to-day training, then dances and sports on the weekends. They spent so much time in the pubs the barmaids poured the beers before they got there. He finally received a longer leave to travel north of London to Tuddenham in Suffolk and visit his brother Hank. They gave him an RAF jacket and snuck him into the officer's mess for a few drinks.

"Don't worry Harp. At least you don't have to fly through a hail of flak shells every night."

Harp was the nickname Danny gave him in school because he never let things go. He hated it. Hank was flying with the British RAF instead of the Canadian Royal Air Force. Hank's Ninety Squadron would be flying tomorrow night. He was surrounded by the Brits.

"Why don't I just go on a run with you? It sounds like a piece of cake. You haven't had trouble so far, right?" Ardagh said, picking up his pint of Guinness. One more wouldn't hurt. "All those guns to protect you. You don't even see the Jerries. While we're down in the trenches with them, fighting them off."

"Piece of cake? What's that?" Boyle asked. "Been in it? You've mucked about already? Have you?"

Ardagh put his head down, staring at his hands. He had done nothing. Four years of training in the Lake Superior Regiment. He was now a twenty-two-year-old corporal and led his section, running around playing make believe. He wanted his turn to fight. Enough with bloody games. The anxiety of the wait was too much to handle, living in a frozen state, watching Marv's feet tangle in the chair alone. All they did was talk and talk about what it would be like to fight.

"No. It's been four years and I've done nothing. Training like a toy soldier. I haven't made up for anything," Ardagh said.

He found it hard to imagine his brother flying up there, risking his life. He remembered the first time he saw wave after wave of bombers fly overhead. It was an impressive force. Then later, watching so many limping back home with smoke coming from an engine or visible pieces of the plane missing. He looked up with a mix of pride and fear for his brother. Living near London, they all witnessed a plane getting shot down or crashing hard with no parachute. The bravery of the air force gave the resolve for all the troops to push harder in training. They often bought the first pint for any air force pilot at the pubs.

"I'm sure I could handle one of the guns," Ardagh said, putting his hands together, pretending to fire a machine gun. "I'm a better shot than Gerry... Hank."

"He thinks it's easy," Hank said. "Typical foot soldier, brown job."

"I think it's a jolly idea. A mascot. Our own lucky charm," Boyle said, grabbing Ardagh's shoulders. He picked up his pint and raised his glass above the crowded officer's mess bar.

"To our rabbit's foot and the Crazy Rabbit!"

The crew crowded around the table with their pints of beer raised and clanked the glasses over Ardagh's head. Hank had his childhood crooked smirk. It always led to a fight or a wrestling match. Was he kidding? They were always like that. Taking a joke a little too far with each other. He knew better, so he continued to play along. Ardagh raised his glass to a louder cheer.

"At least he isn't a tart," Boyle said. "A soldier like Harp could help us fight our way out if we get shot down, so won't be a totally useless tit." The comment made everyone laugh, and they raised their glasses again.

"Fort William boys don't back down on anything," Hank said, lifting his glass. Ardagh caught his eyes, they looked as if he was asking him to come. He felt something inside turn with excitement. Ardagh wanted to be there for his brother. He looked around the room. All these men had been through it, risking their lives on several missions already. He was lucky to be around them.

"Never," Ardagh said, lifting his glass in the air and finished his pint to more boisterous applause.

Everything from then on was a blur.

He woke up beside Hank's bed with a heavy hangover. They had a hearty breakfast of eggs and beans with coffee. Food was not in short supply before each mission, Hank had told him. You never knew if it would be your last. Hank smiled and winked. This was the first suggestion that his boasting the night before would come back to haunt him. Ardagh swallowed hard as the eggs got caught in his throat. Was Hank serious? He really carried jokes too far. Ardagh ate his entire breakfast, soaking up the last pieces of eggs and beans with his toast. His head started to clear. Boyle hadn't touched his meal.

"Well, he's a cool cucumber," Boyle said as he got up. Hank held up his hands, pretending to fire his guns, and laughed. It was fun to be around them.

They marched off to a large hangar and listened to the commander describe the mission. Ninety Squadron was to attack Stuttgart and the factories that built Daimler Benz aircraft engines. The plan was to fly south, cross the English Channel, and head north of Paris in a direct line to Stuttgart. Drop their gifts to the Führer and then return along the same route. The dangers typically started when they first crossed the Channel, and then on the target, followed by nearing the Channel again. Over four hundred planes, along with a fighter escort, were getting ready for the mission. "Safety in numbers," the commander had said.

Ardagh assumed Hank wanted to spend more time with him and let him see what they really did. They hung out all afternoon and had an evening meal of eggs again. It was dark when they walked back into the changing quarters, handing him a wool jacket and jumpsuit to put on. It took him a moment to understand they were serious before the fear swelled into his stomach, and Ardagh had to run to the toilet. He could hear the chuckles behind him as he ran out.

Ardagh stared into the toilet, his head spinning. Pieces of egg and toast clung to the sides. He lifted himself to his feet, staring down at his eggs floating in the water. He needed to decide. It was his decision to put himself in harm's way for the first time. He knew he would have to face it at some point. Why not now? It was stupid, but the only way he could get rid of that empty feeling of shame and guilt was to attack it head on. Hank told him the one thing he would learn about flying in a bomber was that you had lots of time to reflect on life. It would be a lifetime experience he would share with Hank.

*Fort William boys don't back down on anything.* He would not back down now. *Never.* He flushed the toilet, walked back into the room to the cheer of the crew and climbed into the gear. He looked at Hank's face. There had been a lot of growing up in the Cadieu household over the last four years of war. Lots of things he still couldn't face or talk about. Now he was with his brother and would find out what Hank faced on every mission. Ardagh would be their lucky charm.

The Lancaster was an impressive plane. He had never flown before and had nothing to compare it to, but it looked massive when he approached it. Just before they snuck him into the bomber, he stared at the large-eared rabbit that covered the plane's nose holding a bomb in one hand, ready to drop it.

*The Crazy Rabbit* said it all. What nut job would want to go on a bombing run where the casualty rate was something like twenty-five percent? Hank told him not to worry. They were destroying the Germans in the air, and things had gotten more manageable, but this was high-risk gambling. *What would Ma say if she lost us both?*

The Royal Air Force Lancaster bomber shuddered as it lifted into the air. A familiar smell of burning fuel filled the cabin, and Ardagh felt his stomach sink. The weightlessness gave way to the loud drone and vibration of the engines, but that feeling stuck with him. It was the same sensation he'd had floating on the sheet of ice that convinced him to crawl off to safety. Jim had yelled at him to get away. He tried to get Jim out but failed. Everything spiralled down and fell apart after. Jim always said things happened in threes. Ardagh had his three. It was supposed to be all behind him. If he couldn't get past Jim's death, how could he get past the rest of it?

"Here we go," Ardagh heard through the headset. He felt the bomber pull upwards and the change of rhythm of the four engines. Ardagh stared up at the backside of the big-eared, skinny nineteen-year-old kid hanging in the top gun turret seat. Some things never changed. He'd opened his big mouth. How stupid he sounded. There was no turning back now. He felt a flash of heat and sweat rise through his body.

The Lancaster continued to climb, and his mind searched through the darkness as he examined the glow of dials above the navigator's seat for a reason he was here. He heard the landing gear lock into place. Maybe it was because his brother didn't look all that impressive in his air force uniform. He had to salute the bugger because Hank was an officer, but still.

The trace of rubber mixed with oxygen, and the steady drone of the engines, was not so bad. As Hank moved the turret around, Ardagh felt the swoosh of cool air and vibrations of the hydraulics. The Lancaster started into a slow turn, then levelled off beside another bomber and Ardagh sensed his own fears resurface. What was he thinking? He shifted in the jump seat and stretched his arms out to relieve the tightness in his chest.

The pilot, Boyle, leaned into the cabin and gave Ardagh the thumbs-up signal and a pat on the back. "Nice guy," Hank had said over the eggs and beans. "The best pilot in the squadron. Never gets in trouble and has luck so far up his ass it sparkles on his teeth."

Ardagh watched the navigator hunched over his maps, plotting their course, ignoring the bounces and constant buzz of the engines. There were flashes ahead of them in the dark under the clouds. Hank explained what they would be up against when the bombers crossed into France and the Kammhuber line, as they called it.

The German night air defence system named after Colonel Josef Kammhuber was a series of control sectors equipped with radars and searchlights combined with night fighters. German air defences continually strengthened along with the Allied bombing missions, but they always had an answer to it. They set the bomber stream up to counter the German defences and provide a constant stream of bombers that overwhelmed the fighters.

Were the flashes anti-aircraft guns or lightning? He couldn't tell. Ardagh tried to turn his mind off. He was in for the ride. His stomach grumbled and reminded him he lost his dinner earlier. What would he give to have a burger and fries right now? It always reminded him of Jean. His first love. Jean loved to quote movies. *Well, here's another nice mess you've got me into.* It was the perfect Laurel and Hardy movie quote.

It seemed so long ago, almost five years now, meeting Jean to get a burger and fries at the McKellar Confectionery. It was his comfort food, a hamburger with special Coney sauce, fries with gravy, and a Coke. He loved to watch Gus Kelos, the owner, line up hot dogs on his forearm as he poured the Coney Island sauce onto them. Ardagh couldn't get enough of Jean or their fries. They would sit trading turns, taking one French fry at a time and dipping it into the ketchup. He missed those moments. He always let Jean take the last French fry.

He missed her more than the fries and wished he had just been more level-headed. There were many things he would like to do over or take back, and she was the first. She was stronger than him and wouldn't have hesitated to jump on a bomber.

"France," Boyle announced over the intercom, waking Ardagh out of his dream.

Ardagh braced for the first blasts from anti-aircraft fire and shards of steel to come through the thin metal skin side of the plane marking the crossing of the Kammhuber line. But nothing happened. Boyle reminded them to keep an eye out for fighters and stay alert.

The bomber crew settled in for the long flight, and Ardagh tried his best to stay warm and move around. They brought out some sandwiches, cheese and crackers to pass the time. He snacked on a piece of a chocolate bar he had brought as his potential last meal. They had reached the European continent, and he marked down mentally another achievement in a short time. First time flying and first time to Europe. Lots of firsts, hopefully not the last.

The stream of bombers flew deeper into France, passing over Paris, closer to their eventual target of Stuttgart, Germany. The cabin of the Lancaster was dark except for the flicking on and off of the navigator's flashlight. It reminded Ardagh of an usher at the Royal Theatre in Fort William. Those were the simple days, before everything fell apart. The newsreels of the bombers. Now he was in one. A lot happened at that theatre. The start of a push into a new direction in his life.

They had finished the movie and the lights of the theatre turned on, and the crowd shuffled toward the exits. Ardagh had followed Jean, holding her hand as they moved down the row to the aisle. He felt torn between staying with Jean and working for his dad or signing up. The Germans had taken over Norway.

Ardagh stepped ahead of Jean, pulling her down the aisle, out into the packed hallway, in silence. The crowd was loud, and he noticed there was a group of men in uniforms walking slowly ahead of them, blocking their way. The uniforms made Jean afraid and uneasy. A reminder he would leave her at any moment.

*Are you going to join?* It was a question everyone was asking, and it was a constant fight he'd had with Jim and Jean.

His dad had lined up a job with the grain trimmers to build up some seniority and he worked for his dad at the ice company, harvesting blocks of ice with Jim. It was another frigid January night. The icy wind from Lake Superior whipped up over them, and the warmth of the theatre disappeared. Jean had listed off all his friends who had joined or were about to join.

Even his older brother Wilf was thinking about joining. His brother had it all. He had married Mildred just after coming back from Scotland, where he had played professional hockey and he had a full-time job with the railway with two kids. Wilf had promised to watch over him if he joined. The pressure to sign up was mounting.

It was a busy Saturday night. They walked along in silence, watching the cars roll by.

He knew what was at stake. Jim had come back from the first war and was a drunk. But Jim was like an uncle to him. He had hung on every word, listening to his advice. But there were some days when Jim couldn't function and there was nothing behind his eyes. He didn't want to end up like him.

But she had been right. He should have listened to her. She had seen him changing his path before he knew it. It was the pull of loyalty to his friends over her.

Ardagh noticed the bomber's slow turn that marked the final line and new direction leading to Stuttgart. He had changed his path, which he hoped would lead him in the right direction. If he had been stronger back then, his life would be different now and he would have avoided the turn of fate that had struck him down. Now he had a new girlfriend, Eileen. His British billet. What would she think of him if he told her his full story? They accused him of running away when he hit Joey in the car. It might make him feel better, but would she still accept him knowing this?

# Chapter Two

# Labour

Bruinisse, Schouwen-Duiveland Island, Netherlands
March 1944

Koos rode hard, pushing her bike to the limit. She ignored her hair blowing across her face and the ache from her scarred leg. She needed to get home fast. The German trucks had just passed her and the town was surrounded with makeshift road blocks. It could mean only one thing. They came for the men, more workers. Slave labour to help in the German factories. The hunger of the Germans for men was insatiable. Her thoughts were only with her brothers. Her father could keep them from harm's way for the moment, because they were fisherman and were needed. But how long until they came for one of them? David, the youngest of her brothers, had no kids and was at the most risk of being taken away. He hid the last time, giving her father the time to fight it. The Germans were smarter and more desperate than they were before, with many more spies to help them. So much had changed since the start of the war. Life was getting more and more difficult under the German occupation. Bruinisse was now part of the Atlantic wall, Hitler's new defensive line to prevent the Allied army from landing in Europe. The Germans restricted anyone from leaving, and they occupied schools with anti-aircraft guns, which disrupted normal schooling. Public transport was diffi-

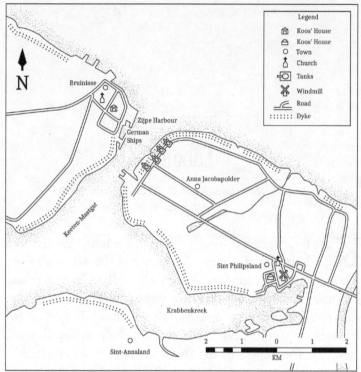

**Legend**

| | |
|---|---|
| 🏠 | Koos' House |
| ⌂ | Koos' House |
| ○ | Town |
| ⚲ | Church |
| ⊡ | Tanks |
| � | Windmill |
| ⌒ | Road |
| ⋮⋮⋮⋮ | Dyke |

Sint Philipsland, Netherlands

cult, and the increasing influence of the Dutch Nazi party, the NSB, terrorized day-to-day life. Their eyes and ears were everywhere. All it took was a note or a comment to the Germans to instigate an arrest. David would have to find the right place to hide with the many others or be taken away.

The sky was bright behind the clouds, and the ocean was calm. The winds that normally swept the island of Schouwen-Duiveland had not shown up in the early summer afternoon. Koos made the sharp turn onto Beursstraat at full speed, a narrow street crowded with buildings on her left and a cafe to her right. As she reached the intersection, a man jumped out from behind the corner of the building; it forced her to step on her brakes and swerve to avoid him. It was Pieter Jansen. He looked afraid. It was the same frightened expression he'd had when Joost rescued her. Her grip tightened on the handlebars, and she pushed on the pedals to get her speed back. Seeing Pieter annoyed her. She wished he was gone. The Germans should take him. It was hard for her to hide her bad thoughts after what he had done to her. It felt childish now, considering their current life. He could be taken. Life was so simple, four years ago, before the war, when she just had to fight off boys like him in her school. It was her first dance and piece of freedom that had ended in disaster.

*** 

"Make sure you're back before eight," Abraham said from the dinner table.

"But, Papa, the dance goes on until nine. The whole class will be there," Koos argued as she stood in front of the door, looking at her mother for support. "Please," she mouthed out the word to her mother.

"Oh, dear, let her have some fun. It's just down the street. She'll be fine," Koos's mother said as she waved Koos away.

Koos could only hear the grunt from inside, and she was away smiling to herself. She was certain someone would ask her to dance, and she nearly skipped the entire way to the school for her first secondary school dance.

The hall at the school was full, but divided between boys and girls. Koos dressed like the others in their traditional dress and wooden clogs. The clap of the clogs echoed over the top of the voices as they moved around.

Koos looked across the hall, and her eyes immediately fell on Joost de Lange. It wasn't hard. He was the tallest of all the boys in her class and, in her opinion, the best-looking. She turned away and adjusted her white cotton bonnet then the ties to her skirt. She noticed another boy's stare; Pieter Jansen.

He was shorter than Koos and wore round silver-framed glasses that made him look smarter. Koos was still not sure he was that bright, even after several years at school with him. He was always watching her, it seemed. The kids all gathered into their assigned groups for the first song of the evening, which was a traditional dance that involved the entire school. They had been practising for over a month to get it right. Koos giggled as her classmates all linked arms. Pieter slid in beside her as he had done at every rehearsal. She didn't mind. The thought of Joost on her arm made her stomach ache. The music started just as everyone finally connected, and they didn't hesitate to dance. All the girls stomped their clogs and clicked their heels, and the several circles spun around. They completed three different songs, kicking and stomping and changing partners, until the music stopped for a break. The next stage of the dance was about to start, and she hoped for a partner.

Koos stood alone, looking for a partner, watching her friends move about on the dance floor. There were several small groups of boys and girls waiting to be asked. She was surprised Pieter had not asked her and was off with a group of boys across the hall. Pinocchio's "When You Wish Upon a Star" was about to end, and she watched as Pieter circled the dance floor toward her. As he approached, the song ended, and he stepped close to her but said nothing. The next song, "In the Mood", by Glenn Miller, started. Without thinking, Koos grabbed his hands and jumped in to join the rest of the kids. The dance party flew by fast after, as she twirled around with Pieter for more songs than she could count. He pressed up against her several times, but Koos didn't mind as the songs rolled one after another. She smiled at her friends, and they laughed as they bounced across the floor, the banging of the clogs occasionally drowning out the music as the kids moved. At eight o'clock, the music stopped for a break, and many of the younger kids left and made their way home. Koos stood now with just a couple of friends and watched who stayed behind. The chatter of the crowd got quieter. Koos spun and danced in front of her friends, caught up in the night's excitement as she saw Pieter walk over. Was he brave enough to talk now?

"Hello, Koos. That was fun. Are you going to stay longer?" Pieter asked, as he looked away at his friends.

"Yes, I am," Koos said with an eager nod.

"Will you come for a walk with me? It's hot in here," Pieter stammered out, then added, "We could cool off for a bit before the next songs."

"Sure," Koos said. Her girlfriends giggled at each other as the pair walked away.

"Don't mind them. They're just jealous."

Pieter remained quiet as he led her out. They walked down the short hall and turned back down along another hallway, deeper into the school.

"Where are you going?" Koos asked. "The front door is the other way."

"I want to show you something first," Pieter said as he pulled her into an alcove leading to a classroom door. He didn't hesitate and pushed in for a kiss. Koos sidestepped him and shoved him out of the way, but Pieter held her arm and pulled her down. He fell onto her, and she felt him grope her. He leaned in, and Koos felt his wet lips on her cheek, searching.

"Get off me!" she shouted and shoved. Despite his size, Pieter had anchored himself between the narrow walls and pinned her down, continually groping and trying to kiss her. She closed her eyes and tried to fight him off, but it was no use.

"Stop! Stop it! Leave me alone," she cried. She opened her eyes as a flush of heat pulsed through her, and she hit him. Then a shadow stood over them.

Joost reached down and grabbed Pieter by the collar, throwing him aside like a wooden peg doll. Koos could hear a childish grunt as Pieter slammed into the wall, and his clogs scattered down the hallway. Joost glared down. His eyes were dark, and Koos could feel his energy making her face flush red and skin tighten across her body. He stomped over to Pieter and lifted him again, and said in a calm voice, "What were you doing, little pig? Don't you have any manners?"

Joost lifted him against the wall, leaving Pieter's feet dangling so that they were eye to eye. Koos watched him squirm against the wall, his lips quivering. The only word Pieter could get out was "Don't," before he was thrown again down the hallway and into the opposite wall. He cried out again as Joost stood over him and punched him in the stomach and face. Koos stood up, staring down at the scene as blood splattered the wall. "Stop!" she shouted.

Joost held Pieter by the shirt with his fist raised, ready to strike again. He let go, and Pieter slumped to the floor, whimpering. Joost walked over to Koos, breathing heavily, his fist covered in blood. He looked down at his hands, then at Koos.

"Are you okay?" Joost asked through a shaky breath, moving closer to her.

Koos stared into his heaving chest, blood-covered hands and finally his face. "You didn't have to hit him so hard," she whispered, looking down on Pieter, who was still lying with his face in his arms. She could see his back lift with every deep breath. He was still alive. Joost wiped his bloody hands on his pants.

"So, I should've just let him..."

"No! But..." Koos said. "I don't..."

Joost moved closer and reached up, fixing her bonnet. "I'm sorry," he said. The colour in his face lightened. "Can I walk you home?"

They stepped around Pieter, who was still moaning on the floor. Joost walked alongside her down the hall and out into the schoolyard.

"Only to the corner," she said. His eyes flickered brighter, and she knew he was keen to help her.

They walked in silence the short distance to the street corner close to her house. Her mind was still racing, and she was lost for words. She looked up at him but was too nervous for her eyes to meet his. Her arm still felt sore where Pieter had grabbed her.

"Thank you," she said before turning and running into her house, the tears building as she ran straight to her room.

Koos buried her head into her pillow. How could she be so stupid and trusting? She screamed into the pillow, smothering her tears. She would never let that happen to her again, she promised herself. Her thoughts turned to Joost. How did he get there so fast? Was he watching over her? What did that mean? Her head spun, thinking about it. She sighed, wiped her face on the pillowcase and sat up. Her cheeks stung, and it felt good to let go of her emotions. She knew what she wanted to do with Joost, and she felt her cheeks redden with the thought.

*** 

Koos snapped out of the past at the sounds of grinding truck brakes. She stopped to confirm what she heard and looked down the side street at the German truck and a motorcycle parked in front. Soldiers were climbing out of the truck. She turned down the street and pedalled closer to get a better view of what house they were going to. The soldiers lined up and marched away from her. She climbed off her bike to watch. There was another man watching and, as they passed him, she realized it was Joost. She wanted to shout a warning, but held her breath. Her chest pounded as she watched the German boots march in unison. They continued past Joost to the next house, and he followed them. Joost didn't look afraid. What was he doing? She had never stood up to her father until she met Joost. He was part of her awkward step toward becoming a woman. It was April 1940 before the Germans had arrived and changed her path. It was right after the incident with Pieter that she was finally unafraid and had stood up to her father.

***

Koos remembered where she used to sit in school, the second back of the front row. It had turned out to be her favourite spot. Close enough that the teacher knew she was interested, but far enough for her friends not to think she was too eager. What caught her by surprise was Joost picking the seat right behind her. Now, after last week's fight with Pieter, she thought there must be a reason. Did he know she had a crush on him? He had hardly said a word to her, and their eyes rarely met. She had long ago given up, resigned to the fact she wasn't his type. He towered over her. Tall and muscular. Much more mature than the other boys, he would sometimes show it. She didn't think he was a bully, but he would never back down from a fight. All the boys at this age seemed to want to blow off a bit of steam. He was no different. But now he had rescued her from Pieter. Everything had changed. They suspended Joost for three days for the fight. Pieter as well, but he didn't return for over a week because of his injuries. Or was it pride? Koos had gone to school the next day but was grounded by her father and prevented from going out. The sentence was still under review two weeks later, but she had found a way around it.

Koos had spent the days while Joost was suspended staring at herself in the mirror, trying to figure out her advantages and strategy with Joost. She was of average height among the girls in her class, just a couple of inches over five feet tall. She was blessed, her mother would say, with full, curved hips that would produce many kids someday. Her breasts were small but filled out her dresses. She had clean skin and a pleasant face with high cheekbones that surrounded a straight-rounded nose, short full lips and soft brown eyes. She had finally decided that her eyes were the most attractive of her features, along with her dimpled smile. The safest place for her was in the classroom among her friends. She would simply say hello in class.

It seemed like yesterday, but it had been the day he returned. Joost had come back from the suspension after the dance late to class. She had then finally caught his eye as he rushed in. He said hello, and the entire class heard it, followed by a groan from a few friends around her. The teacher had to settle the class down. She still couldn't remember what they had studied that day. Her inner argument of what to do next consumed her thoughts. She decided on a simple smile and hello at the end of the class. It worked. The following days passed by, and the little things continued to escalate to her liking. She arrived earlier and earlier. The conversations lengthened to where they started walking home together to finish them.

Today was the day she would let him kiss her. She had decided a week earlier, but then her father noticed them walking together one day. He had warned her about Joost. He wasn't from the right family. They were a Dutch family that leaned more favourably to the fascist Germans. It was the first time she learned it was a reason not to date. She had laughed it off when he said it. She was the second youngest girl in her family of eight. He was just trying to protect her.

They knew there was not much time left before the Germans would arrive in town to take control, but nothing had happened. Every day that went by, the tension grew in Bruinisse. A young girl of fifteen should not be caught out on her own. Who knows what would happen? That was the chain that held her captive. "Who knows what would happen and when?" her papa would say. He was tired, she could see, but did they see her? How tired and restless she was, trapped without cause or reason. Her brothers could come and go as they pleased, but not Koos. She sat looking out their window, trapped. At first, she tried to read, to listen to the radio for escape, but as days turned into weeks, her patience turned into lethargy and she daydreamed of simply going for a walk. If only she could ride her bike again. It was a short forty-five-minute bike ride down the Rijksweg to the town of Zierikzee.

Eventually, her short walks from school to home had turned into longer and longer walks with Joost. Her fights with her parents became louder and more open. She wasn't afraid to push the limits.

"Why can't I talk to him or see him in town, Papa?" Koos asked.

Her father reached for his napkin and gently wiped his large moustache clean of the fish chowder remnants that hung like raindrops.

"Another time," was all he said.

Koos pushed her untouched bowl away, creating a tidal wave of chowder that slopped onto the table.

"Unfair; even Pieter gets to go out!" she said. She still wasn't sure why she said it.

"How dare you speak this way to me? Up to your room!"

She had been through this injustice many times before. Her small sweater-covered shoulders heaved uncontrollably as she walked deliberately away to the stairs. No tears. It was always better not to fight.

As she reached the first step of the narrow staircase, she took a full deep breath and calmly turned around to her parents and older brother, who still sat at the kitchen table. No tears.

She looked into her father's eyes, and with a steady voice that echoed her mother's, she said, "I'm not a little girl. I'll go next time. I can talk to Joost."

And she turned and moved up the stairs to her room. As she reached the door of her room, she heard her mother say, "Well, she has grown up fast. You can't keep her hidden away forever."

\*\*\*

Koos hid back and watched Joost follow the group of German soldiers with mixed feelings. She remembered diving headfirst into her bedroom, smothering her face into the pillow to hide the stream of tears, but she remembered her promise to herself from then on. She would do what she wanted, but she would also look at Joost in a different light. It had been their first family argument. She listened more to what Joost said and did.

Yes, Joost had admitted their family agreed with the Germans' position, but he was a born and bred Dutch. If it came to it, he would sign up to fight. He was too young now, but he would follow his brothers, who both were in the Dutch army. This had settled it for her.

How silly she had been to think otherwise. As they left school for their walk, another group of boys challenged Joost to a fight. She still didn't know why he always got into fights, but, as usual, the fight did not last long. Joost's strength and height won easily. The other boys had run off. Although he won, the hurt look in his eyes had drawn her further in. She had been tricked then.

Koos listened to the boots of the marching soldiers and the shouts of orders in German behind her as she turned around and headed back down Kerkstraat. What was Joost up to now? She struggled to take a deep breath as she dropped her bike on the street and entered the house. Her father, Abraham, stood in the living room. His stare told her nothing.

"Go to your room and don't come out," he said.

"But, Papa, where is David?"

"Go!"

"They are down another street. There may be time," Koos pleaded.

"Koos," David said as he stepped down out of the stairwell. He wore a knapsack on his back and a cap covered his dark hair and face. He reached out and wrapped his arms around her, squeezing her, then let go before she reacted.

"You need to hide in the attic, there is no time," Abraham

said, and he grabbed his arm, pushing him back up the stairs. "They aren't coming for you, but if they catch you out on the street who knows what could happen? I wouldn't be able to help you. Now go!"

"But, Papa, they won't catch me. I can't stand to stay here!" David pounded the wall, shaking the room.

"They've blocked the roads. I've seen them myself," Koos said.

David pulled off his cap and wrung it in his hands. He looked up the dark staircase. The attic stairs hung cold, like a corpse from the ceiling.

"I can't hide like a rat. I would rather run for it. Anything would be better than being dragged out by the NSB," David fumed.

"I'll go look," Koos said and moved to the door before anyone answered.

# Chapter Three

# Stuttgart

Somewhere over France
March 1944

Ardagh looked at Hank's backside. He was sitting on the sling seat in the mid-upper gun turret of the Lancaster. Hank's hand appeared holding an opened tin can, which he threw at him. Hank peered down through his mask and gave him the thumbs-up. The tightness among the crew was one thing that Ardagh noticed right away, as if Hank wasn't his brother. The awkward feeling as if he were a stranger. This had stuck with Ardagh until the moment when the tin can hit his leg and spun away. He felt the simple act bring them closer. He looked back up and waved, giving Hank the thumbs-up sign back. At least he had this time with him, he thought. The sweat rolled down his back, and he tried to take in extra oxygen through the mask. Yeah, it was great to get closer to Hank. They were in this together.

Ardagh had developed a closeness with his own crew that was not unlike Hank had with his, but he knew it still wasn't the same. They were in a life-or-death battle and death came easily in war. Death had come without warning to his regiment during training, but it was still hard to fathom. How many would not come back as they battled through Europe? How close would the survivors be at the end?

He couldn't help but think of Private Bond and Private Marchuk, killed simply from a ride in the back of a truck on exercise. These were the first significant casualties of the war for 'A' Company, and they were still in Canada. All because the guy driving didn't know the roads and how the vehicle full of men and equipment was top-heavy and unstable. They went right through a T intersection, skidding and bouncing like a hockey puck on its end, then slapped into the woods, twigs snapping all around them. The truck's weight crushed the poor bastards as it rolled, and the entire platoon went flying out the back like hockey sticks sliding off a wall.

He had a lot of faith in Boyle to steer them right after meeting him over just a few beers. He guessed war was like that. Just like they relied on the truck driver to make sure they were safe. It seemed like forever since Debert, Nova Scotia. They blamed the accident on loose gravel. Dead from the loose gravel and a four-ton truck falling on you. It really made him think, and they were told to prepare for many to follow when they finally fought the Germans.

He wanted to see what it was like to put yourself in harm's way and to get it over with. He was tired of playing games, always preparing. Hank climbed onto the bomber every week. Now he knew what Hank's crew experienced and why they drank so much.

"Target," the navigator announced over the intercoms.

They finally reached Stuttgart. The mission targeted the city's centre and the narrow valleys that hid the factories that produced the Daimler Benz aircraft engines. These engines powered the Messerschmitt fighters.

"Ready in 30 seconds," Boyle said. "Bombardier, take over."

Ardagh sensed the bomber slow down.

"Steady... Keep weaving..."

It rolled slightly and dropped into its bombing run at

twenty thousand feet. For the next agonizing two minutes, the bombardier controlled the plane. The pathfinders had dropped the red and green flares to identify the target. They were high above the scattered clouds that had formed over Stuttgart. The German anti-aircraft made the clouds look alive with little lightning bursts. The engines droned on and Ardagh focused on the vibration on his back, waiting for the signal that the bombs had dropped.

Ardagh looked through the cabin. No one moved. It was quiet over the intercom. The flickers of light increased as they flew over the target and experienced the shell bursts rumble around them. The sense of doom for those below. He tried to shake off the thought of what was happening below. He stomped his feet and wrapped his icy hands under his armpits. His thoughts fell to that last night on the ice with Jim and his first experience with death, remembering Jim's words. *I'm just saying it's a big sacrifice, whether you die or not.*

He recalled Jim's expression as he stood leaning on the ice pick. The wind blew in gusts down the frozen Kaministiquia River, whipping up the snow and dancing across the open water where they had harvested the ice. It was hard not to forget.

Jim was a giant, well over six feet and close to three hundred pounds. He had fought at Vimy Ridge in the first war, so when the discussion came to the war, he was serious. Ardagh could smell the rum on his breath when the wind blew in his direction. They had been cutting ice and his dad had left him to work alone with Jim while the rest of the crew worked the ice at the other end of the river. They were always rotating back and forth as the river refroze in the spots that were harvested. Ardagh enjoyed the time he spent with Jim, who was always full of advice and endless funny sayings. Like Jean, Jim loved movies, but always misquoted them, followed by a silly wink and a nod. Ardagh knew now that he had made the mistake of asking him his opinion on whether he should sign up. Jean was worried Jim would convince him to sign up. He had told him the opposite.

Ardagh felt so small then as he pulled the blade back and forth in the ice. He was nearly a foot shorter than Jim and about a third of his weight. They agreed he needed to build some muscle, so Jim let Ardagh have as much time cutting as possible while he sipped his rum. The war had taken its toll on Jim and he constantly drank, which fed a short temper that got worse as he drank. Ardagh knew how to handle him the best, and things generally worked out well. So, his father let them work on their own.

*Something dies inside you, no matter what.* Jim had warned him what would happen if he signed up. A lot of dying and things he will be ashamed of doing to survive.

Ardagh remembered staring into Jim's eyes. It was the first time Jim had shown a hint of emotion. It was the most he had ever talked about the war, other than how to shoot and heat up the tea. Nothing that hinted at the experience he had gone through. The vision of Jim's torn look burned into his memory before Ardagh's world cracked and fell apart under him.

Ardagh's blade got stuck in the ice and Jim had pushed him out of the way to give him a hand. *Let me do it. You need to be stronger, kid.* The ice gave out a loud crack as Jim pushed the blade deep into the ice before it fell out of his grasp.

Everything after happened in slow motion.

Jim's angry grunt, as he reached for the handle of the blade. The crack of the ice as it gave way. Water splashed up from the cut in the ice and covered Jim's boots. Jim slipped and fell to his knees, then, with another grunt, he disappeared into the black water.

All went quiet.

Snow whipped over the water and blew up into Ardagh's face, blinding him. He wiped his face and looked out across the ice before he crawled as close to the edge as possible. Jim emerged, letting out a loud, wet gasp. His head and shoulders floated above the water. Ardagh watched Jim's arms flail as he tried to hold on to the edge, but pieces of ice kept breaking off.

Ardagh crawled on his knees over to the ice pick and swung it around. He crawled back toward Jim, dragging the ice pick beside him. Water soaked into his gloves and his hands weakened as he pushed the pole toward Jim. Ardagh's knees were wet and stuck to the ice.

Ardagh looked down at the remaining ice that lay between them and crawled forward a few more inches. The ice cracked again, and his pants stuck to the ice. He pushed the pole out further.

Jim's hands slipped off the edge, and he fought to stay above the surface. Ardagh moved forward another foot and thrust the pole out, this time lying flat on his stomach. Jim grabbed the pole and Ardagh held the full weight of Jim on the other end. Jim pulled himself up onto his elbows. He wiggled his shoulders and grunted like a walrus. Ardagh watched him struggle to pull himself up. Their eyes met as he clung motionless, poised on the edge of the ice. He shifted his elbows one more time before sliding back down into the water. Ardagh could only see Jim's hands and the top of his head. The pole was now loose in his hands.

It was no use. He needed to get help. The water crept up to Ardagh, and now his arms and chest were wet. Jim's deep voice yelled, "Go! Go!"

Ardagh still couldn't remember letting go of the pole or whether Jim could hold on to the edge of the ice. Ardagh just ran to the distant lights across the lake. The other group was only a couple of football fields away, but the wind was in his face. He yelled for help as he ran, but to no avail until he was almost on top of them. His father and the other men had all turned to run then, knowing something was wrong. It was all too late.

The Lancaster rattled and bumped as if happy to let go of its burden.

"Bombs away," Boyle said over the mike.

The two five-hundred-pound bombs and the single thousand-pound bomb dropped onto the target. They had a smaller load than usual to make room for the extra fuel for the longer journey into southern Germany.

Ardagh tried to shake off thoughts of Jim. A sense of relief washed over him as the bombs released and the plane lifted with the reduced weight. The bomber seemed different after the bomb bay doors closed and the engines picked up. The crew, as if awakened from a sleep, moved about in unison. Hank moved the turret left, then right, followed by the tail gunner, and the navigator's light flashed on to mark the location.

"Tee up the flash," Boyle ordered.

The bomber banked into a long turn. Ardagh remembered from the briefing that they needed to do a camera run to show the results of the bombing—the glow of the fires burned through the clouds. They still needed to go back over the target one more time. The biggest danger was colliding with other bombers rolling over the target area.

Ardagh tried again to see anything through the navigator's window. Nothing. Everything was in a fog, and he felt alone. He sat back down and tried to take it in. But his mind again wandered back to sitting alone in his father's ice truck. His hands were cold and stiff then too, but from the icy water, as he tried to look through the foggy window.

They had covered Jim's body with a tarp. They were now carrying his lifeless form to the ambulance, struggling to move his heavy, soaked body up the low shoreline. He could still hear Jim's voice inside his head. "Get out of the way. Let me do it!" His big arm knocking him aside and stepping in front of him. The front attendant slipped, and Jim's arm fell out from under the tarp and hung down from the stretcher, bouncing along as they walked. The window fogged up again as Ardagh's cloudy breath filled the truck in muffled silence.

*It's not your fault.*

Stupid blade. But he should've been strong enough to do it himself. Who else was to blame? Ardagh was the only one there, and he couldn't help him. They shoved Jim's body into the ambulance and placed his arm back under the tarp. These little things were etched into his memory. Putting on his cold and wet gloves, he had felt nothing, like someone had carved a void into him.

Ardagh stared down at his hands. They were cold now in the bomber and he shoved them under his armpits. The Lancaster lifted and sped up as Boyle announced, "Clearing off, stay alert."

Boyle pushed the Lancaster lower to ten thousand feet to help avoid the night fighters and settled into the bomber stream, back to England and safety. It was time for the great migration back to the base of the four hundred bombers that had just pounded Stuttgart and the Daimler Benz factory. This was the dangerous part, with the squadron weakened by the long journey with no air cover. The night fighters would target the weaker stragglers or damaged planes. They stayed alert, stoically staring into the dark sky. The navigator watched the Fishpond radar display for any sign of approaching German night fighters. This display could show the difference between friendly bombers and fast-approaching German night fighters. Ardagh yawned and stretched, trying to relieve the constant strain. No one let up or relaxed. The feeling of helplessness wrapped around him like a cold blanket, and he shifted and stared through the rear of the cockpit. He was just a powerless spectator like he'd been with Jim, but this time there was no place to run. He needed to learn how to overcome it.

# Chapter Four

# NSB

"Koos!"

Koos hesitated at the door, a sense of doom on the other side. She stared back at her father. His voice was sharp and commanding in her ears. She groaned and turned around, facing him fully, a silent plea in her expression, to go outside. She needed to do something to protect her brother. Stony silence faced her, and she moved back into the living room and sat in her father's chair, forcing herself not to cross her arms.

This was how it was. *We need to protect you because we can't afford to lose another.* She fought it her entire life. Over-protection. But now they lived in a different world. A world where the Germans ruled. Anything could happen. Most days were quiet and people went about their business as usual, hiding in a world of fantasy. The Germans were good at it. Lull you into sleep, then strike. Just like today. Their fate could be sealed already and they wouldn't know it. It was for the Germans to decide, unless they acted. At least try to act in some way.

Her parents lived in constant fear before the war of losing a child. Before Koos was born, her parents had lost two children to pneumonia. After four years of war, their fears had grown worse. Now they were about to lose another son. How could they let her out there, alone? Especially after what had happened at the start of the war. She had defied her father then. She had gone with Joost, despite her father's warnings, along the dike to watch the ships sail through the narrow passage between Bruinisse and Anna Jacobapolder. The Germans had not arrived yet. She remembered the walk along the dike. The fear and anticipation of kissing Joost. It seemed silly now.

\*\*\*

Koos walked along the dike through the fading evening light with the wind blowing in her face. She liked to walk on top of the dike through the green grass. She could walk back down, protected from the wind, but she enjoyed looking out, dreaming of what lay beyond the dike. It gave her a sense of freedom every time she made the climb and reached the top.

Joost, her boyfriend, followed. It had been her own choice. Her decision to make, to be with him, not her father's. She felt good about it. But why did her father's voice fill her head? Stay away from him, he warned. She had to stay up late the previous night with her father to watch the French Navy destroyers come into Bruinisse. Her father, always well dressed in his dark suit and hat, planned to visit the docks and welcome them. He was the proud Rentmeester in charge of the fishing grounds, dividing up and managing the local fishermen, collecting taxes for the use of the fishing grounds. They also owned three houses and the two fishing boats. He wanted the family to show respect for their newly arrived guests. The French Navy had been patrolling the Eastern Scheldt between Bergen op Zoom and Bruinisse, looking to see if a German invasion force was preparing to attack. He warned her that the Germans were about to come to Bruinisse at any moment and to stay home.

The last few days had been the most strenuous the family had ever seen. First, the sound of aircraft overhead, followed by the thumping in the distance as the bombs had fallen. Her father assured her it was the airbase in Haamstede and that they would be safer to stay put, but they packed what they could carry just in case. He said with confidence that their small port town was not strategic. Bruinisse was a tiny fishing village and had no military presence. But now the French Navy had shown up, it caused the entire town who had not yet fled to come out of their homes to cheer them on.

The declaration of war had happened quickly, and the German attacks had taken place across the entire country. The war in Europe was not unexpected. They covered it in her classroom with her teachers ever since the Germans attacked Poland. They followed every German strategic takeover of towns and cities in Poland on maps posted on the classroom walls. The teachers told them it was inevitable they would attack France and England. Belgium and Holland were just the innocent bystanders in this European fight. The concern of her mother and father deepened, but they stayed positive until the bombs fell.

The bombing and air raids were constant, with airplanes from both sides battling overhead as the family hid in the cellar. The town had not been attacked, but the tension and alarm of another German raid remained high. It was shocking how fast the Germans had moved across their small country. There was a rumour they had already reached Sint Philipsland just across the harbour. A disorganized Dutch army regiment had entered the town, taken up positions and billeted in the homes, but then suddenly left. This left everyone in the village hoping that the war would not come their way. Many fled to the smaller towns inland, closer to the middle of the island, for protection, but then the bombs had dropped to the west. The plan was to escape to Dreischor and stay in the local church, but they stayed put with all the uncertainty. The school remained open to keep a semblance of normalcy to Bruinisse. They practised what to do in air raids.

The whole world changed with the shocking announcement that left the country in anger and despair. The queen had fled to England, leaving all behind. Koos sat beside the radio with her family and saw the look of fear across her mother's face. It was the first time Koos saw her mother cry. She was surprised at her normally stoic and strong-willed mother's show of panic in her voice when she stood up and paced the room.

"What will we do? What will we do?" her mother asked over and over while wringing her hands until her father stood and held her. They had not shown such affection toward each other in all her years.

The next day, an abrupt announcement of the unconditional surrender of the Netherlands to Germany came over the radio as she was helping her mother with supper. It was only a few days, not even a week, from the declaration of war. There was a sense of relief that the bombing would stop. Of course, they hoped the Germans would treat them fairly. But then, by the end of supper, more news that their province, Zeeland, in the most southwest part of the Netherlands, bordering Belgium, would continue to fight. The French decided it was an important area and it would help protect them against the Germans when they attacked into Belgium and the city of Antwerp. The war was not over for them, and the French were preparing to stand and fight the Germans in Zeeland. This caused a second panic, and another wave of families had fled to the inland countryside.

Now, Koos followed behind Joost, continually looking over her shoulder for her father. The town was small, and not much went on without everyone knowing. Walking with Joost would add to the gossip. That wasn't her concern. What if her father saw her and confronted Joost?

Koos watched Joost stride ahead of her. She was glad for her father's stubbornness to stay near his boats. She smiled to herself, taking a deep breath of the salt air. Her cheeks flushed, and a warm wave of heat flowed over her. She picked up her pace and grabbed his hand, pushing against him. Joost pulled her close, putting his arm around her, and continued to walk along the dike, staring out to look for signs of any new ships arriving in the harbour.

She was safe in Joost's arms. Now she would get her first kiss. She nudged him again with her hip, pushing him to look at her. Instead, Joost pushed away from her, breaking his grip. "That's the *Hydra*! It's a Dutch minelayer. I saw it earlier steaming through the channel. Maybe they have news of the German whereabouts."

"Oh, who cares, Joost, let's continue our walk. My father might be there."

Joost ignored her and picked up his pace.

"Come on, Van den Berg, don't be afraid. Looks like they are about to dock. Let's go see," Joost said. She didn't like it when he called her by her last name. He only did it to make fun of her and put her down.

The narrow harbour was only a few hundred yards from their house. They were able to reach the dike near the dock-yard before the slow-moving minelayer made another broad turning sweep in the narrow channel that separated them from the Sint Philipsland peninsula.

Suddenly, its three-inch guns fired at the Sint Philipsland dike on the other side of the channel, sending up enormous dust clouds. They stared in shock as the feisty Dutch ship fired round after round into the embankment, and smoke-filled bursts of dust flew into the air.

"What are they shooting at?" Koos said.

A few seconds later, returning fire came from across the channel behind the dike in response to the *Hydra's* salvos. They followed the tracer bullets across the channel directed at the exposed Dutch ship.

"The Germans," Joost said, in shock as they both stood on the dike.

The *Hydra* was a prominent target in this narrow channel. The captain had initially slowed down to fire into the German patrol that sat out in the open on the dike, but then, in a panic, sped up when the Germans hit them several times. The captain tried to pick up speed to get away from the onslaught of machine-gun bullets and antitank fire. Still, several direct hits landed, causing a cloud of smoke and fire to erupt on the slow-moving minelayer.

As the assault on the Dutch boat continued to unfold, they just stood staring on top of the dike and watched the show.

The ship moved close to them, spewing smoke and fire. Koos could see the crews both fighting the blazing fires and trying to return fire at the Germans across the channel. The Germans hit the Dutch ship again. And this time, a gigantic explosion engulfed the minelayer. This finally awoke them to the danger as the ship brought the fire toward them. They both instinctively dove to the ground behind the dike.

Koos crawled across the dike into Joost's arms, clutching him tightly as the shells hit the other side of the dike, causing dust and dirt to rain down on them. Koos held onto him as they tumbled together further down the back slope of the dike embankment. She endured the concussion waves as each shell hit the other side of the dike.

Joost grabbed both of Koos's wrists and pushed her away. He stood up, jumping with fear, and ran across the street and behind the first home. He was gone before she knew what had happened.

More shells suddenly hit the dike. More dirt and rocks sprayed her, and she dug herself deeper into the dike wall.

Then as the gunner changed his aim, and she could now hear the Dutch ship being torn apart by another explosion. Metal shrapnel fell around the streets and homes.

Suddenly, like a switch, silence; the firing stopped.

The silence continued for some time.

A distant rumble of explosions woke her into action. She crawled to the top of the dike, her entire body aching, and the ringing in her ears blocked out all but the loudest noises. Koos could see the stern of the Dutch ship as it moved away in the distance, smoking and burning heavily. It was floating lower in the water and listing to the port side. There was still smoke coming from the other side of the dike from the shells that had missed the sinking ship. She could just make out soldiers standing on the other side of the channel, observing their success.

One thing was guaranteed, the Germans were here, and they weren't friendly. They meant business. It was incredible to think how fast they had reached the coast, in less than a week. It would only be a day or two before they crossed the small channel and occupied the town. There was virtually no one to oppose them.

Koos turned and rolled onto her back. A sharp pain exploded from her ankle into her chest as she moved. She closed her eyes, feeling the pain throb through her leg before she lifted herself onto her elbows, and looked down at her foot. Koos watched in horror as bright red blood gushed from her leg and pooled in the grass and dirt. Another pulse of pain shot up her leg and blood flowed down into her shoe. Pain surged into her temple with every pulse. She collapsed and looked up at the hanging grey clouds and black smoke. The sky flickered darker as she tried to focus. She dug her fingers into the wet grass, trying not to think about the blood pouring from her leg, and she pushed her back against the cold hardness of the dike and let out a soft cry before a knife of pain engulfed her. She remembered hearing her name and holding her breath, clenching her teeth as a light breeze picked up her hair, then everything went black.

\*\*\*

She was more ready now, than back then. She remembered the

shock and surprise when the Germans fired on the minelayer and the explosions rocked the shore and how they had just stood there, trying to take in what was really happening. Was this really happening? Her father had come to her rescue right after Joost had run. Now she knew what to do and how to act. She was not afraid to stand up to the Germans or the NSB, the Dutch Nazis.

Koos stood up and ignored her father as he yelled her name again. She opened the door, and the smoke blew into her face. She stepped onto the street, closing the door behind her. What she saw and felt would last her lifetime. She knew these senses that filled her were permanent, as if something died inside of her. The pulse of rage rolled up through her clenched fists and over her arms and into her face. The stench of diesel triggered the feeling she wanted to strike out. It would never go away. How could he, and why? What had she done to him?

Joost stood in the garden across the street as if he was trying to hide. He had a look of surprised guilt on his face and, under his boot, there were crushed tulips in full bloom. A truck was only a few yards away, its fumes of dark smoke pouring out the exhaust pipe. She could see a few men sitting dazed in the back. One with his face bloodied and shirt torn, his once greased-back hair sticking out. He was holding his knee and blood dripped from his chin. The Dutch Nazi soldiers climbed out of the truck as other soldiers marched down the street to their house.

Joost had betrayed her family. He was a snitch. Koos's eyes blurred, and she felt the tears fall down her cheeks. The door opened behind her and she heard the screams of her mother as David brushed by her onto the road. As she stared across at Joost, she made a promise to herself to never trust another and to stand up against the Germans. She vowed to make the traitors pay.

# Chapter Five

# Night Fighter

Somewhere over France
March 1944

Leutnant Jahn shifted in his seat and trimmed the engine of his Messerschmitt 109 when he saw the Lancaster ahead of him, outlined in the dark night sky, just three hundred yards to his starboard side. He hadn't been searching long since the radar tracking had placed him close to the bomber stream. He had swept north and south until he spotted the faint shadow below the clouds. Night fighting was a combination of luck and artistic license. Interpreting the radar signals and navigating.

They had lifted off for a second time that night from their base in Coulommiers, just southeast of Paris. His primary task was to follow the stream and report back positions for the night fighters to attack. It was a large stream of bombers, and he had let the first few pass by, hoping to find a wounded, easier target that was limping back on three engines. So far, he had only seen four engines spinning. Jahn looked down at his fuel gauge, tapping it as if to waken it from its sleep. He knew this had no technical merit but was a superstition he followed. Fuel and time in the air were always a precious commodity. When his fuel gauge hit low, it would be time for him to take on this stronger Lancaster before heading home.

He followed his prey and kept his distance. This was his five hundredth mission, and he had five kills to his name, but being careful had got him through this far in the war. He floated three hundred yards to the port side above his first victim, feathered the engine back and watched the top gunner's movements. The gunner was moving his turret back and forth and had not seen him yet.

***

The Fishpond display indicated a night fighter approaching, and the navigator announced, "Fighter in the area. Port side."

"Affirmative," Hank said, "Three hundred yards out, port side. I see him."

There were no clouds in the night sky to protect them. The moon was bright. Ardagh stood and looked over Boyle's shoulder to steal a glimpse. It was no use. The night fighter was on the port side of the bomber. He sat back down and took in a large gulp of oxygen from the effort. He looked at his watch. It was two in the morning.

The navigator motioned for him to strap in, and Ardagh struggled to pull the clip into the buckle. He tried to take a deep breath of oxygen through his mask, but his chest tightened. Hank was right. He had a lot to think about. Would he get the chance to change his path? It was out of his control now. The engines droned on, and Hank's turret swivelled back and forth. The navigator switched on his pocket lantern and marked up the map, plotting their progress and recording their position.

The night fighter kept its distance, tracking them. It felt like they were a swimmer watching a shark circling. Hank had explained that sometimes the night fighters would just track them, then fly away. They were trackers for other, more experienced night fighters. What would this one decide to do? The longer the night fighter waited to attack, the better the odds were.

Ardagh held on. He felt the strain as each gunner checked in over the headset as they waited to be attacked by the Messerschmitt. A surge of anger and frustration built up into him, and he wished he could strike out. But it was hopeless and out of his control. He hated the feeling, and he tried to take a deep breath, burying his face in his hands. His mind wandered to Jean sitting across from him at his house right after Jim died. *You can't hide from it.*

It was a cold windy day in April, with the leaves from the previous fall swirling around the yard. Jean had shown up at his house in a fur-lined coat and thick red lipstick on. Her blue eyes looked frozen over and snow-covered. He hadn't left the house for weeks after Jim died. Ardagh had gone to the funeral with Jean, but they had only spoken briefly. He had gone out once with his pa, but hadn't called her. He hadn't even thought to, and he didn't know why. Did he care? His mind was blank and disconnected. That was when he told her. His thoughts had gone to Jim, floating in the icy water.

Jean sat down on the couch, arms folded. She still hadn't taken off her coat. Ardagh chose his pa's chair opposite to her. Only a stained wooden table separated them. Glenn Miller's "In the Mood" played on the radio in the background. The song never seemed to end, and they both sat waiting for it to finish until his mother came. She placed two cups of tea with cream and sugar on the table and said, "I'll be upstairs if you need me, dear." She turned off the radio before heading up the stairs. Jean had let out a sigh and crossed her legs.

Ardagh had done everything he could. Jim had told him to leave him to get help. He would hold on. Jim would understand. Ardagh would sign up. That's when she told him. *I won't sit here and hold on, hoping you will come home to me.*

Ardagh looked up at Hank in the turret. All he could do now was sit and hold on. He knew now that she loved him and was trying to make him stay, to save him from this.

"Port side, three hundred yards. Steady," Hank said. The turret shifted to the right, tracking the night fighter.

That was the last conversation he had with Jean. It was over. He knew now that he was in love. It was his first love and he couldn't recognize it then. It still hurt. When he told Eileen his story, she laughed at how sweet he was. Said that it was normal to dream of your first. But then you grow up and life gets harder. He couldn't tell Eileen the real reason. It hurt too much. The fallout of leaving the theatre. The twist of fate that would carry with him.

Ardagh had gone over that moment a million times since. It changed everything in his life. His decision to leave the theatre. It was a few weeks after they had broken up. His former love was sitting off his port side in the theatre, Jean. The feeling of waiting for her to notice him as he sat gripping the armrest, wanting to have the strength to rip it off and smash the guy's face sitting next to her. He had gone to the theatre with Danny. Ardagh looked at Danny with his oblong face and tight lips. His face was expressionless. Danny always kept things calm. How could she be with someone else so soon?

Ardagh glared across at Jean and then at the guy next to her. Only four seats separated them. Would she notice him? He shrunk into his seat. Time stood still, and it was like his chest was filling with water. Danny elbowed to go, but Ardagh pushed him away.

Ardagh wanted to stay, but she turned and caught his stare. Her sad glance at him was as direct as a blowtorch to his face. She was with a real man. Someone who was strong enough to stay with her. Ardagh was gone, dead to her. The hurt of her perception washed over him, and he had a strange awareness of not belonging.

He had stumbled out of the theatre. Danny followed right behind. He looked at his taller, lanky friend. His worried look told him he wanted to say something, but Danny held his tongue. They shared everything together, they may as well share this disaster. Ardagh walked to his father's car and said, "Let's go to my sister's. They'll have beer."

Ardagh parked the car in front of the house and, before he could get out, little Marv and his buddy Joey were out with their wagon to greet them.

If he had only stayed and fought through it. His life would be different. Jim had told him everything happened in threes. He could have saved Jim if he had been stronger. One thing had led to the other. He had lost Jim, then Jean, but then the third was unspeakable. If he'd stayed at the theatre and stood his ground, or watched the road. If only. Joey. He now carried this with him. It changed the course of his life, and he was determined to fix it. There was only one way he knew how. He had his reason. So, he and Danny had signed up to join the war against the Nazis.

*\*\**

Leutnant Jahn looked at his gas gauge and tapped it again; thirty minutes of fuel left. He had followed them for almost twenty-five minutes for the kill. Now or never. He had given his last report of the location of the bomber stream. Jahn liked the waiting game because it dulled the defences of the bomber crew by creating panic among the air gunners. He watched the top gunner until he moved his turret in his direction. The bomber would typically dive away to avoid the stream of bullets. If he was accurate, it would be over quickly, and he would head back to base and have a night of well-deserved sleep. The most vulnerable point of attack on a Lancaster bomber was the port or starboard quarter at the rear of the plane. Staying level and at speed with the bomber made it more difficult for both gunners to react. As the turret moved to face him, he pulled up and then throttled full as he steered into the quarter port side and pressed the trigger. His fire ripped into the side of the bomber.

***

Ardagh jumped in his seat as he heard Hank's gun going off in short, controlled bursts and a calm voice over the headphones. "Quarter port side and closing fast."

"Roll to port!" the tail gunner, Hill, yelled.

"Brace, brace!" Boyle said as he pushed and twisted down on the controls. This put the Lancaster into a controlled spin toward the ground, instead of turning away from the approaching night fighter, performing the standard operating procedure under an enemy attack. Boyle turned the heavy, slower-moving bomber into the oncoming night fighter. The quick manoeuvre shortened the distance between them and the approaching night fighter, giving him a brief exposure to the top side of the Lancaster. But it was also unexpected.

"Quarter port!" Ardagh heard Hank through the headphones with excitement.

The steady rhythm of fire came again from the turret above, with another rain of shell casings falling into the open bay.

Then a loud cheer, "Attaboy, Hank, give it to him!"

Hank's turret stopped firing.

"Jammed!" Hank said in frustration.

***

Jahn heard the bullets thud into the side of his cockpit, and he broke away from his attack. The bomber dived into him instead of away and he needed to pull back to prevent ramming into it. He was too close as they spun and dove downward together. He let the fighter drift back to the port quarter side and the tail before he pressed the trigger, ignoring the return fire.

***

The tail gunner, Hill, fired as the bomber plunged into almost a free fall, and the night fighter pulled into his view. The shell casings flew about the fuselage as Hill continued to fire.

Ardagh held on as the bomber twisted. A sensation of falling enveloped him, and his stomach lifted into his rib cage. The interior of the fuselage erupted as bullets raked the outside of the plane and slammed straight through, ricocheting fragments of metal spraying around him.

"There's smoke, ammunition has blown!"

"He's down, he's down! Great shooting! Confirmed, confirmed!" As the entire crew erupted the voices filled Ardagh's headset.

The dive only lasted a few seconds before they levelled off. Ardagh coughed and choked on the spit in his respirator mask. He ripped his mask off, spitting and coughing, then pulling in oxygen from the air mask. Heaving, he puked out the entire contents of the earlier sandwich on the bottom of the fuselage. Ardagh struggled to wipe out his air mask with the sleeve of his jacket and finally gave up. The cold spit and puke froze around the edges of his cheeks, and his face stung. As he filled his lungs again, the stink of burning fuel and puke filled his senses. He blew and expelled the foul air out of the mask.

"Settle... settle..." Boyle said. "Not all at once, boys."

"Steady... I see the bastard now... Good shooting, boys... confirmed."

\*\*\*

The Messerschmitt 109's cockpit canopy, riddled and shattered, blew off and the underbelly filled with flames. Leutnant Jahn's lifeless body lay against the controls, and the plane rolled and banked out of control.

\*\*\*

"Great work, boys, Hank and Hill, just splendid... just splendid!"

"Let's get home. Stay alert."

Ardagh looked down in the dark shadows of his boots to the pile of shells on the floor.

*Breathe*, he told himself. He knew now what he needed. It

was to control his own destiny. Take charge of what lay ahead and not look back. If he let his past hold him back, he wouldn't survive and what he left behind would be for nothing.

## Chapter Six

# Dutch Nazi

Bruinisse, Netherlands
April 1944

"What's this patch for?" Thomas asked.

"It's showing I'm in the SS," Joost said.

Joost's nephew sat cradled on his arm and the child's little fingers explored over Joost's grey-green uniform as he stood outside the Ferry House Cafe. He was to leave for Sonneberg, Germany, in the morning to join a newly formed Dutch SS Panzer Grenadier Regiment. There was no turning back. The day was brighter than usual despite the low clouds that always sat on the island. He gave Thomas a long hug, ignoring his squeals, before placing him back down on the sidewalk. He had promised to buy him one last treat before he left for training. Thomas stared into the window eyeing the chocolate-covered Stroopwafel. Joost decided he would buy one for himself, too. He didn't know when he would be back.

They entered the cafe feeling the warmth of the bakery and taking in the sugary aroma. Thomas jumped up and down as he held on to Joost with both hands, shouting, "Stroopwafel!" The five round tables of the cafe were full, but quiet. Only Thomas's shouting and stomping feet could be heard.

Joost shook Thomas's hand. "Quiet, or you won't get any," he said as he turned to look. They all were staring at him. He recognized Pieter and another classmate and nodded to them. Pieter shook his head in response, and his face reddened. Pieter stood up as if thinking about saying something, but he just pulled at the sleeve of his jacket, avoiding eye contact. Joost had served his suspension after fighting Pieter. They had even hung out for a time afterwards, considering each other friends, but now, after Koos's brother was taken, nothing was normal. Pieter moved through the tables with his head down and pushed by without a word. Joost knew the response he would get from signing up. His father was the Chief Engineer of the water board and founder of the island National Socialist party and wore the SS pin, but this was something else. His father had opened the sluice gates and started the flooding of the land, but that was the Germans' decision, not his. But why did Pieter ignore him almost in shame? They shared the same views about the NSB.

A couple stood and put on their coats, walking out, leaving full pastries on their plates. The other tables cleared out, except for one man who sat alone. It was his old schoolteacher, Mr Van Hulst. He was in a heavy sweater and wore high rubber boots as if he just walked off a fishing boat. The chair creaked as he leaned back, stretching. Their eyes met and Mr Van Hulst smoothed his short moustache and removed his thick glasses to rub his eyes as if ready to give one of his classroom lectures. It was funny. Joost would miss those times more than ever when he sat cold and alone at the front, but now it was too late. He left Thomas at the counter and sat down across from the teacher.

"You couldn't resist your father? I thought you were better than that," Mr Van Hulst said before Joost settled into the chair. His deep, smooth voice left you in no doubt about his authority. Joost had hung on every one of his words in class. He was always there for advice, no matter what. His directness stung the most, but Joost and Van Hulst had an understanding.

"But it was expected. Wasn't it? The gossipers, to answer them," Joost said as he waved his arms in the air.

"But going from snitch to soldier is more serious. They shoot those that run. Most likely death awaits you," Mr Van Hulst said.

It was not just one blow, but two. Those that run. Joost held the edge of the table, resisting the urge to throw it across the room. He would prove them wrong.

"I was never... I didn't," Joost said, slapping the table. "Snitch, for what reason?"

"Maybe you were set up?"

"But why? For what purpose?"

"Revenge or jealousy. Who knows why people do stupid things like sign up for another country?"

"A united Europe, we'll defeat communism," Joost said.

"United Europe, please. You're running away. You should stay and fight the Germans. Then you could win Koos back, but not this way."

"Stroopwafel!" Thomas shouted and stomped at the counter.

Joost pushed the chair away and hurried back to the counter, scooping Thomas up.

"Two Stroopwafels," he ordered over the counter. Joost felt a hand on his shoulder.

"Don't come back," Mr Van Hulst said before walking out the door.

The cafe was empty and silent. Joost paused and took in the scent of fresh cinnamon and chocolate flavours in the air. The young daughter of the baker glared at the door from behind the counter and in a soft voice said, "Two Stroopwafels."

Joost stared down into the counter, examining the cakes, re-thinking his choice. What would he like? It was the same question he had asked himself over the past months. Ever since the

*Hydra* accident and even more so now, since David was taken. Events seemed to transpire against him. The accusations of being a snitch and siding with the Germans pushed him over the edge. The pressure from his father to follow him into the Dutch Nazi party and join the Dutch SS regiment. Joost paid and picked up the Stroopwafels. They stepped out onto the sidewalk. The wind had picked up, and he felt the cool breeze. He knelt down and handed one Stroopwafel to Thomas.

"Let's walk along the dike," Joost said, grabbing Thomas's hand, "and enjoy our Stroopwafels."

\*\*\*

Koos stopped pedalling and glided to a stop. She planted both feet on the ground, straddling her bike, and her jaw dropped. Thomas was holding a Stroopwafel in one hand and a Dutch Nazi in the other. It could be only one person. They were walking away from her out of the Ferry House Cafe. She could tell by his walk that it was Joost. So, he had finally done it. It surprised her how it happened so soon. But now he would no longer be part of her life. They had all read how many of the Dutch SS soldiers had died already on the Eastern Front. He would not last long, she hoped. She held on to the image. Joost holding the tiny hand of his nephew, enjoying his Stroopwafel. *Is this what war does to us? Makes us have these bad thoughts? Thomas would lose an uncle.* She tried to erase the thought of Joost. What did she want to happen? What would happen to her brother? It was war and he would pay. It wasn't her choice but his, and he would have to live with it. She turned her bike around and pushed the pedals. Slow at first. Then, as hard and fast as she could go. The wind picked up and swirled around her. She leaned in, fighting it. She needed to get ready for tomorrow.

# Chapter Seven

# Wrong Way

Farnham, England
April 1944

"Cut him some slack, fellas", Danny said as he watched Ardagh march down along a hedgerow to the river away from the carrier. They sometimes compared themselves to Bing Crosby and Bob Hope. He felt like he was watching Bob get lost. It was cold and wet despite the time of year. April might be hot or cold, depending on what part of England you were in. They were now training in what they were learning was the cold area. It was another chance to show their strength as a fighting unit and test the NCOs. So far, no one had been killed in action or captured during this drill. The Lake Superior Regiment was manoeuvring around the flank of the Algonquins, and they had lost contact with their platoon. The fake battle was almost over, but they still had a few more hours to capture the remnants of the Algonquins and link up with the remainder of the regiment.

"He hasn't got a clue, is all I was saying," Woods said. "Watch, he'll quote another movie and we'll go in the wrong direction."

"You've confused him enough already," Danny said as he pulled his helmet down. His large forehead and narrow, long face made it look like his helmet was too small, and he was always tilting it down. "Let him sink or swim. If he doesn't learn now, we are in shit up against the Germans for real."

"We've been in England for two years now, and two years of training before that. You think he'd know where he was going by now. At least Wilf knows left from right. He's lost without his big brother," Wilson said. "We're a motorized unit, for Christ's sake. We're supposed to move fast, not plod around through shrubs. On the farm, my dad would call it slowpoking around."

"He's probably dreaming about his old lady. Picking out the right walking stick for her. What's her story, Danny?" Woods asked.

"She's old enough to be his mother, I'd say. Short story there," Wilson said.

"You're both just jealous, is what that is. She lost her husband, so give her a bit of respect," Danny said. "She's good for him, which is better for us. So, fuck off."

***

Ardagh walked along through the mixed green and yellow reed-covered riverbank. It was cold and foggy, just like he had seen in the movies. The only sound was his feet crunching under the grass. He still found it hard to believe that he was in England and wearing a uniform. They were billeted in Guildford, southwest of London, close to the regiment's training grounds at Farnham. The billet house sat at the very end of the street, next to the Guildford rail line across from the busiest intersection and main road into London. He could hear the rail cars rolling by and the gears grinding as they slowed down at the corner. He was lucky for a kid from Fort William, and it suited him just fine. Besides, he was in England and didn't care where he was. It was all part of the grand adventure. It did not surprise him he had ended up in a similar home to his own so far away. The row house tucked away between the rail line and the river was only a thirty-minute stroll to Guildford Castle.

He was so close to the Wooden Bridge pub he could taste the pints of beer and hear the barmaid pouring them.

Eileen Moody and her sister Lily were the highlights of his new life in England. This was definitely worth the sign-up fee. The long, hard days of training went by steadily, like a shift at the grain elevators. But the nights were theirs, mostly. Leenie, as he called her, which she loved to hate, was always leaning on his shoulder at the pub. He and his buddy Danny Payne were fortunate to be billeted to their house for two years now. At first, it was awkward. Both Eileen and Lily were quite a bit older than them. Eileen's husband had been killed in the early battles in France. Lily had just moved in to help support Eileen through the tough times.

Ardagh thought back on how childish he must have seemed to Eileen at first. He had grown up a lot from the days before he left Fort William. Of course, neither of them had any clue about what they were going through for the first several months. They focused hard on training and getting used to their new surroundings. They rolled into a training routine with hard days away, followed by binges of pub crawls and touring where they could. His path toward Eileen came about over time and was not much different from those of some other guys in his platoon. They both lived together, and she had comfortably replaced her late husband with him on the daily routine of cleaning, dinners or packing him a bite to eat. After a few months of this routine, they became closer and closer. She sat next to him on the couch while they listened to BBC news. He would thank her with a brief hug after dinner.

She gave him a 'good luck boy' wave and smile every morning before they went off to train. She listened and advised him about the girls after the dances when he came home empty-handed, frustrated and alone.

Then he discovered that Lily and Danny were a couple. They had kept it a secret for several weeks, but couldn't hold it back any longer. Ardagh laughed at himself, thinking back on it. He had already known for weeks before they even knew. They soon were going out together as a group and it wasn't a surprise or shock when one night at the pub across the street, Eileen and Ardagh stumbled back together. He kissed her on the step, telling her how much he loved her, then abruptly passed out on the couch. It was a surprise when, in the morning, she crawled into his bed. He hadn't noticed her flirtatious behaviour until then.

Ardagh had come back after the bombing run with Hank gripped with a mix of fear and newfound knowledge of what it took. His brother had shot down a night fighter and they'd lived to tell the story. He was riding high with confidence. He had told no one and was toying around with keeping it that way.

He rolled back into the same day-to-day routine, and they continued their training throughout the English countryside. The excitement of flying with Hank faded and turned into feelings of fear. Failure at Dieppe by the Canadians raised the question of whether or not landings could be successful against the great Atlantic wall Hitler and Rommel had built. The Germans had almost four years to prepare for them. With the landings in Africa and in Italy, the gossip through the platoon intensified. Their fear grew when they saw the large number of casualties, and they talked about who were most likely to get killed. The non-commissioned officers seemed in Ardagh's mind to take the full swing of it. He was now a corporal and soon to be a sergeant. He was an Original, having signed up early. Now he was second-guessing himself and the extra duty and potential sacrifices that lay ahead. He had long conversations with both his brothers about whether to sink back into the ranks or to accept promotions. Ardagh didn't mind the pressure to command, and the increased responsibility that came with it. He knew he could do it, no problem. He had the skills and could operate and shoot anything. His years of hunting and fishing, living in the wilderness for days camping, gave him a leg up on many men, despite his age. But he desperately wanted to prove it.

Other men relied on him to make the right decisions. Life or death. He had a good crew: Danny, his best friend from high school and Johnny Wilson, the same age as him, a farm kid from Mossbank, Saskatchewan. Then there was Bill Woods. He was a year older and from Toronto. A big-city kid. Ardagh felt like he was always having to appease him and show that he knew his stuff. Bill didn't tolerate laziness or complaints. He was the short, stocky type. He didn't like to think outside the box and had joined up later, which gave Ardagh his only edge over him.

Ardagh wished he had a fishing rod and was back home, but he needed to decide what direction to head. Time was running short. The rain picked up, and the visibility was less than a football field. It seemed like every river and field looked the same.

He had worked hard to get promoted and was on the list to become one of the youngest sergeants. This wasn't the time to blow it. Eileen had pushed him hard to step up. This was his chance. He had argued with Woods that they needed to go right and follow the hedge. But Woods was convinced that after rounding the bend and cutting across through the forest, they were already turned around and should head left and follow the river to stay in line with the regiment. The English countryside was a mess. It was full of winding roads, hedgerows, and river canals. They were continually lost. They had removed all the road signs to prevent the Germans from knowing where they were if they ever invaded in the hopes of slowing them down. It was also great training for actual combat. There were no signs that said 'Germans here'. If Private Woods was right, they would head straight into the enemy lines and be considered killed in action.

Ardagh was certain it was the Wey River he was looking at, and they would link up with the rest of the unit if they continued right along the hedgerow. Jim had always told him, know where you are; if you head in the wrong direction, you could find yourself in no-man's-land. It was instant death, he said. He had paid extra attention to Lieutenant Brown when he pointed out the landmarks at the operations meeting. Brown knew Joey's family and Ardagh always felt judged by him. He was a tall, steady figure with grey eyes and a serious look about him, a real professional soldier and he carried high expectations of his unit. He was the type of leader that pushed you to be the best because he expected the best. This added to Ardagh's need to prove that he could do it and get over his past mistakes. Ardagh looked again at the river, trying to remember what Lieutenant Brown had showed him.

Ardagh turned back and climbed through the hedge then tripped on a tree root, falling head first. His elbows sunk into the mud. He got up, brushing the dirt and wet grass off his uniform. They had all seen it. He was like a stupid little kid playing in the woods. What were they all thinking? Watching him fumbling around.

He checked his pockets and felt the pocketknife. He picked the grass and mud off his elbow. It brought him back to little Marv, climbing off his bike to meet him, then falling flat on his face. Trying to act tough, brushing the dirt off with a tear forming but holding off. It was the last time he saw his parents and his little nephew. It had been after two years of training and two years after sitting in front of the judge watching Marv pick grass off his pants.

He had felt bad for having to run out and miss his mother's last meal. Her worried face. *What if he didn't return?* She had said. No one had ever raised the chance that he may not return. It was like a goalie guaranteeing a shutout before the game started. You just never said it.

Ardagh had moved to the door, and as he stood looking at her, he had his first wave of sadness. Would he see her again? Of course, he needed to bury the past and create a new future path for himself. Lots of hard work and uncertainty ahead, but he would be back. He looked down at his soldier's boots and thought about how life events had overtaken him. He noticed a slight tug on his pant leg and saw Marv poking him. Marv was holding a knife.

"You can borrow my knife. It'll protect you," Marv had said. "I'll get it when you're back."

Ardagh had seen the relief in his mother's eyes, then. He had winked at her and picked up Marv. His father had walked in naked except for a pair of dirty shorts. His dark tanned skin matched Marv's except for a red patch around his neck and shoulders. He looked like a larger version of his grandson. Ardagh slipped the brown jigged-bone-handled knife into his pocket and walked back to his mom, still holding Marv, and they all hugged together.

He felt a pain stab through his chest. Poor Joey. Marv hadn't said a thing, but he knew it was Joey's knife. He had lots to make up for and to prove. He would give it back when he returned.

Ardagh looked at the men waiting for him in the carrier. He missed his family. What was he thinking? He patted his right pocket again, feeling the pocketknife. A numbness fell over him.

"You finished playing in the shrubs? Find the fishing hole?" Woods asked, standing behind the Bren gun in the carrier. Danny looked worried.

"What do you think? Should we continue up right along the river?" Danny asked.

What if Woods was right? Ardagh marched to the rear of the carrier and climbed in. What would Jim do? He thought of Bob Hope, who played Ace Lannigan in the *Road to Singapore*. It was his first movie after Jim died. Something Jim would have laughed at.

"I just want you to stand there and admire me for a while. I just got an idea," Ardagh said. No one laughed. The rain poured hard, and fog rolled through the opening of the hedgerow like a steam engine. Ardagh studied the map again. "Let's head up left along the river for another mile. We should hook up with everyone there."

"I knew you would come around," Woods said.

Danny started the engine and shifted into gear. Ardagh pointed and signalled to head out.

"Good work, Ace," Danny said.

## Chapter Eight

# Roadblock

Bruinisse, Netherlands
April 1944

Koos's basket was full, but it didn't slow her progress. She enjoyed the early morning sun. The sky, a rare blue, had only a thin swish of cloud that disturbed it. Her grandfather, an old fisherman, would tell her it would rain tomorrow. There were very few on the road between Zierikzee and Bruinisse. She had left early in the morning, and it took less than the forty minutes she had planned to reach Zierikzee. The eggs, bread and flour in her basket she had traded for the mussels her brother had given her. Under the German occupation, it was supposed to be illegal and considered black market to trade, but many did it.

Since the Germans had taken her brother David, she had decided that she needed to do something. She went to her Reformed Church minister for help, and he put her in touch with a store in Zierikzee. She wasn't certain, but she thought they worked with the National Organization for Helping People in Hiding or the LO for short. It was better she didn't know, the Minister had told her, but they would appreciate her help. He had told her she was brave, and the thrill of helping made her push her bike faster. She was standing up not only to the Germans, but to Joost. She couldn't help her brother anymore, but now helped support those still in hiding.

The night before, a group of Kriegsmarine, or German Navy, warships had entered the harbour and docked for the night. Kriegsmarine sailors had taken up the cafe and bars while their ships were loaded with fresh supplies. Koos pushed her hair from her face and blushed as she thought about the lieutenant she had met. She spoke German well enough, and she wasn't afraid to talk to them. He had stopped her to ask for directions, as she was one of only a few people out on the street so early. She had cursed at her stupidity, believing that she would go unnoticed in the early morning, but it turned out to be the reverse. The tall Kriegsmarine lieutenant had made her feel at ease while she held her bike between them. She had given him her name without thinking and he asked her where she lived. To her surprise, he had offered to drive her back to Bruinisse, but she refused. It would look terrible for her, she had told him, embarrassed. He had laughed, to her surprise, and she continued on her way. We are not all bad, he told her as she pedalled away.

Koos heard the car long before it reached her. She moved to the edge of the road but continued to pedal. The sun was now above her and she saw clearly that it was a black sedan with a Dutch NSB flag on the front. It could be only one person, coming from Bruinisse. Erwin de Lange was Joost's cousin. But to her surprise, it turned out to be Pieter Jansen.

"What are you doing out here, Koos?" Pieter questioned, without saying hello. Pieter was nothing, just a schoolboy. She shook her shoulders as if to shove him away, remembering how he tried to kiss her neck and pin her to the ground at the dance. His hands searching before Joost rescued her. What was he searching for now? He didn't work for the police, but what was he doing in Erwin's car? Koos's first instinct was to tell him to go away, and that it was none of his business. She stared at the hood of the car. The flag flapped in the wind. Koos knew not to lie, but he was not to be trusted. Had she trusted him before? She was told by the minister to tell as much of the truth as possible if questioned; it made it more difficult for them to catch you.

"I was just at the store. My papa sent me," Koos said and pointed to her basket.

"Do you have your papers?"

"Of course," she said, padding her coat pocket. She would not pull them out for him. "Are you the police now, Pieter?"

Pieter looked at the flag at the front of the car and the corner of his mouth raised just enough for Koos to take notice before he said, "I'm helping my father in the garage and testing the car out for Mr de Lange, that's all." Koos could not think of how to respond and shifted her bike to point down the road. She glanced at her blurred reflection in the car's side and felt the heat from the running engine. Pieter was difficult to read. Why did he ask for her papers? Was he joking or was there another reason?

"I'm not with the NSB. They are fools," he added, breaking the silence. "There is a new roadblock up ahead. Erwin. You should be careful."

Koos gripped the handlebars tighter and stepped on the pedal. Erwin was the school janitor before becoming a police officer with the Dutch Nazis. Single and in his late thirties. Erwin leered over the boys in her school, and whenever she saw him, she felt uncomfortable. It surprised Koos when they accepted him into the Nazi unit. She refused to smile at Pieter and show any courtesy. Did he suspect something or was he just being his usual self-serving pain?

"I know," she said as she pushed on the top pedal and pulled away. She didn't look back as the car sped away. She looked down at her basket of goods and tried to recall how they were placed. A letter and ration cards for the minister were tucked beneath them between the basket and the cloth. They would have to rip the basket off to get to it. She had the right papers if checked to ensure getting past a check stop unless they found the ration cards. The Kriegsmarine lieutenant was her first practice test, and she had passed. Now the first real test was ahead of her. Her thoughts went to her brother and what he must face every day in Germany. Was he safe? This was nothing compared to what he must be going through. The Germans had proven that even her father couldn't protect her or the family. She was on her own.

The sounds of another car woke her from her thoughts and grew louder behind her. She pulled over to the side and watched Pieter race by back to Bruinisse. Maybe he was telling the truth, she thought. She could now make out the first house on Rijksstraatweg and the corner of the intersection that marked the edge of Bruinisse. There were five soldiers with two cars parked alongside the road. She knew one of them must be Erwin de Lange, the others she didn't know.

Koos felt the handlebars loosening in her grip and tried to fight off her body's urge to sweat. She let go one hand and smoothed out her dress, drying her palm, then switching. It was no use. It only made it worse. She tried to recall, earlier in the day, what had stopped her nerves when she met the German lieutenant. It was how relaxed and comfortable he was, as if on vacation, just a tourist asking for directions. She stayed present in that moment and remained calm. He had cursed at his stupidity when she told him the store was right in front of him, thanking her as if she saved him hours of searching.

Erwin shouted loud enough to make her step on the brake to stop. She climbed off her bike and walked the last several yards to the roadblock, taking her time. Afterwards, she would realize how this had saved her life.

***

Leutnant zur See Wilhelm Clausen had the looks and the enormous smile infectious to those around him; it instilled confidence. He sat in the supplies truck cab along with his blonde-haired quartermaster, Heinrich Muller, as it sped along toward Bruinisse. Heinie handed him a canteen of water. The taste of schnapps was lingering, and he took a full drink from the canteen, swishing it around in his mouth. The last thing he could afford was showing up with schnapps on his breath. He had been told that his new promotion and command of the AF 92 would take effect once the ships construction was complete, and he had been given a few days of leave in Zierikzee. It was mid-morning and just a short twenty-five-minute drive from Zierikzee to Bruinisse. He was returning from his leave nearly half a day early and hoped it wouldn't go unnoticed. The truth was, he didn't know what else to do other than get back. His father had told him that these little things mattered in the German Navy. So far, he was right.

They turned right onto Rijksstraatweg, which took them directly to the Bruinisse harbour and his ship. He looked across the flat farmland and dreamed of being back in the crowded streets of Berlin. He was born in Katowice, Poland, but couldn't remember it. He was just a child when their family moved to Kopenick, a suburb of Berlin where the Dahme and Spree Rivers met. He had changed his name from Spilka to Clausen just before the war to improve his chances of getting into the Nazi party and a posting on a submarine. It was his mother's maiden name. He thought it all had been a waste of effort until he found out about his new post and the command of the AF 92. As it turned out, his experience as an artillery corporal in the 50th Infantry division, Wehrmacht, had helped to get him the posting to the Navy Artillery Flotilla. The converted landing craft, essentially moving anti-aircraft guns on water, was a better fit for him than being a submarine commander. He preferred Wilhelm, but after four years of war and building close relationships with his men, he was now happy to be called Willie.

The truck made the turn and sped up, then braked. Willie woke out of his deep thoughts and saw the roadblock ahead. He expected them to be waved through once they saw his uniform, but a hand lifted for them to halt. There were no other cars or trucks on the road, but a lone girl on a bike. She was the same girl he had met in Zierikzee. The roadblock wasn't even German but Dutch SS. He wasn't sure if it was the hangover or the insulting hand gesture from the ill-fitted Dutch SS private that angered him more. So, he climbed out of the truck to see what the holdup was. She couldn't have been here long.

The leader of the Dutch SS group was a skinny weasel of a man who tried to carry himself as if he were larger than his black uniform and sergeant stripes. For Willie, he was the type that was losing the war. His hands were deep into her basket, and he was about to throw the food out onto the road. A pulse of anger flared inside him.

"Koos," Willie said without thinking. "Why are you letting him wreck my dinner?"

The weasel stopped what he was doing and stared up at him as he approached. He noticed a twitch and his jaw dropped slightly. Koos turned to look at him and her cheeks were bright. His anger melted away for a moment until he looked back at the Dutch SS weasel.

"This young woman is delivering special goods for the Kriegsmarine and should not be disturbed," Willie said, trying to sound official. "What is the purpose of this?"

The weasel put the food back into the basket and said, "We are checking for black market goods. And…"

"She's just a girl," Willie cut in. The Dutch SS weasel looked Willie up and down trying to piece things together. Willie could see the smoke coming from the top of his head. He wasn't as bright as his uniform, Willie thought. He reached down and picked up the scattered apples that had been thrown on the road, putting them back in Koos's basket, then covered the basket again with the towel she was using. Everything was back in its place. The Dutch SS weasel stepped back, studying the scene, trying to decide how to act.

He walked around to the other side of the bike and said, "You're interrupting a search of the police authorities on a Dutch civilian. Please step aside while I complete my task. You can have the girl if I decide she can proceed."

Willie moved between Koos and the Dutch SS weasel. He towered over him, nearly a foot taller.

"I'm Sergeant Erwin de Lange. In charge of this squad and ordered to complete searches at this roadblock; if you have an issue, take it up with my superiors."

Willie widened his stance and crossed his arms and said, "Are you allowed to search Kriegsmarine supplies?"

"Of course not. That is not our authority. You're free to go with your supplies."

"Thank you very much, sergeant. We'll be on our way then," Willie said. He turned to look at Koos and he could see the worry in her eyes that he was abandoning her.

"Excuse me," he said as he grabbed the handlebars of Koos's bike and abruptly climbed on, and pedalled away. "Kriegsmarine supplies coming through."

He waved at Heinrich. Thankfully, he was from Munich and had the same mischievous streak as Willie. The supply truck started up and moved forward, following Willie pedalling the bike.

"Are you coming?" Willie said, turning back to Koos and laughing. Koos hesitated, then looked at Erwin, who signalled his defeat and gestured to her to go.

They were nearly at the ships when Willie stopped and got off the bike. The supply truck sped up, and Heinrich gave him a wave and thumbs up before he drove off. The dust settled on the road and it was quiet around them.

"Thank you," Koos said.

Willie stopped and handed her the bike. They walked again in silence. The wind was calm and Willie looked back out onto the water and his ship that sat in the harbour, trying to think of what to say. Was he tired from the night before? His mind was blank. Was he nervous to speak? He was never one to lack words in any situation.

"Can I see you again?" Willie finally asked.

"I didn't need your help," Koos said.

"I know, but it was fun to put him in his place, wasn't it?" Willie laughed. "That's worth something."

"He was our janitor at my school. The war has changed people."

"I thought there was something odd about him, but still can't place it."

"I think he likes you more than me, and is enjoying the power the uniform has brought him. He is mostly harmless, but dangerous at the same time."

"This is a strange town. I like it." Willie laughed.

"Try living here your whole life. With parents that watch your every move," Koos said as she straddled the bike. "I need to be home or my parents will worry. They're fiercer than Erwin."

Willie put his hand on the handlebar, brushing the side of Koos's hand. He felt awkward holding the bike to prevent her from leaving. His confidence faded.

"Only if you promise to see me again," Willie said, but it lacked any authority. Koos pushed on her pedals and it forced him to let go. She pedalled away and then swung back toward him.

"Maybe later," she said, and then turned around, pedalling away. He watched her disappear down the road. He still had almost a full day of leave left, and now he knew what he was going to do with it.

# Chapter Nine

# Stripes

Farnham, England
April 1944

A rdagh sat with his section, staring down at his meal in silence. What a mess. They hadn't gone more than a few hundred yards after he had climbed back into the carrier and a squad from the Algonquin Regiment hidden along the river had killed them. Woods had been wrong. The Lake Superior Regiment had done well, and they were finally looking forward to a few days of rest and relaxation. All except Ardagh and his carrier section. They were the small black mark on the battlefield. His stupid mistake had wiped out his carrier.

"You lost in your dinner as well?" Sergeant Anderson asked as he sat down across the table.

"We weren't sure you guys would make it to dinner, being dead and all." He chuckled at his own poor joke. That was his type, the type to rub your nose in it, thought Ardagh.

Sergeant Anderson was a six-foot-two-inch burly former logger with tight, muscular arms and large, square, athletic shoulders. The perfect-looking type of sergeant you would want to lead a squad. He had it all.

Ardagh stared at him, trying to hold back his words. The sergeant looked and played the part, but he was about as sharp as the mashed potatoes on his plate.

On the other hand, Ardagh was still fighting to break the one-hundred-and-fifty-pound mark, baby-faced and shaved every day, hoping proper facial hair would finally grow in.

"Sir, it wasn't my fault," Ardagh said. This was his first test as a corporal. As part of the test to command your own Bren carrier, you needed to know where you were and where you were headed. Not being able to handle his crew was the problem, not just getting lost. Woods had convinced him to go the other way. The fault was only on him. This was his first real lesson learned as a leader.

"Do you think we'll go over soon?" Ardagh asked, trying to change the subject.

"Rumour has it. It will be in May or June. It all depends on the tides for the beach landings," Sergeant Anderson said, as if he was a meteorologist. "But based on what we have been practising, I doubt we'll be part of that."

"The second wave, then?"

"Based on the manoeuvres we just did, I would guess we are a breakout group once the beachhead is established, so it's important we get it right. We can't afford to screw up and go in the wrong direction, now, can we?"

"I knew which way to go, but the guys convinced me otherwise," Ardagh said as he stared down, mixing his potatoes. He already recognized it was a mistake to place the blame on the others before he finished his sentence. He looked over at Danny. His face was hard to read as usual, but he knew what he was thinking. His deep-set eyes looked hurt, like he was ready to sing "White Christmas". They argued over which way to go, and Woods had won. Danny's cheeks turned red, and he went back to eating.

"That's why you're a corporal, corporal," Sergeant Anderson said, a little too loud for Ardagh's liking. "Isn't that right, Danny boy?"

"I know, but the entire group was insistent."

"But you had all the information. Your crew was just guessing. Never forget that; it may save your life someday."

Sergeant Anderson leaned in over his meal and stared down at him and Danny, pointing a fork full of green beans and mashed potatoes.

"If you make the same mistake in actual combat, you're all dead, but maybe you will get lucky and just get yourself captured to save the rest of us." And with that, he swiftly scooped the potatoes into his mouth. Ardagh stared into his plate, mixing the butter into his potatoes. Sergeant Anderson wasn't as dumb as Ardagh thought.

The advice struck him hard, and he mashed the potatoes, keeping his peas separate on his plate. He liked his peas separate from his potatoes. When everything got mixed up, there was nothing to taste. He expertly smoothed the potatoes into a small mound before finally scooping them into his mouth. The advice and potatoes were both hard to swallow.

"It's okay sometimes to screw up. Better now than later. It's how you learn."

"I can't afford to make any mistakes. I shouldn't be a corporal," Ardagh said. "It's too much."

There, he had said it.

The week had been the most difficult he had faced, and it was like finding your way through lumpy mashed potatoes. The training was getting more whipped up every day, and he didn't know when he would be hit with a lump that shouldn't be there.

The words from the infantry training manual stuck in his head and swirled around every time he climbed into a carrier. "You must think at the speed of twenty miles an hour rather than three miles an hour, since safety will depend on the good use of the ground." He had stopped and argued with the rest of the crew and only saw a sideways glance and reluctant agreement. He made the wrong turn, and it was losing Danny's trust that made him sick to his stomach. What if he got him killed? This wasn't a game. He understood that now, watching the bombs fall all over England. It was actual life and death. He had survived on the bomber and experienced it firsthand.

Did he have what it took to be a leader? The manual highlighted the key strengths of the men they wanted. They must be quick, possess initiative, intelligence and resourcefulness and have a trained eye for the country. So far, he had failed on all fronts.

Woods and Wilson's questioning stares haunted him whenever he thought he was safe. They didn't have to say it. He read their faces. "You'll never be in charge of anything, ever."

He had felt so sure of himself when he rode on the carrier as a private, but was it him or the confidence of his corporal that he carried? He could drive the carrier, fire the Bren gun, and he always had an instinct for where they needed to be.

Danny looked up from his meal, still chewing, and said, "Don't be a punter!"

"Punter, that's a good one," Sergeant Anderson laughed.

The empty chair between himself and the rest of the crew left him exposed and alone, so with his head down he left the table, hearing laughter at his back.

Ardagh walked out of the mess hall and into the park, and the cool air hit him across his face as he picked up his pace. His meal turned in his stomach and grumbled along with him. *Are these the mistakes that get you killed, as the sergeant said, or are they why we train and train until you don't get it wrong? One mistake won't kill you, will it?*

He thought of Joey when he stepped outside, and the cold ran through his body. The fog had rolled in, and he could see nothing of what lay ahead. So, he followed the gravel footpath through the old park that wrapped itself around their mess hall. He was used to the cool, damp weather, like walking along Lake Superior in the fall. He did all his thinking on his feet.

Keep moving, and you would find your way, Jim had always told him. He made his way through the park and stretched out the minor aches in his legs from sitting in the carrier all day.

The gravel crunched under his boots, and he dropped into a steady march. He stared down at the path, watching one foot fall in front of the other. The stiff wind brought his thoughts back to Jim and the look of fear on his face. The feeling of panic when he realized what he had done to Joey. He pushed it out of his mind, but it went to the look on the faces of the crew when they realized they'd run right into the pretend enemy and were ceremoniously told they were killed. The only Bren gun in the company. What could be worse?

"How are you doing, son?" the padre said.

Ardagh looked up, startled. He had almost walked into him. *Where did he come from?* Ardagh thought. *Jesus.*

"I'm fine, sir," Ardagh said as he shook off the surprise.

"I have been watching you circle the park several times now."

"Just clearing my head, I'm good... sir."

"You know, I'm always here to talk, Corporal. I'm new to you fellas, but I hope over time to get to know each one of you; the battles ahead will be difficult, and you'll need all the support going, not just orders."

"Yes, sir," Ardagh said, shifting his feet, kicking his toe into the gravel.

"No need to call me sir... just Padre... alright?"

"Padre," Ardagh said. The padre was an impressive figure. They said he was in better shape than anyone in the regiment. He was not your typical minister. He oozed discipline and strength in God.

"Yes, now let's walk together, and you can tell me all about it. Is it a girl?"

Ardagh started back down the path, gripping his hat in his hand, and sighed, looking somewhat surprised again at the padre.

*Jesus.*

"Well... I don't know exactly," Ardagh said. How was he going to get out of this one, he thought.

They walked along the path until they both saw a bench, and the padre sat down and patted the seat beside him.

"Come, sit down beside me and let me tell you a story. Maybe that'll help."

Ardagh sat down on the bench.

"It's not that bad. I'll be better, Padre."

"Well, let me tell you anyway, just in case later you may need it."

"Great, Padre."

Ardagh gave a deep sigh and looked out into the fading daylight and quiet open field.

"Great, now listen, I'm not from Fort William or Port Arthur, but I've some experience that I hope can help you."

"I'm from Fort William."

"I realize you boys are proud of which town you come from. It's quite remarkable, considering they are right beside each other. You're more competitive than the Germans, I'm afraid."

"We've got to fight for everything coming from Fort William. I guess that's why it matters, Padre," Ardagh said frankly.

"The thing you must always remember, you're not alone. The men here are just like you. They all have their stories or struggles from where they come from. Some were leaders in their own right before the war, some are still running away from their past. Some men are just followers by nature. Others can only lead. All the training and the schemes that higher-ups create are there to test you and test what you have in you. When the shooting starts and we are in action, we have to be ready. Not just some of us, but all of us. No weak armour. Whatever demon you're fighting, whoever you're carrying with you, you need to finish that fight and focus on the task at hand."

Ardagh looked down at his feet, but he could sense the eyes

of the padre on him. *How did he learn all this stuff? Does he know why I signed up and had to get away?* It was a simple decision to escape his troubles. His brothers were happy to get away, but not him. Joey still stayed with him despite the time that passed, like a sprain that wouldn't go away. If he put any weight into what happened, the pain would flare up again. They could never understand. It would always be there. They were not there, and it was easy to judge him and his actions.

"I'll be alright, Padre," Ardagh said.

"There are always hurdles holding people back, no matter who you are. Recognizing that is the biggest step, so you can figure out a way to get over or around it. Sometimes it takes a stronger person to realize when they are ready or not. The lieutenant won't hold you back later if you show the initiative and strength of a leader. We all realize the stakes are high, and mistakes are deadly. It is to be respected, the risk. So don't beat yourself up about it. The rest of the platoon will appreciate you more for it. Besides, with all the changes over Christmas and the establishment of the new motor regiment, we are now a pretty strong unit, and we are short on drivers, from what I understand. They'll not think little of you if you volunteer to switch back."

The padre was never known to mince words, and Ardagh realized he had given him an out.

"Thank you, Padre. I've tried to learn and have been getting the hang of a lot of things here. It has been... a whole new life so far from what I left."

The padre patted his shoulder and said, "You're welcome, son." Then he stood up and walked back along the path into the darkness.

Ardagh sat staring into the dark field. The chilly breeze was threatening to break into a gust. The padre was right. There was a lot more for him to learn before he could take the next step. He needed to figure out how to control the fear. The thought of the looming battles and what that meant fell just out of his reach every time he tried to visualize it. As much as they had trained, they still hadn't been shot at for real. Would he stand up under fire? What was his character? He felt a flicker of fear remembering the bomber and Hank. He didn't like the idea of taking a step backwards. It was Jim and Joey all over again. But he didn't want more blood on his hands. The wind picked up, flipping his collar up against his cheek, triggering a shiver. He stood, stretched his arms, and headed back along the path. Eileen would be waiting for him with some hot tea. He pushed away the fear and thoughts of the past, but a dull pain remained in his stomach. It somehow always stayed with him. He picked up his pace, feeling his legs warm and loosen, excited to curl up with a blanket and cup of tea and enjoy the warmth of Eileen's couch. He would decide tomorrow.

# Chapter Ten

# Ferry House Cafe

Bruinisse, Netherlands
April 1944

It was early afternoon and Koos had yet to shake off the excitement of the morning roadblock. The Ferry House Cafe was full. The scent of fresh cinnamon brought Koos back to her school days. Mr van Hulst sat alone at his table in the corner. She hurried over to him, taking her jacket off, and sat down, folding it on her lap. So much had happened in such a short time and she had lots to tell him.

"So," van Hulst said, placing his newspaper on the table. Koos pulled the envelope from beneath her jacket and slid it under his newspaper. No one could see.

"Would you like some tea?" Mr van Hulst asked.

"Yes, please."

He stood and walked to the counter and ordered a tea. Koos looked down at the folded newspaper, worried. Why didn't he hide it away? She tried to remain relaxed. She was sure it meant nothing, and this was a test. He returned with the tea, and she told him everything that had happened to her in the day.

"Well done," van Hulst said. "Maybe you can learn something from this lieutenant."

"Really?"

"Yes, you may learn their movements. What is their next port they are heading to? That could help."

"I'll try, but..."

Koos held her breath as the tall Kriegsmarine lieutenant entered the cafe and stood at the counter. She turned back to van Hulst and said, "I think I should go."

"Stay calm, there is nothing to worry about with the German Navy," he said before placing the newspaper back in his bag along with the envelope. "This was just an easy run. Something for you to learn on. You have nothing to hide."

She didn't believe him. Why did he need to put it away, then? She looked at his hands as he rubbed them together and she realized he was more nervous than her.

"You must go if he asks," van Hulst whispered.

"I... I can't."

"You must make him happy. You're already in deep. Find out what they are doing here. It might be useful."

"But..." *What would people say?* she thought.

"We can't be caught," van Hulst whispered as he looked down at his bag.

Koos's heart raced. What if they were caught? *Her brother was caught.*

Koos turned to face him and leaned into the table. "I want to do more."

Van Hulst leaned back with raised eyebrows. His glasses slid down his nose. "Yes, of course," he said.

"Hello, there." She heard the voice over her shoulder. "You certainly get around."

Koos turned in her chair, and to her surprise, smiled. She stood and grabbed her coat to show she was leaving. She was more afraid of being seen with him than of being caught. If she was friendly to one German, she was friendly to them all. That was what the town would think, right or wrong. The town was never wrong.

She would do more. She turned to look at Willie. He had the look of a sailor with a great catch. She stepped toward him, and gave an awkward greeting, unsure if he was a friend or foe.

"I was just leaving," she said and moved to the door of the cafe. Willie jumped ahead of her, pulling the door open and said, "Let me join you. Walk with you, then."

"It wouldn't be right," Koos said, her cheeks warmed. What was wrong with her? She wasn't afraid. She was happy.

"Ah, you're worried what people will say?" Willie looked over at van Hulst.

"That's my dad's friend. Only, my father."

"Walk with me," Willie said, holding the door open. Koos walked through the door, and he followed her out onto the sidewalk. She watched van Hulst leave the cafe in the other direction. Willie stuck out his elbow, but she ignored him and continued along. He dropped his arm, and they shuffled down the street like two strangers. If only her father saw her now, she thought. Her mind was racing. What could she learn that was valuable?

"Thank you for earlier," Koos said. "Erwin is jealous of our family and now thinks he can push us around."

"I hope he won't be a future bother. But I doubt it. I would suggest staying away from him. If you can."

"Yes, I know you're right. We'll probably have to go soon away. If they plan to flood the island."

Willie moved close to her, and they walked side by side. They continued along in silence for a while before he spoke.

"I'll be back before then, I'm sure."

"Do you like coming here?"

"No, and yes. I would rather be out to sea than trapped in the harbour here. But our ships can't handle rough water. So, we need a safe place to hide. This is as good as it gets except for when the tide is out. It's hard to defend ourselves," Willie said. "But I'm liking the locals. So yes, mostly."

"Someday I would like to travel and see the world. But I don't know what I would do if I had no place to come back to. I have been here my whole life. It's been my whole life," Koos said. Her eyes blurred, and she sniffed to clear them. "I don't know anything else."

"The war will end sooner than you think. We are just holding on to delay the inevitable and hope to survive," Willie said. "Where I come from, there will be not much left for me. Berlin has been a major target for many months now. My family is..."

Koos stopped and let Willie get ahead of her. She had lost track of where they were headed. Now, they were just a block away from the front of her house.

"Tell me more about your family. Let's walk along the dike," she said, turning back, heading toward the dike. "You can show me your ship."

They walked back along Kerkstraat to the dike and then climbed to the top of it, heading south toward the harbour where the flotilla sat. The clouds had rolled in and covered Bruinisse with a low, bright blanket as far as you could see. The wind was calm, making it a pleasant afternoon walk. She thought of Joost, but pushed him to the back of her mind. What would they or the Resistance want to know? She had no time to ask. But if she asked too many questions, he might wonder about her. All of this had happened in such a short time. She felt overwhelmed. What would her mother do? Make him feel at home, she used to say to her papa. It always worked with his business meetings at home. It often surprised Koos what it revealed over the many dinners they had. That's what she would do. Make him feel at home. But how?

Koos picked up her pace and bumped into Willie with her hip, letting out a giggle. "How big is your ship?" and hooked her arm under his.

Willie pressed back. "Sailors don't like to talk about the size of their ship."

Arm in arm, they walked along the dike like they were on a Sunday walk. Koos pushed her hip into him and she enjoyed the brief contact. Would he want to kiss her? She would have to decide if it happened.

"Is this what you always wanted to do?" Koos asked.

"I wanted to... I wanted to be on a submarine but was too late. The jobs were given to the more experienced sailors. But I'm happy where I ended up. The work is dangerous, but we have a great crew that is well trained. I'll get my ship in a few months, and most of the men will join me."

"Are you ever scared?"

"We are constantly on alert for British dive bombers or ships. We were originally meant to transport men and equipment for the invasion of England. But retrofitted to patrol the coast lines. But the ships don't do well in bad weather, so we mainly move around Zeeland, between here and Ouddorp."

They continued along the dike, and now she could see the flotilla of four German ships ahead. Men were busy moving around on the decks of the ships. She watched the anti-aircraft guns with men manning them and practising. She counted almost one hundred men moving around the dock and the decks of the four ships. There was a small group of men along the dike that protected the ships. Some were standing and some were lying down. Willie was watching them as well.

"What are they doing?" Koos asked.

"It's a platoon of infantry that helps protect the artillery boats when we are docked. They are practising. We always have to be prepared. Every harbour is different. This one is too close to Anna Jacobapolder. We could get attacked from the other side of the bank."

"I guessed that."

"How would you know?"

"I was here when the *Hydra*, a Dutch minelayer, was attacked by the Germans in the strait from the other side."

"Ah, so you have seen it happen. I should be concerned then."

Koos looked across and remembered the *Hydra* attack. She knew what he meant.

"But the ships are behind the dike. When they attacked the *Hydra*, it was out in the open. I was standing here when it happened. Look," Koos said, stopping and pulling her dress up to show her scar on her leg. "I was wounded."

She twisted her leg back and forth to show him. Willie looked down at her leg and then up to her thigh. She pushed her dress back down and felt the redness in her face. She grabbed his arm again, dragging him along.

"Well, there is little protection behind the dike. We're too low and can't fire our guns when the tide is out or too high and exposed when it is in. So, we need to always be prepared for anything," Willie said. He stopped and held her arms, examining her. "It looks serious. Does it still bother you?"

"Sometimes, but only when I ride my bike."

Willie pulled her tight and kissed her before she could react. Koos tried to push him away, but she had learned a lot. If she could handle Pieter, she could put up with Willie, and she stopped resisting. It was just a kiss. Willie pulled away when they heard the cheers from the ship. He let go of her and turned to walk away, only to get a louder cheer. Koos grabbed his hand, pulling him back toward the ships to further cheers.

# Chapter Eleven

# Goodbye

Guildford, England
April 1944

Ardagh woke with a start. He was back in Guildford, the row house away from home. His shirt was dripping from sweat. It was the morning after his two-day leave following his disastrous training exercise. Two days of binge drinking with Danny had blown over him like a storm cloud. Remnants of a bad dream floated in and out of his thumping head. The nightmare had only changed slightly. It was a confused mix of being stuck in the bomber, not knowing which way to go while trying to pull Jim out of the water and steering clear of Joey. It was just snapshots of moments that brought out his fears. The taste of last night's beers still lingered, and the stench of alcohol hung in the bedroom. He felt the urgent need to piss, but the colossal headache clouded his brain.

He gently sat up in bed and swung his feet onto the floor, still dizzy and sweating. His fear of combat and the feelings of panic while flying in the bomber poured down on him. He knew everyone was afraid, but he couldn't get out of the storm of fear. Another set of chills still swept through his body as he stared at the wall with a mixture of anxiety and the lingering buzz from the alcohol. He thought back to his long conversation with the padre. His advice was simple: if you don't think you can handle it, you aren't ready. All his long discussions over pints of beer and this had been the best advice. What was he thinking? Another wave of nausea overwhelmed him, and he lay back on the bed. Today would be a slower day. The regiment was shipping out to a new location to complete preparations before they loaded onto the ships for the invasion of Europe. It might only be a few months before they would finally have to face the Germans. His life would take another turn.

He had awoken with the word 'Channel' loud in his ear as if he had headsets on. It had momentarily cleared his headache and gave him a sense of relief, and he could breathe. It wasn't until the bomber had crossed the English Channel that everyone could celebrate their return from another mission. Today, he would talk to Lieutenant Brown and convince him he could lead. He needed to keep his stripes and prove he was someone. It had been four years since he left Jim on the ice and ran. He had to stop running from Joey. He could still hear Jim's voice in his head. *You need to have a reason if you are going to make the sacrifice or you won't survive.*

Ardagh eased himself out of bed and got dressed. He heard Eileen's familiar voice in the kitchen as he climbed down the narrow stairs.

"Something seems different with him," Eileen said, ignoring Ardagh. "Almost grown up, in a way."

"Who's grown up?" Ardagh asked as he put his arms around Eileen and squeezed her tight.

"Hey, get off, you!" She squirmed away. "What has gotten into you? You seem different, is all we were saying."

Ardagh stood thinking, and the sweat crept into his lower back again. *Do they see right through me and my fear?* Could he really tell them how he felt?

"You look... you look stronger... older," Lily said. "No, tougher."

"What did you get up to when you were visiting your brother?" Eileen asked.

Did he look stronger?

"Just hungover. Nothing you need to worry about," he mumbled as he sat down at the table. Eileen placed a hot cup of weak tea on the table in front of him, and the first sip provided little relief to the throbbing in his head, but he forced himself to take a second gulp.

"Well, whatever you did, or are doing, keep doing it, my love." Eileen put her hands on his shoulders and rubbed his neck. "It may keep you safer when things get tough." She leaned down and kissed him hard on the cheek. "I have seen that look in the other boys who have come back from fighting."

"Thanks, Leenie. I will."

With a deep breath, his body relaxed and settled down. The cloud that hung over him parted slightly, and the tightened anxiety that had gripped him for the past three days loosened, but just enough to focus on the day ahead.

"I think we are moving again to get ready to leave for France."

"Oh, dear," was all Eileen could respond as she let go of his shoulders and sat down next to him.

"So that's it," Lily confirmed. "That's what we have noticed. You're worried about what's coming next. You'll be okay and have nothing to worry about."

"No, it's something different altogether."

"You've trained for so long, and we've seen you get stronger every day," Eileen said, trying to sound confident.

"You have a great section and lieutenant," Lily said. The two women looked at him like his mother did when he left Green Bay. His head throbbed again, and he slouched over his cup and took another slow drink of tea.

"It could be another year before I'm back, maybe longer, unless I get wounded," Ardagh said, hanging his head low over his hands.

"Oh, my luv, don't say such a thing," Eileen said.

"It's a long time to wait for someone," he said and regretted it right away. It was a small door that opened to let Eileen go.

"So, you think I'm going to just forget you?" Eileen asked. This was a continuation of the fight they'd had the night before. He had only left for a moment to go to the loo. Another soldier, a Canadian sergeant from Toronto, sat beside her. Ardagh was very drunk by this time and wasn't afraid to say something. The sergeant apologized and abruptly left. But it set off the 'what if' when he is gone discussion. It was not new to her or many of her girlfriends. It was a different time, and life moved along fast and sometimes out of your control. There were enough songs written about it to fill your whole day. He was still young, and he wondered if she had made a mistake in falling in love with him. This was when their age difference exposed the weakness in their relationship.

"I was waiting for him, but he died fighting. I didn't expect to meet anyone else for the rest of my life until I met you. We talked about it last night. What else do you want from me, luv?"

Eileen got up and turned her back on him. "I don't want you to leave like this, thinking it's over, it's not. I love you. If you want me to sing "*We'll Meet Again*", I won't."

It was her strength and up-front nature that attracted Ardagh to her. She was a strong woman and rarely backed down. Much like his mother, he guessed. She had a fire in her eyes that made her more attractive rather than less, but he was still hurt. Hurt that she would talk to anyone, and especially the night before he was to leave. How could she?

Danny had warned him she was not who she seemed. She had moved pretty quickly to replace her husband, and she wasn't too sad to see him go. Eileen had told him this over beers one night. Danny was so mad. He told Ardagh they both should dump them. Ardagh was more serious with Eileen and it hurt him to hear this. He knew Danny wasn't long-term with Lily. It was one of the few fights they ever had. They agreed to never fight over a woman again and made up while they were off together on their last training exercise. It had come full circle last night and struck him hard when he saw her smile at some nameless sergeant. It was brief but said a lot.

"I'm not your husband. You will still go out every night doing nothing but drinking and dancing. You'll meet someone else. It's war." He got up, following her to the sink and pulled her close.

"Why'd I do that?" she said. "I think it's more about you, about your fears of what lies ahead. What if you meet a French girl that you just rescued? What then?"

"Oh great, now the eggs... Ruined, along with the day," Lily announced as she lifted the frying pan that sat on the hot plate.

"I have sacrificed everything for this war," Eileen said, throwing the dishtowel down. "Now this." She pulled away from him and ran up the stairs. Ardagh could hear the door slam shut.

"You better just go, for now," Lily said. "She'll be fine, and there will be time enough for a proper goodbye. I'll have to say goodbye to Danny, I suppose."

Ardagh gave Lily a deep hug. He had forgotten about Danny. He could feel her shake in his arm.

"I'll tell him, don't worry."

His head throbbed. He drained the last of his tea and groaned. Lily turned and busied herself with the dishes, and he knew that was his cue to leave. He grabbed his kit bag and left the house. He looked forward to the ride to the base. The morning was cool and clear as he climbed onto his motorcycle and kicked it alive. He was glad to get away and move on, despite the fear of what was ahead. He made up his mind and would not back down, not again, not for a girl. Ardagh realized that their time together couldn't last, and by the time he had turned onto the main road to the Farnham base, he knew he was right. He pushed the motorcycle's accelerator to the max, feeling the cold air hit his chest. It was time for him to focus on what lay ahead. He would convince Lieutenant Brown he could lead.

Ardagh arrived at the mess hall early, grabbed a cup of coffee, and sat alone. He wanted to prepare himself before he met with Lieutenant Brown. He was still hungover and needed to be sharp.

"You need some ham and eggs to get rid of the hangover, soldier?"

Ardagh jumped out of his seat and saluted to Lieutenant Brown as he stood up to acknowledge him.

"Sorry, sir."

"Well, you're looking a little green, staring down into that cup. Sit back down. I just wanted to let you know we talked it over," Brown said, standing over him. Ardagh stared back down into his coffee. He knew what was coming. It was the look of judgment just like when he sat in court for his sentencing. He was given a two hundred dollar fine and a second chance but it felt like a life sentence to not be punished. This was the real punishment.

Brown's voice deepened as he leaned over him and said, "We don't need someone like you leading when the shooting starts. Everyone looks at you different. Don't ever forget that. You need to be better. Showing up hungover is not a surprise."

Ardagh stared into the darkness of his cup. So that was it, back to a private. He felt empty and alone. How could he be so stupid?

"Sorry, sir, we let it get away from us last night. I've resolved to not choose that path again." Ardagh tried to talk strong but it came off flat. The blow of removing his stripes was nothing compared to admitting to his past. *Someone like you.*

"Well, I hope so," Brown said as he moved off to another

table.

"Thank you, sir," Ardagh said to himself. He took another large gulp of his coffee and got up. His head still pounded and his eyes felt tight. It was another stupid mistake, and he needed to be alone. He had let Jim down again, the pole slipping from his hands. He felt blind to what was ahead. Why couldn't he see Joey? He would have to fight for a second chance, pay attention, and get past it when the shooting started.

## Chapter Twelve

# The Catch

Bruinisse, Netherlands
April 1944

Koos sat on the top of the dike, running her finger along the edge of her scarred right leg, as she looked out across to Sint Philipsland. She was in the exact spot where she witnessed the German attack on the *Hydra* four years ago. She fared better than the crew of the ship. The *Hydra* had beached outside the range of the Germans, unloading the wounded sailors into lifeboats. As they made their way to shore, the Dutch coastguards had fired on the approaching lifeboats, killing one sailor before the friendly fire stopped. Later that year, the Germans salvaged the *Hydra* in desperate need of steel.

Koos still felt a chill in her body when she thought back to the aftermath. She had lived most of her teens at war. She was now a woman, eighteen years old, but was still treated like a little girl despite the risks she took to deliver the ration cards for van Hulst. Koos felt double-cursed, being a girl and the second youngest in the family, but it also helped her get past the constant German checkpoints.

The Allies had attacked the Germans in Bruinisse several times over the last few weeks. German boats would arrive at their tiny fishing port, British fighters would spot them, and the air raid sirens would send them to the church basement more and more frequently. But Koos's house miraculously re-mained intact after every exciting return. The Germans had not been so lucky. Several of their small ships had been sunk in the harbour. The rumours were that they would be moved in the next few days, and the town and polder flooded to make it more difficult for the Allies to capture Zeeland.

They had sat by the Dutch Radio Orange for several days now, listening for every detail of the Allied progress, but they had yet to land in France. Rumours ran rampant that there would be a second front. The Allies would land in Western Europe before the summer. Hope for the end of the war and food shortages grew stronger. Liberation would happen some-day. It had been a tough year and was getting worse. Her father would always joke, "You can't have a food shortage if you have no food."

She looked across the channel to Sint Philipsland. When the time came, they planned to move in with her eldest broth-er just across the narrow channel to Sint Philipsland. Koos had been to the stylish Dutch house many times over the last few years, and they had already moved things over, just in case. She was worried that it would put an end to her work with van Hulst and the Resistance. She knew she could do much more.

A German artillery ship moved into the narrow channel within shouting distance of Koos. She watched the young sailors on deck move around, preparing the warship to dock. Two of them stopped and waved to her. She waved back out of surprise that they had noticed her. Then she saw him. He walked out from the bridge. Willie looked taller than she re-membered. She waved to him and he saluted back to her. It made her laugh. They watched each other as the ship steamed by and she wondered what he was thinking. How long would the war continue? What was in store for both of them?

Her father's boat had sailed by moments earlier with her older brother and father aboard. The family had anxiously awaited their return, as the fish were desperately needed. There was always a risk the Germans or Dutch Nazi would confiscate the fish, but now that the Kriegsmarine had come to their port, this guaranteed it. She felt the need to act and to do something. She didn't know what, but anything was worth a try. Would Willie help them?

Koos hurriedly jumped onto her bike and pedalled hard to get to the dock before the Germans. She saw that Erwin had already made it to her father's boat. He stood above them with his hands on his hips. She had not seen him since the roadblock. His uniform looked ridiculous on his thin, non-muscular body. Almost feminine. He didn't belong in the scene of fisherman and Kriegsmarine men standing around.

As she approached them on the dock, she could hear her father saying, "But we still get to keep some of our catch. That is fair."

A second man dressed in a Kriegsmarine uniform, who looked like the one who was with Willie, stood next to Erwin with a clipboard in hand.

"We need it all. What are the totals? We need to keep proper records," he said in a very harsh Dutch tone.

"Hello, Pop-pa!" Koos called out and waved with excitement. "Hello, Erwin, how are you? What a great catch. There is certainly lots to go around."

The Kriegsmarine quartermaster did not look at Koos and said again, "We take it all."

Erwin pursed his lips, then put both his hands on his cheeks and squeaked with unnatural pleasure before he said, "Well, that's too bad. I'll make sure nothing is left behind." He bent down and leaned closer to the edge of the boat, placing both of his hands on his knees, and said, "Your son can help me search all the hatches."

"Heinie, let's get moving. We do not have time to waste," came a powerful voice. Koos held her breath as Willie walked up. He wore a white captain's hat and a large leather overcoat. She recognized the look of mischief on his face. When he caught Koos's eye, he shoved his hands in his pockets.

"I'm trying, Willie, but he refuses, and this idiot isn't helping," Heinie said as he pointed at Erwin.

Koos moved in front of Willie. She was glad to have a thin floral dress on and her hair pulled back. Her cheeks reddened, and the wind had flattened her dress against her body. She knew her father would disapprove and would be shocked by how it revealed her body. But they needed the food. The whole village needed the fish. It would go a long way to feed many families. They only could fish sporadically, when the weather and the fighting didn't get in the way.

"You can't take all our catch. Our family will have nothing to eat. Please let us keep some," Koos said, trying not to sound too desperate. "If we don't eat, how will we continue to fish?"

She stared into Willie's grey eyes. She watched him rustle his hands in his coat as if searching for something. Willie blew out a deep breath. He looked at the boat and then back at her. She pressed him again, knowing he was just acting, playing along to make fun of Erwin. Her father stood staring and unaware.

"It's all we have...." Koos looked at her father. His face was expressionless. Stern. "Just enough for us to keep going, that's all. Something..."

Willie looked down into the boat at the catch. He shrugged. Then counted out the baskets, estimating the fish catch. Willie waved over Heinie and said, "I didn't tell you to take it all. Just some. I'll get rid of the idiot, and you just take what we really need. Okay, that's an order."

"I don't care about these people. They are being shipped away. We may never see them again."

"I'll always care. The Dutch are people, as you say, and deserve better. We may need more fish next time we are here,"

Willie said. He had lived in poverty as a boy after the first war, moving from German Poland to escape the Russians. He knew their hunger and what it meant. But how could he say no to Koos?

"Help them take the rest home. Even if it means you sending one of the Gefreiter."

"Yes, sir." Heinie saluted.

Willie turned to Koos. "You may keep some. Heinie will figure it out."

"I will be happy to help bring your share," Erwin announced. "It would bring me great pleasure."

"Stay out of it!" Willie said sharply, and turned, walking back to the ship without waiting for a response.

Koos waved back in triumph at her brother and father. She had won, although an easy victory. Her father only nodded, and her brother continued on with unloading. Koos walked back to the house, tears forming in her eyes. What else did they want from her? Nothing was good enough for them.

*** 

The street was busier than normal. The town was preparing to leave. Pushed out to make room for the flooding, and the new defensive positions the Germans were building as part of the Atlantic wall. They would stay for now, but she didn't care. Koos had gone home, but listening to her father talk about Erwin and the fish was too much. She couldn't stay in the house. She was angry with her father and brother. They gave her no credit. What could a little girl do? Her father was clueless, but her brother should know better. She could only think of going to the Ferry House Cafe. Hopefully, van Hulst was there.

She reached for the door of the cafe, her head down, mulling over what to say to her father. It was no use. The handle slipped away from her and she stumbled through the door. Willie stood behind it, laughing.

"You too!" Koos said, regaining her balance and storming

by. She sat at the first table and checked the room. No van Hulst.

"What did I do?" Willie said and sat down.

Koos didn't answer at first. She looked at him. His charm was infectious. He obviously made a good leader. Should she stay with him in the cafe? What did it matter now, anyway? No one cared about her.

"What's wrong? You look sad," Willie said. "Let me get you a cup of tea."

"Okay."

"Now we're talking. That's good."

Willie went over to the counter and came back with two cups of tea and a Stroopwafel.

"You need something to help your sorrows. What's wrong?"

"You wouldn't understand."

"Please, is it because your father treats you like a little girl?"

"How did you..."

"I was there, remember, and saw his look, and I saw your look. I may be German, but I'm not stupid."

Koos laughed. He had a casualness about him that made her comfortable. It made her inner struggle dig into her. How could she betray him? But he must know the risk of his job. It wasn't just about him. The Germans and NSB had to go. They had destroyed many lives. Her brother. Was he alive?

"How old are you?" Koos asked.

"Thirty-one. I have no wife or kids. The war put a stop to that for now."

Willie reached for her hand and she let him.

"Will you be back?"

"I was just promoted and will take over a new ship in the First Flotilla. The AF 92. It will be ready in July. I suspect we'll be back here again."

"That's wonderful." Koos looked away. The cafe was now nearly full. What could she learn from him? She would not be here again if they forced them to leave.

"We'll help protect against the invasion when it happens."

"Is this what you want? Are you afraid of the responsibility?"

"It won't be much different from what I'm doing now. I'm ready. But there may not be much time to train the crew. It's rumoured the invasion will happen soon."

"They are forcing us to go, but my father wants to stay for now."

"Then, I hope, we'll meet again." Willie squeezed her hand.

"Is your ship bigger and stronger? Will you be safe?"

"It's new and an improvement to the others. Here is the ship. It's bigger." Willie said, drawing an imaginary outline. "There are guns here and here for protection." Willie showed her, pointing at the table.

"Where do you sit?"

"Here on the bridge."

"I'm happy for you, but sad at the same time."

"I know. But the war will end soon. One way or another. Life will change and I will come back."

Would he? She wished they all would leave them alone. Koos finished her tea. He seemed so nice. It was confusing.

"Let's go for a walk and you can tell me more," Koos said as she stood up and stretched. It had been a long day. She could see his eyes explore her body. She would kiss him one more time. They left the cafe holding hands. She didn't care about the stares.

## Chapter Thirteen

# Stars

Bretteville Le Rabet, France
August 9th, 1944

"My dad used to take me out in the truck away from the lights of the house," Wilson said.

"What the heck does that have to do with climbing onto these tanks?" Woods asked.

"He would take us into the field to stare up at the stars and the northern lights," Wilson said. "Just reminded me of home, that's all."

Ardagh looked up at the stars. It was a clear night and the first time he had seen stars since leaving Canada four years ago. He laid his Enfield rifle on the hard steel of the Grenadier Guards Sherman tank before pulling himself up. He climbed to the back of the turret, feeling his way along. It was pitch black, just before four in the morning. Danny climbed up and fell in beside him with a grunt. He knew what that meant. No one was happy to ride on top of the Grenadiers' tanks when they had their own armoured carriers that could move faster. It made no sense that 'B' Company of the Lake Superiors would have to catch a ride on their very first attack. But orders were orders.

They had been up on the front lines with sporadic shelling and limited sleep for more than a week but had not fired a single shot. 'A' Company had taken a mauling a few days earlier in an attack, losing several men killed and wounded. They knew it was war now. Ardagh's stomach tightened, but he shook it off, giving Danny a hard elbow. Danny was always a bit of a beanpole but had gained a lot of muscle over the last year. He was lucky to catch him under the arm. Danny didn't wait to give it back. Wilson and Woods flopped down on the back end of the tank. They slapped each other on the backs like hockey players on the bench before the puck was about to drop.

Ardagh mentally checked over his equipment as the tank fired up. They felt the vibration of the motor below them and got a whiff of diesel. This time, he knew it wouldn't take off into the air. He checked his footing and pictured how he would jump off if they were hit. This time he would be in control versus being thrown around in the tin can of the Lancaster. He ran his hands along the length of his rifle and checked the bolt action. The smell of fresh oil filled his nostrils. He knew the rifle was clean and ready to fire.

Ardagh looked over at the tank next to them and Wilf gave him a quick wave then an exaggerated salute. It felt good to have him close.

Twenty tanks rolled forward toward a stand of trees in front of Bretteville Le Rabet. Ardagh could taste the dust that flew up from the tanks ahead, but it was not long before they jumped off and spread out through a wheat field surrounding Bretteville Le Rabet. The sun was just coming up and he could see for miles in every direction.

Ardagh followed the track of the tank for a few paces before walking into the dry, golden wheat. He brushed his hands across the tops of the wheat and pulled at the ears as he walked through to find his position. The tanks spread out across the field ahead of them and searched for targets.

"Want me to go find a tractor so I can swath some Germans?" Wilson said. "It makes my heart hurt to see all this grain go to waste."

"Maybe you should think about gophers and dig in right away, just in case," Danny said. "They had to see us coming. I can almost see Paris from here."

"There's no dust in Paris." Woods coughed.

"Get ready to move up into the tree line when the tanks move," Lieutenant Brown said, tapping Ardagh on the back before disappearing into the wheat.

"It's like I'm back home. Golden fields for miles in every direction," Wilson said. "Could have been practising this whole time back in Saskatchewan. Good place to start our first fight."

Ardagh sat up, bent to one knee and peered through the sight of his rifle into the forest ahead of them. "Looks like the armour might have scared the Germans off," Ardagh said. "We should get moving soon." The sky was clear blue, and the sun had fully appeared. All was quiet. He could feel the warmth on his face as he squinted through one eye, looking for a target.

"Probably your stench that scared them off. You were letting them rip all the way here. Stay down, and wait for orders," Woods said. "You never know."

"Nothing to see. The tanks will cover us," Ardagh said as he looked down at Wilson next to him. "You might get to fire your rifle finally."

Ardagh flinched at the sudden sound of gunfire, followed by a ricochet hitting the side of the tank in front of him. He put his arms up and flopped to the ground all in one motion and pressed himself into the ground. A short burp-burp of a machine gun sounded, followed by bullets hitting the front and sides of the tank. No one responded, as they all kept their heads down. The shooting slowed to sporadic sniper fire, which pinned them down while they waited for orders. The calls for a stretcher came out across the exposed line of men in the field. Ardagh looked over to Wilson, just a few feet away.

"Wilson, you alright?" Ardagh heard no answer. He crawled

over to him. Blood pooled around his helmet. He rolled him over. A bullet had smashed through the bridge of his nose.

"Jesus!" Ardagh yelled. "Wilson..."

Danny crawled over and pulled off Wilson's helmet. Blood spilled out, soaking into the crushed wheat behind his head.

"Wilson... Wilson... Can you hear me?" He made no sounds. His body was lifeless. The bullet had killed him instantly.

Ardagh's stomach seized, and he held back the urge to throw up. One minute they were talking, the next he was dead. A lucky ricochet off the side of the tank had taken Wilson. The bullet was for him. Had he done everything right or had he attracted the attention by kneeling in the open?

A shadow formed over him and he looked up. To his surprise, it was Lieutenant Colonel Murrell along with another group of men with stretchers.

"Grab the wounded and follow me back over the road!" Murrell shouted down the line. He was standing fully exposed to the fire. The men stood and followed him through the wheat field, carrying the wounded across the road to safety. Ardagh was surprised at how many were wounded and needed help. He looked over at Sergeant Anderson on a stretcher. Blood covered his ripped open upper chest. His hands gripped the sides of the stretcher, his muscular arms and shoulders ready to burst out of his uniform. He turned his head toward Ardagh, but there was no light in his eyes. A pulse of blood flowed out of the wound as his chest heaved and he fell back dead. Ardagh's thoughts went to his fork of mashed potatoes and peas. Maybe you will get lucky, he had said.

'C' Company moved up and forward through their position and continued the attack on Bretteville Le Rabet. Ardagh looked out across the wheat field following the progress of 'C' Company. He held back the urge to run out into the field to check on Wilson. Was he still dead? He guessed they had already passed by Wilson's body. The tanks moved forward, firing into the trees, with 'C' company following. Ardagh scanned the ground ahead of him and wiped the sweat off his forehead. He had seen Wilf make it across the road to safety.

The only remains of his first battle were trails of crushed wheat that headed off toward the line of trees and, somewhere out there, Wilson's lifeless body. He looked over at Danny, their eyes meeting before he shifted his back to checking over his rifle. Woods was lying on his back with his arm covering his face and his elbow sticking up. Ardagh watched his chest move up and down. He tried to focus on what was next. They would have to go back out into the field and follow 'C' Company into the town. He would have to get past Wilson at some point. Anderson and Wilson were gone. He needed to see what was ahead and to never let his guard down again.

## Chapter Fourteen

# The Flood

Bruinisse, Netherlands
August 1944

"That's good information. You've done well," van Hulst said as he stood up. "I'll reach out when I get there." The cafe was cold and empty. The shelves were bare. They shouldn't have even met. She had delivered the last of the forged ration cards and there was no reason to be there but to say goodbye.

"But I want to come," Koos said in desperation. "I know I can help. Please."

"You will hear from me in a few days. Be patient. Go with your family for now. We'll have more cards to deliver in a month. We are all leaving today as well."

She realized it was just words. They were all the same and treated her like a child still. The Germans had finally forced the rest to leave. Over the past several months, she had made many deliveries of fake IDs and stolen ration cards with no problems. They needed them for those in hiding, and she knew she could do no more. Now van Hulst was going back to Amsterdam to continue the fight without her. If she was a boy, it would be different. Koos stood in his way.

"Please."

"Listen, you have done well. I'll pass along the information about the ships. I'm sure it will be useful. You've risked enough for now. Off you go," van Hulst said, signalling her to move along. Koos turned away and walked to the door, holding back her tears. *Don't cry now, you're too strong for that.* She would show them. She hoped in Sint Philipsland she could do something. Van Hulst followed her out onto the street.

"Be careful of Pieter," van Hulst said. "He is NSB. He turned your brother in. We know this for sure now. Watch out for him."

Koos took a step back. How could this be? She saw Joost, not Pieter. The statement hit her hard, like a slap in the face. It wasn't Joost, and now he was fighting for the Nazis because of her. But he still signed up. It made little sense, but now she had two enemies instead of one.

*\*\*\**

Koos stood beside her father in the wheelhouse of the fishing boat. He spun the wheel and turned the ship in the narrow strait that separated Bruinisse and Anna Jacobapolder. They were going only a short distance to Sint Philipsland. Koos looked back at Bruinisse and her heart sank as she scanned the dike. The fishing boat was now in the same place the *Hydra* sat when it was hit by the Germans almost four years earlier.

Koos felt like the *Hydra*, getting hit from all sides. She had never been so depressed in her life. She always thought that leaving home would be the start of a new adventure. A change in her life that reflected what she had accomplished. She had been working so hard to earn her way. The respect of her father and mother to go off on her own. But now she felt like a kid being shuttled away to safety. Or was it safe? They were headed to her older brother's house to live through the next phase of the war. She had lost the one thing that kept her going. To resist. Resist against the Germans, however she could. That was all thrown away now. Van Hulst would go off to Amsterdam to continue his work and they left her behind. A child is left behind, not an adult. Her father prohibited her from going. She had one last conversation with van Hulst and told him every-thing she learned from Willie. It was the one thing she clung to. Something to be proud of, working for the Resistance and fighting the Germans. He didn't know whether it was useful to them, but she hoped the British now knew where to look to sink their ships. It was bittersweet, as she found her feelings for Willie remained strong. He would survive, she said to herself. Although it was war, not everyone would die. Maybe once it was over, they could meet again.

She had come a long way from the first time she stood up for herself. She looked at her dad, driving the boat again, in command. Did he give her the credit? She didn't think so. It had been her idea to help protect her brothers in the first place and put more fish on the table. She remembered sitting at the kitchen table as they always did. David was still with them, be-fore he was taken. It was after the *Hydra* attack and she had forgiven Joost, but her father demanded she stay away from him.

*\*\*\**

"You need to stay away from that boy," Abraham said, pound-ing his fist on the table.

Koos put her head down and remained quiet, knowing fighting didn't help her cause.

"Like I said, Papa. He won't let us keep anything. As soon as we get to the dock, he is standing and waiting," Koos's brother David continued. David was the youngest of her older broth-ers and was now fishing with her other brother, Dies, when-ever they were allowed out on the water by the Germans.

"But he is a useless fool. God will punish him in the end. Just ignore him and keep what you can."

"It's no use. He won't listen to me. He thinks I'm still a kid at school and he is the headmaster, but he was only the janitor."

"I guess we'll have to think of another way. We could sneak in during the night."

Koos lifted her head and sat up. She would give him back his own advice. "I have an idea, Papa," she said.

Abraham turned and gave her the not now stare, but her eyes pushed through it and knocked it aside. She hesitated as her eyes met her mother, then fell back on her father.

"Why don't you fish with them?"

"Don't be silly," Abraham jeered and waved her away. "I don't go on the boats anymore. What would people say?"

Koos wanted to get her point across.

"But he wouldn't say no to you, Papa, would he?"

\*\*\*

Her father had never looked back after that. He seemed prouder today than ever before. He was doing something. She had felt the same until she stepped on this boat, fleeing her home. Now she would be back under their command, trapped and stuck in her brother's house. The war was coming to them now that the Allies had landed in Normandy and were battling the Germans. There was new hope that they would be free before Christmas and it was safer to be away from Bruinisse.

They were one of the last few families to leave the island. The bombed harbour was too close to home to take any more chances. Sint Philipsland was inland and safe from bombing and they would anchor the boat beside her brother's house on a small dock. She only took a few things with her. It seemed as if she was leaving her entire life behind.

## Chapter Fifteen

# Scratches

Ecorches, France
August 1944

"Go! Go!" Jim yelled. Ardagh pushed back from the edge of the icy water and let go of the pole. He stood up and shook off the wet snow from his mittens and ran to his father. He had to move quick before Jim froze to death in the water. The snow picked up off the river and blew into his face. His dad seemed so far away down the frozen river. The ice cracked under his feet. His legs were heavy. It was a struggle to keep moving, fighting the wind and the snow. He couldn't go any further. He closed his eyes.

"Harp! Watch out!" Danny yelled. Ardagh opened his eyes. He was at the steering wheel of his dad's car. The white flash of a Toronto Maple Leafs jersey in the headlights. He tried to swerve out of the way, but the steering wheel wouldn't budge. The boy pushed the wagon closer. He tried again with both hands. His whole body shook as he pulled at the steering wheel. It broke off into his hands. The car plunged forward, out of control. He heard glass shattering around him.

Ardagh awoke with a start and opened his eyes. A dim light filled the top of the trench. He could hear the rain falling and it was cold. He wiped his eyes and massaged his jaw. His teeth felt sore. The dream was the same one he had after he landed in France. Before Wilson died. It seemed like a long time ago, but it had only been a couple of weeks. Now his regiment was trying to prevent the escape of the German forces, desperate to leave what they called the Falaise Pocket. Ardagh saw what the RAF bombers had done to the retreating Germans; long lines of wreckage. He had seen fields of slaughtered horses, pieces of men, arms, legs, and bodies strung over miles. Twisted body parts and animals sat out for days, covered and bloated with flies. The stench of death hung over their current position, and yet he still dreamt about Jim and Joey.

Ardagh stretched his arms and legs. The pain in his back-side and legs was excruciating, after sitting and crouching for hours. His trench was covered with logs and dirt to help conceal his position. Ardagh shifted, from one side to the other, trying with limited success to scratch his legs against the side of the trench wall. The bug bites from the past couple of days were full of pus. His new game was to squeeze until the blood popped out after the pus. He was just circling one bite between his thumb and forefinger, about to squeeze, when a machine gun started up near him that jolted his whole body. He stood up, hitting his head on the low log roof, and looked out across the open field while trying to stretch the sleep from his stiff legs. Ardagh rubbed the top of his head and checked his hand for signs of blood.

He looked over to his left at Danny, who gave him a thumbs-up. What would he do without him? He had always thought they were close friends, but the last few weeks brought them to a whole other level, sharing everything about everything. Just a quick glance at each other, and they knew what the other was thinking. He now understood even further what Hank's looks and glances with his flight crew meant at the pub. They shared the fear and the excitement of combat together. It was hard to explain the strong emotion or connection. He read about the stories of war vets and the bonds created through fighting.

He could understand it now. It would be the silver lining he would bring back with him after the war if he survived—the deep friendships of the men in his platoon.

Ardagh missed Wilf. His older brother was one of the lucky ones, LOB—left out of battle. He had a minor hand injury and was getting it stitched up. But it allowed Ardagh some space. He was ready to prove himself without his brother around.

To his right, Lieutenant Brown, had his Sten gun out, looking around as he crawled out to check on the platoon. The fire Ardagh recognized was well off to the left, and he saw no movement in front of him. His position was above the town of Ecorches, France. He could see down a minor road that snaked uphill toward their position, and he studied the small church of Ecorches for signs of the enemy. The defensive line on this slightly rolling hill was good. They tucked themselves in behind a hedgerow, with an unobstructed view of any movement up the road. If the Germans were heading east to escape, this was a natural route for them to go, so they set up the Bren guns and mortars to focus on this road. The dead Germans and destroyed equipment lay scattered all around them.

"Get the PIAT ready just in case," Brown ordered, stumbling by Ardagh's position. Ardagh lifted the British-made Projector Infantry Anti Tank (PIAT) gun onto the front of the trench along with a bag of rounds. He had fired it a few times, but without success. This time, it would be different.

The grinding sounds of tank movements were loud in the distance. Ardagh listened to the steady fire of German machine guns and now the whistle of bullets hitting the surrounding trees. The lower position behind the hedgerow gave them some protection from the fire. The 22nd Canadian Armoured Regiment (CAR), camouflaged behind them, darted up to look for targets. Sergeant Larry Reynolds, an old-timer from Manitoba, came running past along with Woods, Kohler and Nie. He then saw Danny jump up and join them as they moved along the hedge. Ardagh jumped out. His arms strained lifting the PIAT, and his stomach tightened as if squeezed by a bear. He reached the team and ran ahead. He saw a German tank hidden in the tree line fifty yards away. Ardagh stepped out of the hedge's cover, lined up the sights of the PIAT on the far-right hedge that ran perpendicular to the hedgerow and fired. Nothing happened. He tried again. Still nothing. Beads of sweat rolled down his neck. His hands were slippery. He fumbled with the PIAT, trying to get it to fire. Sergeant Reynolds moved in beside him and said, "Give it to me."

Ardagh handed him the PIAT. Sergeant Reynolds pulled out the round and threw it away and grabbed another from Ardagh's bag. Ardagh moved out of the way and Reynolds fired the PIAT. The explosion left no doubt that it hit its target, and a firestorm of metal flew across the field, which was already scattered with dead and bloated cows. He felt the heat of the burning tank on the tops of his hands as he lay in the grass.

The sergeant rolled back behind the hedge, grabbing the tail of another round, calmly loading it into the PIAT. Ardagh watched Reynolds, hoping to get another chance as they continued to move further down the hedgerow. With no comment, Reynolds jumped back out, exposing himself for a second time. Still, this time, they all immediately jumped down beside him and started firing in the same direction further up the hedge. Ardagh held his breath, watching the turret of the German tank move to engage the group as Sergeant Reynolds lined up the shot. Would he fire before the tank saw them? It was a game of life or death. "Shoot," he heard himself say. What was he waiting for?

Sergeant Reynolds's second round amazingly struck the second Tiger tank that sat behind the first burning Panzer. Men from the Tiger tank exited the turret and were immediately hit with a wall of fire from the platoon. The explosions further ignited the first tank. The Tiger lunged left, shaking, lifting as if to race forward, a ball of flame spewing out from underneath the turret. Sergeant Reynolds then crawled further up the hedgerow and caught a German ammunition half-track trying to pull out, and fired at it. The ammunition exploded, scattering debris again across the open field.

The men backed up, crouching into the cover of the hedge. Sergeant Reynolds, jogging back along the hedgerow, waved up to the tankmen of the 22nd CAR. Ardagh grabbed his rifle, fearing that another tank would break through the hedge at any moment. He stumbled next to the 22nd CAR tank, along with Danny and Woods.

"There's a third tank just thirty yards behind the first two. Can you take it out before they run?" Sergeant Reynolds said as he ran up ahead along a ditch carrying his loaded PIAT. The rest of the small group instinctively rolled in behind the tank as it leaped forward. Ardagh reluctantly followed, staying with the group.

This time, however, the third German Tiger tank was more prepared. The 22nd CAR tank moved into the open to engage the last tank. The German tank fired first but missed to the right. Shrapnel raked across the tank as the hedgerow disintegrated.

Ardagh hid on the right side of the Canadian tank, with Kohler and Nie standing on the left side. The concussion of the shell landing so close threw him in the air, slamming him against the tank. His left leg hit hard on the tread of the tank, and his helmet was knocked off. He climbed onto the rear of the tank for protection.

Shrapnel shredded the men around the tank. Without hesitating, the Canadian tank fired into the third German tank with great accuracy. They were in a strong, elevated position that provided the perfect sight line in the close engagement. The German tank stood no chance and, like the others in its group, erupted in flames. Again, the machine guns opened up fire, with a flurry of bullets hitting the hedgerow.

Soon firing stopped on the other side. The veteran Lake Sups showed restraint holding fire, and the shooting died down instantly. The explosions and burning continued across the field in the German hedgerow when a small white shirt appeared, followed by a second and third. They watched as the remaining twenty or more German soldiers emerged from behind the hedge with some hesitation. The Lake Sups stayed disciplined and maintained order as they let the Germans approach, hands in the air. They had learned the hard way over the last month not to trust the enemy. The intense fire and popping sound of burning tanks along with smoke covered the battlefield.

Ardagh slid off the tank and groaned, covered in blood. The first thing he thought of was Danny, but he was having trouble seeing clearly the scene in front of him. He tried to shout out his name, but it forced out a brutal coughing spree of spit and blood. He rolled over onto all fours, spitting out the blood and dirt that covered his face. With effort, he looked up, and there were two men with him, lying motionless. Both Private Kohler and Nie were dead. The German eighty-eight shrapnel had taken its toll on the group.

Danny was on his knees, collecting himself and staring hard down at the other two men. They looked at each other, and a wave of relief and guilt hit them together. Ardagh rolled onto his back, coughing and wiping his eyes clean.

"Shit," Danny said, which made Ardagh lift himself and look.

"What?" Ardagh choked and winced from the pain in his leg.

"Reynolds."

Danny pointed to the shallow ditch beside the tank. The sergeant lay sprawled out, still clutching the PIAT in his hands, his body crumpled and filled with hundreds of bullets. The hidden German Tiger's machine gun had caught him by surprise out in the open and torn into him before he could fire the PIAT.

Lieutenant Brown approached, along with Woods and several of the German prisoners. "Take them back to the battalion for questioning, Woods," Brown said. "How did he see those tanks?"

"Reynolds saved the platoon from being slaughtered," Ardagh said, amazed. "He knocked out two Tigers and a half-track. Reynolds is a hero. It happened so fast, sir."

"Don't forget to grab the PIAT, Danny," Brown said. "How are you doing, Harp?"

The slap of the real question hit him hard. He stared down at his legs. He had done nothing. Reynolds died a hero. He felt his face flush, full of anger and shame. He would do something next time.

"My knee feels like they hit it with a sledgehammer..."

Ardagh stood up but fell in pain as he put weight on it.

"It's nothing, just...."

"Scratches..." Brown said, completing his sentence.

Brown stared hard at the dead men on the ground and blew out a heavy breath. Brown hesitated, brushing the dust off his uniform, trying to form the words.

"Let's get you back and checked out just in case," Brown said in a low voice. "We lost a... It's okay, Harp."

Ardagh knew he didn't mean it. He knew, but was too tired to say it. He had failed to fire the PIAT and had done nothing. It should have been him.

## Chapter Sixteen

# New Uniform

Sint Philipsland, Netherlands
August 1944

Joost stood in front of the cafe window, trying to decide whether he should go in. The dull glare of the cloud-covered sun reflected off the glass prevented him from seeing inside. He squinted again, cupping his hand over his eyes. It was his first leave and visit back to his family. His family had left Bruinisse like many others and found a place to stay in Sint Philipsland. He decided to go to the cafe to check out the pastries. Then he would walk on the dike to look across to Bruinisse and where he had watched the *Hydra* attack. But he really hoped to see Koos. Her brother's house was nearby and he was hoping by chance to see her. He felt his pocket and the folded letter he brought for her. She would be happy to see him after she read it. He wanted to win her back.

The time walking back and forth from school with Koos seemed old and stale. But these trivial moments of his past he wished he could still have, even for a moment. Normalcy. Just a walk. No fear. No stress or anxiety. These were the feelings he could name that plagued him now, every day. The sounds of death and destruction filled his head. Reliving the sheer terror of shells landing around him with every slamming door. The stink of bloody, torn bodies of Russian and Dutch soldiers. No one could understand the harshness of the front. There was no mercy. He was one of the lucky ones to have survived the Russian front. The entire unit was nearly wiped out in retreat of the Russian advance in Estonia in July and they were now refitting in Schlochau, Poland. He had only been to the front for a few weeks. The shrapnel that took a piece out of his thigh gave him the time off to come home, but he would be back to the front soon enough.

Why had he signed up? Why did he join the Nazis? Koos had stopped talking to him. Was that enough? He had explained to her why he ran, thinking she was behind him. That he had returned to get her, but was too late. Her father was there, and Joost knew then what that meant. She had forgiven him, but he had lost her.

Then her brother was taken as a labourer. He would never forget that day. The trucks of SS soldiers pulling into the town. Fascinated, he followed them. Watched as they lined up and marched in separate squads, going from house to house. This time, he wasn't afraid and followed along. He even spoke to them. He marched along with them, some not much older than him. Then they came to Koos's street, and he continued along. Joost tried to warn her and ran out in front of the squad. Stay back, they warned him and pushed him aside just as they reached the front of Koos's house. He stood back in shock at what unfolded next.

He watched Koos come out of the house. Tears covered her face, the look of loathing and fear. The shock and surprise at seeing him. Her family shouting and arguing with the sergeant in charge. Koos's brother David came out of the house and was loaded into the already full truck of men.

"I'm sorry."

"How could you?" she said. "Why?"

"I didn't. What do you mean?"

"You know," Koos said. "Get out. Go away. I hate you."

"But..."

It had only taken him a few days to decide. The rumours and accusations were harsh, and it felt isolating for him to stay. They said he was a Nazi snitch. He had gotten angry and re-membered the moment walking back along the dike and what he said to himself. *If that's what they think, then watch what I'll do next.* He volunteered for the new Dutch Nazi regiment the next day. His father was proud of him. Joost would finally get away from them and their lies. He hoped it would be an ad-venture, but more so that it would gain him some respect and show he had no fear. He needed to prove himself, and it was his own choice if he wanted to show he could fight. Besides, he would fight for Europe against the communist. He believed in the Europe of the future, a united Europe. He needed to regain his honour.

He cupped his eyes again to see inside, but it was empty. It was no use looking for her, and he felt foolish thinking she would want to see him, anyway. Maybe Koos was gone. Joost stepped back from the window, and saw her reflection. He turned to catch her.

"Koos, Koos!" Joost shouted. "How are you? It's been..."

"What do you want?" Koos said, folding her arms.

"Is this the hello I get? I just wanted to say hello. Are you well?"

Koos stood on the road just off the sidewalk but still only a few steps away. She stared at him. He had forgotten how dark her hair was, and the shape of her chin. He smiled and removed his cap. She stood her ground as if ready for a fight.

"How are you? It's been so long," Joost said. His throat felt dry, and his voice cracked as he spoke. "Will you walk with me? Like old times. Before all of this. I'm only here for a few days. I promise I won't bother you again."

"I can't. You know this. You know why," Koos responded in

a flat tone.

"But so much has happened. Only this time, please."

"Why? What has changed? Do you think because you have a uniform on you can do as you please? It'll only make it worse. Why did you come back? You should be ashamed of yourself. Look at you! No one likes you or cares about you," Koos said.

"Koos, please, listen to me, just for a short walk. The things that I have seen, you would not understand. But I'm begging you. It may be the last you will see of me. Most of the men I fought with have not made it. You must hear me out. What if there isn't another chance? You can't believe I did anything. What was it I did? I was just a boy."

"You know what you did. I may never see my brother again."

"What if I told you I have seen your brother? Would you talk then?"

Koos stepped back on the sidewalk. She stared up into Joost's eyes with no expression, holding her breath, and her hands clasped in prayer. He knew then that he had won.

"Are you telling me the truth?"

"I knew you wouldn't believe me. I told your brother that," Joost said, reaching into his pocket. "So, I had him write a letter. I'll give it to you if you walk with me."

Joost followed Koos in silence for several minutes, watching her hair bounce in the wind and dress move over her hips. He felt a tinge of excitement. She stopped and turned to him. "Why did you do this? Why go to the trouble? It won't change anything."

"I knew you wouldn't talk to me, so I asked around to find him. It wasn't hard if you have connections. Like I said, I have survived a lot. I know you will never believe me now, but I was simply there, just like you. I didn't do anything wrong. People just needed someone to blame. I followed the soldiers that day. I wanted to show you I wasn't afraid anymore but... they ostracized me. In the end, I signed up to get away. What did it matter?"

"Joost, you signed up for the SS. Do you know what they have done to people, our people? What you did or didn't do means nothing. You're the SS."

"But I'm not. I'm in the Armed SS. We are like the army. We are fighting the communists. It's not the same."

"People only see the uniform. That is what you represent."

They walked along the top of the dike. It brought him back to his school days. It felt good to be alive simply following a path. Joost looked out onto the channel, remembering the battle over the *Hydra*. It was so minor compared to what he had seen and experienced since. Yet, he had trouble letting it go and releasing the shame of it. Nothing compared to the bug-infested Russian front. The chaos of fighting and living in a trench watching a tank rolling over you, hoping to survive. At least he fought back. The adrenaline of watching a shell penetrate the armour of the tank and the explosive aftermath. But it still never replaced what he lived here. This moment forever marking the loss of his youth. The turning point of his life. Could he ever get it back?

"I miss our walks," Joost said, breaking the silence again.

"It must be difficult. To come back and see not much has changed," Koos said.

"It's a comfort for me. Will you still be here?" Joost said.

"The war will be over soon. The Germans are losing in the east. Almost our entire unit was killed or captured. We are now trying to start a new unit. It's just a matter of time. I'll come back for you if you wait."

"I don't know you anymore. We both have changed," Koos said, stepping away from him. "Besides, why me? I'm sure many German women would want you."

"I don't, I haven't," Joost said, reaching for her. He raised his hands. He stood as if preparing for a hug, then put them back to his side. "There has been no one else, Koos. I don't know why, but that is how it is. I'm still struggling with the past."

"So much has happened to us. It has changed what you are and the uniform you wear. How can you take it back?" Koos said, turning away from him.

"Listen, the war will be over, and life will change again. What then? What will you do? This is a small town. There is so much more. We could go away somewhere new, like Berlin or Munich, away from your family. You will always be 'little Koos' here. You need to grow up and see something different from riding your bike around this pitiful town."

"Easy for you to say," Koos said. "World traveller of evil. It's evil what you're doing. I would rather die here alone than do what you have done."

"I'd ask you to wait for me, but I know you will and are. You've no other choices after the war. Everything I do is for you, regardless of the Germans. There is nothing else here in this God-fearing backward town. When the war is over, and I'm back. It won't take long. If I survive, it'll be for you. You'll be here."

"Of course, you're right, Joost. You're always right. Look at yourself. Time will not heal these wounds. You need to go now," Koos said, turning her back to him.

"Koos, I'm sorry. We can't change the past. I just know. I'll be back, and it will be for you. And someday, you'll see..." Joost said, stepping toward her. He put his hands on her shoulders and kissed the top of her head. Her shoulders relaxed, and Joost let go, turning and walking away. He would be back, Joost said to himself.

## Chapter Seventeen

# Glaitkit

Guildford, England
September 1944

Ardagh jumped off the bus and hobbled along the last block, cutting across the rail line. His knee still hurt with every step, but he didn't care. He was back, at least for a couple of weeks, maybe more. The doctors told him to exercise daily and stretch. The stress of the last few months fell away with every step closer to Eileen's row house, tucked in beside the Guildford rail line. He could almost taste the fresh pint he would have to celebrate at the Wooden Bridge pub as he limped past it.

"Can I help you, mate?" the young British corporal asked, answering the door.

"Is Eileen here?" was all Ardagh could muster. He must be a billet, just like himself. Ardagh stared up at the taller, dark-haired corporal with bright blue eyes and a wily curled smile. Ardagh decided not to wait to be let in and walked past him into the small sitting room with the bay window. A blanket lay messed up on the couch with two empty teacups on the table. Not much had changed since he had left only two months earlier. How could it have?

Eileen stood at the stove with her back to him and said over her shoulder, "Who is it, my luv?"

When no one answered, she turned and saw Ardagh just standing and staring through her.

Ardagh stumbled out of Eileen's house and across the street, heading to the pub. The pain in his knee disappeared, and he crossed the street and rail line quickly, reaching the pub door with his heart in his throat. The expression on her face said it all. It was so unexpected. The feelings of fear, anxiety, loss, and pain over the past month of fighting hit him at once. He guessed it heightened your senses when you had come closer to death, and feelings came to the surface more readily. He didn't know why he ended up at the pub, out of habit, but he needed to get out of there.

He should have known better. All the signs were there, and he didn't listen. Danny had said to watch out for that one. She was a war profiteer. It was a standard description for loose women taking advantage of the next new boy that could buy them stockings and fur. In Eileen's case, he said it was a pint of beer and a shag, and they both roared. Now it made him sick.

Her husband had died early in the war, so you couldn't blame her for taking advantage. After many nights at home with her, she finally came out of her protective shell. How does a widow act in the war? How long do you mourn? When the bombs fell over London, the loneliness and fear had gripped her. At the start of the war, no one thought England could be bombed as savagely as it was and come so close to the brink as it did. So, when Ardagh showed up at the door, despite their age gap, she clung to him. He still remembered the night she told him she loved him.

They were running to the shelter, sounds of bomb blasts mixed with sirens in the distance. Eileen had reached out and grabbed Ardagh's hand. He remembered her red-painted fingernails. She collapsed into his arms and leaned into him for warmth and a hug before she kissed him. Ardagh learned this was planned, of course, later on, as she had described it to his brother on how they met. Why did she pick him? His brother had asked. He was there for the taking along with his innocent smile, Eileen had said, I love him, and they laughed. The training days, as the boys referred to them now, seemed long ago, a fairy tale, an innocent time.

She still wanted to be friends and would take care of his things, she said. How many guys had heard that one in this war? Well, he still cared for her, which again was a crazy thought. Was that because of the time and fear of being forgotten if something happened?

Ardagh entered the pub, and as he sat down, the young Scottish barmaid that ran the place swooped over with a surprised look.

"Harp!" Mandy spouted. "You're back, eh!" she said as she jumped and bounced around the bar to give him an enormous hug and full kiss on the lips, to his surprise.

"Tell me everything!" Mandy said, still clutching him in her arms. Ardagh could feel her curved hips, and the softness of her breasts pressed into him. He held back the urge to kiss her hard again, and the image of Eileen standing at the stove deflated him.

"I just broke up with Eileen," Ardagh said finally. "She has a new toy soldier."

There, he had made it official.

"The bitch!" Mandy said, pulling away to get a good look. "But who cares about her? You know she's not for you?"

With the excitement of a lioness about to pounce on her prey, Mandy put her arm around Ardagh and pulled him close.

"Tell me what you can about the war, the battles. What happened to you? Why are you here? Where is everyone else? You can't just... keep me sitting here without something," she said in her coarse Scottish accent. Her auburn hair was slightly longer than Ardagh remembered. He looked at her and thought about Wilson. Wilson loved Mandy, but was too afraid to talk to her. He looked at her and only saw blood.

"I got wounded," he mumbled, "and I'm on leave to rest up."

"Crivvens! Where, lad? Are you going to be alright? So sorry."

"Just my knee and some minor scratches. I'll be fine," Ardagh said and stared into his beer. "The boys are good, but I miss them already," was the best he could muster. His eyes felt like they were glazing over, and he looked away.

"Dinna fash," she squeezed him once more. "Let me pour you a pint."

'Don't worry', he had heard that phrase a lot in this pub over the training years. It took a few more pints of beer to understand her Scottish phrases. She hopped down and poured him an official pint to the rim of the glass, his first on leave.

"Slainte!" he bastardized her Scottish cheer and took his first long, hard drink. The lump in his throat cleared. "It's going fine, I guess. The Jerries are tough and determined. Young fanatical kids are what we are up against." His hand trembled slightly as he raised his glass to his lips, and he focused on steadying the glass before placing it back down. The bitter taste brought back memories from when he first arrived in England. How could he or anyone describe what he had seen in such a short time?

"It's hard to believe, but the SS kids are more dangerous than any of them. The fight is really just getting started now that we have a foothold in France. What should I do about Eileen? She wants to be friends. After all this." He gulped his beer a little too fast, and it poured down onto his shirt. "Shit," he muttered.

"She's daft and glaikit. Forget her," Mandy said as she walked away down the bar. Ardagh watched the arch of her back and her hips sway. He was hoping to be with Eileen tonight.

Ardagh sat sipping his beer, trying to wash away the events of the last week. He felt like nothing. No girl and the aching feeling he let his friends down. When they had finally made the trip across the Channel in July, they were supposed to be eased into the battle. It seemed like a blink of an eye to him now. The indoctrination to the front lines in a quiet section of the front seemed like starting kindergarten. He wished he could do it over, do it better. Next time, he wouldn't let them down. Losing Eileen was God's way of punishing him.

It seemed strange not to be with his platoon. He had spent day and night for four years non-stop with them. Suddenly they were gone from him. It was a relief to be out of the fighting, but it was all the day-to-day banter he missed. When he left the hospital, the advice from the doctor was, "Don't worry, you will have plenty of time to get back to them. Have fun, so you'll have stories to tell. They want you to enjoy the leave, and besides, it will do you good!"

Ardagh rolled out of the pub without saying goodbye to Mandy. She was too busy with customers to notice. Besides, he was on a mission. Ardagh stopped and undid his trousers. The stream hit the wall, and he changed his aim to the gutter. The plan was to confront the British corporal and win back his lady after he took a piss. He stood with his forehead against the wall of the pub. This always happened to him, getting dumped for something better. He would show him who was better.

The lights of the row house were off, but that didn't deter him. They were always in a blackout. He banged on the door.

"Eileen, it's me!"

There was no response, so he tried the door. It was open, and he fumbled inside, knocking over the coat rack and tripping on the table.

"Shh, shh... you will wake everyone up," Eileen said from the hallway. "I was almost there. Why didn't you wait?"

"Where is he? What does he have that I don't? I didn't do anything, is that it?" Ardagh asked, his words slurring, but he continued into the house.

"Come on, luv... off you go. I don't need any of that here," Eileen said, pushing Ardagh back to the door.

"Come on, Leenie, I miss you... Where is he?"

"He is not here. Now, off you go."

"You're lying... Where is the bastard?" Ardagh said, pushing past her into the sitting room and falling into the couch. Eileen stood in front of him, staring down, hesitating to move. Finally, she pulled the blanket off the top of the couch and sat down on the sofa beside him. She put her arm around him and held him to her chest before wrapping the blanket over them.

"I did nothing..." he groaned.

"It's okay, Harp, you'll be alright. There... there... luv, it's a fine mess today for both of us."

Ardagh rolled onto his side, and they both fell asleep.

\*\*\*

The Canadian Club in central London looked packed full, like every night he came out. Most of the tables around the crowded dance floor were empty. Couples danced shoulder to shoulder, shuffling together to Bing Crosby's "Swinging on a Star". Ardagh wondered what Danny was doing now as he watched two more pints appear on the table. Hank reached for his first and took two long sips. Ardagh watched and waited for him to put the beer down before he took his own sip.

"I don't get it," Hank said. "I thought she loved you!"

"I think she loved the idea of me."

"So, you just got up and left in the morning without a word?"

"What else was there to say? It's war, I guess." But he knew what to say. When he woke in the early morning on the couch and looked around, everything was different. Eileen had gone back upstairs, and it had all become clear to him he was past this. He had moved on without her and had seen the worst of life. It was what Jim had talked about. How would she or anyone understand what he and the other guys had gone through?

Bodies torn and ripped apart. Nothing left, just a body. He couldn't even talk about Wilson or explain it. Danny understood with only a glance. Would he ever find anyone else who could understand him like that?

The music started up again and half the crowd jumped up to the dance floor. There was a mix of army, navy and air force all paired up to dance. The familiar Glenn Miller song, "Pennsylvania 6-5000", made Ardagh tap his feet under the table. Hank's feet hadn't stopped tapping since they sat down, Ardagh noticed.

"How many more missions do you have left?"

"Ten if I'm lucky, one if not."

"Ha-ha, funny guy. What does Boyle think?"

"He says we'll get through."

"How does he know?"

Hank took a long drink of his beer, his hand steady.

"He just does. Okay? He just does," Hank finally said, wiping his face.

Ardagh stared down into his beer. He was right; instinct and experience kept you alive. He thought back to when he first landed in France and how he felt now. The things he would tell himself, what to worry about and what not to, would be so different. He guessed it was the same with every new mission for Boyle and Hank. Things they could control.

"What will you do afterwards, have they said?"

"I have a good shot at getting home and becoming a trainer in Winnipeg. You get a bit more seniority for being in the RAF instead of the Canadians. So, with some luck, I could be home right after Christmas."

"Cheers to that!"

"We are dropping bombs deeper and deeper into Germany. The war must be close to the end. Will you have to go back over?" Hank's hand trembled slightly, lifting his beer.

"In the next few days, I head back to France and then back

to the regiment. I can't wait. This is the longest I have been away from the boys. Who knows where they are?"

"Another pint is in order then," Hank banged his glass on the table.

Ardagh stared down at his full pint of beer then at Hank's empty one. "You get one, I'm fine."

Hank came back with two full pints and sat down, tapping his foot to the music.

"Are you alright, Hank?" Ardagh asked.

"We're scheduled to fly out again next week. Germany again for sure. I don't know... It has been a rough patch since I last saw you. Remember back when we were kids, and you and Wilf climbed Mount McKay. I came with you and then chickened out. I always regretted that. The feeling you guys did something I never did. That's why I joined, I guess. But now, I don't know. Why is that?"

"You know why I joined," Ardagh said, taking a long drink. "If I survive and comeback with a medal will anyone care? Will that make up for Joey?"

"So much has changed," Hank said, lifting his beer glass and swirling it around. They both watched it swirl faster and faster, the beer touching the top of the glass threatening to spill over the edge. "People forgive and forget."

Ardagh watch Hank drink his beer, spilling it down his chin, "I should get my head examined for joining, I know now it won't change things. Brown will never forgive me. But I hope someone will after all this. I feel like I'm missing out now, being away from my squad but nervous to go."

"Wilf will be there at least to help you. I have no one. They're all Brits. I want to go home as soon as I can."

"Wilf, you can have him." He missed him as much as Woods and Danny.

"Don't let him hold you back. He knows you're the smarter one and talks you up to everybody. He will support you no matter what. You should be a sergeant by now."

Now, he felt ready to go back, and none of that mattered. He would help however he could for his brother, and for his friends. He knew now combat was that way and was smarter for it.

"Easy for you to say. It's difficult with the older guys."

"But you know your stuff. If you get the chance, take it and when you come home, you'll get a better job, for sure. Jim would have been proud. No one will judge you." Everything Jim had said was true. It didn't surprise him now. But would anyone accept him.

***

It wasn't yet eight o'clock when they stepped out onto the damp street. Ardagh was now holding Hank upright, trying to use the lamp post as an extra crutch.

"I can't do it anymore," Hank slurred. "Won't survive. I'm too young to die."

Hank slumped to the sidewalk with his head in his hands.

"You'll be fine. Stop sounding like a baby."

"What do you know?" Hank shook his head and pushed him away.

"I know enough. Now shut up before I leave you here." Ardagh lifted him back up and held him up.

"What... Just like Jim..."

"Leave it alone," Ardagh said, raising his hand as if to hit him in the face. "Say it again!"

"You're still afraid and you haven't gone through what I have. You never know when you're next."

But Ardagh had seen more than his fair share, like Reynolds's crumpled and torn body full of bullet holes. Kohler and Nie went left, and he went right, death one way, life the other. He might never see his brother again.

"Things are different now, for all of us." Ardagh tried putting his cap back on his head and stood Hank up on his own.

"I want to die."

"Don't be silly."

Hank let go of Ardagh and hugged the lamppost. He was too drunk to stand on his own. Ardagh heard the sounds of a bus as the driver pushed the accelerator. He watched the dim lights of the double-decker bus as it sped toward them down the road. Hank let go of the lamppost and stepped out onto the street in front of the oncoming bus. Ardagh grabbed him by the collar just as the bus slammed on its brakes and came to a stop.

"You're standing in front of the bus stop, you idiot. Tough to get run over when you know it's going to stop."

Ardagh dragged him back onto the sidewalk and they stumbled down the street with Hank laughing and hollering.

"Maybe it's best you let the Jerries try to kill you. You might have more success."

"At least I'll be shooting my guns when it happens," Hank said, holding up his hands, pretending to fire.

Ardagh watched his brother stumble down the street. He remembered how lost and shaken he was standing on the ship crossing the Channel. Only leaving with a sore knee and bug bites. Angry with himself for letting down Reynolds. Ashamed to come back. Now he knew he was lucky to get a chance to come back to the start. It felt different, and he saw things he didn't before. He had been given a gift. The doctor was right. He had thought just simply pushing things away and taking control would save him. But it wasn't so simple. He had to learn what he could and couldn't control to find the right path. Jim had tried to tell him. He told him when he learned the sounds and sights of things, he would be ready to follow his instinct. *You will learn to see what is ahead. Once you have lived the fear and danger of combat, you will know how to follow your instinct to survive.*

# Chapter Eighteen

# Koos Returns

Bruinisse, Netherlands
October 1944

Koos stood on the dike and watched each German ship leave the Bruinisse harbour one at a time. She had arrived too late from Sint Philipsland with her father to find Willie. But now she hoped to see him one last time, although from a distance. They were new ships she hadn't seen before, but of the same flat landing craft style that Willie had shown her. The last ship was much bigger than the others and had AF 92 painted on the side.

She studied the tall man standing on the bridge, looking across to her. She waved, and he waved back. It was him. He was still alive. She felt good that she had done her part, but it hadn't killed Willie. Koos's mixed feelings had haunted her over the last few months. Her hate for the Dutch SS traitors and what they did to her brother. Her disdain for the Germans they dealt with day to day. And then the pang of what if things were different, would she like Willie more? It confused her some days, but she could put each in its own logical box and not dwell on each too long. Willie's box was the one she spent the most time in.

A little rain fell, and she flipped her hood up. There was no wind, and the clouds sat lower than usual. The AF 92 was now directly in front of her as the rain picked up. He looked so close high above her on the bridge and he pointed to his eyes and then to her to say I'll see you, and waved again before putting his hands back into the pockets of his raincoat.

She examined the repaired damage on the side of the ship. With the war raging down the coast, the attacks in the area had increased over the past month. He would head into more danger than ever before. She might never talk to him again.

She watched the trail of the ship's wake as it moved off in the distance and gave one last wave, even though she knew he couldn't see her, and walked back to her house in Bruinisse to collect more of her belongings.

***

Willie watched the tiny figure in the distance standing on the dike. The rain fell heavily from the low dark clouds above them. There were so many things he wanted to tell Koos. It was terrible luck to get his command right as the invasion started. He had no real time to get to know the crew and train. It was a few months since he last spoke with her. The flotilla had little experience together, but a lot was expected of the AF 92. It surprised him now how much he missed their long talks. But they had received orders to pull anchor just after he noticed the fishing boat cross the channel. They were to pick up remnants of the 15th Army group escaping the Canadians along the coast. At least she was able to see his ship. Would she like the name they had given her? Der *Lowe*, the *Lion*. They were now an iron ship with credit for sinking a British transport ship. They had sailed right into a column of British ships heading back to England and fired several torpedoes at them, sinking one ship and damaging another. British fighters pursued them while they retreated, but the *Lion* fought back with its lethal anti-aircraft guns on the approaching British Spitfires, knocking out two of them and sending the third turning back home with smoke trailing. He knew she wouldn't approve, but she had run to the top of the dike and waved. She wouldn't be proud of what they had accomplished. But maybe, after the war, he would meet her again and things would be different. He hoped for that day soon.

***

Koos opened the door to her bedroom. Nothing had been moved or taken since she had left. She sat on her bed and took in the familiar smell of her room. Her father only gave her a few minutes to gather more of her things. They had only so much room in her brother's already crowded house. She had argued with her father that she left everything behind except for her clothes and he wouldn't know what she would want to bring back for herself and her sister.

She felt like she was in someone else's life, sitting in her room. Her dolls were in the same spot on her desk, staring back at her. The quilt was still on the bed. Everything was clean and organized. Just a small layer of dust that lifted into the air exposed through the light coming from the tiny window. She knelt and spread her hands over the quilt on her bed, remembering the names she had given each coloured Dutch girl that was sewn inside the squares. Their faces hidden by a bonnet. Her room was a child's room. Somehow, since leaving Bruinisse for just a few months, she had grown up or had gained a different perspective on life. Everything in the room seemed foreign or from another time. She stood up, looking around, and went to sift through her sister's things. Her room was similar, and she filled a bag with everything her sister had asked for.

"Are you ready?" her father called up the stairs.

"Yes, coming."

Koos went back to her room for one last look. There was nothing she wanted. She stood at the top of the stairs. Yes, nothing. She held the bag full of dolls and toys for her sister, double-checking everything before heading down.

"Didn't you take any of your things?" her father asked,

looking into the bag.

"No, I have what I need."

Her father put his arm around her and gave a quick squeeze of her shoulder, and they walked out of the house.

## Chapter Nineteen

# Mortars

Wildert, Belgium
October 20th, 1944

The padre made his way from man to man as they sat in the cool wet grass along the road. The yellow and red trees over the road were a sharp contrast to the grey morning. The low clouds kept the chill in the air, and he could just make out his breath as he spoke.

"Hey, Padre," Wilf said. "Nice of you to join us, sir."

"Boys, I have some great news for you two. Ardagh is back. I just saw him at headquarters. He won't make it to this dance, but I think in a day or two, depending on how you boys fare, God forgiving."

"Took him long enough," Danny said. "How does he look?"

"A little quiet, but eager to get back at it. He said he has some news for you about Hank." The padre nodded to them both and continued down the line.

"What do you figure, Wilf?" Danny asked.

"He is coming into a bit of a mess, with little time to prepare. We'll have to make sure he doesn't get ahead of himself. Guns blazing, trying to make up for lost time," Wilf said.

"Will he stand up this time?"

"I'll watch over him. Don't worry, Danny."

"Yeah, he'll be fine. I'm not worried."

The tanks fired up down the line, and the platoon stood up, signalling the start of Operation Suitcase.

\*\*\*

"Hold here," Ardagh said as he knelt and peered around the corner of the farmhouse. Their section was on the far flank of a small village called Wildert. The intense fire coming from the surrounding houses had stopped. 'B' company had split up, with Ardagh's platoon on the far-right flank and his section farthest to the right of all. Ardagh, Danny, and Wilf all volunteered to jump ahead to the next house, and they were now past the first line of defence of the Germans.

Danny raised his finger to his lips, signalling to be quiet. They both listened to German voices coming from inside the house. Ardagh looked back and saw Lieutenant Henderson waving to both of them to come back. He risked another look around the corner of the house and, just then, three Germans appeared and, unaware of their presence, dashed across the backyard into the next house. Ardagh spun around and crawled along the side of the house, pulling a grenade from his belt. Danny followed and smashed a hole in the window at the front of the house, and Ardagh threw the grenade through it. The rest of the section ran to the house as the explosion rocked the inside. They waited a few seconds, then entered through the front just as the remainder of the group joined them.

The Germans ran from the other house and Ardagh dashed through the back door, followed by Danny and Wilf. They reached the house and threw another grenade through the open door. Ardagh looked back just as rifle fire came alive from the neighbouring house. The other group was too slow to follow and were now trapped by the German fire. Wilf, Danny, and Ardagh were alone and too far out in front.

"Shit," Wilf said.

"Why didn't they follow?" Danny asked.

"The Germans are trying to counterattack and fight it out.

We'll have to wait for a tank," Ardagh said.

"Screw that; we'll be prisoners or dead first," Danny said as he peered through the window. Ardagh made a plan as a squad of Germans moved into the house next door.

"You go first, Danny, then you, Wilf, head to that hedge and clump of woods then circle around. Do you see the low green wooden shed? Let's meet there. It doesn't look like anyone is on our other flank yet," Ardagh said, pointing into the woods.

Danny didn't hesitate and hurried back out the front door, opposite to the house with the Germans. Wilf waited.

"Go now!" Ardagh ordered. Wilf turned to argue. "Go!" he said again. Wilf disappeared out the door. Ardagh watched him dive into the hedge. He stood up to move through the door but hesitated. A red tricycle like the one Joey used to ride lay tipped over beside the door. He wanted to reach down and pick it up, set it right. But he noticed movement in the corner of his eye and froze.

"Halt! Don't move!"

Ardagh turned, staring at a German with a rifle pointed at his chest. The English shocked him the most, almost Canadian, but not. He didn't know what to do. Dive through the door and take his chances or put his hands up. The German decided for him, as he was too close.

"Hands up!"

Ardagh dropped his rifle and put his hands up. They pushed him through the back door without checking him and into the next house. One of them shoved him up against the wall, holding him by the neck. The young German paratrooper pulled out his knife and showed it to him before pressing it along his face. Ardagh looked at the patches of unshaven growth on the German's face as the blade slid along his own. They both had trouble growing a beard. The paratrooper brought the blade down to his chest. Ardagh held his breath, waiting to feel the pain of the blade slice into him. The paratrooper leaned into him, their noses nearly touching. Ardagh's mind raced. What about the gun he kept in his side pouch? Could he get it in time before the blade entered his chest?

Ardagh moved his hand to his belt, letting the paratrooper choke him. He heard a couple of quick orders, and the German released him. The paratrooper grabbed him by one arm, dragging him through the door into the backyard. The German in charge followed behind, and Ardagh heard the click of a rifle bolt.

They cut through another backyard and a set of red-coloured hedges past a smouldering half-track behind a house. Ardagh grunted, holding back his anger. He was still alive. He had a chance. They had only moved through one backyard and there were lots of potential places to escape. These were elite German paratroopers and fanatics. Several paratroopers lay strewn along a hedge separating the backyard. The fighting had been at close range, and they looked to have been ambushed. It would be easier for them to shoot him. There wasn't much time. The further away from the front line, the harder it would be to escape. It was him or them. He wasn't ready to put his hands up and he couldn't run away from it. He remembered what Jim had told him. *You'll know when it's time, trust me.* He had to do something.

"Schnell!" the paratrooper yelled as he pulled his arm along. The kid had big, thick, muscular arms, and reminded him of Sergeant Anderson. Ardagh let the German pull him along, and was almost lifted off his feet, as they stumbled across the yard. There were no sounds of gunfire, and it seemed like everyone was taking stock. They continued through another backyard. Ardagh looked over his shoulder at the paratrooper behind them. He had stopped to light a cigarette and fallen a few yards back. It was now or never, Ardagh thought as they approached another hedge. There was more distance between them now.

There was a good chance the German would fumble for his gun and Ardagh would be away through the hedge. He put his hand into his pocket, gripping the handle of the revolver, and felt for the safety. The shriek of a hawk shattered the silence from behind the next hedge. It flew over them, holding a mouse in its claws. They both turned to watch it glide over them. Ardagh pulled the gun from his pouch and without hesitating fired into the chest of the German and pushed past him through the hedge to the next house. He waited for the crack of the rifle as he ran to the side of the house. He reached the side wall and crouched, listening. Ardagh could hear the heavy boots of the second German across the grass as he approached around the corner of the house.

Ardagh fired as soon as he appeared. The German fell to the ground, and Ardagh ran over him and back through the nearest hedge, circling back to where they had come from, looking for the clump of trees and green shed. Ardagh fought through another hedge, hoping he judged the right direction. He moved fast across another backyard and through the hedge, focusing only on what was ahead of him. He saw the house they captured him in off to the left and the corner of the green shed just in front of him.

"What took you so long?" Ardagh heard as he rounded the corner. Danny jumped up and grabbed him, pulling him down.

"Shit," Ardagh said. "You scared the crap out of me. Why didn't you keep going?"

"Didn't want to leave you... brother," Wilf said, his voice sounded flat and tired. His face at first looked pale and grey but now the colour was coming back.

Ardagh touched Wilf's shoulder, it was good to be back to see his face again. "You're still ugly as ever."

Ardagh told them what happened, as they moved through the houses and on to the main street. They spotted the tanks of the Grenadiers and rejoined their platoon.

"Back home," Danny said, though his lips didn't move. "Try not to surrender again." Their section walked back into the same house. Wilf handed Ardagh his rifle back. The Germans had pulled out. Ardagh would be with them if he hadn't escaped. The Lake Superiors had taken the town and orders were to firm up where they were. They moved the carriers up along with the rest of the company.

"I didn't surrender. I told you I shot two of them."

"Right, I'll believe it when I see it," Wilf said. Ardagh wondered if he would have done it without his brother beside him, knowing he was there waiting for him. They all knew it was different fighting close up. Ardagh was happy to be back and alive with his brother next to him, safe.

"Do you need anything? I'm gonna grab some food from the carrier," Wilf said as he walked to the open door. He stopped and turned back waiting. Danny waved him off but Ardagh felt his stomach growl.

"Sure," Ardagh said, following Wilf out of the house.

The sun was now low, and it was getting dark, which left little time to get settled. Ardagh watched Wilf take a deep breath of the fresh air and stretch his arms out as he started back to their carrier. Ardagh could still feel the tension in his body and he tried to shrug it off, rolling his shoulders, taking in the cool fall air. The whine and moan of the first mortar was like a breaker going off in his head, and he ran, diving, under the closest carrier. The German mortar landed to his left, and he curled up, hoping the hot metal would miss. Two more rounds landed around him in succession. His brother disappeared into the smoke. Everything went yellow and red, then black.

# Chapter Twenty

# Kubelwagen

Sint Philipsland, Netherlands
November 4th, 1944

Sergeant Joost de Lange drove across the small bridge into Sint Philipsland. His driver, Stabsgefreiter or Corporal Hans Burg, stopped as he crossed the bridge, unsure of which direction to head. By any measure, Corporal Burg was a thug. His chief assets and skill were his fists and his ability to fight with them, not driving. Joost had convinced Hans to join him on this out-of-the-way errand only on the strength of the promise that he could smash some skulls. Corporal Burg had seen no action yet and was green. He was eager for a fight. They had promoted him because of that hunger for violence and taking on the nasty business of shutting down the Resistance. It was rumoured that he had been on firing squad duty.

"Left, follow the dike," Joost ordered. The Canadians would be here soon. It surprised Joost not to have seen any German forces in the village so far.

"Yeah," Hans said. He was not one to have long conversations with. On his first visit back, he had bumped into Koos in front of the cafe and they had walked along the dike, but he hadn't found out where she was staying.

"I'm not sure of the address, but I think it's just down from the cafe."

Joost enjoyed these simple decisions. He was lucky to be

alive. The same fate or luck didn't belong to his unit, the 4th SS Panzer Grenadier Brigade Nederland. The Russians completely decimated the regiment on the Eastern Front. They didn't care to make prisoners of the Dutch Nazis. He had lived a lifetime on the Eastern Front, quickly getting promoted through the ranks to sergeant. The last promotion nearly got him killed. Pieces of shrapnel were still in his body, causing havoc with his muscle system and breathing.

The fear had never left him. The first time was with Koos, and he ran. Even today, the thought of that moment stuck, and he could feel the familiar wave of fear all over his body. He carried it with him everywhere he went. It was the shame of running. It almost got him killed several times. They thought he was brave. It was all a lie. He had run, not just from the *Hydra*, but from her too. Thoughts of her carried him through the bug-filled summer and rains. No matter what he did on the Eastern Front, he couldn't shake the thoughts of being with her. Now the throbbing pain from his wounds reminded him daily of this weakness. He became more hardened with each day that passed. He had more prominent and longer mood swings. The doctors told him it was the stress and anxiety from the front lines, but Joost knew it was something else. He had risked coming back to Sint Philipsland to see her before the war's end to correct a wrong. He needed to see her and some-how change the past to fix his future. Their future together meant everything to him.

He was lucky to have survived the massacre and to be back in Holland. His family had fled long ago out of fear of retribu-tion for supporting the Nazi cause. They were safe in Germany, but she wasn't.

He imagined her excitement as he walked up to her house and held her. She would pack her things and go with him. She would not hesitate, and he was confident that they would find her. It was a small town; everyone knew everyone. Sure, his uniform would scare people into silence, but he was a local.

He would go to the cafe and simply ask. What would be the harm in that? They moved along Zuiddijk, which followed the outline of the medieval village and the dike. He would start searching at the only cafe on Voorstraat.

"Pull over here," Joost said. "We'll check inside. Stay here. I don't want to alert anyone yet."

Burg just gave a broad grin and nod of his head and leaned back on the car, lighting up a smoke. Joost started across the street to the cafe, looking up and down the road. Then his eye caught movement from the house on the opposite corner of the street. He stopped and stared, not believing his good fortune. Koos's mother, Janna, was walking out of the front yard carrying a basket of clothes. No need to ask anyone now. He stood and watched her. Then she now noticed him, but put her head down and continued on with her task. He moved across the street with giant strides to intercept her. She felt his presence and stopped.

"Hello, madam, do you remember me? I'm Joost."

"Oh, hello, Joost. Yes, of course. How are you?"

"Well, I could be better, but I've been one of the lucky ones," Joost said, pointing to the scar on his face.

"Yes, well, that is good."

Janna shifted her basket to her other hip and put it between her and Joost. Joost smiled back at her, standing in her way. Joost wanted to hit her. She was also to blame, but he suppressed the anger boiling below the surface. Not yet, he told himself. She will change her tune. Koos first.

"Well, thank you for your kindness. How is Koos doing?"

"She's not here."

"I didn't ask you whether she was here, just how she was doing."

"Her wound has healed. She is fine."

Her words stung him to the core. He saw Janna's eyes widen

in fear. He held back the urge to strike her across the face. In Russia, he wouldn't have hesitated to shoot her. He took a step back. Joost tried to remain in control.

Lowering his voice, he said, "Well, that's good. It's been a long time. God forbid if it hadn't healed by now. I have some great news for her. Is she around?"

"She is out."

"So, she is here, but out?"

"No, she is not here."

He had all he needed. So, he smiled and stepped back again.

"Well, tell her I said hello. We'll be on our way. Thank you."

Joost turned without waiting for a response and crossed the street. He watched as Janna turned and ran back into the house. He nodded to Burg, who threw his cigarette onto the road and jumped back in the car.

"Head further down the dike road, then pull over. I don't want them to see us. We'll wait here for a bit and watch the house."

They only had to wait a few minutes before she rode into them.

\*\*\*

Koos hurried on her bike in the fading light down Zuid-dijk toward her brother's house. The long ride gave her time to think. She had argued earlier with her father and mother and had left to clear her head. It was late, and she was pushing it. As the sun set, the words of her father, "Stay away from the Germans and be home before dark. There is a curfew," crept in her thoughts. She wasn't a kid anymore, and she didn't need to be lectured. Her father had only followed the rules; it was sickening. They'd left in a rush only a few months ago when the Germans flooded their home in Bruinisse, but fortunately, she could bring her bike. It was her prize possession. Now, her thoughts were consumed by what would lie ahead when the Allies arrived. They had already landed in France, and they hoped it would all be over by Christmas.

As she rounded the road along the dike, two German soldiers stepped out onto Zuiddijk. She continued pedalling,
keeping her focus on the two soldiers just ahead of her. They
seemed to be waiting for something, maybe her, but why? She
had nowhere to turn. The dike was on her right, and several
homes lined the street on her left. She slowed as they both
stepped into the middle of the road. One carried a rifle and
pulled it off his shoulder. The other placed one hand on his
hip, where a gun hung on a shiny belt. They were both very
young and dressed in grey-green uniforms. Koos had seen
these uniforms before, but not in a long time. It was only when
they looked for men to fill their ranks that the Dutch SS had
torn through her town. They had convinced a few to join. Anger built up inside her, thinking about it. The war was creeping
closer to them every day, and they should be free from this.
*Why don't they just leave us alone once and for all?*

"Halt," said the blond, the taller of the two soldiers, with a
hand on his hip.

"Joost," Koos said, frowning. As she approached, she noticed a thick bubble-like scar that followed the line of his chin.
It was still bright pink and ran from his ear along the edge of
his chin. It created a jagged appearance that outlined his face.
His lips hid any expression as she tried not to stare. Joost's
movements were like his face, broken and disconnected. He
shifted, looking uncomfortable, constantly moving in place as
she approached.

"How are you?" he asked, but didn't wait for a response.
"I've some glorious news for you."

She was warm despite the cool breeze that flowed down
along the dike. Her legs were stiff from the long ride, but she
stayed rigid and held her ground. She felt sad. What happened
to him? He looked as if he was in constant pain.

"This is Hans, my driver. I'm a sergeant now. Are you heading home? It's getting late," Joost said, trying to sound concerned.

"It's just over there in the corner," Koos said, pointing. She hoped he would understand. She was close to home.

"Your mother says you're well."

"You've talked to her?" Koos asked.

"Yes, but I wanted to share the news with you. I've talked to your brother, and he wants you to visit. I could take you there now," Joost said. His tone puzzled Koos. What was he up to? What did he really want?

"Maybe another day. It's too dangerous." She spoke just above a whisper, but the words echoed danger inside her. *It's not for me, but for him.* She could see his Iron Cross and Wound Badge on his lapel. He fought twitches in one leg, and he leaned on his gun. He shifted to hide it; it didn't work. She took a chance and took a deep breath, slowly blowing the air out of her lungs. She had nothing to hide.

"Joost?"

"He really misses you."

"Yes, are you okay? Where have you been?"

"That's not important now. You must come with me."

"But why? The Canadians are coming. They're close. We'll be free."

"Please, don't make this more difficult than it is. You'll be home in no time."

Before she responded, the other soldier grabbed her by both wrists, pulling her off her bike. Joost grabbed her around the waist. She held back a scream, uncertain what to do next. Koos could feel him hard against her, and she screamed and kicked at the other soldier, sending them both tumbling to the ground. As they landed on the ground, his hands came free, and she elbowed him hard in the chest. Koos struggled up on her knees and his grip tightened. She felt the tug on her skirt as she tried to stand. The other soldier had regained his footing and stood over her. She never saw the right hook that landed on her jaw.

***

They both stood over her limp body, breathing heavily. Koos lay still, sprawled out on the road. Joost reached down to check for a pulse. Thankfully, she was still alive. He had more to say to her.

"Throw her in the back seat. Let's get out of here."

Burg picked up her limp body and carried her to the car. Joost grabbed her bike, rolled it up and over the dike, and briefly watched it roll into the water. He looked around to see if anyone had seen them. Sint Philipsland remained quiet. They needed to get out of here fast and find shelter for the night, but not in this town. Not with the Canadians coming.

Burg had turned the car around and was waiting for him. He jumped into the back of the Kubelwagen with Koos. She lay slumped behind the passenger's seat on the floor of the Kubelwagen. He could see her chest moving with every shallow breath. Before he knew it, they were heading out across the bridge. He had made it.

## Chapter Twenty-One

# Luger

"Look, it's moving! It's alive! It's alive! It's alive!" Ardagh mimicked. "He looked like Frankenstein." It reminded him of Jim pretending to be Frankenstein, chasing Ardagh around the house when he was a kid. The dark clouds in the distance and the hint of rain gave him an uneasy feeling of what lay ahead. The wind blew his collar up and it flapped against his face.

"What are you talking about?" Danny said. "Keep your eyes forward and hands on the Bren."

"Wilf. He looked like Frankenstein when I saw him." He had to talk about it. It was the only way to move on. Wilf would be safe at least.

"Yeah, he was pretty messed up. We were lucky. They nearly got us all," Danny said.

"He seemed in good spirits. I'm glad he is getting out of here. He told me to step it up now that he's out of the way, and take care of you guys," Ardagh said. He tried to push the image of torn flesh and exposed bone of Wilf's leg out of his head. Wilf's encouragement to step up came from a whisper and forceful grip when he pulled Ardagh close. Eileen had pushed him to step up, but now after the fighting they had been through, it was real and meant something.

"We're going to miss him on defence for sure. I doubt he will play hockey again with the wound he had," Danny said, pointing at the Bren gun.

"I think that was the last thing on his mind. He was pretty doped up. I'll miss the old fart," Ardagh said, levelling the Bren gun down the road ahead.

The column of four Lake Superior carriers moved cautiously down the road, open flooded farmland on either side. They could see the small, classic church spire in the distance as they crossed the canal bridge connecting the peninsula to the island town of Sint Philipsland. The initial view from a distance was old, just like every town they had entered with low roofs and stone walls. However, the first thing that caught their eye was the water tower immediately to their right. Snipers were always the big unknown. They were there to slow the advance and cause as much grief as possible, and it worked. They were as frustrating as hell and deadly. The water tower was not the best hiding spot and provided no cover. But it didn't mean they hadn't seen them coming for miles.

Ardagh's carrier led the section up the narrow, slippery road to test the German position. They stopped about a half mile after the canal bridge and waited for a response from the Germans, parking on the back side of the dike wall that lined the road to get a better view of the village. Ardagh checked his Bren gun and peered down the road through its sight.

He had only been away for a few weeks, but the changes surprised him. He was getting more settled into his new platoon after a week of fighting. His new platoon leader was Lieutenant Henderson. He was a straight shooter, intelligent and accomplished, replacing Lieutenant Brown, who was wounded a week earlier, along with Wilf. Ardagh had mixed emotions about Brown leaving. Brown had pushed him, and he wanted to show him he had changed. But after the last few days he felt relieved to have a second chance and not be judged.

"Do you hear that? Sounds like a jeep," Ardagh said.

In the distance, he could make out a tan grey Kubelwagen, or jeep, moving fast along the road at them. The sun was almost setting, but it lit them up from behind. It amazed him the people in the jeep couldn't see them. Maybe they were reconnaissance from another troop. Were they beaten to the punch?

"What do we have here?" Danny remarked, exploring through the field glasses.

"Let's move down onto the road, Woods," Ardagh ordered.

"Fire a burst over the top of them, Ardagh."

"Right, but are they one of ours? They would have fired a flare."

"Just a quick burst above their heads will get their attention. Silly buggers."

*\*\*\**

Koos blinked to gain her focus, trying to open her eyes. Her head hurt and she could feel the vibration of the moving car every time Hans stepped on the gas. She tried not to move. She was crammed below the back seat. Her head was against the back door, looking up at Joost staring out the back window. She closed her eyes to give herself time to think. How far had they gone and how long was she unconscious? Her cheek was throbbing, and she wondered how swollen it was. She shifted her shoulders to ease the pain in her back.

"Take the first left after the bridge," Joost said. "You can open your eyes now, Koos, and get one last look. Come sit next to me."

Joost patted the seat next to him and clicked his tongue like she was a dog. Koos looked away and wrapped her arms around her knees, drawing them in, curling into a ball to fit into the footwell of the back seat. She shook her head in silence, feeling the car lurch and gain speed.

"Come on, Koos." Joost reached down and grabbed her

arm. Koos locked her arms tighter and anchored her feet.

"Don't make me..." Joost leaned down, lifting her feet off the floor. She kicked her feet just as Hans slammed on the brakes and the front windshield exploded. Glass and blood sprayed into the back seat.

\*\*\*

Ardagh leaned on the Bren gun and, as he pulled the trigger, Woods released the brake on the carrier, causing it to lurch forward and changing Ardagh's aim. The fire from the Bren gun rolled up along the road and into the oncoming car's grill. The car swerved and plunged into the watery ditch, leaving its tail sticking up.

"What... Fuck," Ardagh said. "Now, why did you do that? Jesus!"

The car smouldered in the distance. The lack of any movement and fire from Sint Philipsland suggested they had a free run of the town.

"Way to test the defences, Harp," Danny said with the usual straight face.

\*\*\*

Koos lifted her head from behind her knees and glanced up at Joost. Blood was pouring from his shoulder as he pulled out the Luger and pointed it at her. Koos looked at the driver, who lay slumped against the window, his face covered in blood, not moving.

"Don't move," he said.

"It's over, Joost. Give up."

He just glared at her and licked his lips. His red scar stretched like a second smile, and he snickered. "Shut up, let me think."

She could hear the sounds of tanks speeding up toward them. Would they shoot again just to make sure? It had to be the Canadians. She would be free if she survived. Joost put the barrel of the gun to his temple and gasped. Blood gushed out of his open wound, and he coughed up blood. He wiped his face and spit onto the seat beside her.

"Don't do it," Koos said. "Surrender."

"What do you care?" He coughed and leaned forward, looking out the shattered windshield. The tanks grew louder until she heard the gears grind to a halt. Joost slumped down into the seat. His face was only a few inches away from hers and he put the barrel to his lips, signalling her to be quiet.

***

Woods let go of the brake and moved up the road, followed by the remainder of the section. It was his mess to clean up now. Ardagh grabbed his Sten gun and jumped out to inspect the damage. It surprised him that no one had jumped out to yell or return fire at them. It looked like a German Kubelwagen, with its roof cover on. Its nose pointed into the ditch and a small trail of smoke floated out. All else was quiet. He thought about Wilf and his last close-in fight. He was lucky then. His hands felt wet. He flipped off the safety as he approached the driver's side, ready to fire a burst. He could see the broken windshield and tight group of bullets that had cut through the back of the canvas cover. The driver's head leaned against the bloody window, not moving.

He saw movement in the back seat and crouched down below the armour plating as he heard a female voice cry out. The pop-pop of a handgun disrupted the silence and bullets tore through the canvas above him. Ardagh pulled back the firing bolt of the Sten gun, ready to let loose a burst into the back seat. He reached over and grabbed the handle of the door, pulling it open. Bullets hit the side of the door and he sat back behind the rear wheel, out of the field of fire. He could hear the whimper of a girl and then the click of an empty chamber, followed by silence. Ardagh stepped in front of the open door to face a German lying on his back, blood covering his chest and the barrel of a Luger. His grotesquely scarred face had a strange smile. He saw a girl curled up on the floor of the back seat next to him. Their eyes met, he wanted to reach out to her. The German turned his gun toward her. Ardagh clenched his teeth and set his stance as he fired a burst into the chest of the German.

Ardagh stared back at the young girl, his Sten gun ready to fire. Her hands were over her ears, and she was swaying back and forth. She closed her eyes and let out a scream as tears streamed down her cheeks. Ardagh looked at her empty hands and shouted, "All clear!" and Danny came down the bank. He pulled the back door open to see the result of Ardagh's shooting.

"Jesus," he said and reached in, pulling the girl out of the Kubelwagen, dragging her up by her jacket. She didn't resist and scrabbled along with Danny. They reached the road and Danny pushed her onto the ground. She stared in awe back at him, tears still streaming with a soft squeal as she wheezed.

Ardagh opened the driver's side door. His hand shook as he grasped the handle. He had survived another fight at close quarters. He coughed and wiped his mouth. The driver was a Dutch SS corporal. The Bren's 303 calibre bullets had almost torn him in half below the neck and chest. Behind him sat the now dead sergeant, Dutch SS, not German. Ardagh stepped back and looked in through the rear door to get a closer look. He couldn't have been more accurate. The results spoke for themselves. Only half of his skull remained, and the blood and brain splatter covered the entire back of the seat and door. He grabbed the Luger and walked back up to the carrier.

"What do you make of this one?" Danny asked as he approached.

Ardagh stared down at the young girl. She was sitting with her legs crossed, blood splattered across her face, with a glazed look. It was strange. If she were with them trying to escape, she would be angry and upset. But she bowed her head, clutching her hands together, and gave out a half crying laugh. She sounded relieved and almost happy.

"Do you think he was trying to escape with his girlfriend?" Danny said.

"Don't just stand there, Danny. Get some water," Ardagh said, waving his arms.

"Oh, in love already, are we?"

"Fuck off and get the water. She looks like she has quite a shiner on her chin. A little water would help clean up the mess."

Ardagh poured the water onto his handkerchief and pressed it to her forehead, cheeks and neck. She just sat peering up at him in silence. She must be in shock, Ardagh thought. She didn't resist his efforts to clean her, and stared at their badges.

"Well, good evening, Fraulein," Danny said, smiling down at her.

"How do you feel?" Ardagh asked.

The girl stood up. Ardagh's eyes locked onto hers. This time it wasn't the look of fear, but of wonder and happiness as she wiped her tears from her cheeks.

"We're Canadians," Ardagh said, pointing to his sleeve and the blue Lake Superior badge. Koos immediately laughed and nodded her head, wrapping her arms around him.

"Definitely Dutch, Harp, we got here just in time."

"I think from the village," Ardagh said.

Lieutenant Henderson moved up to join them. They watched as he jumped down from the carrier. "What have we got here, boys?"

"Two dead Dutch SS and one girl, who we think is Dutch. Maybe some funny business, but not sure. She seems happy enough to see us, sir."

"Harp had an old-style shoot-out with the SS sergeant."

"Good work, Harp!"

"Okay, throw her in the back for now, and let's get moving before it's fully dark. Apparently, it looks like the Germans have left the village. Let's move out!"

Ardagh lifted the young Dutch girl, cradling her in his arms, carefully placing her in the back of the carrier, and retook his place behind the Bren gun. They waited for the rest of the section to pass by them before they followed. He turned to look back at her one last time, and she was smiling at him like it was the best day of her life.

## Chapter Twenty-Two

# The Potato

Sint Philipsland, Netherlands
November 5th, 1944

The noise and excitement outside her room left her anxious that she was missing out. Her brother's house was empty but for Koos and her father. She sat, lonely up in her room, looking out the window onto the courtyard where the Canadian soldiers were gathering for breakfast. Her bed was made, and she wore her favourite chequered skirt and sweater with roses. The war was now in their backyard again. Koos had been eager for the troops to arrive and for the locals to see their heroes. But the events still shook her. There was great excitement in Sint Philipsland with the Canadian boys, as her papa called them. Her papa had been very clear about staying away from them and keeping her distance. She belonged to a solid Christian family, spending every Sunday at their church. There were many stories of girls romanced by the soldiers. She hoped this would be so for her, or at least that she could meet some of them. Canada was such a far-off adventure. She wanted to meet the men who had saved her again. These rugged farm boys were the talk of the town.

Her mother, Janna Marina, was her hero. It did not surprise her when the soldiers showed up at her door. Her mother welcomed them fully and had the same feelings as herself. She had raised eight kids and supported her husband through two wars. Koos marvelled at her strength and energy. Her mother immediately invited the men to the house. With the makeshift canteen across the street, the area became a central gathering point for them. Her mother was now off searching for supplies to help them.

She still felt exhausted. The last night's events had left Koos in shatters. They had saved her. However, the excitement of the impending freedom had the town beside itself. Everyone was out in the streets hugging and kissing, and the chatter was loud. No celebrations in the past could compare to the feelings of the townsfolk today. No one had questioned her about why she was riding in the back of a carrier. They just assumed, like the rest, that she had been taken up with the celebrations and overstepped the usual boundaries. Her father and mother knew better. They had been searching the town in fear that she was taken.

Koos was at the age where all she could remember was the fear and danger of being under occupation. She was just a young teen when war broke out. The collapse of Holland had been so swift, it was hard to remember how it happened. She examined the slight scar on her leg that remained from the *Hydra* attack. It all seemed so long ago, standing on the dike with Joost as the Germans destroyed the small Dutch minelayer. Joost running, leaving her on her own, and then being rescued by her father.

It was the years of waiting to be free, the slow changes and dwindling rations that tortured them. Eventually, one thing after another was taken away. The lack of food and ability to move about freely became overwhelming. It made people do funny things. So many turned collaborators for a piece of bread. Pieter was one of them, but for revenge or just because he could? She was proud that she had helped the Resistance and her family. She was doing something. Now she felt like she was just hiding out. The last two days had gone from fear to joy. The Canadians had arrived at the right time to save her, and Joost had paid with his life. She wondered what would happen to Pieter. Had he fled with the others, or would they capture him?

The Canadian soldiers parked their many strange vehicles in an open field on the north side of the road into town. She secretly hoped that they would get to have one soldier stay with them so she could learn everything about them. Koos looked at all the faces of the soldiers lining up for food outside her window. She would never forget his face, the face of her rescuer, his light blue eyes. He had cradled her and lifted her into the back of the carrier. His eyes had locked onto hers with a look of concern before they lit up. Where was he from? What was his name? She had spent the last few weeks since the Allies had landed on the beaches practising to improve her English for this very moment. A wave of nervousness flashed over her, and she suppressed the thoughts of holding and kissing him that filled her mind. She was now eighteen and a full-grown woman. The years of the occupation had kept her tied down with the dangers of the German soldiers and her parents' control.

She was young, just a teenager. "Still a baby," they said. "Their little sister Koos."

"We want nothing to happen to you. Besides, you're too young."

She wasn't clear why she had such passionate feelings, even before she met any one of them. But her dreams over the past few months were extreme and vivid. Just thinking about her dreams caused her to ache inside. Was there a reason or destiny in the war and hardship they had gone through? Would this set the stage for the rest of her life? She wasted hours daydreaming and walking the dike and paths around her home, wrestling with these questions. What would it be like to be free again? She was now free after four years and her liberators were here. She would finally meet her heroes. Apprehension filled her and tightened around her stomach like a wet rope. Not letting go, every thought added a knot and complicated her feelings. As she searched through the crowd of men, the shock of freedom became real. The knots grew tighter.

She'd spent the last night in bed and all morning recovering, but was now getting worried she would miss seeing her blue-eyed rescuer and his friend again. She wasn't sure how long they would stay and feared she would miss them. Her father was excited to hear about German ships spotted in the Zijpe harbour across the muddy channel. They would certainly go there next.

"There were up to three ships of the Kriegsmarine for the taking," her father said. "It's our chance at some payback!" To think this tiny little harbour of Zijpe would see such a battle. "What about our home?" her mother asked.

"It's already lost from the flooding, the bloody Germans," her father muttered back, "We'll show them."

Staring out at the canteen, she continued her search for her hero, watching as the soldiers lined up for food.

***

"Hey, Harp, how's the love life?" Danny said at the front of the breakfast line. Ardagh had yet to see the girl again after she disappeared into the crowd when they first entered the town the night before. It was still early. There was not much to see in Sint Philipsland other than a church, a water tower and a windmill dating back a few hundred years. They had built dikes hundreds of years ago around a mudflat that created the island and built the town on the southeast corner. Voorstraat or Main Street to the church, which was at the centre of town, was lined with a couple dozen homes and shops. They'd set the canteen up at the end of Voorstraat near the dike and the little yellow windmill. Ardagh had used up most of the morning looking for her among the groups that watched their every move.

Danny always knew how to push his buttons. Ardagh turned and, without comment, threw a potato off the counter, and it sailed harmlessly over Danny's head but straight onto the side of the house across the street.

"Nice throw, Harp. Good thing the Dutch have small windows, or you would be in big trouble with our neighbours!"

"Fuck right off, Danny!" Ardagh said as he elbowed past Danny with an enormous grin.

The door to the house across the street opened, and a curly dark-haired girl walked out to pick up the potato. Ardagh shuffled and picked up his pace to beat the girl to the evidence. He reached down but was too slow, and the girl promptly snatched it off the road.

"Hey, sorry."

Before Ardagh could stand up, he heard the harsh voice of an older man in Dutch who said, "Koos nu het huis in!"

The young girl pivoted on her heels and hurriedly ran back into the house, but not before turning to get a full look at Ardagh. She had given the slightest of smiles before her hair tossed over her face and hid the bruise on her chin. She ran past the old man into the house. The old man strode up to Ardagh, smoothing the large moustache that hung over his upper lip and chin. The old man gestured for him to move on.

"Strike one, Harp!" Danny said.

"He never was a great hitter."

"Or fielder," someone from behind Ardagh said, and they all laughed. Ardagh retreated, backpedalling to the platoon and the safety of the canteen.

"I think she was the girl from the Kubelwagen," Ardagh said.

"Well, maybe the healing has begun," Danny patted Ardagh on the shoulder and gave him a half-hearted hug.

"Not a bad day's work in the Canadian Army. This will make the papers."

"Young love found in Dutch town over rescue and potato incident."

"The old guy didn't seem overly pissed, did he?"

"No, I think it was all a bluff protecting his daughter. I saw him earlier during the celebrations. I think he is one of the fellows in charge of the town."

"Chocolate may work, always worth a try, to break the ice," Ardagh said with a sheepish grin.

"Did you catch her name?"

"Nope, I thought he might have said it but wasn't sure, not strong with Dutch yet."

"At least she wasn't wearing those ridiculous hats and dresses the older women wear."

"They are very friendly, and happy to be free."

"I've got a feeling we're not in Kansas anymore, Danny," Ardagh said.

The girl had a look about her he couldn't place, a hidden strength. It was the smirk he had seen as she walked away. It was the first girl he had met since landing on the continent. The bruise reminded him she had been through a lot.

Ardagh stared off, thinking about the house on the corner. Danny had already started calling it the potato house just to needle him further. He would have to walk by for a visit when he had time off. Having chocolate as a backup plan or flowers wouldn't hurt. The Dutch hadn't seen proper food for some time. The night before was the first time he had seen such an exciting celebration. All the ladies came out with their funny white hats and dresses on. It was quite the sight to be seen coming from Fort William.

Ardagh sat down with his meal, looked over his plate, and smiled at the comfort of having a hot meal. The crowded table of soldiers remained silent but for the clanking of spoons on the plates. He tried to picture and name men who had been killed or wounded over the past few weeks through the heavy fighting. His mind was blank. The platoon had new recruits that were green; they arrived without names. With the constant action, they didn't have enough time to learn them. It was nothing like he'd expected before the invasion. He had been thrown into managing the Bren gun because of the losses. The originals with the most experience were handed the most important jobs, and he took command of the section.

Ardagh looked over his section; they needed rest. For the first time since leaving Canada, he felt at home. He was glad to be back with the boys. Despite the jibes, he realized they'd missed him. It wasn't often that the wounded returned. No one ever really knew the full details as men came and went. They were thought to be either dead, or lucky to move on.

Ardagh smelt the fresh ocean breeze roll into the protected courtyard. There were bursts of wind that whipped up around them constantly. He could sense a large storm blasting the Atlantic to the west, but it had yet to rain. The town was on the south side of the island and somewhat protected from the storm. Instinctively, he glanced at the upper window of the potato house and noticed her staring down at him. He wanted to wave but held off, for fear that Danny would disrupt the moment.

"Hey Harp, why are you smiling?" Danny said.

"No reason," Ardagh said as he turned and shoved Danny away. "Let's get cleaned up."

Ardagh watched Danny and the others in the platoon head back down the street to the carriers before he turned around. He wanted to walk past the mystery girl's house one more time, hoping to catch another glimpse of her, but instead he saw her walking up to the top of the grass-covered dike across the street. He hurried to catch up to her.

Before he could say anything and without turning around,

she said, "Hello."

"Hello, I'm Ardagh," he stammered.

"I'm Koos," she said in a heavy Dutch accent. Ardagh showed surprise on his face.

"You speak very good English. Can I join you?" He tried to remember if he or Danny said anything inappropriate when they first rescued her. His face grew red, trying to untangle his buddy's conversations. He sat and hoped for the best.

*** 

She nodded and abruptly sat down, staring into the grey water. The pair sat behind the dike. Dangerously close to Koos's house for her safety, but far enough for some privacy. She had spent a lot of time in this spot over the last two months. It was her safe zone. She could see the tiny yellow windmill and listen to the water gently lap up onto the shore. Most days like today were windy, which covered up the noise of the neighbourhood. Many times, her father had to climb over the dike to get her attention. She normally wore a scarf to keep her hair down, but today she wrapped it around her neck to show her face to him.

Koos turned and looked at Ardagh, and tried to say his name properly, "Ardagh... thank you for saving my life."

"Well, I don't know about that. I'm sorry. I almost killed you," Ardagh said, squinting to study her face. She wanted to kiss him. She was so excited to be free from the Germans. It had all happened so fast and they had waited so long. Her heart was pounding. She looked at him, studying her. *He is searching for something,* she thought.

"Why do you say that?"

Ardagh turned away, checked his rifle, and then set it down, rechecking the safety and pointing it toward the water.

"You never know what to expect with the Germans or what is waiting ahead of us. We've seen a lot of death and destruction. Accidents happen, and people die. Some make bad decisions or get in the way. It's very complicated sometimes. We only meant to warn the driver, but the carrier lurched and, well, you were lucky, I guess. I think war is like that."

"So, I got in the way, and you fired on us?"

Ardagh pulled on more dry grass in silence. He looked like some boys in her school. Not as fierce, on his elbows fiddling with the grass. Ardagh finally threw the grass, and they watched it blow across the dike before he spoke. "Can I ask you something? I need to know."

"Yes, anything."

"Why were you in the car? Are you... were you friendly with the Nazis?" Koos looked at him. He seemed hurt, like something from the past had resurfaced. Like he was about to be let down again. She held her breath, but she wanted to scream. She had risked everything, and he was worried about himself.

"A Nazi, you think... I'm... really?" Koos asked before she slid away down the dike. Her eyes filled with tears. She brushed down her skirt as she got up.

She turned and fired at him, "How could you think of such a thing?"

"Sorry... Sorry, I didn't mean to offend you, but we found you in the car with two Dutch Nazis."

Ardagh stood up, ready to retreat. They stood staring at each other. Koos looked up at him. He was her hero. Why was she fighting him? This was her moment of truth. What she said next would determine her fate with him or not. She could dismiss him and never see him again, but she had waited too long for Ardagh, or someone like him. This was a chance. A chance to leave this place and go on a new adventure. She was tired of fighting, of holding her ground with her father, her brothers and mother. Did she need to fight him as well? She just met him. He looked at her differently than others. She enjoyed his gaze. What was so different?

She said finally, "You need me to explain. Please sit back

down with me... Please."

Ardagh hesitated, then laid his rifle back down and sat. She sat beside him and turned her body to face him.

"I only knew one man in the car. The sergeant. His name was Joost. He was a classmate. Before the war, I had a crush on him. It didn't work out. When the war started, he joined the Dutch Nazis and went off to fight. I hadn't seen him since August and he'd changed. He was severely injured. He came back to the village I think because he was out for revenge. They threw me into the car, and he was taking me away from my family. I didn't know where he was taking me. But I guessed why."

"You were in rough shape when we found you. How does your bruise feel? I'm glad you're feeling better. We've seen it a few times. The chaos of the battle, the panic that follows. The Germans do crazy things. They're realizing that they may lose."

They sat silently, staring at the grey water and sky. Koos felt sad, everything was moving so fast. Would he stay or move on and continue to chase the Germans? They could be gone tomorrow.

"I hope it ends soon. We've had enough," Koos said as she moved closer to him. She enjoyed his warmth as his shoulder rested next to hers.

"We hope by the spring."

"Where are you from?" Koos asked. Ardagh stared at her, looking unsure how to answer.

"Fort William," Ardagh responded, shifting his feet and crossing them. He was on his elbows, stretched out beside her. He grabbed a handful of grass. She had seen none of the soldiers without a rifle. After these many years of war, it seemed normal.

"Fort William, where is that?" She turned away, looking down, watching his rough hands picking at the grass.

"It's sort of in the middle of the country at the end of the

Great Lakes, let me show you," Ardagh drew with his finger in the grass, "This is Canada, these are the Lakes, and Fort William is here."

"Is it far?" Koos said as she shifted back onto her elbows. The bruise on her chin felt warm, and she let her hair hang over her face.

Ardagh turned to her, and she instinctively brushed her hair from her face. "Yes, it is far, a two-day train ride from the coast. But it would be a beautiful trip if you were with me."

Koos smiled and followed along, "Are Nazis allowed to go to Canada?"

"Only the pretty ones," he said, shaking his head. "I think I could sneak you in."

Koos giggled and held his hand, staring into his eyes and taking in his smile. She was happy for the first time she could remember. She would never forget this moment and how it changed the course of her life forever.

"I'm glad I found you. Even if by luck. Sometimes things are meant to be," Ardagh said, lifting her hand up.

"You don't have to say that. I'm happy you're here. You saved me. It means something. I think. It's been a hard time. My father says it'll be another cold winter. You can't imagine how you've saved us."

"I've so much I want to tell you. The last year for me has been an adventure. Until now, I wondered if I was nuts."

Koos looked back at the top of the dike and saw another soldier was now walking down toward them.

"The lovebirds," he said.

"This is Danny. He was with me when we found you. Danny, this is Koos," Ardagh said. Ardagh looked nervous and stood.

"Yes, I remember. Nice to meet you again," Koos said as she got up with Ardagh. She moved close to him. It felt normal to her, like they had always been.

"Something's up. We have to go get ready," Danny said.

Ardagh turned to her and said, "I'll be back." He touched her hand and walked away, but it was enough for her.

***

Ardagh watched her pass by one more time, mesmerized. They had stood down. There were rumours of German ships across the channel, but no one could verify it, so the platoon had all come back to the canteen to have an early afternoon tea break. The sun was high, a bright blur through the clouds. It still threatened to rain, but the wind bursts had died down and the air hung heavy. Koos was riding her bike following the dike, then through the city centre and around. Passing by him every ten minutes. A young boy rode up on his bike and Ardagh reached into his pocket and pulled out a chocolate bar. He gestured a trade for the bike. The boy let go of the handlebars and let the bike drop where it stood as he snatched the chocolate bar from his hand. Ardagh climbed on the child's bike, knees sticking out awkwardly as he pedalled in Koos's direction. He caught a brief glimpse of her before she made a turn along the south dike. Ardagh stood on the pedals and sped up. By the time he reached the corner, she was making another turn down Schoolstraat that headed to the church. Ardagh was catching up to her and figured he would catch her before the church.

He reached her only a few houses before the church and sat back down on the seat and glided as he approached her. *Enjoy the moment,* he thought. Her back was straight and rigid as her legs pedalled away. She looked elegant and at ease. Her brunette hair bounced and fluttered in the breeze. The Dutch rode their bikes everywhere and seeing a girl on a bike was a common sight now, but it was still a novelty to him. He smiled and decided he would pass by her and pretend he didn't see her.

Ardagh pulled alongside of Koos but kept looking ahead. He just got his front wheel in front of hers when she picked up her pace. She cut into his path so fast he had to turn away quickly to avoid a crash. He pulled back behind her and sped up again. Her straight back and hips were in the same position with no effort. It was as if nothing had happened. He picked up his pace but couldn't catch her. By this time, he was back at the canteen. He was pedalling as fast as he could. Koos was a few bike lengths ahead and out of reach. A cheer rose from behind him as he passed the food line. He picked up his pace again, but to no avail. She turned the corner with grace, her face expressionless. His heart sank. *Maybe she doesn't like me,* he thought, and he stopped pedalling. He glided around the corner and almost crashed into her back tire but managed to weave past her. He looked back, and she was laughing. Koos pedalled up beside him and put out her hand. Ardagh reached for her but only brushed the tips of her fingers. He corrected his speed and reached out again. She pulled her hand back and laughed. He looked forward and weaved away from a parked truck, just missing it. She reached back out and this time their hands met and held. Her hand was warm and soft. His body relaxed as he enjoyed the moment. He stared at her rosy face and the twinkle of mischief he had seen before. The scent of her perfume made him feel excited and alive. He wanted to hold her.

They glided to the corner, holding hands. She said something in Dutch and tugged him closer. He pulled his knees in to avoid hitting her bike and she looked down at him and stuck out her tongue, making a funny face. Ardagh copied her and for the first time in a long time, he felt like a kid again.

Her pedalling carried them along. They reached the churchyard and laid their bikes on the grass. Laughing, they climbed over the low fence and fell to the grass. They sat together leaning on their hands.

"Why are you biking in circles around the town?" Ardagh said, pointing his finger looping it in the air.

"It's the only thing I can do."

"I know, but why?"

"I don't know, it just makes me feel good. Whenever I ride my bike. I just... I don't know... feel in control of my life and where I'm going. Does that make sense?"

Ardagh nodded and sat up. "I wish I was in control of something. Maybe after the war when I'm home."

"When the war is over, I'm going to ride all over Europe. Just because I can."

"Oh, you can?" Ardagh asked, teasing.

Koos moved closer to him and lifted her chin toward him. Her expression was serious except for the glowing cheeks.

"Yes, I can," she said and leaned in, kissing him on the cheek.

"There you are!" a familiar voice blared over his shoulder, making him flinch, nearly bumping heads with Koos. He jumped up and watched Danny marching toward them with a mixed look of amusement and seriousness that told Ardagh he wasn't just interrupting. There was a reason.

"Again?" Ardagh asked.

"We gotta go, they confirmed, ships in the harbour across the channel," Danny said, breathing heavily.

"Are they artillery ships?" Koos asked. Ardagh looked at her with surprise. There was more to her than he thought.

"What do you know?" Ardagh asked.

"I lived in Bruinisse. It's a long story, but I know those ships," Koos said. She told them everything she had learned from Willie and about the AF 92 as she followed them back to their platoon.

Ardagh and Danny searched out Lieutenant Henderson to pass along the information Koos had given him.

"We are going to wait until it's dark before we fire on them," Henderson said. "Colonel didn't want to show our hand, and they have a lot of firepower."

"We need to move quick, sir. The ships will be stuck at low tide and unable to return fire," Ardagh argued. "If we go there, we'll find out for sure, and then we can let them have it until the tide comes in."

"How do you know this?" Henderson asked.

"His girlfriend told him," Danny said, elbowing Ardagh. "But she was telling the truth. She even knew the make of the ship and type. She lived on the other side and saw them harbour there several times."

"Come with me and tell Captain Styffe," Henderson ordered.

# Chapter Twenty-Three

# Hands In His Pockets

Bruinisse, Netherlands
November 5th, 1944

"Sir, here is the weather report and Captain Steine's orders," the ensign said. "It doesn't look good for the next twenty-four hours. We are to stay put."

The weather was not cooperating and the 1st Artillery Flotilla remained stuck. The seas were too choppy for the converted landing craft. Finally, orders to move from Bruinisse to Ouddorp had come across the wireless when the enemy fighter alert had ended. However, as they checked the weather reports, the channel was terrible. Ironically, that's how it was. Of course, the enemy fighter planes would disappear with lousy weather. They couldn't fly in these storms, and they knew the flotilla couldn't move either without a significant risk of being lost at sea.

But now they had an additional threat. The AF 47 reported approaching Sherman tanks and carrier troops across the narrow channel on Sint Philipsland. The Canadians had arrived at last, and their quiet shelter had been discovered. They had a platoon of seventeen men with one machine gun, a Panzerfaust, and rifles to protect the flotilla. They were ordered to disperse along the opposite dike, facing Sint Philipsland.

Willie had ordered his men to their stations as he scanned the shore opposite his position. His ship, the AF 92, was in an awkward place tucked in behind the other ships, the AF 44 and 47. They gave him some protection, but Willie knew they were in for it. Their only choice was now to stand and fight.

Willie looked at the weather report and Captain Steine's orders and then his watch, but it didn't change the situation they were in. It was mid-afternoon. This put them in a perilous situation, with the Canadians pressing from the east. He had spent lots of time learning from Captain Knuth sailing along the northern coast of Germany and Holland, knowing the waters saved them a few times from being destroyed. The speed of the AF 92 helped outrun their prey. Quick thinking with fast fly-by-night attacks in open water was his strength. Staying on the edges was the key, and not getting caught among your enemy. It was the simple plain advice passed down from their admiral, sometimes easier said than done. They had created lots of chaos, but barely escaped in the waves and stormy weather of the channel. This cat-and-mouse game happened everywhere along the coast.

Silence filled the bridge as they looked across to the peninsula to Sint Philipsland. The three officers stood around Willie, stress and anxiety across all their faces. Heinrich had brought a bottle of schnapps. He needed to keep them calm. They had plenty from the supply they were carrying. The troops they rescued carried all sorts of treasures and left some behind as a thank you. They even had women's undergarments for the girls back home. Heinrich took good care of their stash and made sure everyone got their share.

"Let's have a schnapps!" Willie ordered as he set glasses on the table. Heinrich opened the bottle and filled up the glasses.

Willie lifted his glass and said, "To a long life and adventure. Heil Hitler!"

The schnapps burned Willie's lips as he contemplated how

he would get out of this one. He didn't want to surrender his ship but he wasn't a fanatic who would ask his men to fight to the last man. He poured himself another full glass of schnapps.

"Tell the men to stay alert. We stay in position until the weather changes," Willie said, still holding his schnapps to his lips. He tilted back his head quickly and downed the schnapps, smacking his lips.

Lieutenant Hans saluted and said, "I'll tell the men to remain at their stations, and inform them we're staying put." His voice trailed off as he bowed his head and left the bridge.

Willie peered through his binoculars and observed the top of the dike across the channel. Out in the open, several half-tracks with machine-gun mounts faced them.

"Half-tracks!" Willie said to the others on the bridge, "See... there." He pointed to his second-in-command. "Let's hope that's all they have. Request to AF 47 to move out of the harbour to engage. If we move right away, we still have a chance."

They watched as several tanks appeared on top of the dike just over a mile away.

The communication came back. "Hold your position."

In other words, stay put and hide was the simple response relayed by the communications officer from the AF 47 captain. The first mistake he realized now was to be in this harbour in the first place, so close to Sint Philipsland. No one had told them that Sint Philipsland had been taken. It was suicide to be trapped in the harbour.

"We are sitting ducks if we don't move now," Willie said to the crew on the bridge. "This couldn't get any worse. The tide is too low, and the AF 47 couldn't fire on them if he wanted to! Let's be ready to move regardless if they fire on us."

Just as he spoke, the Bren gun carriers opened up and fire rained down on the AF 47. Willie looked back across the channel and now saw Sherman tanks roll up into view onto the dikes.

"Shit," he said to himself; they still couldn't directly engage, and they were stuck in behind the other two ships. So far, the AF 47 was holding on, undamaged, but it was an excruciating time to wait for the tide.

"Quickly, what time is the tide coming in?" he asked. The strain in the look on his face told everything.

"Sixteen hundred hours. We should be fully above the dike in another twenty-five minutes, Captain," was the professional response from his second. The men on the front deck were readying the guns. However, they were pointlessly aimed at the two ships in their way.

"It may be too late by then," he said coldly.

A barrage of artillery fire rained down on them and finally found their mark. To their horror, the entire bridge of the AF 47 disintegrated and collapsed. The smoke cleared enough for them to watch the AF 44 receive a direct hit, and the munitions caught on fire. Willie didn't need to wait for orders.

"Full ahead!" Willie ordered. Without hesitation, the ship lurched forward and crept away from the two burning vessels. The crew on the bridge looked on quietly in shock as their comrades fought to put out fires or throw themselves into the water and swim to safety.

"Move out to the harbour entrance and engage the enemy where possible." The communications officer repeated the new orders from the AF 44.

Willie looked across to the communications officer with a grim expression. "Tell them aye-aye." The officer repeated his answer as they all watched the scene in horror. Both the AF 44 and 47 were on fire and continuing to take more punishment, with mortars and tank fire crashing around them.

"Full ahead," repeated Willie as he stuffed his hands into his pockets. He would not let the mistakes of others fail him and his men. They had been in many sticky situations in their short tenure. Still, they always came out successfully when they were the most aggressive. Should he have just done what he thought was right and ignored the delay? Hesitating was a disaster. They were taught in their naval classes to be aggressive.

The ship drifted past the burning bridge of the AF 47. *What a waste,* he thought. If they had moved when the instinct had told him, they would at least be clear of the harbour and a challenging target. It felt good to be moving and let the boys fire at the enemy, at least. Go down fighting, they had been taught. You never knew the outcome.

*** 

Ardagh stood up in the carrier's front, looking across the channel to the burning German ships, reloading the Browning. He looked to his right and left at the line of tanks and carriers across the dike. They had parked three tanks of the British Columbia Regiment beside him. The tank commander gave a casual salute before he looked down and gave orders to the gunner to fire. The other two tanks in the troop were well spaced out along the dike and firing non-stop. They had a superb view of the harbour and the three enemy ships across the channel. The two six-pounder anti-tank guns on the other side of his carrier had successfully hit one ship and were setting up to take aim at another. It was like they were out on the practice range. Everyone wanted a piece of the action. It hadn't taken Captain Styffe long to order them to move Six platoon up along with the troop of British Columbia tanks to engage them. Lieutenant Henderson had given the standard signal and wave to open fire. There was no direct fire back, and the troop of tanks and carriers took their time adjusting, then firing and adjusting again. It was still before sixteen hundred and the tide was yet to fully come in. Koos had been right. The Germans couldn't fire back because they were below the dike wall of the harbour.

"Look at these guys!" he said to Danny and the crew. "Watch out for return fire. We can always move back behind the dike."

The farthest ship made a move to get out of the harbour. The gunners from the tanks and six-pounders couldn't adjust quickly enough and Ardagh watched the shells land without success. He felt his stomach turn as each six-pounder and tank failed to register a hit.

"Keep firing!" Lieutenant Henderson said. "Get your range."

Ardagh climbed out of the carrier and went to the mortar team while watching the six-pounders and tank fire. He realized they were too close to the tanks and on the wrong side of the dike road to hit the exit of the harbour.

"Let's set up over on this side, boys," Ardagh ordered. "It'll give us a better angle and some more room to adjust."

The mortar squad quickly moved back and set up.

"Lead it a bit. We only have a few minutes before it will be out of the harbour," Ardagh instructed.

They shifted the mortars and fired. The first set of mortars salvos were too far ahead, but they fed them again. Ardagh watched as they found their mark. This lifted the entire group and, as if on cue, the fire became more effective and accurate.

The German ship finally moved into the open and began firing back. Ardagh could hear the ping and zip of machine-gun fire, and the anti-aircraft guns pounded into the dike. Like a line of dancers, the carriers and tanks gracefully stepped back behind the dike for cover.

The mortar team adjusted again. The simple manoeuvre inadvertently improved their accuracy, and after just a few salvos, a gigantic explosion from a direct hit blew into the sky over top of them. They didn't hesitate or pause fire, and a second explosion followed.

Ardagh peered through his binoculars as he sat beside Lieutenant Henderson and Danny.

"It's a hit!" Ardagh said over the continued firing of the

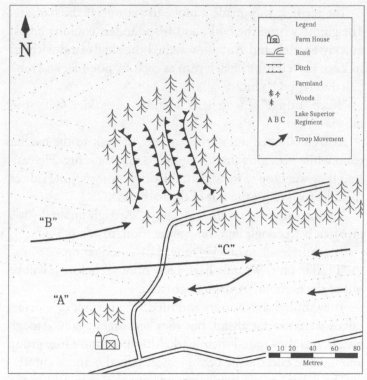

Legend

Farm House

Road

Ditch

Farmland

Woods

A B C   Lake Superior Regiment

Troop Movement

"B"

"C"

"A"

0  10 20    40    60    80
Metres

Battle of the Gap

mortars and tanks. "Look, the front of the ship is sinking." He pointed without taking his eyes out of the binoculars.

"You're right, Harp. You can still see the bridge above the water, but the ship is smoking and on fire," Lieutenant Henderson responded.

A full salvo of mortars and tank fire was suddenly unleashed and directed toward the now sinking ship. Seconds later, a massive explosion greater than the previous one erupted and debris flew into the air. The German fire instantly stopped. Several more explosions in the distance lit up the sky.

The tanks and mortars continued to fire and pound the Germans on the other side. Ardagh dropped his binoculars, got up onto his knees, and pulled out his small pocket camera. He lifted it up, and sighted the small lens on the scene across from them.

"Damn, they're too far away!" Ardagh said, looking through his camera. He moved the camera along but could only make out black smoke and fire. "Yep, too far."

"Harp, get your ass back behind the dike!" shouted Lieutenant Henderson. "Before you get your head blown off."

"It would be nice to get a close-up picture. You don't see this sight often. A group of Kraut ships sinking."

"Not a bad idea, Harp, if you don't listen to my orders, I might send you over alone!"

Just then, Captain Styffe strolled up as if on the practice range to ask how it looked.

"We think there are at least three ships badly damaged, but it's hard to see from the smoke and grey backdrop on the other side, sir," Lieutenant Henderson said.

"Well, get your platoon organized back in town. We are planning a raiding party to check it out. Since this is your show, your platoon will lead!"

"Yes, sir," Lieutenant Henderson said, trying not to laugh.

"Something funny about that?" Captain Styffe asked.

"No, sir!" the lieutenant saluted, then peered over at Ardagh, giving him a wink.

As the captain left, Ardagh smirked and said, "I guess... I won't be alone..."

# Chapter Twenty-Four

# Admiral Styffe

Sint Philipsland, Netherlands
November 6th, 1944

"Jesus, watch out," Ardagh whispered as Danny stepped on his heel. "Is this safe?"

"Nothing like a crowded boat with loaded rifles... I always used to say," Danny laughed.

"Straighten up, men," Lieutenant Henderson ordered.

The sun still had a few hours before it would shine through the low clouds when forty men from number Six and Seven platoons boarded three fishing boats for the dangerous trip to check out the damaged Kriegsmarine ships. Ardagh thought it was a big gamble to invade an island with no backup or plan. But the Lake Superiors were riding high with confidence over the last few weeks. The Germans were on the run, becoming more of a rabble than the army they first faced in Normandy. The captain's exuberance over discovering ships in the Zijpe harbour a short distance across the channel was too tasty of a sandwich to not bite further into. It was the Dutch Resistance that insisted that the Germans were on their backs, and they gave the Lake Superiors the rundown of all three ships and men. Their mortars and tank fire had sunk the Kriegsmarine artillery and transport ships, they said, and caused many casualties. If they moved fast enough, they could capture the small port and verify the sinking of the German ships. The enthusiastic locals thought highly of the Lake Superiors and believed they were giants. By the end of the morning, they could be heroes or Hun prisoners. In the exuberance of being set free after five long years, were the locals overconfident in the Lake Superiors' achievements? Ardagh had seen the balance between success and failure. Reynolds's PIAT attack or the ricochet of a bullet that killed Wilson. Firing first to rescue Koos. Sometimes overconfidence got you killed, or aggression was enough to carry the day. History was full of these wins and losses. The victors celebrated while the losers burned. The Lake Superiors would soon find out which fate awaited them.

The two platoons only carried ammunition and weapons. No life jackets were available, but it was a short distance. No one questioned it. They travelled lightly, expecting to return before nightfall. Ardagh, however, packed his camera just in case, hoping to get a shot of the evidence for home and family. Otherwise, no one would believe that they'd sunk anything but fishing boats.

The tiny little fleet of borrowed boats set sail from the Sint Philipsland port at the peninsula's eastern end. The leading boat's captain was Koos's father, and he was eager to do his part. He was a very confident and comforting figure with a large moustache and a bright twinkle in his eye. As they pulled away from shore, he burst out with a short song under his breath about family and kids.

The little fleet and 'Admiral' Styffe's plan, formally "the Captain Styffe plan" was simple. They set the plan up for the two platoons of 'B' Company to manoeuvre without being seen from the approach to the east. Number Six platoon would provide covering fire as number Seven platoon advanced on the town of Bruinisse. Number Seven platoon would first determine the strength of the units they were up against just in case and be prepared to hightail it back. Hopefully, the Dutch were right, and the ships wouldn't be able to follow. Ardagh was still uncertain whether that part was thought through. But the Admiral had assured them that there were no other German ships in the area. The burning and explosions observed during the evening from Sint Philipsland gave the Lake Superiors encouragement to finish the task. The mission was a go.

The makeshift fleet hugged the eastern shoreline of the small island until they reached the peninsula near Anna Jacobapolder. They moved at under five knots, but only needed to travel a thousand yards to reach the shore, less than ten minutes of exposure to the enemy. The sounds of the motor and boat cut through the water. They remained quiet, waiting for the familiar sound of the German MG fire to engulf them.

Ardagh looked around at the other men as they got closer to the smoking ships in the harbour. They were out in the open channel, so presumably, the Germans would see them coming. It was still slightly dark as they approached, directly toward the planned landing just south of the town. They had discussed this in depth before they all boarded the tiny fleet of boats. Ardagh couldn't help but joke, "There are a couple of extra bathtubs in my billet we could use, sir." He got a few giggles from his section, but just a hard side stare from Lieutenant Henderson. *I must drive him nuts,* he thought. *Oh well, it might be over quick if we don't get moving to solid land.*

Ardagh reached into his side pouch and pulled out his pocket camera. He only had a few shots left, and he thought if this moment wasn't one of them, he didn't know when there would be a better time. He snapped the shot and received a quiet but sharp voice in his ear.

"Christ, Harp, this isn't a cruise holiday, for Pete's sake. Get ready. They could let loose on us at any moment."

"Ready, boys," Lieutenant Henderson said again nervously.

They pulled up and jumped out onto the shore, taking cover behind the dike wall. Ardagh had already set up the Browning and slammed in a belt of ammo. The three ships were still smoking heavily, with the largest half capsized, and the damaged bridge sat exposed above the water. Bruinisse was covered in a smoky haze and grey low clouds hung as if trying to push back the top of the smoke billowing from the ship. A cold, light rain soaked the wet grass on the dike. Ardagh caught the hint of fresh ocean mixed with smoke. The two groups fanned out onto the embankment, number Six platoon setting up to create a protective bridgehead, and number Seven platoon lined up in single file patrol to push into the town and explore for the enemy.

As they sat and listened for any German movement in the town, the grey darkness slowly faded into a silver shine. The rain had stopped, and the sun was fighting to appear. This was the closest they had come to getting a glimpse of the sun since entering Holland. They could now make out the identification of the one ship still sitting above the surface: AF 92, in white block lettering. The flags were still flying. The ship pumped out thick, dark smoke from its inner hull around the exposed bridge deck. No fires were visible above the deck of the artillery ship. The AF 92 sat just one hundred yards offshore, tantalizingly close.

The patrol stood up in unison like a choreographed line of dancers. They moved over the wall and dashed to the closest cover. There was no light coming from the small window of the house at the edge of town. Ardagh sat behind his Browning, watching as each group kept leapfrogging from one building to the other and came out with Dutch civilians at each house. He heard the odd momentary burst of Sten gunfire as they moved deeper into town. But it soon became clear that the larger force of Germans must have fled out of town as their makeshift fleet approached.

Captain Styffe ordered the platoons off the dike, leaving a few behind to protect the boats and a small boarding party to check out the AF 92 Kriegsmarine ship.

Lieutenant Black, along with Corporal Shaw, Corporal Mitchell and Ardagh, climbed into a rubber dinghy and paddled the short distance to the burning AF 92 Kriegsmarine ship. The sporadic gusts of wind swept up off the dike as Ardagh dipped his paddle into the water. It triggered a flashback to his days out on Lake Superior. Normally, they would never have gone out in this weather, but they hadn't thought twice about checking the Kraut ship. The ensign pennant was still flying from the top of the ship's bridge; if they could get hold of that, it would be proof of the ship's taking. They tied the raft to the sinking ship and went on board.

Smoke continued to pour from below, so they decided not to spend too much time aboard in case it blew. Ardagh was the first to the bridge to observe the carnage and devastation. There was a perfect hole where the shell penetrated. The bridge's interior looked like the inside of a blender, equipment and body parts torn apart. It was eerily quiet, with a pool of oily water that marked the deep stairwell down to the lower bridge. A mix of muddy water, blood and tissue covered the remaining floor. Corporal Shaw stepped through the carnage of the bridge to access the ladder and climb to the mast. He quickly untied the rope and expertly pulled down the ensign. A loud cheer erupted from the shore. He rolled it up into his tunic and climbed back down to the bridge.

"Poor bastard," Ardagh said as they searched for other trophies. "Look, this must be the captain," he said, staring into a blank, handsome face with his eyes still open and a half grin staring back. His white cap slightly tilted to the side; he lay awkwardly.

"His hands are still in his pockets," Ardagh said.

"It's as if he didn't see it coming," Corporal Shaw said. The bridge shifted, and the ship let out a deep growl from below, followed by a vibrating shudder, as if it was listening to them.

"Let's not join him, fellas," Lieutenant Black said, "get out of here before it blows."

# Chapter Twenty-Five

# Heartbreak

Sint Philipsland, Netherlands
December 1944

"Can I have your autograph, sir?" Ardagh chimed as Lieutenant Henderson walked up to the platoon. They gathered around the front of the Bren gun carrier. Ardagh stood on the back of the carrier, holding a copy of the *London Times* for everyone to see.

"Do you need any help, sir, when we cross, or can we all just pack up and head home to our ladies?"

They held back laughter as the lieutenant walked up to the platoon.

"Yeah... Yeah... Yeah..." the lieutenant said. "You guys can't let anything go, eh? It's been a long while since we sunk those ships. You found another old article, Harp?"

"Oh, no, sir! Nothing like that; that's old news!" Ardagh said as he shook the paper above his head. "Did you know Crevecoeur means heartbreak? And well, it was heartbreaking to the fellas when we read yet another story from across the globe."

"The higher ups were surprised to find the Lake Superior Regiment, led by number Six platoon, captured a fort," Danny said.

The lieutenant just gave Ardagh a sideways glance as he

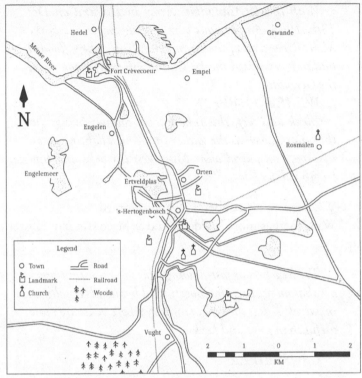

Crevecoeur, Netherlands

kicked the grass.

"Congratulations, sir!" fired Ardagh and saluted, followed by the other men.

Lieutenant Henderson threw his arm over Ardagh's shoulder and neck affectionately, squeezing him in a half nelson, and grabbed the paper. Lieutenant Henderson laughed and handed the newspaper back to Ardagh in victory. Ardagh cleared his throat and grinned as he read the story word for word out loud to the boys.

*Amphibious War Waged Along River" By Douglas Amaron, Canadian war press correspondent. Canadians Battling in Flooded Area.*

*With the 1st Canadian Army in Holland on Dec 13th, 1944. Amphibious war is being waged along the Maas River west of the Nijmegen salient, where flooded flatlands separated the 1st Canadian Army troops from the Germans.*

*WEAR LIFE BELTS*

*Bleak and wet, this inhospitable country brings out the sailor as well as the soldier in the men fighting across it. Troops on patrol wear Mae West life belts and hip-length rubber boots.*

"Where were my rubbers?" Danny chimed.

"Wait, there is more," Ardagh said as he continued. "Listen up!"

*The treacherous fast-flowing Maas is a constant menace that on occasion has overturned boatloads of soldiers in patrol. This is the type of country where boats are more useful than jeeps and tanks.*

*CROSS RIVER*

*The German positions now are all north of the Maas River, but enemy patrols frequently cross to the Canadian side. Just as the Canadians make nightly sorties into enemy-held grounds.*

"They make it all sound so easy. Of course, it was all me, so make sure you all know that next time when we are fighting the Jerries!" said Lieutenant Henderson, waving his fist.

"Hear it is; wait for it," Ardagh said. "*TWIN THRUSTS*!"

"Twin Thrusts!" Danny said. "Sounds like Harp and Woods at the pub chasing the nurses!"

Woods didn't hesitate to punch Danny hard in the shoulder, sending him hollering.

"This is good. Stop crying, Danny," Lieutenant Henderson

ordered as Ardagh continued to read.

> *Twin thrusts by troops of a central Canada battalion brought about its evacuation. One platoon commander, Lieutenant Buck Wright of Kenora, Ontario, attacked north along the road, skirting the east side of the canal while another platoon under Lieutenant Tommy Henderson advanced from the east along the Maas River.*
>
> *The attack, launched last Friday and supported by a barrage from the artillery and tank regiments, halted when Wright's men came to a demolished bridge on which the Germans directed intense and accurate mortar fire. Henderson's men soon encountered a minefield...*

"Let's forget about the minefield," Danny said, rubbing his shoulder.

"It's pretty good," Ardagh said. "I think this story is literally in every newspaper around the world. What are we going to do next? First, a couple of battleships sunk, then a fort!"

"Anything else they need cleaning up?" Danny asked, straight-faced. They all laughed. "How about a Nazi airfield or the Siegfried Line? Why didn't they just send us to capture the dam bridge?"

"We need a Field Marshall to capture... maybe," Woods said. "Somebody should get a medal."

"Sounds like there will be lots of time for us to add a few medals and souvenirs," Lieutenant Henderson said. "The big push to the north into Arnhem failed. The Germans are tougher than we think. They are still firing rockets to London."

"Where to next?" Ardagh asked.

"Well, we get a few days of semi-rest here as a reward for the naval engagement and the fort, so enjoy the rest while you can and visit your girlfriends!"

"After all, tomorrow is another day!" Ardagh said, quoting *Gone with the Wind*. "And she's not my girl yet...."

"Oh, come on, Corporal, you have been goo-goo for the past month over her. What's her name again?"

"Corporal?"

"That's a funny name," Lieutenant Henderson said, shaking his head.

"No, no, you called me Corporal," Ardagh said. "Didn't you?"

"Oh yeah. That's right, I forgot to mention. I think you've done a fine job since you've been back. So, I recommended they promote you. Keep it up and we'll make you a sergeant. No promises, though. You will stick with your crew and same platoon since we are short already. Good work, Harp," Lieutenant Henderson said as he handed him the stripes and shook his hand.

"Thank you, sir. I won't let you down," said Ardagh, looking over at Danny, who gave him a wink and a nod. *Did Danny have something to do with this?*

Woods gave him a pat on the back and said, "Now we're in trouble."

"You won't be seeing Paris for a while, so enjoy it here. We still have a long road of fighting ahead," said Lieutenant Henderson. "You boys are dismissed until tomorrow evening."

The platoon didn't waste any time to head out. Ardagh felt a little taller as he marched down Voorstraat toward Koos's house.

\*\*\*

It had only been a few weeks since they had seen each other, and he had changed somehow. Koos couldn't put her finger on it, but just the way he carried himself as he walked toward her was different. They had traded several letters and her emotions were spilling over at seeing him. The last words in his letter went through her head. "I want to hold you."

\*\*\*

"Wow," he said, pulling her in. "How have you been?"

She lifted her chin as she leaned in and kissed him hard on the lips.

"What do you think?" she said, then shoved his chest hard with both hands that sent him staggering back.

"Of all the gin joints in all the towns in all the world, she walks into mine...." Ardagh mimicked Humphrey Bogart and wrapped his arms around her.

"It has been horrible waiting to hear from you." She sighed with relief. She enjoyed the warmth in her cheeks that lasted even as he touched her hand. "I never thought it would be this tough to wait for you, especially after hearing the rumours of what is happening at the front."

She searched him as if he were a prize bundle. "But never mind. I'm glad you're here now," Koos said, nuzzling into his shoulder, and taking a deep smell of him. His sweat, the wetness of his uniform, the mixed scent of gunpowder, cooking stove and cigarettes was awful, but it was a dream to have him back and safe. "Let's get you cleaned up."

"I can't wait to have a hot bath," he said, embarrassed. "Sorry for the smell. It was another tough few weeks, but we took a fort, so all wasn't that bad."

"Well, my father and uncle would love to hear all about it, I'm sure," said Koos, expecting another hard kiss.

"Top secret, loose lips sink ships," he smirked, moving in for the big kiss.

"Move on, you two," Lieutenant Henderson shouted from across the street. "I'll see you at eight hundred hours, Corporal."

"You're a corporal now?" Koos asked.

"Yeah, I just found out, but it's official. I don't know if I like it, though. They seem to get killed more often than not," Ardagh said, looking down and kicking a loose rock on the ground with his dust-covered boot.

The grey clouds blocked the sun as they walked to the front

yard of Koos's house. Ardagh wished the canteen wasn't so close by. There was a good chance he'd get more work to do, and heckles from his platoon.

"Let's go to the church," he said as he grabbed her hand. They spun as if dancing, and she bounced off his shoulder as they walked along the short row of houses hugging the street toward the church. Unlike Fort William, where every home had a large yard, these houses were, like all the other Dutch towns he'd been through, all sandwiched together. It was a short walk to the churchyard, and she nodded, waved to others along the way as if they were in a wedding procession. He enjoyed the simple moment of walking with a girl. It seemed like the entire town was out to greet the Lake Superiors. The stress of the last few weeks enhanced every moment with her. *She will be the talk of the town, and the other girls will be jealous,* he mused.

They jumped up over the low wall protecting the church's yard and collapsed onto the grass. A few other couples were lying in the churchyard, reconnecting, which made them feel at ease again.

"Wow, I didn't know they were together," Ardagh said, grabbing a handful of grass and tossing it onto Koos.

"That's because you were too busy with me," Koos said, throwing the grass back at him. "You stink like a dirty pig," she giggled.

\*\*\*

The hot bath and meal following some deep questions from Koos's uncle and father was a dream to Ardagh. After the stress of intense battles, a normal family existence seemed overwhelming. He wasn't sure how to handle it and often felt like he was drifting into a different world, only to be thrown back whenever Koos touched his hand. She would put her hand on his thigh and squeeze, which sent excitement through his body. He had not experienced this intense of a feeling toward another. What would happen next? Her family was crammed into her brother's tiny home like a pack of sardines. When would they get time alone? So, the evening went from drifting thoughts of her body against his to anxiety at not being able to hold her close. He knew it was a big decision for her. It would be her first time, and he didn't take it lightly. He hadn't been Jean's or Eileen's first. This was new to him, and they were playing for keeps. Koos was the only one who had been through what he had. She lived through the fear of dying in that jeep with the Dutch SS. He would never forget her expression before he fired, killing Joost. It had created a strong bond between them.

\*\*\*

Koos felt nervous for the first time sitting beside Ardagh. Her palms kept getting wet, and she was constantly wiping them on her dress. She had to go pee twice. Her father and mother had talked about going for a walk, but hovered around as if they knew what she was thinking. It would be their only chance with the house empty. She had never gone all the way with a boy but had decided it would be Ardagh. She never wanted to leave his side. Her feelings were deeper than she could explain.

Then, as if her father could read her thoughts, he announced it was time for them to check on the boats, and they all got up and left the house. They were finally alone.

Ardagh looked deeply into Koos's eyes, and a large smirk crossed her face, and she said, "I know what you're thinking."

"You do?" Ardagh said in a whisper. "How are...."

Koos jumped up, grabbing his hand and pulled him off the couch, and said, "Follow."

She wrapped his arm around her waist and dragged him toward the stairs and into her bedroom.

"What if they catch us?" Ardagh asked.

"They won't. They went for a walk, but we don't have much time," she said as she pulled her hair back and held back a giggle.

"Are you sure?" he asked, embarrassed. But he was ready and wanted to be with her forever.

"Yes," she whispered. And she pulled him down onto her bed.

They lay there just breathing and listening to the house and the stillness. No thoughts, just the two of them. Time seemed to stand still, and they rolled and faced each other, and kissed. She pulled him in and held his lips to hers in a deep kiss. They rocked, holding each other, and she watched tears fall from his eyes. She kissed his cheeks and whispered, "I love you."

"I love you more...." Ardagh said, as if in a dream, not holding back.

\*\*\*

Ardagh sat with Koos on the outside of the dike, staring at the calm water and grey sky. The deep green grass at their feet. Rob sat beside them, eating his chocolate bar. Ardagh rarely had time to reflect on life, it seemed. He figured Koos's nephew was about the same age as his nephew, Marv. Her parents were still not back from their walk, and he felt a strange mix of relief and anxiousness to get back with his platoon. These were the same emotions he'd had before he left. He was excited about their future but also afraid of it, just like when he last saw Marv and left for England. He had told Marv the story of the Sleeping Giant, hoping it would help him understand. Now he knew what it meant. It was a reminder of sacrifice.

\*\*\*

Ardagh enjoyed the bounce of the 1939 Dodge suspension as it bumped across the train tracks. The tracks followed the Lake Superior shoreline, marking the entry into the cabins at Green Bay. He enjoyed the twenty-minute drive along the shore. It was the only time he had to get his head straight while visiting on leave from the Lake Superior Regiment. He only had a few more days left, and he was trying to make the most of it with as much time at his parents' cottage as possible.

Ardagh made the first right turn onto the narrow dirt road that led to the line of cozy cottages wedged between the narrow beach and rail line. His father's truck sat parked in its usual spot beside the path to the outhouse and a woodpile. He wouldn't bother to walk inside the small green three-bedroom cottage, as he knew Marv would be at the beach, most likely playing in the sand.

Marv ran back to his yellow dump truck and shovels that were scattered about the beach, as Ardagh stood watching him. He sighed and stared out onto Lake Superior and the range of tree-covered hills in the distance. The sun warmed his shoulders. The water was calm and short waves rolled gently onto the sandy shore. Little minnows grouping together moved with no urgency or care. He wished life was so easy.

"Hey, little Marv, come sit up on my knee. Come on, tough guy, want to fight?" Ardagh said to his tanned nephew with his arms outstretched. Ardagh sat in his old wood beach chair staring out onto Lake Superior. The sky was clear blue with only a couple of high, light clouds in the distance. He had an unobstructed view of the Sibley Peninsula that stretched across the lake and protected Fort William and Port Arthur. It always amazed him how much it looked like a Sleeping Giant lying down in front of his cabin. Where else in the world could you have such a view?

It gave him a sense of excitement and anxiety at the same time to think of what lay ahead and wonder where he would end up.

Marv let out, "Rrumm... roooom..." and plodded straight into Ardagh.

"Hey, tough guy," Ardagh said and lifted and tossed him in the air, then down again.

"Again?" Marv said as he lifted his arms and stared up at Ardagh. "Again?"

"Uh, okay, skin and bones, okay?"

Ardagh grabbed both his arms and swung him in circles until he went dizzy. Marv stumbled around in circles with his arms out to balance himself, mumbling, "uh erg dz ugh," then falling on his bum. Ardagh then pounced like a lion on him to unleash massive tickle blows under his armpits, to the great delight of Marv.

"Stop, stop," Marv cried. Then just as Ardagh stopped, Marv said, "Again... Again."

Marv looked at his uncle, smiling.

"Are you going away again? When will I see you?"

Ardagh wanted to talk about Joey. Tell Marv he was sorry, but he didn't seem to care. Would it matter what he said? Maybe telling Marv a story would help him understand when he gets older. Something to carry with him. He forced a smile and said, "Yeah, I have to. But in the meantime, you can look at the Sleeping Giant and give him a wave. He is a Great Spirit, and good luck."

"Where is the Sleeping Giant?"

"Do you see the man lying out in the lake?"

"Where is he, Uncle Ardagh?" Marv questioned, looking down into the water.

"No, no, no silly, not in the water, but floating on the water. Can't you see him right there?" Ardagh stretched out his arm and pointed to the peninsula that expanded across the horizon.

"See... he is sleeping."

"He's sleeping? I don't see him," Marv said.

"No, no, no little guy. If you just look into the distance, you can see a giant man sleeping with his arms crossed on his chest, see?"

Ardagh pointed again and tried tracing the outline of the giant with his finger.

"You're silly, Uncle," he said, squirming on his lap. "There is nobody sleeping."

"I know, you can see his shoulders, body, the head. Do you see it? Next time you're in town, ask your mom. Has no one told you the legend of the Sleeping Giant?" Ardagh asked. "Sometimes at night you can hear him snoring away and the waves build up on the lake and smash onto the beach."

"Will he snore tonight, Uncle Ardagh?" Marv asked.

"No, not tonight. You know he has been asleep for a long time. Now, do you see him?" Ardagh picked him up and pointed again out onto the lake as the sun shone down on the tree-covered plateau in the distance. "When you look at it from where we are or anywhere along the shore of Fort William or Port Arthur, it looks like a giant man sleeping with his arms crossed on his chest. Ojibway legends have the giant being a Nanajibou, the Great Spirit of the deep water, who turned to stone after the location of a secret silver mine was disclosed to the white man."

"Why? Why did he turn to stone? Can we wake him?"

"No," Ardagh said, waving his hands. "Or at least I don't think so.... good question! I guess... I hope someday." Ardagh didn't want to upset Marv too much. "The story goes that the Great Spirit of the deep water rewarded the Ojibway with a silver mine to help protect them from the harm done to them by the white man who destroyed their way of life through disease and firewater."

"What's firewater?" Marv asked.

"It's alcohol, like your papa drinks, and makes him funny," Ardagh said. *Maybe this is too deep for the kid,* he thought.

"Anyway, little guy, there was one big condition to having the silver mine. Don't tell the white man! Should the white man find out, he warned... it will turn me to stone."

Ardagh grabbed Marv and tickled him. "Little stone Marv."

"I don't want to turn to stone!" Marv said.

"The Ojibway soon prospered from the silver and were

known for their beautiful silver jewellery. The Sioux became jealous and tried their best to find the location of the hidden mine, but failed."

"The Sioux are bad!" Marv said excitedly.

"Well, they were just jealous. I think the Ojibway were doing better than them, which is bad, you're right. Never be jealous and always work hard, and it will reward you. You never have to steal to get ahead. Remember that!"

"Okay," Marv said.

"Do you want to hear the rest?"

"Yes, please!" he said, or more like 'pweese' as he squirmed again on his lap. "You don't have to go pee, do you?" Marv shook his head, looking down.

"Finally," Ardagh said, "they dressed a scout to pretend he was an Ojibway tribesman, and he soon discovered the entrance to the mine. On the way back to tell the Sioux chiefs, he stopped at a trading post and used some silver to trade for food. The white man was wise and wanted to know where he had gotten the silver. So, they got the Sioux scout so drunk on firewater that they convinced the scout to take them to the location of the mine."

"Who is the white man?"

"Us."

"Are we bad, too?" Marv said.

"Well, that's a longer conversation," Ardagh said, shifting in his chair. "The Great Spirit of the water was watching the scout and the white man, and upon the discovery of the mine, the Great Spirit started a great storm. The storm killed the white man and sent the Sioux scout adrift in his canoe and he went crazy. When the storm cleared, a giant stone now blocked the bay in the shape of a man. This was the Nanajibou, the Great Spirit of the deep water, turned to stone as he told them would happen. The silver mine landed at his feet and was protected forever from the white man."

"And so now he is sleeping?" Marv said, crinkling his nose.

"Yep, and sometimes he snores. That's what creates all the thunder and why some people now want to call the town Thunder Bay! Because of all his snoring!

"Nanajibou was a hero. He would sacrifice himself and turn to stone to protect his people. That is what the soldiers are doing today, so always salute or wave to any soldier you see."

Ardagh lifted Marv in the air and threw him high, catching him before he hit the ground. Ardagh crouched down, held Marv by the shoulders, and looked into his eyes.

"Now don't forget to wave to him every day I'm away. It will bring me good luck. Do you promise?"

"I promise."

"Okay, off you go, little guy." And he smacked Marv on the bottom and sent him on his way. Marv jumped into his little red one-seater pedal car and drove off.

"Brum... brum... brum... erhhhch... neeeeer."

Ardagh turned and gave chase, shouting, "I'm going to blow you up with my fighter plane!" He spread his arms out, chasing and yelling at Marv.

"Neeer... neeer... neeer... rat-at-tat... rat-a-tat-a-tat... neeer... neeeeer." Ardagh fired imaginary bullets at Marv as he raced away from destruction.

*** 

Ardagh sat back in the grass, staring out across the water. The winds picked up, and the anxiety rolled over him like the waves lapping up onto the shore. It was always there with its consistent rhythm. Rob came roaring by again for the tenth time, pretending to fire his rifle. The waves rolled relentlessly, hitting the dike and dissipating away.

As he sat staring in a daze, he thought again about the Sleeping Giant, trying to remember how it looked. Now, three years later, he had seen lots of sacrifice, remembering and carrying a piece of them with him every day. The stone giant seemed so large back then in the background, with the sun beaming on it, when he did not know what his future held. Ardagh could still remember the high pitch of Marv's voice. It was just like Rob's.

"What are you thinking about?" Koos asked.

"He reminds me of my little nephew, Marv," Ardagh said.

"But you look sad."

Ardagh thought back to the days before he left and it was still difficult to think about. Should he tell her what happened?

"I was just thinking about the Sleeping Giant."

Ardagh looked at Koos and felt his eyes water. He would tell her about Joey someday, but not now. Would she leave him if she knew?

"I'll tell Rob the legend of the Sleeping Giant, just like I told Marv. Maybe someday you'll come and see it," he said and squeezed her hand. He knew it would help him if he told her the story. He was stronger now and had survived a lot. But he couldn't tell her everything.

## Chapter Twenty-Six

# The Gap

Hochwald Forest, Germany
March 1st, 1945

The padre stood next to Lieutenant Colonel Keane, who sat beside the radio set inside one of the communication carriers. Keane, still in his clean uniform, looked fresh from his leave in England, but his face said it all. So far, it was a one-sided conversation. He prayed the brigadier would postpone the attack. It was cold, wet, and raining. The black German mud exhausted them and covered everything. A night's rest looked as far off as an English pub. The Lake Superiors had finally entered Germany and captured Uedem on their way to the main objective, the German Rhine River. They had been fighting steadily for four days and now sat with the Grenadier tanks at the edge of the Hochwald Gap, an opening that led to the Rhine River. The tide of the battle was running in favour of the Canadians, but it had slowed and could at any moment turn against them. Brigadier Moncel had called the Lake Superiors back for one more job, to attack into the Gap to keep the momentum.

"The men haven't slept or eaten in the last 24 hours. They are exhausted and muddy. In addition, the Kangaroo transportation hasn't shown up. I don't know where they are. The Jerries still behind us have held them up," Keane said into the

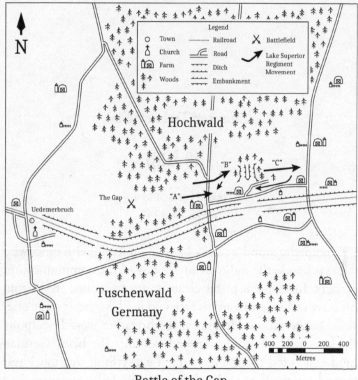

Battle of the Gap

wireless, hoping the brigadier would understand the risk they faced. He and his executive officers had just driven in carriers through a snow flurry to get to 'D' Company's HQ. They had been hit with a mortar barrage while they waited for the Kangaroos to show up. The fighting HQ and 'D' Company set up beside a farmhouse less than a mile from the Hochwald Gap entrance.

"Just come and see for yourself, sir. We can't expect them to go on foot. Yes. I know we have the Grenadier tanks for protection. The men are exhausted. We don't even know who is on our flanks. It'll be suicide." Keane stood up as he listened to Brigadier Moncel's response. He ran his fingers through his

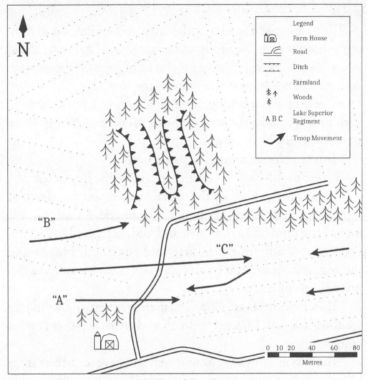

Battle of the Gap

hair and sat back down. He pinched the bridge of his nose then moved to smoothing out the ridge of his eyebrow with his thumb as he listened. His body shuffled in the cramped carrier. The padre could see he was losing the battle. Keane shook his head.

"I know we need to keep the momentum. The mobility of the tanks and Kangaroos are impossible with this mud." Keane rarely pushed back on his orders. They knew many men would lose their lives this morning if he lost this argument. There was no other choice.

"Yes, sir. We'll work out another plan if the Kangaroo transportation doesn't show up," Keane said and hung up the wireless.

The padre gave the sign of the cross and whispered to himself a short prayer, "Be strong and courageous. Do not be afraid or terrified because of them, for the Lord your God goes with you; he will never leave you nor forsake you."

At one in the morning, sixteen Kangaroos finally arrived with orders to take the small fighting group into battle. There was no turning back now.

"This is a bloody mess," the padre said.

"I tried to dissuade the brigadier, to give the boys a rest..."

He sat on the back of the signals carrier, staring down at a small patch of mud that hung from his clean uniform. He flicked the mud off his uniform and said, "I pushed back hard, Padre, but Bradburn got in first, and convinced him to give the Algonquins a rest. If I only had made it back sooner, such a price for going on leave."

"They'll understand, Bob. The men love you and would do anything for you. I'll send them off and try to pep them up for you."

"The Algonquins have fought well and have seen their share of fighting, but our boys have been at it too long already. No food for almost two days and no sleep. This is going to be a mess. We don't even have a full company, never mind a regiment."

The padre sighed. He'd had many of these conversations over the past several months. More than he'd thought was possible. He had heard and seen it all. The strain of the commander, having to send men to their ultimate deaths, and the struggle of the men to follow the orders given, knowing the potential consequences. With each battle and engagement, they gained the experience and knowledge to understand the outcome and worked together to prevent the worst but achieve the objectives given to them.

Every death was etched in the background of each success.

This task they both knew would not end well, but there was no other regiment that could step up to the task in front of them. The padre knew these small talks helped the colonel clear the fog and the strain that went with the pressure of his life and death decisions. He hoped this would help him make better decisions that affected the men and save lives.

"The brig says he will come and see them off. Thank the men for me. They're the best we have. We'll have a longer break after this. I promise." Keane stood up, ignoring the mud that covered his boots and climbed back into his command carrier to get the latest signals, hoping for a change in plans.

"I better get to them," the padre said when the thunder of mortars stopped. He walked off into the cloudy dark morning across the farmer's field that stretched out to a row of trees marking the forward jump-off line.

It took two hours for the Kangaroos to be readied and loaded. As tired and weary as the men were from the many days of fighting, they could still laugh, and waved to the padre, shouting, "Here we go." Even though they knew the task ahead meant almost certain death and destruction.

As the padre approached the jump-off line, he could make out the outline of the Kangaroos. The Kangaroos were a gutted tank, the entire turret removed, ammunition storage removed, bench seats fitted in the turret ring area, and the driver's compartment separated. They held up to twelve men more if they clung to the sides. Men were already loading onto them.

He picked the farthest row of Kangaroos to the left, which turned out to be 'B' Company. Ardagh, Danny and Woods stood at the back of the first Kangaroo checking each other's equipment.

"Hi, Padre," Ardagh said before the padre could say anything. "Come to join the show?"

"Just some straightforward advice from our Lord, Corporal. Stay out of the mud if you can, and a short prayer," the padre said. They all bowed their heads as he spoke.

"Cast your cares on the Lord, and he will sustain you; he will never let the righteous be shaken."

"There is no mud, Padre. Just another beautiful spring morning," Danny said. Mud hung from the bottoms of their coats, and they looked heavy. "So much for thinking at high speed in this muck."

"At least we won't get lost. You're not in Kansas anymore, Toto," Ardagh said.

"Another quote, it never gets old," Woods smirked.

The familiar sound of a mortar round filled their ears, and they dove for cover under the Kangaroo. The padre fell in beside Ardagh as the shells landed further to the rear.

"I guess we must be quick, possess initiative, and have a trained eye for the country. I can't believe I was so worried about all that crap. Sorry, Padre."

"You have come a long way, Harp. All the boys have. Don't be afraid to lead if you have to. We need more men like you."

"If I only had a brain."

"The nerve," Danny said.

"Now, I'm the Tin Man?" Woods said.

"Our Lord will take care of you, you'll see," the padre said, ignoring them. He rolled out from under the Kangaroo. "Lord, be gracious to us; we long for you. Be our strength every morning, our salvation in time of distress."

It was three in the morning when the wet and tired group moved out. The padre had tried to make it to every man, diving for cover and jumping from one slit trench to the other. The padre was their tower of strength, always ready, willing, and able to come to their help through thick and thin to assist in their evacuation when wounded. And to bury them.

The mud was thick, and the going was slow. Up in the start line behind the cover of the tree line and anti-tank ditches, there were some quiet moments.

The men had not hesitated to climb into the Kangaroos to get on with the task ahead of them. They had joked and laughed at each other, most likely more out of exhaustion than anything.

The padre climbed into a trench at the start line and took note of what lay ahead. He had a spectator's view of the battle that he feared would forever mark the war for the Lake Superiors. It was a very narrow alleyway sloping downward into the enemy positions bounded by a high elevated railway embankment on the right and a well-protected forest to the left. He felt safe behind the tree line that sat just into the Gap. His eyes followed the muddy road on the other side of the tree line that ran from the forest on his left to the rail line on his right. They would be stepping out into the open. A few hundred yards before the rail line, the road turned down the middle of the Gap through a narrow valley with the ground gradually sloped downward, only interrupted by two gentle rolling hills toward the bottom. There, along the road and tucked into the hills, were three farmhouses. The padre knew that 'A' and 'B' Company's objectives were on either side of these smouldering farm homes and a clump of bombed-out trees. The more difficult task was for 'C' Company to push through the two other companies' objectives and, if possible, to reach an area just south of the rail line.

The padre watched as the three columns, along with the tanks of the Grenadiers, moved across the road and down into the Gap. They were well under strength after four days of fighting with less than half the men they should have. Each Company loaded easily into the sixteen Kangaroos. A flare lit up the sky, and he could see the outline of the Kangaroos as they moved to their objectives. Flashes and explosions filled the darkened morning. He smelled the acidic stench of burning wood and the combined intensity of the whiz bangs and pop-pop of the counter fire overwhelmed his senses.

Suddenly, the padre saw the left column that was 'B' Company light up as one of the Kangaroos was hit, fire spewing out. The lead Kangaroo did not stop, but men piled out of the last Kangaroo. Now, fire lit up the other column next to them, but it disappeared into massive explosions of mud and fire that continued around them. He watched as the 'C' Company Kangaroos followed down the slope into the narrow alleyway into what the padre imagined to be a hell storm. Soon they were all consumed amidst the explosions and columns of flying mud and debris that could be seen throughout the narrow valley. The padre slid back down into his trench and prayed.

*\*\**

Ardagh looked up into the darkness, watching the flashes of thunder overhead. His makeshift column was heading into a hail of mortars. Sounds of metal clanged against the Kangaroo. Sliding. Accelerating. Stopping. A hard left turn. An explosion rocked the frame, followed by a loud bang. Flames shot up beside the Kangaroo. Ardagh stood and peered over the edge of the open bay. Fire and smoke filled his vision. The column stopped.

Ardagh was the first out of the Kangaroo, charging up the steep ravine. As he crested the top, he saw figures thirty yards ahead running away. He fired a burst into them, and they fell. The rest disappeared into the early morning. He looked down into the ravine, and could only account for a dozen, including himself and Danny, who had followed.

"Just us?" Ardagh said. "You two cover our left flank. You guys, thirty yards right of them, I'll sit in the middle with the Bren and Danny. Woods, take the rest and split up to my right. Dig in or use what you can find."

No others were left.

"Jesus, where is everyone? We didn't have enough to start in the first place." Ardagh peered over the edge of the temporary slit trench. He had dug into the side of the steep gully, expanding the original German trench to reduce the risk of taking a direct hit from the mortars that were consistently raining down. The Bren gun was laid on top, ready to fire.

"Stuck in the mud, we're getting fucked," Danny said. "The other two Kangaroos were hit. Not sure who is left. You're the only Bren for now, and they know exactly where this gully sits. The Jerries have it sighted. These guys don't monkey around. I'm surprised by how deep it is."

"Keep digging. We don't have much time before sunrise and a counterattack. I'm going to get more ammo for the Bren."

*I need to think things through,* Ardagh thought. He assessed the situation as he climbed back down into the gully. The remnants of 'B' Company had successfully moved down the left side of the Gap in a cavalry-style charge to the burning copse of trees. The thicket turned out to be a steep horseshoe-shaped ravine that provided protection from the shelling but not counterattacks. Ardagh had dispersed the men along the gully ridge that looked out onto an open farmer's field. The two remaining Kangaroos sat safely thirty feet below at the bottom and entrance of the gully. Three tanks of the Grenadiers protected the entrance to the gully, but could not climb to the top and provide support. They would fire mortars first before they counterattacked. He needed to be quick before the Germans returned. He moved to the nearest Kangaroo and grabbed two boxes of ammo for the Bren and started back up the side of the gully.

"Here, give me a hand to carry up the ammo," Ardagh said. "It's like climbing Mount McKay."

"You've never climbed Mount McKay in your life. You will be sergeant now for sure, your lifelong dream," Danny said. "Harp a sergeant, who would have thought? Of course, by default, since there is no one else."

"Fat chance, Danny boy," Ardagh said. "Besides, I forgive you."

"For what?"

"Middle school."

"You're kidding me now?"

"Yep, I'm making it official. I forgive you."

"It took this much shelling and mortars for your forgiveness? It's just a nickname, Harp... Jesus. I hope I never cross you again."

"I'm glad you're starting to see it my way," Ardagh laughed.

"You need to discuss your deeper issues with the padre," Danny chimed as he turned and headed down the ravine.

"Be quick, Danny. The mortars may come any minute."

Ardagh watched Danny slide down the steep slope of the ravine and disappear into the darkness. The whining sound of the first mortar woke him into action, and he crammed himself deep into the slit trench. Shit. Did Danny make it to the Kangaroos? The entire forest shattered around him, with splinters of trees falling into the trench. A shell landed next to a large tree, which fell back over the corner of his slit trench. Constant sounds of whizzing shrapnel and metal hitting the Kangaroos and tanks filled the gully. The familiar popping of machine-gun fire was followed by the sounds of trees being shredded. The fire stopped. Ardagh crawled out and stepped up onto the firing step, and checked the Bren gun. He shouldered the Bren and wiped his face with his free hand. Sweat trickled down the side of his cheek, and he brushed it against the butt of the Bren gun as he looked through the sight. There was no movement in front of him. He felt a tap on his shoulder, Danny was back safe and he gave him a thumbs-up in return.

A flare shot up above them, and they could make out movement from their left flank. Ardagh twisted left to look for targets. He saw muzzle flashes in response and felt his elbows sink into the mud as he fired off a quick burst into the group. The light faded away, and he paused. A second flare exposed the group, approaching less than fifty yards to their middle. Ardagh pushed his upper body up into the Bren, letting a short stream of bullets flow into the group. They all fell. Danny continued to fire beside him over to his right in short, controlled bursts. He pushed up against Danny and fired a long burst as the group of Germans turned and ran. The light faded to dark, and the firing stopped.

"I'll check on the boys," Ardagh said, and sprang out of the trench and moved along the ridge. He reached Woods and two others.

"Stay disciplined with your fire. We may be here for a while. Accuracy will keep the Jerries from coming back," Ardagh said, and he left without waiting for a response. He moved between the groups, checking their lines of fire and offering encouragement. It would only be a minute or two before the barrage would kick in again, so he had to be quick.

Just as predicted, the sounds of mortars plunged him back into the bottom of the slit trench. This marked the end of the first counterattack.

Ardagh was happy to see Lieutenant Henderson as he climbed into the slit trench next to him, along with Major Murray. The sun appeared over the horizon, and the scale of the gully had come into view. 'B' Company which comprised only fourteen men, including the lieutenant and major, was spread out across one side of the horseshoe. It would be impossible to defend the entire position. Major Murray had met up with 'A' Company and concluded they were best to move to 'A' Company and regroup.

"Gather the men next to the Kangaroo, and we'll make a dash for Alpha Company's position using it and the tanks for protection. Major Gavelle is hit, and Major Murray is taking over Alpha and Baker Companies," Lieutenant Henderson told Ardagh.

Ardagh and the remaining group from 'B' Company made it to 'A' Company's objective, just four hundred yards south of the gully. Ardagh set up the Bren gun next to the rubble of a German farmhouse. He had an unobstructed view looking up at the bank of the rail line that marked the south side of the Gap. Heavy shells and mortar continued to rain down. The black clouds hung low over the trees with trails of smoke.

"At least we're out of that mud hole," Danny said. "Remember when we used to run down the rail line and place the pennies? I feel like we are about to be that penny."

"Out of the pan into the fire," Ardagh said. He pulled out his pocketknife and tried working the lid off a German ration tin. "Is that the saying?"

"There is no yellow brick road around here," Woods said. Ardagh and Danny both looked at Woods. It was the first time he had played along with their game of phrases. He used it more now to keep his head. They had all been through a lot, but this was the worst of it so far. Woods had always struggled to accept him as a leader. This meant a lot to Ardagh.

He put a hand on Woods' shoulder and said, "Just keep an eye out for the flying monkeys." The group looked thin spread out around the battered farmyard. Bodies of German and Canadian soldiers littered the shell hole and filled his vision.

"I'm more worried about the Tigers. I don't think we have the armour support to take one out," Danny said. "There goes 'C' Company. Poor bastards. One thing to do it in the dark but to attack in broad daylight..."

They watched the Kangaroos and tanks of the Grenadiers move forward, disappearing down the road through a channel that was still protected. Ardagh decided to follow the column to get a view of what lay ahead. The concentration of fire increased, followed by larger and larger explosions. Ardagh moved up along the road to get a better view of 'C' Company, just two hundred yards away. Germans were driving up the hill toward him, overrunning 'C' Company. They'd run right into a German counterattack. The Germans destroyed all six of the

Kangaroos and the three tanks, leaving them burning.

Ardagh fired and ran to the safety of a nearby slit trench when shells exploded in quick succession around the advancing Germans and Lake Superiors trying to get back to 'A' Company. Ardagh slid into the slit trench, only to discover a German soldier occupying it as well. Heavy shells exploded over them, and they both clung to the inside of the muddy walls. It was as if someone had set fire to the rain. Then everything fell silent. Ardagh looked up at the enemy within arm's reach. The German raised his head, sensing he was being watched. A bright light exploded in Ardagh's head as it lifted him into the air. Blackness washed over him.

The smell of blood and the taste of mud woke him. He gasped for air, tasting only mud. The grit made him puke. He opened his eyes, coughing. His arm was wedged under the body of the German. He pulled himself free. The enemy looked like the scarecrow. Stuffing spread everywhere—broken pieces. Ardagh raised himself out of the carnage, spitting the mud from his lips, and stumbled back to his position.

"The tanks and Kangaroos are gone," Ardagh said, rolling into the trench next to Danny. He curled up in the corner and pulled at his sleeves. They were wet and cold with bloody mud. He shivered and scratched again at the damp around his wrists. He threw off his blood-covered gloves and buried his hands in the warmth of his coat. Ardagh stared at the black mud. And his thoughts went back to Jim floating in the icy water of the Kaministiquia River. He could still see his panicked face and flushed red look. His stiff, floating body. Panic and fear in his eyes. Ardagh buried his hands deeper, trying to feel the warmth. His ears were still ringing as he looked at Danny for any signs of fear. Danny's face was wet and covered with chunks of mud, but held the same expressionless look. His eyes flickered and his voice trembled as he spoke, "It was our own artillery falling short."

"'C' Company was overrun. All the tanks were knocked out. We need to keep moving," Ardagh said, closing his eyes.

"They're still coming. This day will never end. Looks like the Jerries are along the rail line, six Tiger tanks at least," Danny said as he pointed.

Ardagh wiped the mud from his face. His legs felt numb and heavy. He stood up and stretched as he peered over the edge of the trench. He immediately saw movement along the side of the rail line. Ardagh looked across the yard to the farmhouse, less than a football field away. Everything came into focus. He examined his Sten gun, then replaced the clip and said, "Let's move up to the other farmhouse and get a better angle on them. Follow me." They both leaped out of the trench. Danny waved to the men to follow. Moving low, avoiding the shell holes, they reached the edge of the farmhouse yard, and the remainder of the platoon filed in behind.

As they set up along a fence line, the remnants of 'C' Company moved through them into the farmyard. He counted just eight men. Corporal Byce nodded to Ardagh with a grim face. Blood covered his uniform. He did not stop his stride and headed straight to what remained of the farmhouse. Ardagh watched as he wrapped the leather strap of the sniper's rifle around his arm and pressed the butt to his shoulder. He disappeared into the farmhouse.

The tattered group from 'B' Company poured controlled fire down the length of the rail line at the oncoming Germans. The rail line stood above them and to their right. But no Germans had made it that far up to give them leverage and outflank them.

"Watch the top of that rail embankment, Danny," Ardagh shouted and, as if on cue, a German poked his head above them and threw a grenade down at the group. A sharp zip and crack sounded. The German collapsed. Ardagh stopped worrying about the rail embankment. Corporal Byce was only one hundred yards behind them with a sniper's rifle. He made quick work of the Germans who dared to move along the rail line.

The German Tiger tanks continued toward them. Knowing his men needed more time, Ardagh scanned the field in front of him and found what he was looking for.

"Stay here," Ardagh ordered Danny as he climbed out of the makeshift trench, Sten gun in hand, and ran into the open field. Destroyed Kangaroos and bodies lay all around him. He stormed across the muddy field, head down through the wet heavy rain and wind, swinging to the left of the oncoming tanks. He dropped beside a dead Lake Superior soldier and grabbed a PIAT from his grip.

Ardagh rolled on his back and examined the PIAT to make sure it was in working order. He couldn't afford to make the same mistake again. He rolled back on his stomach and then crouched on one knee, taking aim at the first German Tiger tank. It was too far away, so he moved, crouching, toward the oncoming tanks. He was now the right distance to the lead tank. Kneeling again, he planted his knee firmly and leaned in, taking good aim at the lead Tiger tank.

Everything around him seemed to stop, and it was the first time in four years that he felt in control. Jim's voice filled his head. "Go, go!" But instead, he took a deep breath and fired. He felt the thrust of the projectile leaving his shoulder and watched it hit the side of the tank. Ardagh threw away the PIAT and picked up his Sten gun. He watched the crew of the tank bail out, but Woods with the Bren gun opened up from the fence line, killing them. Two Grenadier tanks moved up, encouraged after seeing the lead tank knocked out, and positioned themselves in front of Ardagh to take on the remaining Tiger tanks.

Ardagh used their cover to get back to Danny and his men. He climbed back into the trench with Danny and Woods in time to watch the remaining German Tiger tanks fire accurately into the two Grenadier tanks, knocking them both out. Only two Grenadier gunners climbed out to safety.

Lieutenant Henderson ran out of the farmhouse and yelled, "I've ordered some heavies on the old 'C' Company position and the field. Keep your heads down."

They had delayed the Germans long enough to leave them exposed in the open field. Ardagh ordered the group back into the farmhouse just as the first shells fell and explosions erupted around the Tigers and German troops caught out in the muddy field. The Germans lucky enough to be near the Tiger tanks crawled on top before the tanks reversed out of the firestorm.

All went quiet, and snow flurries replaced the falling shells. Soon a thin coat of snow covered those who had fallen.

## Chapter Twenty-Seven

# Canterville Ghost

Oirschot, Netherlands
March 12th, 1945

The movie ended with the dim lights of the makeshift theatre turning on. Some men were slow to get up. It was always like that. Sometimes taking your mind off the continual danger that lies in front of you like a steel-toothed shredder leaves you in a zombie state.

Ardagh shook the black thoughts out of his mind, not knowing how long he had been in the same trance, and stood up.

*The Canterville Ghost,* Ardagh thought, *if only life was so simple. Where is our English castle to stay in? Boy, it would be nice to shake off the ghosts from the past if they were all so friendly,* mused Ardagh. *Why me and not the other guy? There will be many ghosts the guys will need to shake when this is over.* The subtle theme of the movie didn't go unnoticed. Guys stirred in their chairs when Caffy jumped in to save the day. The regimental motto of fearless in the face of danger had hung over the men long enough.

The padre approached with a concerned expression. Not good. Ardagh had seen that stare several times now over the past few months, and it was never a simple conversation.

"Hey Harp, I have a major favour to ask you. You could say

no, but we have no one left with your experience and knowledge of the battlefield," the padre said without expression. Their eyes met, and Ardagh knew he was in, no matter what he asked. This was how the regiment was now. The tough days they experienced together over the past year brought everyone together tighter than family. No stones or thoughts were left unturned. It was the silver lining that none of them expected: the closeness and friendships that formed, especially among the platoon and certain of the senior officers. The padre was that special officer. He was there for you, no matter what. The fear and anguish of battle, the advice for girlfriends, there was nothing you couldn't discuss with the padre.

"I'm in, as long as I don't have to save any ghosts." Ardagh tried to laugh. "Easy to be a hero these days, no shortage of opportunities, apparently."

The volunteer group from 'B' Company loaded into the truck for the brief journey back to the Gap. The padre and Ardagh chose to drive along on motorcycles to lead the group. Ardagh never really looked back on the many battles they'd fought. At least, he tried not to. It was tough enough to prepare for what was next, never mind trying to remember what had unfolded—it was a defence mechanism to stay alive and somewhat sane.

Ardagh felt the engine's vibration, mindlessly following the padre, and reflected upon what they may discover. Everyone stayed deep in their own thoughts. They needed the few men that had made it through the battle to help search out their fallen comrades. The fight in the Gap had been a muddy, devastating mess. There was wreckage over a large area, scattered equipment from both sides, and the area was still covered with mines.

Ardagh only had a blurred memory of the carnage in the mud-soaked areas he dug into, and the few of the men he had seen get hit around him. They drove up the short narrow road that divided the fight between 'B' and 'C' Companies and stopped beside the shattered farm house that had been one of the few places for cover against the German counterattacks. It surprised him to hear the birds chirping. The men were quiet as they shuffled out of the back of the truck.

The forest in front of them stood black like shards of burned matchsticks neatly placed among deep craters. It was still a muddy, torn scene with a mix of scattered equipment, mud, and the odd tree that had miraculously escaped the firestorm. Still cold, Ardagh thought. Still wet.

"What a mess," the padre said as he stepped off his motorcycle. "They put the boys through hell... It's surprising anyone survived."

"Definitely the worst of the fighting we have seen... from painful experience, sir," Ardagh said, trying to sound cheery.

"Let's get to work, son. I know this will be a hard task for all, but it needs to be done."

The padre pulled nervously at his gloves and jacket, turning to the others. "Let's get to work, lads." He waved the others over.

"Where should we start?"

"If I remember the worst of it..." he paused and searched over the burned landscape. A man stepped out of the burned-down farmhouse. He was cradling a crumpled boy in his arms. Ardagh's thoughts turned back to Joey and Marv, describing the accident in the courtroom. Marv had shown that he knew the difference between right and wrong. There was little room for right and wrong to exist in war. Survival was sometimes the only choice. Ardagh had tried his best to make things right. The man stepped through the remains of the broken home, taking his time. Ardagh wasn't sure if the boy was dead or alive. He fought the urge to run over to him and hold the boy. Tell him everything would be okay. But all he could feel was a deep pain in his chest.

"We should start in what remains of the woods and that deep gully over there," Ardagh said, pointing to a devastated area with shell holes surrounding a blackened location of broken trees away from the farmhouse. The group moved off the road, down between rubble of the farmhouse and the gully. They came upon a couple of men lying still next to each other. "That's George Yanchuk, one of the Originals, and Middlemiss beside him."

Yanchuk lay only a few yards from an enemy slit trench, on his back with a grenade still clutched in his hand, killed as he charged the position. In a shell hole beside him, sitting up in a lifelike position, was Middlemiss.

Ardagh stood over Middlemiss and stared down. He could see that he had taken direct rounds in his abdomen, and his hand was clutching his stomach, with dried dark blood staining the front and legs of his uniform. He looked like he was peacefully waiting for Ardagh.

"Never saw these guys when we came through, but we stayed further into the forest, dug into the gully over there." Ardagh pointed past the broken pile of rubble that once stood as a farmhouse.

"Hold on!" the padre said. "There's another one of ours here."

As Ardagh moved in closer to investigate, he saw to his horror the burned body of a soldier with his arms around a German soldier in the slit trench they were attacking. The haystack beside the men had caught fire and burned the bodies where they stood. They'd been in an obvious hand-to-hand fight that ended in both of them losing their lives.

"Jesus," Ardagh said as he tried to process what had taken place and how it could've ended in the way it did. He had seen many dead and wounded over the past several months of combat. No stranger to gruesome, torn-apart bodies and tangled blood-covered battle areas. Still, the closeness of the aftermath hit him harder. It was unusual to see a scenario played out in front of you the way this scene looked; as if it was a movie, and they arranged the layout for the last shot of the fight.

They lifted the men one at a time and laid them on stretchers to be transferred to the rear for temporary burial. It became a very labour-intensive process as they systematically cleared around each body to ensure there were no mines or grenades dangerously ready to explode. They removed rifles, ammunition belts, helmets and all kinds of equipment one carried into battle. They didn't search their pockets for items, as that would be done prior to burial. The padre said a few words and a prayer for each before moving them.

They moved on further, to where Ardagh had spent the better part of the day being heavily mortared and stopping multiple counterattacks. All he could remember was the mud and wet rain, and trying to stay dry and safe. The gully appeared deeper into the farmer's field than he recalled, and split in two. So, it was more like a deep U carved into the side of the elevated farmer's field with the bottom of the U bitten off. This was why the carriers were able to drive up to the gullies, he realized.

He could now understand why they had made it through, or at least how they had a better chance than being out in the open. The gully was very steep, and the dug-in trenches formed a dashed line across the top of the gully and field above, which had protected them from the devastating mortars and artillery. Above them along the ridge were firing positions dug deep as well. This had created a strong, well dug-in, defensive position that allowed them to repel several counterattacks from multiple directions.

"It really caught them out in the open," the padre said under his breath. They worked their way only a few yards into the mud, where four bodies lay as if in a line but face down. He moved up to the first in line. He slowed and paused briefly before he crouched down and pulled off his helmet.

The soldier's face from before the battle flashed across his vision, as if it was just happening. He would never forget it. It made him pause then as he did now. His quick glance and the heavy-faced determined look across the soldier's face and his movement to grab the side of the Kangaroo to climb on. The 'see you later' look, then bravely bantering, "Let's go, boys, and get it done." The padre had naturally patted him on the knee as the Kangaroo jumped off.

"This is Sergeant Lehman and some of his platoon," the padre said. "I saw them off."

"Shit," Ardagh said. "Koos will be upset. He was dating one of her friends."

"These guys are new, other than Sergeant Lehman," the padre said.

"They were pretty exposed coming through here. It's right in the German firing line, piss poor luck," Ardagh said as he looked toward the gully that had been his sanctuary during the fight. The surrounding mud had dried, but it proved to be a more backbreaking task, separating them from the wet ground underneath, holding them in place. They repeated the procedure as before and placed them in the back of the truck.

Ardagh continued back to check out the two Kangaroos that were knocked out and still smouldering black smoke. There he saw two more men from the regiment. The one outside the first Kangaroo had a bullet through his head and couldn't be recognized. He searched through the kit and saw the name Private Carrier. He was new. The other guy who had just gotten into position and was killed, he recognized.

Although he was new and just joined in November, he recalled the guys joking with him as his platoon walked by.

Someone had shouted out, "What do you know? You're just a stupid potato farmer," and he had responded, "I'm not, I'm an oilman, I told you, so piss off."

It was like that with the newcomers before being accepted in. Ardagh recalled laughing to himself as they walked by, watching Carrier return a smile. And then someone else had said, "Well, I guess you know how to make chips then," and they all had laughed.

"He was a hell of a driver," the padre said. "He drove a team of horses to deliver gasoline and kerosene to local farmers in PEI when he was only eight."

"The fish and chips guy," Ardagh said. "It's funny the things you remember of the guys. Brief clips or moments, or gestures they made, but if you asked me about a conversation we had, I couldn't remember a thing." Ardagh sighed while peering into the smouldering Kangaroo.

"I think it's the stress, my son." The padre frowned. "It affects us all in different ways. So young... the lads," the padre said. "What do you mean by fish and chips? He drove a truck?"

"No worries, padre," Ardagh said and reached down to remove his helmet and rifle. "Just a poor joke. We were so tired, we all laughed... just a sad joke."

"What do I tell his mother?" the padre said, under is breath.

They spent the better part of the afternoon searching the area in the gully and the collapsed farmhouse that had seen heavy fighting. The padre insisted they were still missing a couple of guys. In particular, a young kid the padre had taken special care of when he first arrived just a month ago. Private Ash wasn't supposed to be here. He was only fifteen years old and had lied about his age. There was a big fuss about him from above, apparently, as he had run away from home. His parents were pissed and put up a big stink to get him back. The kid still left anyway, and the mother decided it was best they at least knew where he was. Well, the army didn't work that way. If you could fight, you fought. So here he was, pushed up the line to the front. It was apparent after the fight when he wasn't accounted for. The padre was beside himself, as Ash should have been LOB—left out of battle. But the regiment was short of men from the previous night's fighting, and in he went. They just wanted to find him now, so that the padre could look his mother in the eyes, tell her he had done well.

They checked the woods to see if they could find him in there. There were other guys from a British unit looking for men, and they decided to head over to search the area. They worked their way into the edge of the forest, into a small clearing where there was a mortar position. Several German dead and shell casings covered the floor of the surrounding forest.

The British corporal stopped digging and said before they could make a comment, "We have already buried five Krauts, five more to go."

"There was some fight here," Ardagh whistled. "I think this must be Ash. He is young."

The padre bent down and patted him on the back and whispered, "Good job, son... you have done well... I'll let your mom know."

"They must have tried to skirt the heavy fire from our position in the gully and swung into the trees, thinking they could outflank them. Obviously, they didn't realize that part of the front hadn't moved back yet. Right into a heavily defended position," Ardagh said as he peered into the dugout where the Germans were still tangled.

Private Catto was lying next to Private Ash, his hands clutching his Sten gun with shell casings all around him. Ardagh kicked at the shells lying around them. "He really let them have it to the end."

"They sure made it a fight. Two against ten, they died fighting," the padre said. "Hard not to feel proud of these guys, but sad, such a waste."

They walked in silence along the edge of the wood, then headed back toward the gully and crossed the moonscape crater-filled field. They reached a slight roll in the farmer's field and came upon another struggle that had played out like the others. A small group of men had been left exposed in the open and were killed by mortar or artillery fire.

Ardagh helped carry Ash's body to the truck. He was the last one to be moved. They lifted him into the truck. Ardagh held onto the end of the stretcher and pushed him upward onto the rear of the truck bed. His hands felt sweaty under the burden and the pole slipped from his hand, letting Ash's arm swing from beneath the tarp. The padre pushed his arm back underneath, and the job was done.

The truck was now loaded with the dead. Ardagh climbed onto his motorcycle next to the padre and his thoughts turned back to Jim being loaded into the ambulance, his arm swinging from under the tarp. Jim had never left his thoughts. All his advice over the years had brought him this far. He took one last look at the farmhouse. No sign of the boy and his father. A ghost from the past. It was the first time he had been able to go back and see the devastation he had been through. The carnage that he had left behind. To see it clearly afterwards and understand what it meant.

"I need to write this down. It needs to be understood and heard by all," the padre said. "At least for these boys, I don't want it to be lost. Give me a minute. I don't want to lose this moment."

The Padre sat with his notebook and wrote:

Oirschot March 12, 1945

*Dead men tell the story of the battle of the Gap.*

*The mouth of the Gap bore the signs of intense shelling, with the ground pitted and scarred and torn by fire of all kinds. A gully that provided the only protection was cut to pieces outlined by torn trees. The houses nearby were heaps of rubble and still smouldering.*

*There was unforgettable courage recorded here.*

*Private George Yanchuk was within a few yards of an enemy position, lying on his back with a grenade*

*clutched in his hand, killed as he charged. At his side,*
*Private Walter Middlemiss was sitting in a shell hole*
*in a lifelike position. He had been with Yanchuk when*
*a burst of small-arms fire in the abdomen stopped him.*
*He crawled into the shell hole, sat there and died.*

*An unknown Canadian made the enemy position.*
*His arms locked around a German. He was burned to*
*a crisp by a mound of hay that caught fire alongside*
*the slit trench he fought hand-to-hand in. Sergeant*
*Lehman was lying a few yards away, struck down as*
*he brought in the platoon.*

*Stretched out in line lying as they fell, Corporal*
*Gray, Private Donald McDonald, Private George*
*Couture and Private William McRobbie. Further*
*back, where two Kangaroos had been knocked out as*
*they lunged across an enemy trench, two more Lake*
*Superior men lay dead. Private Carrier had been shot*
*through the head as he was debussing. Another, Pri-*
*vate Ralph Silliker, was killed as he raced to take up*
*the first position.*

*Private Ralph Ash and Private William Catto were*
*on the fringe of the Hochwald forest. Trying to skirt the*
*intense enemy fire concentrated on the Gap area, they*
*swung to the left flank to the cover of the woods. They*
*were found in a small clearing... dead. Judging from*
*the enemy mortar shells and casings piled here, these*
*two had run into a mortar position. A British signals*
*unit stated they had already buried five Germans, and*
*five still lay there to be buried. Signs of a battle were*
*everywhere. These two had died fighting.*

*Ahead of the Lake Superior positions, five men of*
*the Algonquin regiment were found: four regulars and*
*one officer. Mortar or artillery had killed these men.*
*The officer had lived long enough to put a shell dressing*

*on one of his men and was crawling to another when he died.*

*Such is the story of those who died in the Battle of the Gap, as it was interpreted by one who went over the field of struggle afterwards and was made to feel both humbled and proud by the feats of men such as these.*

## Chapter Twenty-Eight

# A Name

Sint Philipsland, Netherlands
March 1945

Ardagh slowed the motorcycle as he hit the long stretch of the road and saw the water tower that marked Sint Philipsland, Koos's temporary home with her family. Excitement at seeing her jolted through his body, and he automatically juiced the engine. He sped up, hitting the entrance of the bridge, catching a little air. As he landed, he glimpsed a figure on the road ahead. He released the gas before he reached the other side. Skidding to a stop, he almost hit a blond boy on the side of the road waving at him. It was Rob, Koos's nephew. *Jesus, almost killed you,* he thought. He was a lot like little Marv. They were very close in age. He pushed the motorcycle and rolled across the bridge to meet him. Before Rob could ask, he placed a chocolate bar in his hand.

"Eat it now," Ardagh gestured to his mouth, "so you don't have to share it. I have lots more for the others," and he patted his bag.

"Dank u," Rob said with a crooked grin. They sat in silence while Rob greedily chomped down his chocolate bar. This kid had been through hell in his short life. Compared to what Marv had gone through, it would shock his family. A Canadian kid and a Dutch kid living such different lives. He guessed that Rob didn't know any better, so maybe it wasn't so bad. Hopefully, they would meet someday when all this was over. He wanted to bring Koos back home. It all seemed like a long way off, like a second life.

"You're so much like my little nephew, Marv," Ardagh said to Rob as he tossed his hair. "Little Rob, meet little Marv."

Rob stared up at him with a chocolate-covered smile.

There was a large Canadian contingent protecting the town as the Germans were still in the area and uselessly occupying the other islands to the west. Ardagh studied the several tanks and carriers lined up in the field, surrounded by a group of men, where the Lake Superiors used to park. Hopefully, she hadn't met another soldier while he was away. He felt a dull pain in his chest and climbed off the bike. *That was stupid,* he thought, and tossed it to the back of his mind like a grenade and let it explode away—nothing he could do about it.

It had been over two months since he last saw Koos, and he was anxious to see her. They had given him a few days of leave after the mauling at the Hochwald Gap. He was now promoted to sergeant and was excited to show Koos his new stripes. He had earned them. Ardagh was one of the few remaining with combat experience, one of the Originals. Lieutenant Henderson, now Captain Henderson's had let Ardagh sneak away and have a day or two with his new girlfriend, knowing that he would bear a ton of new responsibility and added risk when he returned. It was an understanding between the two of them after Ardagh's discussion with Lieutenant Brown back in England. So much had happened. His head spun, thinking about it. He had lived more in the last year than in his previous twenty-two years.

Rob jumped on the back of the motorcycle and gave Ardagh a big hug as they sped into town to Rob's house. He carried a surprise for them in his kitbag, enough at least for a modest feast for the entire family.

***

Ardagh sat on the edge of the dike, looking down at Koos's brother's house and the makeshift canteen now being used by the Lincoln and Welland Regiment. It was a cool and crisp late afternoon, and the family was busy preparing the exciting dinner feast of food that Ardagh brought from Germany. Koos had snuck Ardagh away from the chaos of the house onto the dike that protected the home.

He whittled with his little pocket knife on a small shell he'd found on the mudflat beach, carving their names into it. The simple act reduced the uneasiness that had hung over him since climbing off the bike to greet Koos and her family. It was the same feeling that dragged alongside him when he first left France after the September fighting.

He enjoyed the quietness of the Dutch town, away from the constant stress; here, he could take a breath without fear it might be his last. This was the first time since the Hochwald that they were alone together. Koos lay beside him, resting on her elbows, staring at his handiwork; he hadn't felt this normal since that last day in Green Bay.

The short time he spent with her family gave him a mix of happiness and sadness. Happy to have a moment to live an everyday existence but sad for his family that he hadn't seen for so long. So far, they'd all made it through; his brothers and two uncles were mostly left unscathed by the war. Hank was now home and safely training other gunners in Manitoba, very far from the war. The war was nearly over.

His memories before leaving Fort William and the fear and rush to get away all seemed like child's play, but the boy being carried away through the destruction of the farmhouse brought it all back. He thought he had shaken it away. It was something that was in the back of his mind to tell Koos at some point. It was too big to be hidden. How would he tell her about Joey?

"Has it been quiet since we left?" Ardagh asked. The noise of the soldiers in the courtyard was a consistent chatter of men coming and going.

"Yes, don't worry. The Germans keep their distance," Koos said. "You won't have to save me again."

"Rescuing damsels in distress is the main reason I signed up."

"I knew it!" Koos said. She moved in closer and hooked her leg over his. "Why did you join up and decide to come to rescue me?"

"It's a long... something hard for me," Ardagh mumbled as he stayed focused on his carving and didn't look up. Should he tell her now or wait until the war is over? What if she rejected him?

"Who else could you tell? It can't be that bad!" Koos said, rubbing his shoulder. "What could be worse than what you have seen or had to do during the war? We are not children anymore. My parents still see me that way, but those days are long gone now."

She was right to think that, if it weren't for Joey. Her simple touch and warmth against his body relaxed and settled him. Ardagh had thought a lot about Jim's death before they came to France, but not as much since. His advice carried him. It was Joey that he still carried. He had seen so much death and destruction. The worries of the past had fallen away. At the Hochwald, it all came back. First, the little boy, then Private Ash's arm falling out from under the tarp that sparked the memory of Jim. On the drive from the Hochwald, he looked at Jim's death through a new lens. It was what really carried him. But it was Joey that he struggled to overcome and understand.

"I was just a kid then. It was before I signed up," Ardagh started. "My father owns and runs an ice company. I was helping him cut ice from the Kaministiquia River. It was March and cold. I was helping one of the other guys. Jim. He was my mentor, like an uncle to me. He was a big man, strong from lifting the ice, but big and heavyset." Ardagh waved his arms over his stomach. "And we were alone. The group had gone further down the river bank, but he wanted to finish what he was doing. My saw got caught between the fresh-cut ice and the uncut ice. It was thicker than normal, and they were good blocks. He lost his patience with me and told me to let go, and he would grab it. I just backed away, and he moved in."

Ardagh stopped and started back working on his carving, blowing the dust away. He said, "My memory moves in slow motion when I think about it. He just stepped forward to reach down. It was wet, and he slipped. The ice block broke free. He fell on his side and rolled right in, head first. He tried to grab the edge, but it gave way, and he yelled at me to back away. I was in shock as I watched him struggle and couldn't move. I froze."

"Oh, I'm so sorry."

"I had fallen in the same river a few years before with my pa. It was stupid. I was fooling around on the ice while he worked and lost track of where the ice was cut and fell in. It was cold and dark. I screamed just before going under the ice. I remember floating in the darkness, holding my breath. Jim heard my scream and pulled me out with the ice hook. I can still see the shadow standing over me before the hook dug into the collar of my jacket and he lifted me out."

Ardagh shook and gasped as if he just emerged from the water.

"Jim yelled again. I grabbed a pole, and he held on, but I wasn't strong enough to pull him up. He was so heavy, he told me to get help, and he would hold on. I turned and ran as fast as I could."

He folded his knife and placed it back into his pocket, and showed her his paltry attempt at carving a little heart with their initials and X and O's. It wasn't much, but she smiled, hugging him deeply and sneaking a kiss on his cheek. The brief physical contact was only the second time since he'd come back—the first time, her father had abruptly intervened. It was like being shot at, and he stayed clear ever since.

"Ardagh, it's not your fault. It was an accident," Koos said as she continued to hold him.

"He was lying there under a tarp on the ice. They needed four men to lift him into the cart. They said he must have had a heart attack; otherwise, he could have been saved. If only I had been stronger, I could have saved him. One minute we were talking and laughing, the next, he was lying dead under a tarp. I feel like most days I have been trying to pull Jim out of the water. Over and over again. I hadn't thought about it as much, but for one guy killed in the Hochwald. Private Ash. He was only fifteen years old. Do you ever feel that way? Like you have been trying to make up for something but can never do it?"

"I don't know. It's silly compared to you and what you have to go through."

"Please, tell me."

"It's just silly..."

"Please, if it is, I'll only make fun of you."

"Stop it..." Koos pushed him away and Ardagh rolled away.

"Please, I want to know."

"I know you made fun of my name before but I feel it hangs over me... Before I was born, I had two older brothers that both died from illness. They named the youngest Jacob. He was only two. My mother named me after him in remembrance. The nickname for Jacoba is Koos. As I have grown older, it has weighed on me and especially through the war. Am I trying to live up to him or my parents? They won't let me be free. I live in a protected shell. But in danger of never knowing myself. I know it seems silly. It's just a name."

"Koos, it's not silly. You're your own person. I've seen it. You're stronger than you think. Your parents are proud of you.

I see it when they try to boss you around and fail."

"See, I told you."

"No... I'm sorry, it's important to you. I try to live up to what Jim would want me to do. He is someone I'll always carry. Just like you, and it means something."

"My father told me once that we're more afraid of the ones we love being forgotten than we are of dying," Koos said as she folded her fingers into his and he pulled her close.

"I never thought of it that way," he said and kissed her, holding her tight. He thought back to the last time with Jim on the ice. At least the soldiers who died would be remembered, he had said. "That's what Jim feared. Being forgotten. He's helped me in so many ways. I'll never forget. It changed the direction of my life and brought me to you."

Ardagh kissed her again. Koos blew a kiss playfully, pulling his hand into her lap and then pulled away from him. They'd only had a few brief encounters, but were comfortable with each other and knew what each other meant.

Koos jumped up, giggled and motioned him to follow. They moved to the other side of the dike, and nervously he glanced back to the house for any sign of a witness to their act. They walked along the back of the dike until they came across a small fold in the ground, and Koos rolled into it, pulling Ardagh down with her. As if in a slit trench facing the Germans, Ardagh cautiously peeked over the edge, and looked for the enemy. Koos pulled him close again only to say "Quickly," with a quiet groan, kissing him hard on the lips. Ardagh needed no more orders.

\*\*\*

Ardagh stood anxiously by the sink, helping Koos dry the pile of dishes from the family feast. How could he tell her about Joey? After their brief encounter on the dike, they had spent the late afternoon walking through the small town and visited her church. It hit him how serious they were getting with each other in such a short time. He had gotten up from the table to stand next to Koos and successfully wrestled the towel out of her hand to help. His mother would have smacked him on the back of his head if he hadn't. It was the way they were; in a large family, everyone pitched in. He needed to tell her, but he wasn't sure how she would respond. He didn't want this to end.

He looked at the scene and took in the many Dutch conversations that were taking place at once. He couldn't understand what they were saying, but enjoyed the family scene. The long double table laid out took up the room's entire length to fit the fourteen loud adults. Mainly Koos's brothers and their wives and another Lake Superior, a signaller from his 'B' Company. He was happy to have another alongside him to help carry some conversation over the meagre roast beef they'd shared. The kids had sat at a smaller table off to the side but were now long gone outside playing.

"Dank u," Koos said again as she accepted another plate. Her excitement at every dish Ardagh handed her made him laugh.

"You're welcome," responded Ardagh with every plate. Not a big deal to help with cleanup, but her mother was smiling at the same time. He knew he would eventually win the battle of acceptance within the family.

Ardagh looked at Norman Hunt. The short, stocky and loud signaller was a year younger and signed up at the same time as Ardagh, making him one of the Originals. It made Ardagh happy to see an old friend from that first day he had signed up. Norman was struggling to explain to Abraham that they would soon win the war, since they had pushed across the Rhine.

"I think it'll all soon be over, sir. We have captured most of the buzz bomb sites, so you shouldn't see them anymore," Norman said, moving his arm like a rocket. "Nu Veilig, you're safe now from the war."

"Ja, that is good Dutch!" Abraham said. "But we still see them. How is this possible? Is the fighting still difficult?" Abraham looked over Norman's shoulder at Ardagh.

"I hope we're through the worst." Norman said, then quietly continued. "The Hochwald was a terrible fight, and we lost many men, wounded and killed, so we're now training new men to get back up to speed. Hopefully, it'll be over before we're back at it."

"Terrible, we've heard on the radio, with the Rhine crossed and the Russians on the edges of Berlin. We don't want to lose any more of you."

Abraham's face was grim and, still looking at Ardagh, said, "It'd be too close to home for some. We're already so grateful to you for the sacrifices you've made liberating Sint Philipsland. Do many of the men have girlfriends in the other villages?"

Ardagh grabbed another wet dish. Many of his friends, including Norman, secretly dated the Dutch girls, all knowing that the families would disapprove. Ardagh stepped closer to Koos, waiting to hear Norman's response.

"Yes, it'll be tough for some. Many of the men were just billeted with the families and became close on the last visit. It's difficult."

"Well, we would hate for them to leave them behind when it's all over and go back to Canada once they have had their fun. There may be consequences." Abraham now directed his full glare at Norman, and then Ardagh.

Ardagh dried the last small plate, watching the table and straining to listen to her father. He handed the plate to her without looking. The crash of the dish onto the wood floor startled everyone.

"Jesus!" Ardagh said instantly and dropped to the floor to pick up the broken pieces scattered around her feet. "Don't move. I'll clean it up."

"Do not take the Lord's name in vain," Abraham said in anger.

"Well, yes, of course," Norman said, clearly hoping to end the conversation.

"Of course," Abraham said, nodding his point across.

Ardagh picked up the large pieces of the broken plate and Koos swept up around them.

"Jesus," she said in a whisper as she brushed past him to empty the pan.

Ardagh handed the damp dishtowel to Koos's mother and walked over to the table as the conversation quieted. Norman and Abraham, fixed in a staring contest, stood up. He needed more time to tell her his story and what happened to Joey.

"Sorry, sir. We'll head back to our billets, but hope to see you in the morning," Ardagh said. He would let it wait for another day.

"I'll walk with you," Koos said. Her eyes pleaded with him to let her in. He couldn't hide from it anymore.

"I'll tell you the story of what happened before I joined. His name was Joey."

\*\*\*

The sun was just rising, as Ardagh wiped the wet dew off the motorcycle seat before straddling it and starting the engine. He'd already said his goodbyes to his new family and was stalling to plant a lasting kiss on Koos's soft lips or just steal a quick hug so as not to get her in trouble. She seemed distant after their talk. He'd told her everything. Jim, Jean and Joey. How it all unfolded and tore his world apart. He knew his path now. It would be with her if she accepted him. He would lead his men and watch out for them.

"Goodbye, my love," Koos said and solved his dilemma for him by hugging and kissing him. She held him for several seconds before they both heard the cough of her father and a strict-sounding call from her mother, "Koos!"

"Until we meet again," he sang cheerfully as he started the engine and kicked out the stand, righting the bike and gently pulling away. Koos ran alongside, and her hand finally slipped from his.

## Chapter Twenty-Nine

# Catching Squirrels

Kusten Canal, Germany
April 18th, 1945

"I got you, Jim! Hold on!" Ardagh yelled. He pulled on the pole, feeling the weight of him. He closed his eyes, his hands straining against the cold.

"Jim?... It's me, Danny."

"Danny! What are you doing here?"

"Pull me out, hurry!" Danny looked up at him, holding a box of ammo.

Ardagh reached down and pulled him up out of the blood-covered trench. The German's face flashed in his head, then the torn pieces and crushed forehead in the mud.

"I got you." Ardagh looked over at Danny and slapped him on the back. He was driving the carrier, sliding in the muddy field.

"Let's go! Keep moving!" Danny yelled.

"I'm driving as fast as I can!"

"Harp! Watch out! The Leafs jersey!" The carrier lifted in the air to the sounds of broken glass around him.

"Did we hit anything?" It was quiet and dark. They walked along a tree-covered road. He could smell the smoke.

"No, keep going... Just through the wall, right here," Danny whispered.

Danikhorst, Germany

"No! Watch out! Don't step!"

***

"Harp... Wake up," Danny whispered as he shook him. "Wake up."

"What? What?" Ardagh said, opening his eyes.

"You had that dream again?" Danny asked.

"Sort of, no. It was different," Ardagh said as he sat up.

"That's good, then," Danny said as he pulled Ardagh to his feet.

"I think so." Ardagh shrugged. "Are the guys ready?"

"All lined up nice and pretty for the raid. The lieutenant is already moving out with his group."

"Okay, let's get moving, then."

***

Ardagh slid hard underneath the spruce tree, catching a branch square in the face. He settled in and peered across the German Kusten canal. It didn't look good.

"Shit, Danny." Ardagh clenched his teeth and wiped his face.

"Yes, boss... The boats are just up to our left."

"Give the signal to hold. We'll wait and watch the river."

Ardagh looked back to the line of troops behind him undercover in the trees to see if any had seen him hit the tree. He didn't care. It was the least of his worries. They needed speed and the cover of darkness to be successful. So many of these water excursions failed badly.

Ardagh knew enough now to know better. He wasn't the same kid that couldn't lift his weight and ran from his troubles. He would do it right and push back if he had to.

Lieutenant Ritchie was leading the column to his left. He'd come back from the ops meeting with the word that they were to cross the canal in the early morning before sunrise. The boats to be provided. They divided the platoon into two groups of ten. No noise, so they just carried weapons and ammo. But they didn't know the real situation they faced. Ardagh heard someone moving behind them. It had to be Lieutenant Ritchie.

"What's the holdup, Sergeant?" Lieutenant Ritchie asked in a whisper.

It was pitch black, and they had to be close just to see each other.

"It's no good."

"We have to cross. There's no choice. Get moving."

"There are only a few suitable spots to cross, and the Germans know them. They're either mined or sighted. Can you hear that?"

"I hear nothing, Sergeant."

"I can smell the smoke as well. The moment we put a boat in the water, they'll light us up. Remember Corporal Shaw?"

"No, I don't. I wasn't there."

Ardagh had learned a lot over the past few months of fighting and crossing rivers. There were many dangers in establishing strategic bridgeheads. The Germans were still well organized and had laid mines along the river banks. The lessons from the Corporal Shaw incident were still fresh. A similar raiding party had been organized in February along the Maas River. After several men had stepped on mines along the shore, Shaw had made a swim for it. The Maas River was narrow but fast flowing. Shaw's fate was still unknown. His group had crossed the Maas River in February, and, chances were, he didn't make it. Most were killed or captured. Ardagh didn't want to have the same fate this late in the war.

"I was," Ardagh whispered. "This is a narrow canal with steep slopes. They've gun positions along the length of it. I can hear them and smell them. We'll get slaughtered before we are halfway across."

"We have our orders, Sergeant," Lieutenant Ritchie countered, but it came out flat. He knew it was a tough task.

"Let me do it my way, then?" Ardagh asked. A light breeze picked up through the trees they were huddled under. He could detect the smoke again and swore he heard the rattle of horses across the canal. He waited in silence for the lieutenant's response.

"Okay, but be quick about it. We only have a few hours of darkness," Lieutenant Ritchie agreed.

His plan was simple. Make sure the cloud cover was right and there was maximum darkness, and launch the first boat of men with ropes attached, to pull it back if the shooting started. He was pretty confident it would. But he would show the lieutenant without endangering his entire platoon. If no shooting, they would paddle with extreme urgency to the other side, hopefully undetected, and scout the enemy. If everything worked well, it was simple. At least April made it easier, with warmer weather, and he hoped they would have a better outcome than Shaw's unit. The last few weeks had been anything but predictable. Sometimes the Germans were gone and other times attempted to fight to the last man. The Originals were slowly dwindling, and a lot of new fresh faces stared back. Their inexperience made the Originals more cautious as they took time to explain things. The Germans they were up against were more of a mixed bag of troops every day. They had to be prepared for anything to hit them. At least he was in control of the men and how they would attack. He would make the call when to cross. He would not risk a mess up. He just wanted to keep his men safe.

The black silent canal sat in front of them as they bent with tightly fisted hands on the sides of the boat. They hurried to the water's edge and didn't worry about getting their feet wet. Danny and the first boat of men climbed in ready with paddles. They pushed off. Ardagh held the rope, waiting. Nothing. The rope slid further through his hands. The water exploded around them as tracer flashes and flares lit up the sky. Ardagh could see the outlined tops of the German helmets on the other side. Just what he expected. The sounds of bullets zipping into the trees above him and the shock of the bright flashes pushed them into action. He pulled as hard as he could, and the men in the boat back paddled as fast as they could. They had answered the question of what was on the other side and didn't need any more signs to get the hell out of there.

The men scrambled out of the boat, leaving it behind to climb up the steep bank of the canal. They rolled over the top and dove behind the safety of the canal where Lieutenant Ritchie was waiting for him. "What the hell, Harp," Lieutenant Ritchie said. "Let's wait until things die down and give it another shot."

"Yes, sir." It was so dark, he couldn't see his expression. *Was he fucking kidding? Shit.*

"Your call, though," he said, between coughs. The firing had died down, but flares were still being shot up along the canal. Ardagh looked down to watch the front of the boat sink into the water and flip over. Thankfully, none of his men were in it.

\*\*\*

Ardagh stood on the right side of home plate with the bat on his shoulder, waiting for the first pitch. They had turned a German farmer's field into a makeshift baseball diamond. Baseball was a simple way for the regiment to relieve the tension of combat. Danny, expressionless, stood on first base. The sun was in his eyes and he felt the warmth on his chest. Ardagh had yet to get a letter from Koos after telling her about Joey and he struggled to push it out of his mind. He waved the bat above his head, feeling its weight in his hands. *Be patient,* he told himself. He could see everything clearly now. The baseball was pitched high into the air, landing three feet short of the plate, and rolled across. Ardagh bent down, picked it up, and threw it back to the pitcher. "That's how it always is, 'A' Company falling short."

"Nice one, canal boy," Sergeant Burrison said. Ardagh pulled the bat off his shoulder and adjusted his grip.

"Let's go, Harp. Hit it out of the park," Danny shouted. "Don't be a punter!"

The pitcher, Sergeant Burrison, caught the ball and responded with a silent nod, mouthing words to himself. He was from Fort William and didn't like to lose. The score was already nine to five for 'B' Company. Danny had walked on to first base, but the last two were fly balls out to left field.

Ardagh waved the bat over his shoulder as the next pitch came. The ball had a low arc and more speed. Just as he hoped. Tightening his grip and lifting his right leg, he ripped into the ball. The sweet feeling as the bat connected with the ball stayed with him as he rounded first base. Danny was almost at third base when the ball bounced for a second time between the right and centre fielders. Ardagh decided this was it, heading for home. Head down, he rounded third. He knew she loved him. The throw came in high to the catcher as Ardagh plowed his shoulder into him, and the ball skipped his glove, hitting Major Dawson in the chest.

Ardagh untangled himself from the catcher and stepped over him. "Sorry, Sergeant," he said, then gave a high five to Danny. He would fight for Koos, no matter what.

"Fuck you, cheap shot," the sergeant said, shoving him hard. Ardagh didn't hesitate and jumped in after him, pulling his uniform from his shoulders and tying up his arms.

"Attention," Major Dawson boomed before he moved between the two sergeants.

"It's only a game. Come on, boys, save it for the Jerries."

Ardagh and Danny moved back to the makeshift dugout, a row of carriers. "Attaboy, take no prisoners!"

"Alright, boys, that's enough. Looks like some rain, so we are calling the game," Major Murray said. "Nine thirty hours weapons inspection tomorrow, so get to it."

***

The engineers had filled in the enormous crater that blocked the road. It was a natural jump-off point to start the attack east. The massive crater had worked well for the Germans to buy time and build more roadblocks. 'B' Company lined the road behind the tanks and flamethrower, spread out in squads of six, spaced twenty-five yards apart. Ardagh, now in charge of the lead platoon, watched the tanks and Bren gun carriers move forward, firing at anything that looked like a target. The Wasp flamethrower led the group and sent a spray of flames into the woods on the north side of the road. 'A' Company moved alongside them on the other side of the Kusten Canal. Sometimes they would fire across the canal to support each

other, but they took their time. The plan was to widen the
bridgehead across the Kusten Canal. Ardagh let the tanks and
flamethrower get a head start.

Without warning, the Wasp flamethrower exploded. Debris sprayed across the road and down into the canal. The
flamethrower landed upside down—both Private Engen and
Private Giving were killed. The stench of burning flesh and fuel
filled the air. Ardagh watched Giving's arm that stuck out of
the overturned carrier burn, engulfed in flames. His blackened
arm moved. His hand curled into a fist, then his arm, just like
the wicked witch, disappeared under the carrier. Both men had
hit pop flies the day before. The carrier continued to scorch the
surrounding earth as the flames searched for something else to
catch. The canal reflected the orange flames, like a Celtic water
god looking for somewhere to strike.

The engineers moved up again, searching for more mines.
They were on the edge of the crater, on either side of the road.
The Germans were always throwing another twist with a new
trap to worry about.

Lieutenant Ritchie moved up to the front. "Sergeant, take
six platoon and clear the woods north of the road. We'll meet
you back on the road."

Ardagh looked over and examined the tightly packed
woods. The area was a mixture of tall maple, elm and birch
trees just a few hundred feet long that hugged the side of the
road, protecting an open field to the north.

Ardagh was glad to get away from the carnage and do something about it.

"Yes, sir."

Ardagh waited until the first 'stop', a Bren squad had moved
into position on his left flank. The stops were vital to a successful woods clearing, preventing anyone from escaping out the
sides and protecting the advancing beaters. The second squad
had already set up facing the thick woods off the north side of

the road to his right. Ardagh, the platoon commander, stood at the centre of a line of beaters spread out as if ready for kickoff. Each man or beater carried a Sten gun. Behind this line sat two support groups that would move through the beaters to attack any Germans. In unison, the platoon entered the edge of the woods, maintaining their disciplined line. The support groups would take any prisoners out and, after the woods clearing, meet at the other side and head back up on the road. A stretch of the woods was smouldering from the flamethrower, and the smoke blew into the trees.

At the edge of the tree line, he could see the hidden wire coming off the bottom of the rifle that leaned against the tree. Mines were one of the greatest fears among the men. The sound of the click just before the explosion meant death or dismemberment. This trap was too obvious. He raised his hand, signalling for the group to stop. He searched for other signs along the tree line. The standard S mine could lift four feet into the air and spray three hundred and sixty steel balls over a one-hundred-and-fifty-degree radius. The few trenches laid out were empty but for some pieces of equipment scattered about. This rifle was an obvious plant, which meant that there was a more deadly surprise hidden elsewhere. He took out a strip of white cloth and marked the rigged rifle for the engineers to dismantle. The line moved forward. The thin fishing line was just visible, tied across from tree to tree, wrapped around branches. If the booby-trapped rifle didn't get you, skirting around it would lead into the trip lines. He again tied a white cloth to the trip lines and moved forward.

On their left, he could see movement. "Support one... left flank," Ardagh said as he threw a grenade where he thought the Germans would be. It bounced off the side of a tree just short of his target. The support group moved through their line and fired as they charged the enemy. After the firing stopped, several Germans, with their hands up, approached the Canadians.

The beaters continued to advance and another group of German soldiers came out with their hands up.

"I guess canals just aren't your thing, Sergeant," Lieutenant Ritchie said, as the platoon made it back to the column. A dozen stunned German prisoners marched by the firing tanks.

Ardagh knew he was right in protecting his men and stepping up to take the heat if it failed because he knew the alternative could lead to even worse consequences. It was what he had been fighting to figure out for the past five years.

"I was always good at catching squirrels," Ardagh said, but his grin fell away when he looked back to the burned-out Wasp. The padre stood on the canal bank, watching over the digging of the graves for Privates Giving and Engen. They would be buried beside each other forever.

Ardagh's Letter Home:

> *Hello everyone,*
> *Hoping this letter or note lands you all in the best of health, which leaves me the same way. In fact, I'm getting fat on eggs and milk. But I could sure use some of your cooking, Ma. Well, the day is coming and I don't think the day is far off when I will be coming home and if I ever get away from home for a year or more, I will get my head tested. Well, Pa, how is grain trimming? I guess you are quite busy these days. How is the ice delivery and the fellow who delivers it? Say, Eldon, watch Hank. He will be stealing your girlfriends. I see he is already starting on your girlfriends. Well, I guess, Hank, you'll be an instructor. That is a very good job. I wish I could get one of those jobs. Well, the time has come for me to close for the night, so for the time being, I'll say... so long,*
> *Ardagh*

## Chapter Thirty

# Traitor Revealed

Bergen op Zoom, Netherlands
April 1945

The clouds moved in, blocking out the sun just as Koos entered Bergen op Zoom, the winds pushing her along on her bike. Koos had ridden over an hour from Sint Philipsland after hearing they had captured Pieter. Everything was moving fast after the liberation. The Allies had liberated Arnhem, pushed north to cut off the Germans in the west and entered Germany, crossing the Rhine. The collaborators and traitors were being rounded up daily.

Koos entered the Grote Markt and looked up at Sint Gertrudiskerk church with its grey clock tower and red shutters. The market square was swarming with people and she felt the tension in the air. It looked as though the entire town was out for revenge. The square was crowded, and she heard the shouts of the angry mob above the usual murmur.

Koos walked her bike, searching through the crowd, one hand on the handlebars, one on the seat. She recognized a few people from her town. There were several German collaborators and Dutch SS lined up with their hands tied and on parade for all to see. The women's heads were shaved and bleeding. They were the rats that had betrayed them all, helping the Germans. She didn't see Pieter among them.

The Canadian soldiers stood by, watching and making sure things didn't get too out of hand. The collaborators would be dealt with in court, but many wanted to do it now. There was only one body lying on the ground, covered by a bloody jacket.

Koos moved closer to get a better view. She could feel her heart in her throat. It was something she wished for, but it was just that. A wish, thoughts of revenge. It was never real. She stood over the body. The beige jacket was familiar to her. There was a lot of blood. But it was his. The boots confirmed it. It was Pieter. She knew she wasn't the only one that gave his name to add to the list of traitors. She felt cold standing over him. Pieter had made his own choices, so why did she still feel somehow responsible for his death? Koos looked at the other traitors. Women and men standing silent, heads down in shame. They had lost and would pay for what they had done. How many others died because of them?

The crowd grew, and more traitors were lined up to march through the streets before being locked up. She stared down again at Pieter's body. It didn't seem real. She stood motionless, staring over the handlebars of her bike. Waiting for him to sit up at any moment. She recalled the look of fear he had. Did he still have that same look? No one else around her seemed to care. More shouts of anger came from the crowd. She had had enough of it. Her head throbbed, and she dragged her bike out of the way. The front tire caught on a cobblestone, and she screamed, "Out of the way!" to the group ahead of her. They stepped back. She tightened her grip on the handlebars and pushed through the crowd.

The front tire of her bike rolled along, steering over the stones. She focused on the tire, its smooth black rubber rolling over and over. The blur of people moved in and out of her vision. The crowd finally cleared in front of her and she turned onto Fortuinstraat. Shops were on either side on the narrow street and she stopped. Taking a deep breath, she made one last effort to turn and look at the church clock and the crowd before climbing back on her bike.

Koos pushed her bike away from the market, one pedal at a time. She needed time to think and clear her head. Everything that had happened to her during the last four years came rushing back. Pieter had got his revenge on Joost, not on her. Ever since the day when Joost beat him up. It was Pieter who started the rumour that it was Joost who betrayed her brother David. She had seen Joost at their house, but she had also seen Pieter on the street just before. The look of fear on his face was not for the Germans, but for her. She was the collateral damage. They were just kids who didn't understand the consequences were real and fatal. Both Joost and Pieter had paid the full price.

Her own hands were not clean. She had pushed Joost away, tipping him over the point of no return. Willie died because of the information she had given to Ardagh. Same with Pieter. War was complicated and deadly. So was life, going forward, becoming a woman. She knew now what her answer was for Ardagh and didn't need any more time or to see him again. She knew she would be with him forever. Koos made the last turn across the bridge and along the dike to her brother's house. She needed to get home and write a letter to Ardagh.

Koos saw her father in front of the house. The winds had picked up, and clouds darkened the sky. The day had started out sunny but now looked to end with rain. He was probably headed to check on his boat. It was part of his daily routine. She wondered if he would miss these days, despite the hardship. If her brother returned unharmed and if they could get their house back, things would turn around quickly. Then she knew he would miss it. He looked down the street before crossing and saw her riding toward him. He stopped and waited.

"Where have you been?" Abraham asked before Koos could climb off her bike.

Koos sighed. "In Bergen op Zoom."

"You couldn't have been gone long. Did you see Pieter?"

"Yes."

"I hope they hang him."

The words hit her hard. She wiped the hair off her face. She felt like crying letting it all out but she held it in. *She was stronger.*

"He's dead. I saw his bloodied body lying in the market square. It was very crowded, but I could see. There were many people who want revenge. I didn't want to see any more."

"It's over now. Life will get back to normal and these things I hope you never have to see again."

"I don't think I want to stay and see things get back to normal," Koos said. She looked directly into his eyes and pushed her shoulders back. Koos could see her father's eyes water, holding back the tears. Was he getting soft in his old age? She wanted to leave and follow Ardagh to Canada. He moved close to her and examining her face. Would he let her go? She was ready to move on. She had grown up enough to know. Her father lifted his arms and gave her a big hug, holding her tight.

Koos sat in her room at her desk. She could still feel the wind on her face. The look her father gave her when she told him she was leaving and the weight of his hug. She felt free for the first time in her life. The letter to Ardagh would be short and leave no doubt she loved him, no matter what. Ardagh had rescued her and killed Joost, but it was more than that. She noticed the connection growing stronger every time they met. Stronger than Joost, stronger than Willie. They shared their deepest secrets and fears. She was safe with him.

Ardagh had shocked her with his story. He had killed a little boy. Joey. It rolled through her head over and over. He had killed Joey and run from it. The judge gave him a two hundred dollar fine and said it was an accident, but he had run from the scene. A hit and run. He was just a kid then, before the war, like her. It could have been his nephew Marv just as easily. He fought it and Jim's death, but now she knew he was different. He wasn't running anymore. Koos saw it with her own eyes over the past months with each visit. His change into a man. She would forgive his past and be with him for the rest of her life.

Koos pictured herself standing on the deck of a passenger ship heading to Canada. What would it be like sitting on the train heading through the forests of northern Canada and walking the streets of Fort William? Would they have kids? Would she miss the ocean? She had changed so much just from moving across the narrow channel from Bruinisse to Sint Philipsland. She was ready for the next change in her life. Leaving behind the war and breaking away from her parents' grip. They would have to let her go.

He needed to know she loved him. That he was a good man. They would spend their life together.

# Chapter Thirty-One

# Saint Hunters

Danikhorst, Germany
April 25th, 1945

Ardagh looked back along the road at his platoon of men. The grass was now green, and it was a reminder to him of the makeup of his platoon and the changes from the tough winter to early spring. The green rookie replacements could be as dangerous as the enemy. It was a remarkable change from the Battle of the Gap. Their confidence and conviction to end the war were never stronger. It was still not without risk. But Ardagh was confident he had trained them well. He watched over them like a mother hen. He believed if they were trained properly and listened, all of them would have a better chance to survive. The Germans were still very dangerous hard fighters mixed in with those who had lost the will to fight and were easy to capture.

The Lake Superior Regiment was now in the far reaches of northwest Germany, pushing down back roads through rural towns to capture the naval base at Wilhelmshaven. The Germans made consistent attempts to slow the Canadians' progress through snipers, Panzerfaust attacks on the tanks with road mines and booby traps. They still encountered radical defenders that extracted a significant toll. Both sides were fighting, but trying to survive. It was an aggressive yet cautious approach. The end of the war was in sight after the final break-through across the Rhine and the surrounding of Berlin.

Their system to attack and destroy the enemy was at its peak up against a weakened foe. The tanks moved down the centre of the road with men in the ditches throwing everything at the exhausted Germans, reloading and throwing even more at them until they rolled over the enemy positions. They moved on foot along with vehicles of all types, to deal with all situations. They would move warily a few hundred yards, then stop to call up the engineers for their opinion on how to remove the many booby-traps they came across. Their job was to protect and prevent the attacks from the Panzerfaust that had plagued the troop of the Grenadier Guards tanks. It was a proven formula that gave Ardagh confidence in these minor attacks ahead. "Don't take any chances," Lieutenant Ritchie had said. "No need to sacrifice any more men. The war is won and about to end."

It was the same message every day to the men since the battle in the Hochwald. Still, they lost some good ones. Just as they moved out, the message down the line was Sergeant Burrison was killed, leading an attack against a dug-in group of Jerries on the crossroad up ahead. They were to continue the push forward. The bastards were still determined to fight, despite knowing the war was lost.

As Lieutenant Pierce, the leader of the Grenadier troop, move up to blast a row of homes along the road, Ardagh checked over the soldiers he now had in his care. Danny, a corporal now, stood at the back of the line, making sure there were no stragglers. Then, the whole side of the first house exploded more than it should have. Ardagh carefully scanned the ground head of him with a veteran eye.

"They must have hit something big," he said to Lieutenant Ritchie, who sat crouched in front of him.

"Must have been a big mine," Lieutenant Ritchie replied,

without taking his eyes off the house. "We are only an hour's drive from the Wilhelmshaven Navy base. Apparently, they have access to some bigger stuff."

"I hope we'll get a chance to sink some more ships. Wilhelmshaven is the same base the ships in Sint Philipsland came from, according to Danny," Ardagh said. "Crazy that we have made it this far to capture their base."

Lieutenant Ritchie nodded and said, "Remind the men to spread out, but stay close to the road and follow each other's steps. Remember, there're a lot of rookies in the group."

Ardagh looked back behind him as Private Fritz Anderson came into his focus, three men down the line. "Fritz!" He yelled and waved to him to move up.

Ardagh grabbed Fritz's rifle and handed him his Sten gun.

"Stay with me," was all Ardagh said. Fritz's wide eyes and grim face made everyone around him on edge.

Ardagh quickly moved up past Lieutenant Ritchie, tapping him on the shoulder and pointing to his right. He crept deeper into the ditch along the road just past the lead tank.

He crouched, lifting the rifle to line up a target further up in the empty field. The commander of the tank yelled down to Ardagh.

"What do you see I don't, Sergeant?"

A helmet and Panzerfaust lifted out of nowhere in the middle of the field. Ardagh let go a full clip of bullets at the German who was lining up the Panzerfaust. The German soldier fell backward to the ground, and the projectile flew aimlessly into the sky. Ardagh reloaded the rifle and handed it back to Fritz.

A smile crossed his face as he looked up at the commander of the tank and said, "You're welcome."

As they moved up the road, two white flags flashed from other slit trenches on their flanks.

"Stay close to me and do as I say."

Many of the new guys had been killed or wounded over the last few months. It seemed as though the experienced group got smaller and smaller while the new recruits turned over and over—some in their graves.

They were so close to the end. They would take their time today and make sure to get through. The tanks were about to finish their last barrage and signalled for them to get ready to take the position.

Ardagh, out of habit, checked his Sten gun, the rest of the men did the same and got ready to move fast. Lieutenant Ritchie signalled across the road, and the other platoon moved parallel to their own. They were halfway up the road by the time the final heavy firing stopped. Before the Germans could react, they were in their positions and fired a heavy volley at them and a few grenades for good measure. It wasn't long before they could hear shouts of surrender in German and broken English. They expertly moved through and around the houses, kicking the Germans down the road to the waiting tanks. Ardagh's platoon of thirty men now occupied the smouldering German slit trenches and set up a defensive position around the houses. There was still sniper fire coming from up ahead, and their experienced sniper team set up to counterattack.

*So far, so good,* Ardagh thought. No one hurt, and they'd captured ten prisoners. There were another ten dead Germans of various ages lying around them. They roughly searched them and moved the bodies to the side of the house after the tanks had rolled up to provide cover and protection.

They immediately searched for new targets, and the artillery officer with them was calling in coordinates. Danny and Lieutenant Ritchie went into the house while the engineers explored the area, looking for booby traps and mines. Ardagh went from man to man, checking on them before heading back to the half-destroyed and still smoking home. Then he saw the signals carrier moving up the road.

It manoeuvred behind the house, and to his surprise, the padre was climbing out. Fit as ever. *He really should have done all the fighting,* thought Ardagh as he watched him. He was in the best shape of any in the unit, solid muscle. His grim stare gave Ardagh a pause for concern.

"Hey, Harp," the padre waved. "You guys are making great progress."

"Yeah, it's tough going, though," Ardagh replied. "You're nuts for coming out here, Padre. You're liable to get your head blown off."

"I thought I would bring up the mail for your guys, as I know it could be a long night," he said and handed the small package to Ardagh.

"There's one from Koos that you've been waiting on." He gave another one of those looks Ardagh had seen too many times before.

"If you came to tell me about Sergeant Burrison, I already know; it's awful so close to the end."

"Yes, it's sad, but that's not the only bad news, son." A mortar round came crashing down, and they both didn't hesitate to jump into the slit trench together. It slammed into the ground twenty yards into the woods.

"I told you, Padre, this was a bad idea," Ardagh said as a barrage of artillery let loose in the distance to counter the incoming mortar fire.

"I wanted... I felt it was important that you heard it from me... and I thought a welcome letter from Koos would help." He struggled to stand and wipe off the dirt and dust from the slit trench.

"Thank you, Padre... I think... What is it?" Ardagh stared across the trench at him.

"Woods was killed by a mortar round. It was a direct hit, and he died instantly. I'm sorry, Ardagh. I know you were close, and he was with you from the start."

Ardagh stared in disbelief at the padre. "How? He wasn't anywhere near the front! He was supposed to be left out of battle."

"This is how it's going to be, at the end. Just a random shell landed from nowhere like a misfire from the bastards," the padre said bitterly. "No reason other than it's still war."

Ardagh stared at his feet for some time and shrugged. "I should get back to the men. They'll appreciate the letters, and I'll let Lieutenant Ritchie know. Woods had a lot of heart." They had started out rough, messing up during training, but when they entered the real fight, they became as close as could be. The magnitude of the loss hit him a second time. First Wilson and now Woods. Why? He pushed the thoughts aside and shuffled the letters in his hands. "Let's get back to killing some Jerries." The stern expression all the Originals carried came back, and he slapped the padre on the back as he jumped out of the slit trench and screamed at the men. "Get ready to move out!"

Ardagh stumbled into the back of the smoking house through the smashed hole in the wall without any thought but to get away from the padre. He moved slowly as he sat down beside Lieutenant Ritchie and Danny, next to a broken window. He searched through the pile of letters, looking for Koos's handwriting. Lieutenant Ritchie turned and stared at him. "What was that all about with the padre?"

Ardagh handed over the pile of letters, minus the letter from Koos.

"He wanted to drop off some letters and told me a direct mortar killed Woods. He didn't even see it coming."

"Shit... Sorry, Harp... He was close," Ritchie said remorsefully, putting his hand on Ardagh's shoulder. "What a mess, first Burrison and then Woods."

"It's just you and me," Danny whispered. Danny looked at Ardagh. His lip quivered and his once expressionless face twitched. He got up and left Ardagh with Ritchie. He wanted to hug him, but he was gone before he made a move.

"We've lost a lot of Originals lately," Ardagh said, breaking the silence. "Makes me nervous." He struggled to think of what to do next. His legs were sore, and he stretched them out. He fingered the trigger on his Sten gun. The familiar scent of burning oil and wood filled the air. He had come a long way from the bomber with Hank.

"Don't be. We are at a good point. Set up, fire, more fire, move up... fire again... consolidate, collect the POWs, and repeat... it's been working great the last few days. They're on the run, and they know it's almost over."

"Say that to Burrison or Woods," Ardagh mumbled, then sighed. "Only a few more to go." There was no one better than him and Danny. He had survived everything. His men depended on him, that's what Woods would say.

Ritchie raised his voice as he got up and ordered, "Let's get the men fed while the artillery pound at the other position. Make sure everyone drinks. It's warming up."

*Keep moving.*

"Yes, sir," Ardagh said before jumping out through the collapsed wall of the house. He was ready to move forward. Don't look back, worry about what's next, he recalled Jim telling him. Woods and Wilson would expect nothing less of him and Danny.

After he organized the men, he jumped into a German dugout to get away from the others and to read the letter from Koos. The padre was right. He needed the distraction from her to help carry him. Ardagh opened the letter, smelling the faint perfume that she had sprayed on it. Where she got it from, he didn't know, as she wasn't allowed to wear any. He appreciated it more than she knew.

> *Dear Ardagh,*
> *I miss you terribly. I hope you are safe and well. It has*

*been difficult sending my letters, since the Germans have*
*still not left Bruinisse and the island, even after their*
*ships were destroyed. We are all hoping the war ends soon*
*so I can join you forever. I feel closer to you than any-*
*one in my life. My papa says he is fond of you and that*
*you showed him you are a proper gentleman. If he only*
*knew... I am well and in good spirits,*

  *Please be safe.*

  *Love*

  *Koos*

She would accept him for who he was. He reread the letter
several times, relieved every time he finished. She would move
to Canada to be with him. He was itching to get home. Back
to his way of life. He could see the path clearly now. No fear of
snipers or mortars or booby traps. Just a few mosquitoes and
a fishing rod, peacefully walking along a stream or sitting in
a boat waiting for a bite. She wanted her mom and dad to be
proud of her choices and to show how he could contribute to
their way of life. They both had high expectations and would
be family.

He was never more in love in his life. The craziness of his
first girlfriend that had led him into the army was long ago.
She was long gone from his memory. The scar of Eileen that he
thought would never heal had entirely faded away like chalk
on a board. It seemed so silly how he could have been as upset
as he was. Koos had taken out the block eraser and wiped it
all away. He guessed that was what love did—heal, clean, and
conquer all. He would do what it took to make it work. If she
wanted him to stay and be with their family, well, he would
stay.

Ardagh lined up the men and they moved out down the
road behind the tanks that continued to fire as they crept along.
The planes had just finished a flyover and waved their wings.
Up ahead was a line of houses that led to their final objective

for the night. A well-organized German defensive line with a large house faced them at another roadblock. They took their time, capturing each house before reaching the roadblock.

The house at the roadblock turned out to be a hotel and restaurant called Neumanns Hubertus. There they discovered, to their delight, some of the best sausages they had tasted in a while. The cellar was also full of flavourful German beer. It was decided to hold and firm up here for the night. This was well-received by all the men.

Ardagh sat at the kitchen table with a stein of beer in one hand and the letter in the other. Danny sat next to him. Fritz stood holding a bratwurst sandwich and beer. Ardagh wanted to keep a close eye on him as it was his first time up at the front. Lieutenant Ritchie gave him a nod and wink as they watched him devour the bread and sausage.

"Remember Normandy?" Ardagh asked. "The stars and the wheat field?"

"The easy days when we didn't know better," Danny said, straight-faced.

"It feels like we're getting back there again. When this ends, what's next?" Ardagh asked, but didn't expect a response. He stared down again at Koos's letter. How would she do in Fort William? "Hubertus Hotel. Beats a field in the middle of no-where, I guess."

"Hubertus was a saint," Lieutenant Ritchie said, biting into the large sausage on his plate. "Apparently, it has something to do with a Christian saint around hunting, big spirits and bright lights, according to the little guidebook I found on the desk. He was a Christian saint who was the patron saint of hunters, mathematicians, opticians and metalworkers. So, I guess it means good spirits and fun. The Germans so far have given us the silent treatment compared to the Dutch. Feels strange."

"We've been to enough strange places, now hunting gods," Ardagh said. His thoughts went back to his last hunting trip with his father. "It'd be nice to get back to some hunting."

"He must be the saint of good beer and sausage too," Danny said, taking the last bite of his sausage and licking his fingers. "How was the letter from your girl?"

"It's a puzzle. She loves me," Ardagh waved it in the air. "I think she's had too much Canadian chocolate, but it makes sense." *My mother will love Koos when she meets her.* Danny snatched the letter from his hand as he lifted his glass to drink his beer.

"Well, what have we here? Oh, I love you, no I LOVE you... oh, oh..." Danny said as he kissed the letter. "We need something to cheer us up. I'll read it aloud... Dear Knucklehead," Danny started. Ardagh watched Danny. He knew he was upset about Woods, but hid it well. This was how Danny dealt with the stress. It helped them both, so he let him have his fun.

"Go ahead. Read it. There's nothing in there for you... piss for brains!" Ardagh laughed as he made a weak attempt to get the letter before taking another gulp of his beer. It felt good to laugh.

"Wow, little Harp is growing up. Back in the day, you would have murdered me in my sleep for prying. He must be in love, boys! Let's see how she is doing," Danny said. His lips tightened as he placed the letter down on the table like a judge examining the verdict. "Dear Ardagh, blah blah blah... wait a minute...."

"What does it say, Danny?" Ritchie asked.

"It says... my papa is fond of you... Holy mackerel... Koos wants you to be with her?" Danny said, "Wow, congratulations!"

"Yeah, I know that, but..." Ardagh said as he scrambled after Danny and the letter.

"See, boys, he is a knucklehead."

"Yeah, I know. It's love at first sight. I guess..." Ardagh said.

"Well, Harp, we feel sorry for her already!" and they all

laughed as Ardagh continued to stare at the letter. He felt a numbness roll up his face and neck. He knew telling Koos about Joey didn't change the facts. But her accepting him brought him a step closer to getting over his past.

"Lots to think through, today," Ardagh said, lifting his beer.

"Cheers, Harp!" Danny said. They looked at each other and knew it was not only to him but to Woods, Wilson and the others.

"I better take Fritz back and settle him in for the night while I check on the others," Ardagh said as he grabbed his Sten gun off the table and slugged back the last of his beer.

"Watch out for the saintly hunters, and congratulations on the girl. The padre will be impressed. He will want to marry you guys and make it official," Ritchie said.

"That'll be something," Ardagh said as the door closed behind him.

They moved through the grey evening to a group of homes that sat behind the hotel, separated from it by a line of trees on the main road. Ardagh paused, taking in a deep breath. He could smell the smoke again. It reminded him of the Lancaster bomber and the burning AF 92. The whiff of oil and wood mixture, sweet and acidic but dry and choking. He looked down the road they'd just fought over. There was still smoke spilling out from a home. Was it a cooking stove, or a fire left over from the shelling? Was it bacon or meat he smelled? His day never ended. He needed to double-check his men, making sure they stayed out of trouble. He enjoyed the responsibility, the look of recognition he got from the men after he explained why they did what they did. All they needed was to attract a firestorm of mortars because they got lazy with a campfire. They were too close to the end. Did Burrison or Woods get lazy? Or was it bad luck? He better check on it, just in case.

"Follow me, Fritz."

Ardagh searched his pocket for the folded letter. He had

never felt this way about anyone in his life and couldn't count the number of times his mind wandered to her throughout the day. He liked the idea of the padre marrying them before they left for Canada. She would have to leave her family, but it was her dream to travel and finally be independent.

Ardagh stopped as he came to a break in a long stone wall that ran beside the house. It looked like tank fire blew a hole through it and the ground was scattered with debris. Ardagh peered through to the house and saw the pot sitting over the campfire and men sitting around it. He paused and shook his head before he signalled Fritz to continue on and climb through the opening. Ardagh hesitated after he took his first step through. Something seemed off.

"Wait!" Ardagh ordered and Fritz stopped.

Ardagh carefully searched the ground in front of him as he stepped over a pile of bricks neatly stacked in a row, looking for any wires. He looked up to see Fritz standing in his way and, slowly checking the ground, stepped around him. Fritz, without warning, took a step forward. Ardagh watched Fritz put his foot down on the wet grass and heard a click under his boot.

# Chapter Thirty-Two

# Good Men

Sint Philipsland, Netherlands
May 9th, 1945

Koos sat on the dike with her diary and pen on her lap, looking out to the channel. The war was over, and she had yet to hear from Ardagh. There was a light breeze that picked up her hair and tossed it into her face, then died down. She automatically brushed her hair away. This act instantly reminded her of the last time she had kissed Ardagh and held him in her arms. He had unexpectedly brushed her hair off her face and said, *don't worry, we will always be together. I will be beside you, watching over you.* He worried about death. If you see a tree branch move or wind pull your hair, it will be me. *I will look after you.* It was corny. She missed their long conversations. She loved listening to his voice, his explanations, or asking for a funny Dutch word.

Koos and her family were deeply religious and strong Christians. The community had great expectations of the Canadian soldiers that dated the girls. You could have her, but you must stay and commit to her for life. It was the silent understanding. No one saw the risk in it. They had lived the risks for so long through the war. Liberation, the moment and excitement, heartened them to accept these boys as their own. It wouldn't happen to them. Not after what they had been through. It was destiny, their destiny, to be forever together and in love in front of God. Did it matter that they weren't married today? They could save it for later. Live now. Enjoy each other now. Koos and Ardagh believed in being together with no misgivings. It was true and moral for her in front of family, friends and God.

No reason for regrets. Koos looked at the diary. Her thoughts tumbled in her head, as she looked out to the ocean. She would travel across it someday. Today, the clouds were low and dark. She couldn't recall any days like this since before the Canadians had arrived to rescue them. Sunshine filled her every day. She imagined herself on the train, heading to Fort William. Holding his hand, watching the trees roll by. Sun shining in the train car. A new adventure. It helped bury those long, sad days before they'd met—Joost, Pieter and the *Hydra*.

She woke from her thoughts and began writing but only got to "My love Ardagh," and another wave of anxiety fell into her stomach. Now that she was truly in love, was it the fear of Ardagh being killed in action and her sins with him that caused this anxiety and fear? She tried to ignore the dizziness and added words to her diary that described her emotions and her plan for them. She would move to Canada and make it work. It would be heartbreaking for her family and difficult to leave her friends, but she couldn't expect him to stay. What was here for him?

She heard the noise of a motorcycle approaching in the distance and stood up.

\*\*\*

The padre slowed the motorcycle as he saw a little Dutch boy in the centre of the road. He waved to him, pulling over. The padre knew what he wanted. He shut off the motor before pulling off his gloves and goggles.

The padre sat back on his motorbike, stretching his tired arms out. He had been driving since the early morning hours. He needed to be back by the evening. It would be a long day, but he had made a promise and wanted to keep it. The trip gave him time to reflect on the last year and what had unfolded in front of his eyes. Training hard in England, the discipline of the men, keeping them out of trouble, the fear of the unknown hanging over them, the little decisions that they had fought over seemed silly today. They had been through a lot.

He wished he could go back to what he called the innocent times. These men, who were just boys, would still be getting lost in bars, pulling pranks, fighting, being alive and well. His spirit would be alive and well. The cold, hard reality of what they had undertaken hit them in the first battles in France. The cold and wet weather of Belgium and Holland tested their resolve many times. But when they saw how hungry and sick the Dutch people were, they strengthened their resolve to fight against the Nazis. They retested this in the Hochwald and the senseless, stubborn defence of the Germans. The Germans knew the war was coming to an end. Meeting the German people across the Rhine was unsettling. Many of them were quick to put their hands in the air. But as the end grew nearer, the fight became more desperate. To lose so many at the end. The Originals, they were the closest to him.

He'd watched boys grow up into men. They grew up quickly to survive. Many privates gained responsibility and became leaders in their own right. Remarkably, for him, he got to see it unfold in front of him. The leadership was good at recognizing when men could carry the responsibility and promoted them along. It was vital in their success as a unit over the year. The Originals from northern Ontario were fierce and feisty men. They were sometimes stubborn. Stubbornness proved to be the right quality in battle.

He had organized many prayers over the last several months to honour the boys that fell fighting for freedom. Most of them, he knelt over and gave them their last rites. He was in a unique position. The padre stood along with God and delivered prayers to all the men who had fallen in battle. They lost many experienced soldiers, and, like Corporal Shaw, some were still missing. But he had done his best and had written to their families. They did not go alone to God.

He was still writing his sermon and trying to gather words for one last ceremony to mark the end of the war. It seemed always to fall short trying to explain the losses. The drive cleared his head and gave him time to gather the words. He hoped to bring more meaning to the men who survived.

This little Dutch boy waved and gave him a smile. Some things were always the same wherever you went. Kids loved chocolate.

"Hello, son," the padre said. "Would you like some chocolate?"

"Ja, Dank je!" the boy said, as he ran up to the motorcycle. The boy snatched the bar out of the padre's hand.

"Dank! Dank je!"

The padre sat, stretching his legs and arms back to life while the boy devoured the chocolate. The skinny blond boy couldn't be more than seven years old. He looked no different from Canadian kids back in Ontario. Yet, he lived in a different world.

"What is your name?"

"Mijn naam is Rob."

"Now you wouldn't know a young girl named Koos, Koos van den Berg?"

"Ja! Dat is mijn tante."

"Can you take me to Koos?" the padre asked, then gestured to climb onto the motorcycle. The boy didn't hesitate for a second, climbing on the back, and hugging the Padre's waist. He had done this before. Many times, throughout Holland, in liberated town after town, the soldiers entertained the boys, driving down the streets. The men with children back home had easily connected with Dutch kids who were blue-eyed and blond-haired.

As they pulled up outside the house, sunken down behind the 16th-century dike and snuggled beside its neighbour with a small rectangular front yard, the envy of the street, the padre recalled now this busy corner of Voorstraat and Zuiddijk with a canteen and parking for the small but lethal Bren gun carriers of the Lake Sups. It was a convenient location near a sandy beach with a loading dock. It was close to the town entrances and provided an unobstructed view of the peninsula. He had spent many hours in front of the old cafe. This was one of their favourite Dutch towns, as it had made the regiment famous. It was funny in a way how war makes strange partners. They never imagined Sint Philipsland would be the place the regiment had its greatest success, sinking three German ships. The lads couldn't be more different coming from Fort William than from people of Sint Philipsland, but they had built a bond and a common purpose with the town's folk after a few days. This religious town loosened up to some extent. They were now free—no more food shortages or Germans.

The padre climbed off the motorbike and looked along the dike. His eyes landed on the familiar yellow windmill, hoping for a comforting sign, but its sails were still. He took in the fresh ocean air. These were the most difficult conversations. He still struggled for the right words. He knew Ardagh loved her. Hopefully, her English was better than his Dutch. The clouds hung unusually low today. No wind added to the quiet gloom of the polder.

The padre searched the dike and down the street for Koos. He saw a young woman running along the dike in his direction. She gave an enormous wave as she must have recognized the motorcycle and him standing next to it. He waved to her in response, assuming it was Koos.

\*\*\*

Koos hurried along the dike. The motorcycle meant it was Ardagh. He was back and now the war was over for them. No more worry or danger. She broke out into a run, watching her feet fall one after the other carefully along the damp grass of the dike. He seemed to be so far away from her. Her heart pounded in her chest. She wanted him close forever. Tears blurred her vision. She was almost with him. She couldn't stumble now. Koos wiped her eyes and stopped running, catching her breath. She wanted him to see her happy. She looked up at him in the distance, but something was wrong. He hadn't moved. He waited for her. Why hadn't he moved? The soldier stood as if he didn't know her.

***

The padre watched Koos hurry along the dike. What would he say? How could he tell her? Ardagh loved her. She was so young. Would she know when she saw him? She gradually slowed to a walk. He tried to think of what to say. Would she overcome this? *Those born of God overcome the world.* He could now make out her face. It was Koos. Her brown curly hair blew in the wind as she stared down at him. She covered her face and cried out, staying at the top of the dike, swaying like a broken rose, and then collapsed.

The Padre stared up at her, realized his mistake, and hurriedly climbed the dike. He could hear her sobs before he reached her.

"Is he dead?" Koos cried out. She stared up at him, begging she was wrong. Tears streamed down from her swollen eyes, but she knew.

"I'm so sorry for your loss," the padre said when he reached her. "I promised I would tell you in person."

Koos clutched her stomach and screamed into the dark cloud above them.

"It'll be alright," he said, kneeling down to comfort her. He embraced her, holding her tight. "I'm so sorry. Let us pray for him."

Her sobs deepened and shook with every breath.

***

The padre stood at the centre of the stage with the Union Jack at half-mast and the 2nd Canadian Infantry Corps band at his back. The full regiment, along with representatives of the other units that had fought alongside them, stood in a U-shape facing him. Each Company stood together in clean, pressed uniforms, reminiscent of the earlier days, dressed to honour the one hundred and ninety-six who had given their lives. Hundreds of Dutch civilians lined the roads surrounding the grassy field, showing support for the men who had rescued them from the Germans. The crowd and regiment stood silent. The padre started the solemn ceremony with a prayer and hymn followed by the Roll of Honour. He had chosen the scripture 1 John 5:4 mainly to remind the men that "We keep his commandments and whosoever is born of God overcometh the world." They had overcome the world through the last year.

Before the padre started his speech, he slowly looked over the men in front of him and gathered his thoughts. They had been through so much. The war was still fresh. It had ended only a month ago, and life had transformed. The many faces of those that had fallen distracted his thoughts as he read his speech.

"In answer to the wrongs committed by powerful men, good men challenged, good men fought, and good men died."

The padre realized that too many friends, brothers, sons and fathers lost their lives. Too many. He chose not to mention just one. The three boys lying next to each other as they charged a German machine gun, the many broken and distorted bodies he had knelt next to for their last rites: terrible scenes that no one should see or experience. The words seemed to fall short, and he raised his voice to emphasize the importance of remembering them. "This day we honour them and..." These young men in front of him must build on this sacrifice and not

waste it. "As we stand on a bright threshold of a new world..."
They have to carry forward and live to the fullest for the lives
lost. The men must be reminded of the qualities of those fallen
men and make good under God in their lives.

"Selfless devotion, unequalled endurance and superb courage were qualities attributed to the fallen."

His thoughts fell to the last men that died. They were fresh
in his mind. The words that he hoped had comforted Koos but
knew still fell short.

In closing, he prayed. *"May God receive them into His eter-
nal care."*

# Chapter Thirty-Three

# Hotel Hubertus

Assen, Netherlands
June 1945

Koos strolled down Kerkstraat in her new hometown of Assen. She hadn't wanted to leave Sint Philipsland, but was forced to go by her parents. They said it would be just for a year. She hated them for it. But now, after a few weeks in Assen, she looked at things differently. She enjoyed living with her brother and his family. It allowed her to breathe for the first time since the end of the war, but kept some stability of family. She enjoyed looking after Rob while her brother got settled working for their uncle and she still had time for long walks and bike rides that gave her a sense of freedom. Getting away had made all the difference.

The entire family was still picking themselves up from the harsh winter of starvation and joblessness at the end of the war. David had returned, thin and weak, but safe. It pained her to learn that Joost had partially told her the truth. He had helped to protect David by giving him food and talking to the guards that looked over his labour detail. Their family had been spared and were better off than many.

Most of the days flowed one into another. But today, she had a plan, a first step. It wouldn't take much now that she was living further north and closer to Germany. Hard to believe it could be a benefit, despite the realities of her life now. She was closer to Ardagh and his grave site. That gave her some comfort, and she had a plan. It was in her pocket, she reached in again to touch the soft folded paper that would allow her to accomplish it. She quickened her pace, almost skipping along among the open shops as she headed to her new favourite cafe. It reminded her of their cafe in Bruinisse. Everyone was out and about, some holding hands, soldiers in their clean uniforms. There were no guns and tanks, but the soldiers had stayed for the time being. Only the police carried guns, it was almost unnatural compared with the last five years of her life.

*Every day gets better,* she told herself as she stopped in front of the cafe. She stared at her reflection in the window and turned sideways to see the shape of her dress. It was tighter than she liked. She smelt the Stroopwafels, and it brought back memories of her meetings with van Hulst. The cafe in Assen was not far from the Brink, where many of the Resistance had been held by the Germans. After the war ended, the stories of arrested Resistance fighters became known. Nearly two thousand had been shot by the Germans or sent to concentration camps where they died. She was one of the lucky ones.

Koos turned back to the window. The wind picked up and blew her hair across her face. A soldier appeared behind her. Was it him? Was he still alive? She pushed her hair away and turned to face him. But he was gone. She stared back at her reflection and wrapped her arms around her stomach. She knew it wasn't him, but it filled her heart with hope when she saw a soldier walk by the way he did. It brought back the memory of him. That he was real. It was how she found moments of happiness. It kept him close despite the passing of time, and she believed he still lived in her presence. She looked forward to these moments and embraced them.

Her plan to visit Ardagh's grave, she hoped, would help release her and strengthen her memory of him. If she could deliver ration cards under the Germans' noses, she could figure out how to get a pass into Germany. She had taken all the steps and paperwork and befriended the Canadians posted in the town. It didn't take long for her to organize her trip to Germany.

Koos would leave tomorrow. She had tried every day to remember him, how he looked, his mannerisms and gestures. She had hidden away from her family and wrote as much as she could those first few days after learning from the padre of his death. It helped calm her. The words he used, and phrases. She knew enough English, but some were hard to remember from all his favourite movies. She couldn't wait to see his films to better understand their meaning. "We're not in Kansas anymore, Toto," or "Koos, I think this is the beginning of a beautiful friendship," and "Here's looking at you, kid." She practised her English every day, and it brought him closer to her. She resolved to learn how to read and write English so she could write to his family. Every day, she wrote to him her own words, feelings, mood, and future. She only had a few photos of him, and she wanted more. She needed to learn more about him and his life in Fort William. But she knew that if she could see his cross and where he was buried, if she could touch it, it would give her peace and start the healing.

Was it fate that she had the best seat in the house when the Canadians had shown up? The stress on their faces from the front lines had pained her. Although they tried their best to hide the anxiety and fatigue of the fighting, the stories she overheard hung in the air and were thick with a bitter taste. For them to put their lives on the line still made her heart bounce and ache. The love grew strong in those times and was fast to hold and lock in. A gold chest for them to keep forever. They were the lucky ones that found love and the deepest bonds that most would never have in their lifetimes.

She kept her thoughts and memories to herself as a gift or

pleasure or treat, not to be shared. It was the idea of loving Ardagh. She was still in love. It was her way of holding on, the only way to survive and carry her promise to him. What did his life mean if no one remembered his thoughts, views, and dreams of life? He held an enormous burden, protecting his friends, doing his job, carrying on for his buddies. It drove him day after day despite the dangers.

They had their places. Koos still visited them and took in the cherished moments and held them tight.

The pain was still so fresh. Their time together was short, which saddened her. But she still went on. She knew the places she and Ardagh had shared would grow old and change, but her heart, she hoped, would stay filled with joy when she visited them, remembering those moments. She would keep them to herself. She felt a wave of nausea and her stomach grumbled. She pushed through the door of the cafe and sat at the first table. Her body ached as she laid her arms on the table and lowered her head. She would see his grave tomorrow.

*\*\**

Koos was getting close. The Kusten Canal was at her back. She paused only briefly on the German bridge crossing to take in the quiet flow of the water and gather her thoughts. She pedalled her way down the minor German back roads, taking in the flowers and lush tall trees, feeling her way. It wasn't much further. Several homes looked untouched and were quiet. It was only a few miles past the Kusten Canal to reach the crossroad that the lieutenant had shown her on the map. The small town of Danikhorst, Germany, was not more than a small hotel and a few homes.

Was she crazy to want to see where it happened and to visit his grave? She had received the travel passes from the Canadian military and was even given a ride for a good portion of the trip. Now she wanted to ride the last few miles on her own to clear her head and think about what she would say to him.

Although it had been only a few months since the fighting ended, northern Germany was almost unscathed from the war. Many homes had been cleaned up, their bright red bricks stacked neatly beside the houses, ready for the walls to be put back in place. The young men were slow to come back, so she mostly noticed women, children, and older men pedalling along the road. Unaware she was Dutch, many waved to her as she passed, and she instinctively waved back, somewhat stunned, but couldn't think of an alternative.

It was very green, and several of the large trees were still standing along the roadside. It was strange to see, as they had cut so many trees down to create roadblocks in Holland, but not so here. These little things angered her. For all the suffering she had seen and lived through, it seemed none of that had happened here.

As she rounded a long bend in the road, she saw a line of homes and a short farmer's field on the right with an impressive two-story home. She stopped her bike and climbed off to walk the last half mile. A couple of younger women were standing in front of the home, chatting with some soldiers sitting in their jeep. They were easily recognizable as Lake Superiors with their red berets. The scene in front of her was very familiar, and for some strange reason, gave her extra strength and courage. These men were her people, her family. They were her heroes that had rescued them from the darkest days she had ever known.

"Hello," Koos said in English as she approached the jeep. "Can you help me?" she asked the blond-haired corporal sitting in the jeep, ignoring the two young German women who looked like they were similar in age. The frumpy brunette was wearing a tight yellow flowered dress that highlighted her chest, which spilled out. They obviously wanted something from the two men, based on the looks she received as she had walked up.

"And where did you come from?" the corporal with sandy blond hair said as he climbed out of the jeep, stretching his legs, ignoring the two German ladies.

Koos was a little surprised by the sudden questioning manner of the Canadian soldier. Was he trying to pick her up? But an edge of anger in his voice made her wonder.

She inadvertently said in Dutch, "The Netherlands, to see my..." and her voice trailed off. And she whispered, "Fallen... love..." before she stared at the ground. She had lost her confidence now that she had thought of Ardagh.

"I think she's Dutch!" the other soldier said from where he sat in the front of the jeep, holding the taller skinny blond German girl's hand.

"What did she say?"

"She is here to see her fallen love," the brunette said in English. "You poor thing, to come all the way into Germany for your lover."

Koos's eyes watered, though her face hardened.

"Yes, he has fallen," Koos said. Emotions of the long journey overtook her, and tears flowed down her cheeks despite her wiping them away.

"Wait, I missed that. Why is she crying now?" the corporal said. "What is she saying about the fallen?"

The brunette pulled her close and wrapped her arms around her, "There... there, it's okay... it's okay," she said. "We are here for you."

"There are a few Canadian graves in the area, but I know of one that is close by. Hopefully, it's the one she is looking for," the blond girl said.

Koos groaned louder with sobs as her emotions continued to boil to the surface.

"Let's take her there now, so it will help her stop crying."

"Don't be so rude," the brunette said. "It's all good. We'll take you to the grave." She helped her into the back of the jeep.

The jeep, with Koos's bike in the back, along with the other women, pulled up alongside an empty grass-covered field behind a home that stood untouched but by the bright late afternoon sun. Tucked just off the road on the other side of a row of trees sat a lone white cross. It was standard procedure to bury fallen soldiers near where they were killed in action until the main cemetery was commissioned. They all climbed out of the jeep but allowed Koos to approach on her own. She pulled a small bunch of flowers from her basket, and she collapsed in front of the lone weed-covered grave. She placed the flowers on his grave before pulling the weeds that had grown.

His name and rank stabbed at her heart as she stared at the cross in silence. She reached out and ran her fingers over the makeshift cross, slowly letting her fingers fall over the letters, gently outlining his name, then his rank and identification number. She closed her eyes and imagined her fingers falling over his face, his eyes, nose and then his chest. Until now, it had been unbelievable to think he was gone. She laid her head on his chest and felt the cold earth, scooping the wet soil up in her hands, and smelled it. She grabbed the white cross and pressed her hand hard against it, leaving her handprint. Their time together on any timescale was short. Four short, fleeting visits that seemed like a lifetime ago. Every moment was fresh in her mind and alive inside her.

She felt a light flutter and put her hand on her belly, pushing it out as she sat up on her knees. He would live on through this child. *At least she had part of him,* she thought. Now Ardagh had met his baby. And the movement in her was like a sign that he knew. It was all she asked for over the last few months. It would start the healing.

"No one must know," her mother had said. How could she live with herself?

"It would be good for the baby and her mental state if she went away," the doctor said. It was true, her time away living with her brother and his family had helped. She wasn't show-ing, but the sickness had passed, and her energy had returned. She was supposed to give up the baby, that was what most did. But she had a plan that would allow her to be with the baby, and her brother had agreed. Her brother and sister-in-law would raise it as their own. No one else would know that the baby wasn't theirs.

Koos awoke from her trance as she sensed the shadows of the others approach her.

"Do you know how it happened?" Koos asked as she stood up.

"Sorry, we don't, but possibly the hotel owner down the road may have an idea. That was as far as he would have made it before he was killed."

The young German girl elbowed him. "Shh, be respectful."

"It is Hotel Hubertus, in Danikhorst. They are a friendly family, and perhaps you can stay with them," the corporal said in a softer tone and pointed down the road. "They are still picking up the pieces from the war, but they have fixed the roof, and they have decent food, despite the shortages."

"I'll ride on my own. We have come this far," Koos said, pat-ting her stomach. "I'll be back again tomorrow."

"Wonderful, we'll let them know you're coming," the young German girl said, trying to sound cheerful.

"Dank je!" Koos said as she watched them drive off. She would head down a new road and a new place on her own, to the last place Ardagh had been.

Koos smiled and picked up her bike, pedalling hard at first, the breeze hitting her face. Gliding forward, tears flowed down her cheeks as she felt the flicker of life, knowing she would car-ry Ardagh with her forever.

# Epilogue

# Those We Carry

Green Bay, Ontario, Canada
April 25th, 1946

The beautiful Lake Superior spring day felt like the start of something new as they sat in silence, squeezed in around the cottage kitchen table. Robert Cadieu sat at the table with his two boys, Hank and Wilf, at his side. They were real men now, men who survived the war, but each broken in some way. Wilf was still recovering from his physical injuries and Hank from his mental anguish. Robert's daughters, Lila and Elaine, along with their mother, busied themselves in the kitchen preparing dinner. Hank's new girlfriend, Sybil, stood by his side. She was a godsend to Hank and the family. She stormed into their life and brought strength to an otherwise spiralling down Hank.

Danny Payne was to arrive at any moment. It had been a long year since the end of the war, and the news of losing Ardagh so close to the end, made the pain more profound. They had nothing of Ardagh to hold on to, none of his personal effects, which made his death harder to believe. The paper pushers in Ottawa had finally answered Robert's letters. Ardagh's duffle bag had arrived at the armoury in Fort William just a few days before April 25th, exactly a year since his death. They wanted to meet as a family to open his bag. It would start the healing, they hoped.

Danny entered the cottage through the back door carrying Ardagh's army duffle bag and placed it on the table. He turned the opening toward Robert and sat down. They continued in silence and stared at the bag with 'Cadieu' in white block writing across the side. They could hear the kids running and chasing each other along the beach. Marv was screaming, "I got you, I got you!" and a quiet, anxious laugh filled the room as they all turned to check on the kids. Elaine stood up and checked on her son, making sure Marv was okay. Rita walked over and stood behind Robert, restraining herself from the strong desire to grab the bag and wrap her arms around it. She instead wrapped her arms around her husband and gave a deep sigh.

"Alright, let's get to it," Robert said, breaking the silence. He reached over and pushed open the bag, carefully removing each piece, laying them out on the table. It seemed like so little for his young, sacrificed life. The bag revealed a uniform, a knitted sweater they had sent him, his kitbag with a razor and brush, an extra pair of shoes and a box.

The first item passed around was a stack of black and white photos that could easily fit in the palm of your hand. No one touched the German Luger that sat cold and foreign on the table. A small pocketknife was in a grey bag, along with a ten-cent souvenir coin, a five Mark German note, and a penknife.

"Thank you, Danny, for coming. We wish it never..." Robert coughed and blew his nose. "It's still hard to believe..."

"I would like you to know that he didn't suffer. I know because I was there when it happened. We were in a town called Danikhorst, in the northwest part of Germany. It was late in the day, and we had just attacked a roadblock at this crossroad town comprising a family-run hotel and a few houses. Ardagh's platoon led the way and took the position. He was really professional and detailed."

"Are you sure you're talking about Ardagh?" Hank said.

"And you're one to talk," Wilf said with a laugh.

"I know, I know... It's hard to believe from when he left, but it's true. By this time, he was a veteran sergeant that cared about his men, and he always watched out for the new ones. He was helping one of these new guys, a Private Fritz Anderson. Taking him to his position. That was the type of leader he was. Do it himself. We lost a lot of guys because of mines at the end of the war, more than anything else. The Germans left them everywhere to delay us and cause chaos. It did both and made everyone very cautious. Ardagh was with Fritz to make sure he didn't trip into anything. Also, toward the end, we were coming up against Navy Cadets of the Kriegsmarine and their armaments. Some explosions were tremendous. We would fire into builds and set off some of these devices, and the explosion would take your breath away."

"The mortars weren't snowballs either," Wilf said, lifting his leg up to show the deep red scar down his leg. "The Jerries didn't care about anything."

"You're right, Wilf. It was never easy. We were so careful in the end. That's why Harp was holding his hand. He didn't want to lose anyone. He was confident to do the job."

"I wish I had met him," Sybil said.

"You'll have to settle with this big-eared lug instead," Wilf said, slapping Hank on the back.

"Harp had a girl in Holland. Her name was Koos. That's something else I wanted to mention. I have her address for you to get in touch. They were in love and talking about marriage. I read her last letter to him. He was still the same old Harp, a little clueless around love. There's still a lot of chaos and destruction in Europe. There are so many displaced people, and it's difficult to find anyone. She moved away, but I think her family will pass on any letters for you. She was thinking of moving to Canada."

"I'll write," Lila said. "She sounds wonderful. Thank you, Danny."

"I tried to find her before we left, but I ran out of time. The padre kept his promise and told her. She went to Germany to visit his grave but then never came back to her town."

"So, when did it all happen?" Robert asked.

"Sorry, it was just after I read the letter. Harp and Fritz left us, and he was leading him to his position when I heard the massive explosion. I thought for sure they were both dead. But I was wrong. Fritz was lying a few feet away screaming with a large piece of metal stuck in him, and Ardagh was not too far from him. Ardagh was..." Danny took a deep breath, and his voice grew softer as he stared at the table.

"The explosion riddled him with metal and tore him up pretty well, and he couldn't have suffered. I helped Fritz, and we got him to the aid station. Before he left, he told me a bit more about what happened. They walked through a backyard with a low wall, and that's where it happened..."

Danny's face darkened, and he looked out at the kids running along the beach. Robert felt his chest tighten and throat go dry. He tried to look away, but still couldn't believe the story. Knowing more was like a hammer pounding his chest with every additional detail, but he didn't want it to stop despite the pain.

Danny's lips trembled, and he wiped his face and said, "They heard the click of a trigger. He said Ardagh pushed him away at that second, and it saved his life. He swears it's the truth. They both dove to the right, but Ardagh was unlucky."

"God..." Robert said, turning away. He closed his eyes trying to picture what had happened and the feeling of shrapnel hitting his son's body. He wanted to hold him one more time.

"Ardagh saved his life," Danny whispered. "He didn't hesitate."

\*\*\*

Danny left them, and they sat exhausted with so much to take in. Robert gathered Ardagh's things and placed them back in the duffle bag.

"Can I have the pocketknife?" Sybil asked.

"Why?" Robert asked. "What would you do with it?"

"From what Hank tells me, it was Marv's knife originally. Am I right?"

"Yes, you are. I forgot about that."

"I would like Hank to give it back to Marv. Maybe heal a wound that is deep. It would be a start."

"You Scottish are softer than you let on," Robert said, pulling it out of the bag. His eyes filled and he wiped them before he handed the knife to Hank. "Marv will be excited to have it. He'll always remember Ardagh."

\*\*\*

Hank grabbed two fishing rods and walked out to the beach. The kids were playing kick the can, and a group of kids were huddled in jail, waiting for someone to kick the can and set them free. Marv ran past him, leaping over the lawn chair and kicking the can across the beach to a screeching cheer. The jailed kids continued to scream as they all took off again to hide.

"Marv!" Hank shouted. "Want to go fishing with me? We can head up the creek."

Marv stopped in front of Hank. He hadn't spoken to Hank in over a year and had only seen him stop by at his grandma's a few times. A wave of anxiety spread over him and the vision of Joey. Joey loved to play kick the can even though he always got caught.

"I know a secret fishing spot that Ardagh found, and I have something of his to give you," Hank added quickly.

Ardagh's duffle bag and what it contained had consumed Marv's thoughts over the past several months. No one told him when it arrived.

"Did we finally get Ardagh's bag?"

"Yes, we just went through it, and your dad thought it would be best that I talk to you about it. Let's walk to the creek and fish. I'll tell you then. I think that's what Ardagh would want," Hank said as he handed Marv Ardagh's rod. Marv took the rod and turned, heading down the beach in front of Hank. They walked in silence until they were far up the creek.

"This is the spot right here," Hank said as he squeezed through two poplar trees and stepped around a short cedar tree. "Let's throw a few casts."

Marv threw the first cast and reeled it in before Hank. The sun was still high, and Marv saw why Ardagh had picked this spot. It was a flat open area that you had to squeeze into through the woods, but that still got the late evening sun. The creek turned and dropped into a couple of sizable pools. Most would walk by it for a more easily reachable area, but once you were in, there was lots of room.

"It has been a while since I have done this," Hank said. "I think it was with Ardagh just before he left. It's funny how time and things go by before you notice."

Marv threw another cast and said, "Yeah, it doesn't seem real anymore now that the war is over."

"It's hard to talk about for most who have gone through it," Hank threw a cast onto the second level and let the red and white lure float down. "I hope you can understand that someday. I lost a lot of friends, and I sometimes forget their faces, and others I can't let go."

A trout minnow smaller than the lure swam up for a bite and then flipped away back into the dark water and disappeared. Marv copied Hank and threw a cast to the top pond, but reeled into a snag.

"Shoot..."

"Don't worry, I'll pull it out."

Marv peered down into the pond and saw the red lure

caught between two rocks. It reminded him when Ardagh would help untangle his poor casts. He was always spending time with him at the camp, but it was getting hard to remember.

"I'm sorry about Joey," Hank said, almost like a whisper.

"I know," Marv said, watching Hank climb up the creek bank to pull out the lure. He had never used the wagon again, or raced. The street had felt empty since Joey's death. He wished Joey was here now instead of Hank. Hank crouched over the pond, staring into the water, silent.

"Do you want me to pull?"

"Ardagh should have seen him... I think... It was dark... He should have seen him..." Hank said into the pond, letting out a quiet sob. Marv watched his back heave and quiver as he spoke. "I don't know what we would have done if it was you... I'm... sorry."

The memory of smeared blood and the sound of bottles rolling across the street washed out the running water and filled Marv's thoughts. A cloud blocked out the sun, and a shadow covered the fishing hole. He closed his eyes to wash away the scene. He could still see Ardagh's face as he threw him in the water, just for a second.

"It wasn't Ardagh's fault," Marv said, rubbing his eyes. "I told Joey to stay close to the sidewalk, but he stayed in the middle. It was an accident. I wish Joey was here. He would like this spot. He could fish better than me."

Marv opened his eyes and pulled on the rod. The lure was free, and he reeled it back in.

"Ardagh was... I have something for you. Sybil and I asked your grandpa if it was okay. I know it won't bring Joey or Ardagh back, but it helped me through carrying the burden of some of my friends that were lost to have something to remember them by."

Hank opened his hand and showed Marv the pocketknife.

He forced himself to smile, but his hand still shook as he handed it to Marv.

"I understand you gave this to Ardagh before he left. I know he wanted to give it back to you himself. He is probably smiling now as I give it to you."

Marv held the knife in his hands and turned it all around. He opened it and ran his finger along the blade. It was sharper than he remembered, and it had a smear of red on the tip. The sleeve still had dried blood in it, Ardagh's blood. He put it into his pocket.

"This isn't my knife."

"What do you mean? Your dad said it was. The knife was in Ardagh's kit, along with his other stuff."

"The knife wasn't mine. It never was."

"I don't understand. Is this the knife you gave Ardagh?"

"Yes, but it was Joey's. It was Joey's knife. It was supposed to protect him, but it didn't."

The cloud blew away, and the sun reappeared, and Marv felt the warmth hit him. He threw another cast into the lower pond. Hank hooked his lure onto the fishing pole and laid it down.

"Listen, I lost a lot of friends over in Europe and one thing that helped us was to have something of theirs to hold on to, and it helped carry the memory of them and brought you closer. Just like a story they told or a funny word. Even things we did together."

"Like this fishing hole?"

"Yes, if you can piece together enough of these things, carrying memories or a small item helps to always remember them. That way, those we carry with us will lead us through our days and give us the strength to carry on, no matter the odds. We talked about death a lot while we flew our missions. Sharing the memories brought us closer together and gave us purpose. Kept us whole, at least a bit."

Two crows flew into the small clearing and called out to each other. Marv stared up at them. It was better to have something, he guessed, and he patted his pocket. He would try to race again for Joey.

"Can we go back now?"

"Yeah, probably time for supper. Can I show you something else?"

Hank reached into the back of his shirt and pulled out a black gun. A German Luger, just like he had seen in all the movies.

"It's not loaded. You can hold it. It was in Ardagh's kit bag. Danny said he got the Luger from a German SS officer before they sunk those ships. Cool, eh?"

"It's really heavy but super cool!"

Marv held up the Luger and pointed toward the crows, pretending to fire.

"Peeewww... Puusshhh."

"If you promise to come and visit Sybil and me, I'll show you the Luger again. Maybe we can shoot it someday. Do you promise?"

"Thanks, Uncle Hank, I promise."

\*\*\*

They followed the path back to the beach, listening to the crows. Stepping onto the beach, they saw Wilf in the distance and Marv gave an excited wave while running through the shallow water to him. Wilf picked Marv up and threatened to throw him in the water.

"No!" Marv squirmed in his arms.

"Don't worry, it's only water!"

"No, Uncle Wilf, I don't want to lose my knife!"

"Aw, I guess Hank finally gave it to you."

"Did you see the gun?"

"Yes, I have seen my share..." Wilf said as put Marv back on the beach and knelt beside him.

"Can you tell me the story of the Sleeping Giant?"

"Sure, why?"

"We were just talking about Harp," Hank said, giving a half smile and nod. Wilf blew out a heavy breath, looking across the lake. The Sleeping Giant stood out today more than most and the lower sun brightened the image of a man lying with his arms crossed. It was as if God was reaching down to touch him.

"Uncle Ardagh said that the Nanajibou was a hero. He turned to stone to protect his people, and that is what the soldiers did and not to forget to wave to the Sleeping Giant every day. Did Uncle Ardagh turn to stone?"

Hank and Wilf's watering eyes met.

"Yes, he did. I'm sorry we couldn't... There are lots that didn't make it," Wilf said as he put his arm around Marv. Hank bent down and hugged them both.

Marv followed the clouds swirling over the Sleeping Giant. He would never forget playing on this beach with Joey and Uncle Ardagh. He wished he could go back to those days. Marv pulled his uncles close and knew he was not alone. They had also lost Ardagh and Joey.

They would always remember looking out across Lake Superior to their own Sleeping Giants.

# Author's Note

Thank you for reading, *Those We Carry*. It was inspired by the stories told to me by my father Mervyn Saxberg about his uncle's Ardagh, Gerald and Wilf Cadieu during the Second World War. Everyone carries someone with them, and my father was no different. I think it was the main reason he told me the stories of my great uncles. He was deeply affected by what happened during the war and losing his uncle. I only met my Great Uncle Gerald "Hank" and the memories of him are faded and short. The stories came from my uncles and the Lake Superior soldiers my father met while working at the grain elevators several years after the war. As I dug deeper into the stories of my uncles and reading the Lake Superior Regiment diaries, nearly every story turned out to be true. These fascinating accounts captured my imagination and motivated me to write this story.

The theme of carrying those who we have lost became clearer as I developed the characters and tied their stories together. *Those We Carry* is deeper than just remembrance. It is about those we have lost and carrying their legacy, stories, values and ideas. But it can also be simply the things they have said, an object they cared the most about or something they made with their own hands. We hold on to these pieces and it changes us.

My father kept Ardagh's duffel bag. He used it for his hockey equipment, and I remember seeing it hanging on the basement laundry room wall for years until it was damaged in one of the many floods in Winnipeg. Gerald kept Ardagh's German Luger and would show it to my father, telling him the stories of Ardagh.

This is a story of fiction, but I tried my best to stay true to the events as told through the Lake Superior Regiment war diaries and *In the Face of Danger* by Lieutenant Colonel George F. Stanley. The major battles and events are true, but like any fictional story, I adapted them to tell Ardagh's story. Several of the events that Ardagh went through are true but happened to other Lake Superior soldiers. A notable example of this was when Ardagh got captured and he shot the two German soldiers. A German patrol caught Sergeant A. G. Johnson and when they were bringing him back, he pulled out his revolver, killing them. I tried to use as many actual accounts as possible to make the story more authentic to the reader.

One of the most difficult truths within this story was the tragic accident and death of Joey Powley. The details in the prologue are based on my father's memory of the event and newspaper articles. The fictional part of the story is that Ardagh was responsible. I struggled with having Ardagh be the bad guy, but in the end, I wanted a deeper struggle for him as a character to go through in addition to the fictional event around Jim's death. In truth, Gerald Cadieu accidentally killed Joey. It happened after Gerald returned from completing his thirty missions in March 1945. He was charged and found guilty, but received a light sentence. It's a family tragedy that I felt needed to be included and to tell Joey's story.

One of the interesting stories my father told me was Ardagh sneaking onto the bomber with Gerald. We have a family photo of Ardagh wearing an RAF jacket that encouraged me to add it into the story. From my research, this happened from time to time, so I felt comfortable adding it.

In my research, I noticed how detailed and professional the records for the Lake Superior Regiment were in recording what took place, ranging from the weather, to where they stayed, to what movie they watched, to who was killed or wounded. I did my best to capture these details and place them into the story.

I spent five years researching *Those We Carry*, and I travelled to Europe several times. It amazed me to see where these events took place and how they have stayed the same. I would highly recommend visiting the places within this story from Thunder Bay to Guildford, Sint Philipsland, Bruinisse, 's-Hertogenbosch, Hochwald Forest, and Danikhorst. It is definitely worth going and experiencing a few of these places such as the Sleeping Giant, The Spotted Cow, Hotel Oosterschelde, Restaurant de Blauwe Sluis, Landhotel Lebensart, and Hotel Hubertus. I met the owner of the Hotel Hubertus and asked him if he knew of a Canadian soldier being killed near his hotel. To my surprise, he stepped outside the hotel and showed me the spot where Ardagh died, over seventy years later.

I had several conversations and correspondence with Koos van den Berg's family, and I did my best to keep her fundamental character accurate. Her niece, Anja Romijn, was a great help and resource to build Koos's character. Koos's nephew Rob de Raat, still owns the home that she stayed at looking out on to the square where the Lake Superior Regiment set up their canteen. Most of her story is fictional, but her base character strengths are true. Koos was a very caring person, and she looked after her nieces and nephews. She loved to ride her bike, and I carried that theme throughout the story. Koos most likely met Ardagh in front of the canteen. The daring rescue of Koos from Joost and her relationship with Willie were fictional. Although, I like to think because of the small community and the number of times the German ships anchored in Bruinisse that she may have brushed shoulders with the likes of Wilhelm Clausen.

Rob remembered the liberation of Sint Philipsland and his recollections helped me tell the story. It is not surprising to learn there were many soldiers that fell in love in the towns they liberated. The soldiers were looked upon as heroes. There were more than six thousand liberation babies born from Canadian soldiers after the war. The Second World War had an everlasting effect on the Netherlands and to this day they still celebrate their freedom by lighting candles on the graves of Canadian soldiers marking the end of the war.

*Those We Carry* closely follows the battles of the Lake Superior Regiment through Europe. There were many sacrifices made by these soldiers. They came from various walks of life: labourers, mail clerks, farmers, miners, and loggers. My great uncles all died young. It is a common theme based on the research of the short list of soldiers mentioned in this story. They stepped up and defended our country to keep us free at a significant cost. *Selfless devotion, unequalled endurance and superb courage were qualities attributed to these men.*

These were the answers the padre so eloquently referred to in his speech to the men at the end of the war. *In answer to the wrongs committed by powerful men, good men challenged, good men fought, and good men died.* The padre made many speeches after the war based on what I have found in the newspaper archives. The story of the Hochwald Gap battle was centre to his message and the hope that the men carry forward and live to the fullest for the lives lost. Everyone must be reminded of the qualities of those fallen men and make good in their lives.

We know how Koos and Ardagh met. Koos visited his grave for over ten years and corresponded with Ardagh's older sister, sending them photographs of herself at his grave. Koos moved away for a year after the war ended. Her father bought a new fishing boat, which he named *Koosje*. She returned and lived with her parents, taking care of them until they died. Koos never married. On her deathbed, she called out Ardagh's name over and over before passing away. Koos truly loved Ardagh. Was a child the deeper reason for this? We will never know. But we do know Koos carried Ardagh with her throughout her life.

# Appendix

## Main Characters

### "Harp" Ardagh O. Cadieu
(March 11, 1921 - April 25, 1945)

Ardagh was a labourer from Fort William, Ontario. He had four brothers and four sisters. Ardagh signed up in June 1940 and was one of the LSR originals. He loved fishing, hunting, basketball and hockey. Ardagh was wounded once and promoted to sergeant in March 1945. He died leading his platoon, tripping a booby trap after they consolidated their positions behind the Hotel Hubertus in Danikhorst, Germany. Ardagh did not kill Joey. I wanted a deeper struggle for him as a character to go through in addition to the fictional event around Jim's death. This tragedy happened in March 1945 and it was Gerald Cadieu who tragically killed Joey after returning from the war. It's a family tragedy that I felt needed to be included and to have Joey's story told.

### "Koos" Jacoba van den Berg
(September 10, 1926 - January 9, 2006)

Koos never married nor had children. We have speculated that she may have had a child with Ardagh, but it was based on our own dream for them. On her deathbed, she called out Ardagh's name over and over. It wasn't until we reached out to the family and shared the letters Koos had sent to Ardagh's sister after the war that the family learned about their relationship.

We have photos and correspondence from ten years after the war as well as when Ardagh's sister and husband visited in the fifties. So, we know she visited his grave regularly after the war.

## Private Wilfred D. Cadieu
(May 21, 1918 - January 27, 1979)

Wilf was born in Fort William, Ontario and worked for the Canadian Pacific Railway. Wilf signed up in August 1940 and left two kids behind to fight the Germans. He was wounded twice and spent three months in the hospital recovering. By all accounts, he was a great hockey player, playing pro hockey in Scotland before the war. He went back to Canadian Pacific Railway as a Trainman after the war.

## "Hank" Lieutenant Gerald J. Cadieu
(February 8, 1925 - November 12, 1976)

Gerald completed his required thirty missions and was credited with shooting down one German Messerschmitt 109. He served in the Royal Air Force in the 90th squadron. I tried to describe this event as best I could from the records. He returned to Fort William to help train pilots until the end of the war. Gerald was responsible and sentenced in the hit and run described in the prologue, killing Joey Powley. He later volunteered to fight in Korea and served as a lieutenant until September 1952.

## Jean

Jean is a fictional character.

## Rob de Raat

Rob was Koos's nephew, and he still lives in the home where Koos stayed after the flooding in Sint Philipsland. He is a similar age to my father and his stories of the Lake Superior

Regiment soldiers he met during the war helped build his and Koos's story.

### "Marv" Mervyn E. Saxberg
(b. February 16th, 1938)

Mervyn Elgin Saxberg, my father, was born on February 16th, 1938. All the stories he told me about his uncles during the war inspired this story. Joey's accident, described in the prologue, was his best account of what happened. He had to testify against his Uncle Gerald. My father is a retired radio and broadcasting teacher. He was a TV/radio announcer and had his own show in Winnipeg called Sports Action for many years. Marv and my mother Ruth raised four children, Kelly, Kim, Kris and myself. They have fifteen grandchildren and two great grandchildren.

### Danny Payne

Danny is a fictional character based on Robert Payne, one of Ardagh's friends. We have pictures of them together, but I couldn't find any records of him.

### Jim Johnson

Jim is a fictional character. His death was based on how Ardagh's father Robert Cadieu tragically died, falling through the ice while ice harvesting in February 1955.

### Robert Cadieu
(1881 - February 7, 1955)

Robert Cadieu owned the Fort William Ice Company and for forty-three years worked the balance of the year with the Grain Trimmers Association. He was born and educated in Thurso, Quebec. He had five sons and four daughters.

## "Joey" Joseph F. Powley
(January 26, 1938 - March 13, 1945)

Gerald Cadieu accidentally ran over the seven-year-old Joey. The prologue describes what happened from my father's perspective and reports in the newspaper. It was Joseph and Mafalda's second child, who was lost in a car accident. A truck killed Joey's older brother Hector in 1934.

## Bill Woods

Bill is a fictional character, a replacement for Company Quartermaster Sergeant Wilfred A. Guerard. Wilf was related through marriage to Ardagh and was killed on the same day by a direct hit from a mortar. I have wondered whether the news of his death had weighed on Ardagh and caused an additional distraction in his final moments of his life.

## Eileen and Lily Moody

Eileen and Lily Moody are fictional characters. I found Eileen's name in Ardagh's service and pay book along with her address where he was billeted in Guildford. I could not find any significant records of Eileen Moody other than her voting records which confirmed she lived in Guildford.

## Mr. van Hulst

Mr van Hulst is a fictional character. I used the name of one of the more famous Dutch resistance fighters. Jonah van Hulst, who was instrumental in saving over 600 Jewish children from the nursery of the Hollandsche Schouwburg; they were destined for deportation to Nazi concentration camps.

## Private John G. Wilson
(July 8, 1921 - August 9, 1944)

Private Wilson was born in Moose Jaw, Saskatchewan. He was

a farmer in Mossbank, Saskatchewan, and had one brother and two sisters. He played the Harmonica and liked to listen to music on the radio.

## Major Chaplain (Padre) John R. Leng
(August 13, 1910 - March 19, 1985)

The men held a high regard for the padre from Welland, Ontario. He had stayed with them through every battle and was always alongside them to help with the wounded, comfort them through their last breaths, and bury them when they were dead. The note, *Dead men tell the story of the battle of the Gap,* was written by Major Leng. It is one of the best direct descriptions of what the Lake Superior Regiment went through in the war.

## Joost de Lange

Joost is a fictional character based on various Dutch volunteers who joined the Nazis and their stories.

## Corporal Hans Burg

Corporal Burg is a fictional character.

## Erwin de Lange

Erwin is a fictional Character.

## "Heinie" Heinrich Muller

Heinie is a fictional character.

## Pieter Jansen

Pieter is a fictional character.

## Lieutenant Brown

Lieutenant Brown is a fictional character.

## Leutnant Wilhelm Clausen
### (August 21, 1913 - November 5, 1944)

Leutnant Clausen was the captain of the AF 92. He was born in Katowice, Poland. His family moved to Kopenick, a suburb of Berlin. He changed his name from Spilka to Clausen just before the war to improve his chances of getting into the Nazi party and a posting on a submarine. I am guessing that Clausen was his mother's maiden name or a relative. His story with Koos is fictional, but he died as described by the Lake Superior soldiers, *with his hands in his pockets.*

## Leutnant Gunther Jahn
### (d. July 24, 1944)

Lieutenant Jahn was a real German fighter pilot and had five confirmed scores. He was killed at the same time that Gerald's bomber was in the area. It was the closest I could find to confirm Gerald's credited score. I changed the dates of the bombing run to fit within the story lines.

# Additional Lake Superior Regiment
# soldiers mentioned.

## Captain Thomas J. Henderson

Captain Henderson was from Winnipeg and had the honour of being Mentioned in Dispatches.

## Private Norman Hunt

Private Hunt was wounded March 10th, 1945 from a landmine. In 1990, he came back to Sint Philipsland and visited the van den Berg family.

## Private Fritz E. Anderson

Private Anderson was severely wounded when Ardagh was killed. We don't know exactly who is to blame for tripping the wire but I went with the less experienced Private Anderson, right or wrong. I needed to make a fictional choice as to what happened. The Lake Superior Regiment diaries say that Ardagh tripped a wire attached to a booby-trapped bazooka.

## Major Roy Styffe
### (1919 - 1997)

Major Styffe was born in Port Arthur, Ontario and was a career soldier. He led 'C' Company in all the battles told in this story, the destruction of the German Navy ships, Fort Crevecoeur, and the Hochwald Gap battle. Throughout, he exhibited powers of leadership and an unshakable resolve to close with the enemy, which established a standard of conduct among all ranks of his company.

## Sergeant Charles H. Byce
### (March 9, 1916 - November 30, 1994)

Sergeant Byce worked in a pulp and paper mill and was born in Chapleau, Ontario. He received the Military Medal for his actions at the Maas River crossing and later received the Distinguished Conduct medal for the Hochwald Gap battle. The citation noted that *the magnificent courage and fighting spirit displayed by this NCO when faced with almost insuperable odds are beyond all praise. His gallant stand, without adequate weapons and with a bare handful of men against hopeless odds, will remain, for all time, an outstanding example to all ranks of the Regiment.*

## Major Thomas H. Murray
### (Sept 21, 1916 - November 29, 1963)

Major Murray was born in Port Arthur, Ontario. He received the Distinguished Service Order. The citation noted the following; *Here again, Major Murray displayed his outstanding qualities as a leader, assuming command of the remnants of all three companies and going about under very heavy enemy fire, reorganizing them and encouraging his men. There is no doubt that his magnificent example was a major factor in the successful stabilizing of the situation. Throughout this whole battle, and despite his intense fatigue, Major Murray constantly distinguished himself by (the greatest) gallantry in action. He cheerfully accepted the greatest risks to himself and, by his courageous example, succeeded in maintaining the fighting spirit of the men.*

In 1963, Major Murray was a passenger on Trans Canada Airlines flight 831, which crashed shortly after take-off from Montreal travelling to Toronto. All on board perished.

### Colonel Robert A. Keane
(May 14, 1914 - August 16, 1977)

Colonel Keane was a career soldier from Fort William, Ontario. He commanded the Lake Superior Regiment from shortly after D-day to the end of the war and received the Distinguished Service Order, among many other awards for his service. I can't imagine the stress he faced coming back from England and having to push his exhausted regiment into the fierce battle for the Hochwald Gap, knowing it would result in many of his men getting killed. Colonel Keane lived a purposeful life and stood up for his values, fought for his country, and helped those who needed him.

## Additional Characters

Unfortunately, I have minimal information on the characters named below other than they fought with the Lake Superior Regiment and were mentioned in the diaries or reports. I portrayed their participation as best as I could through the records.

## Corporal Thomas E. Mitchell
Corporal Mitchell, from Toronto, was one of the soldiers that went out to check on the AF 92 and recovered the bell and flag.

## Sergeant Milton M. Shaw
Sergeant Shaw was from Chatham, Ontario and was one of the soldiers that went out to check on the AF 92 and recovered the bell and flag. In the story I don't distinguish between the two Shaw's. He was awarded a Military Medal.

## Lieutenant Pierce
Is a fictional character. His name was mentioned in the 22 Canadian Armoured Regiment dairies leading the second squadron tanks with Ardagh's platoon.

## Lieutenant Bernard I. Black
(d. 1990)
Lieutenant Black was listed for an award. Lieutenant Black was called to the bar in 1950 and became a barrister, solicitor and notary. He worked for a time as Assistant Crown Attorney, agent for the Ministry of Justice, and as solicitor for the Municipality of Neebing, and CN Rail. He was a former president of the Thunder Bay Historical Society and took an interest in collecting material relating to the legal history of Thunder Bay.

## Lieutenant Ritchie
Lieutenant Ritchie led number six platoon in which Ardagh was the sergeant.

Gerald "Hank" Cadieu's crew mentioned. Pilot Boyle and Rear Gunner Hill.

# Lake Superior Regiment Soldiers Killed in Action

I found this in *The Lake Superior Regiment magazine,* The Green Centre Line.

> "Uppermost in our minds now are the memories of some of our comrade who have made the greatest sacrifice. We stand beside their crosses and hope that in our future at home we may live lives worthy of their sacrifice. Then, we must press on to the final victory..."

### Private Robert C. Bond
(May 2, 1921 - June 27, 1941)

Private Bond was a labourer from Port Arthur, Ontario. He was married with no kids. He was killed in a truck accident in Grace Bay, Nova Scotia. The truck was loaded with twenty-one men plus large amounts of equipment. The driver failed to make a right turn, and the truck went over an embankment. He was killed instantly.

### Private Steven Marchuk
(April 23, 1918 - June 27, 1941)

Private Marchuk was a labourer from Rainy River, Ontario. He was in the same truck with Private Bond and died of his injuries a couple hours later. Neither soldier was to blame for the accident. He was single, with no record of siblings.

### Sergeant Gordon E. Anderson
(February 9, 1914 - August 9, 1944)

Sergeant Anderson was a logger from Calgary, Alberta. He was single and had six sisters. He wanted to be a police officer. I did my best to describe the scene when he was killed in action. His temporary burial was not found, and he was buried in an unknown grave somewhere near Bretteville La Rabe.

## L/Sergeant Richard L. Burrison
(February 5, 1922 - April 25, 1945)

Sergeant Burrison was a postal clerk from Chauvin, Alberta. He was single, with one brother and one sister. Sergeant Burrison trained to be a paratrooper, but broke his leg on a jump. He received the Military Medal.

## Corporal Hedley M. Shaw
(March 4, 1913 - February 11, 1945)

Corporal Shaw, a native of Kingston, Ontario, had his own business selling grain feed and seeds. He came from a wealthy family and had worked for his father who owned Maple Leaf Milling Company, now Maple Leaf Foods. Corporal Shaw was in officer's training when he returned six hours late on leave and was listed as AWOL. He was then shipped overseas as a private. He was married and had three girls. Corporal Shaw tragically drowned in the Maas River after trying to get help for several soldiers who were wounded and his body was not found until 2011, when his unmarked grave was found in a German Cemetery. I have been to the spot on the river where he attempted to swim and can understand why he would have tried it. The Maas is a deceptively fast-flowing river but narrow, maybe forty meters wide. He also may have been wounded by the landmines along the shore.

## Sergeant James L. Reynolds
(May 27, 1914 - August 21,1944)

Sergeant Reynolds was a miner and cook from Leslie, Saskatchewan. He was married with no kids. He had three brothers and four sisters. Sergeant Reynolds was Mentioned in Dispatches in recognition of gallant and distinguished services. *He crawled forward again and inched his way out of the ditch across open ground, intent on getting a tank at the edge of the*

*woods. After Twenty minutes of laborious progress under a with-*
*ering hail of small arms and heavy gunfire, he got into a fire posi-*
*tion, sighted his quarry and let fly with the first bomb - another*
*direct hit.*

### Private Richard J. Kohler
(August 6, 1920 - August 21, 1944)

Private Kohler was a cook in a Port Arthur, Ontario construction camp. He was single and had two brothers and four sisters.

### Private Russell H. Nie
( January 27 1916 - August 21, 1944)

Private Nie was a truck and tractor mechanic from St. Brieux,
Saskatchewan. He was single and had five brothers and four
sisters.

### Private Royal V. Giving
(November 8, 1919 - April 23, 1945)

Private Giving was a labourer from Kenora, Ontario. He was
single and had a brother and three sisters.

### Private Samuel G. Engen
(February 15, 1918 - April 23, 1945)

Private Engen was a trapper/labourer from The Pas, Manitoba.
He was married with no children and had one brother and two
sisters.

### Private George Yanchuk
( June 3, 1921 - March 2, 1945)

Private Yanchuk was a farmhand from Fort William, Ontario.
He was single and had two brothers and three sisters.

## Private Walter R. Middlemiss
(November 14, 1923 - March 2, 1945)

Private Middlemiss was a truck driver from Yorktown, Saskatchewan. He was single, with no record of siblings.

## A/Sergeant Thomas M. Lehman
(June 7, 1918 - March 2, 1945)

Sergeant Lehman was a farm labourer from Lorenzo, Saskatchewan. He was single and had five brothers and four sisters.

## Private Ralph L. Ash
(May 5, 1927 - March 2, 1945)

Private Ash was a mechanic from Blind River, Ontario. He was single and had four brothers and three sisters.

## Private William J. Catto
(April 22, 1917 - March 2, 1945)

Private Catto was a bushman from Port Arthur, Ontario. He was single, and an only child.

## Private William McRobbie
(June 7, 1924 - March 2, 1945)

Private McRobbie was a mail clerk from Broadview, Saskatchewan. He was single and had two brothers and a sister.

## Private George F. Couture
(December 12, 1916 - March 2, 1945)

Private Couture was a miner from Cobalt, Ontario. He was married with three kids. Private Couture played hockey, softball and rugby. He left school to help his father, who was too ill to support the family.

### Corporal James W. Gray
(October 28th, 1916 - March 2, 1945)
Corporal Gray was a warehouse clerk from St. James, Manitoba. He was a single and played hockey, football and golf. He had a brother in the RCAF and three sisters.

### Private Donald J. MacDonald
(July 22, 1922 - February 28, 1945)

Private MacDonald was a labourer from Cornwall, Ontario. He was single, and an only child.

### Private Ralph K. Silliker
(Oct 16, 1917 - March 2, 1945)

Private Silliker was a truck driver from O'Leary, Prince Edward Island. He was married and had two girls.

# Acknowledgments

I first want to thank The Thunder Bay Museum Society's imprint, Reimagined Press, for publishing Ardagh's and Koos's story. It wouldn't have been possible without the great help and guidance from my editor Tory Tronrud. I would like especially to thank Scott Bradley the CEO of the Thunder Bay Museum for taking on this book. This is a great place for this story to be brought to life. In addition, I had tremendous support and help from Michael de Jonge and Dr Michel Beaulieu. I would like to thank the Thunder Bay committee for their input, Dr. Michel Beaulieu, Temitope Ojo, David Ratz, Beth Boegh, Mark Chochla, Sara Janes, Dr. Thorold Tronrud, Michael deJong, ex-officio, and Scott Bradley, ex-officio.

I would like to thank my father for inspiring this book with his stories from his childhood and uncle's. Of course, my mother for her brains, strength and love. I am very fortunate to come from a family of artists that inspires. My sister Kim and my father the painters, Kelly the film producer, and Kris the musician. Thank you, Kim, for your encouragement, thoughtful advice and taking the time to read my many draft manuscripts. Kelly for encouragement and advice to query the Museum as well as the inspiration from the successful films and stories she has told over the years through ShebaFilms.

I would like to thank Anja Romijn for all her stories, emails, photos and family information that made Koos's story possible. Rob and Henriëtte de Raat for sharing their home to learn where Koos lived and the stories of the war. Edwin Popken, Robert Catsburg, Katy Murdoch, George Romick, and Richard Schoutissen for their superb research help. I am grateful to Edwin, at Battlefield Discovery, for setting up a Lake Superior Regiment tour through the main battles and help explain what happened. He was also instrumental in connecting me with Koos's family and Anja. Thank you so much!

*Those We Carry* took several drafts and rewrites over five years as I learned the craft of writing. There were a number of editors over those years that I relied upon for their assessments of my many drafts: Natalie Morrill, Britanie Wilson, Steve Anderson, Deborah Murrell, Emily Ohanjanians, Scott Stavrou, and Lisa Howe. They were all very kind, honest and most important of all encouraging with their feedback. I learned so much from their advice. I would especially like to thank Steve for his thoughtful insight to change the structure of the story and detailed advice. Thank you, Deborah, for the initial heavy lifting on the amazing copy editing and proofing. I would like to thank Scott Stavrou and Lisa Howe for their input on the final draft. Their writing retreat Write Away Europe really helped set me on a confident path to pursue my writing. Thank you to Stephen Echavia for the illustrated maps throughout the novel and Jerry Todd for the fantastic book cover.

I am blessed to have to two brilliant son's Graeme and Kellen who were willing to listen and give strong impartial advice. My patient little girls Vivienne, Ivy, and Georgia always giving warm hugs while I sat writing for hours at my computer.

Most important of all Jenna, my love – thank you for your incredible love and patience through the numerous versions of this story, providing me with honest feedback that made this story so much better. Thank you for listening on our many, many walks. Your pressure to make it a publishable, readable, stronger story pushed me to improve my writing and get it over the finish line. Love you more.

Finally, I would like to thank all those that fought to protect our country and inspired this story. They all are our heroes.

Scott Saxberg is a successful entrepreneur, mentor, and author. He has founded several companies over the past thirty years. He mentors at New York University Stern Business School's Endless Frontiers Lab and the Creative Destruction Lab at the University of Calgary. His passion for hockey led him to become a co-owner of the NHL hockey team, the Arizona Coyotes, between 2013-17. This is Scott's debut novel. He lives in Calgary, Alberta, Canada with his wife Jenna Kaye and five children: Graeme, Kellen, Vivienne, Ivy, and Georgia.

**scottsaxberg.com**     𝕏 **@ysaxberg**     **Facebook.com/ScottAllenSaxberg**